Praise for the novels of Rick Mofina

"*Their Last Secret* is Rick Mofina at his edge-of-your-seat, can't-stop-turning-the-pages best as he dives deep into questions of truth, justice, and ultimately redemption. A riveting, moving read."
—Lisa Unger, *New York Times* bestselling author of *The Stranger Inside*

"Well-developed characters and an intense pace add to this gripping novel. This latest from a gifted storyteller should not be missing from your reading pile."
—*Library Journal* (starred review) on *Missing Daughter*

"Rick Mofina's books are edge-of-your-seat thrilling. Page-turners that don't let up."
—Louise Penny, #1 *New York Times* bestselling author

"A pulse-pounding nail-biter."
—*The Big Thrill* on *Last Seen*

"*Six Seconds* should be Rick Mofina's breakout thriller. It moves like a tornado."
—James Patterson, *New York Times* bestselling author

"*Six Seconds* is a great read. Echoing Ludlum and Forsythe, author Mofina has penned a big, solid international thriller that grabs your gut—and your heart—in the opening scenes and never lets go."
—Jeffery Deaver, *New York Times* bestselling author

"*The Panic Zone* is a headlong rush toward Armageddon. Its brisk pace and tight focus remind me of early Michael Crichton."
—Dean Koontz, #1 *New York Times* bestselling author

"Rick Mofina's tense, taut writing makes every thriller he writes an adrenaline-packed ride."
—*New York Times* bestselling author Tess Gerritsen

RICK
MOFINA

SEARCH
FOR HER

mira

**Recycling programs
for this product may
not exist in your area.**

ISBN-13: 978-0-7783-3160-5

Search for Her

Copyright © 2021 by Highway Nine, Inc.

This edition published by arrangement with Harlequin Books S.A.

For questions and comments about the quality of this book, please contact us
at CustomerService@Harlequin.com.

Mira
22 Adelaide St. West, 40th Floor
Toronto, Ontario M5H 4E3, Canada
www.Harlequin.com

Printed in U.S.A.

This book is for my favorite sister-in-law.
There, it's out there, Lynn.

SEARCH
FOR HER

I am afraid of all my sorrows, I know that thou wilt not hold me innocent.

Job 9:27–29

DAY 1

One

California / Nevada

Watching flat, desert scrub and distant mountains drifting by her window, Grace Jarrett reflected on her life.

You think you're in control, but you're not.

You never know what's coming.

It was strange, she thought, you meet the perfect man, get married and have a daughter. You're living your dream, believing it will last forever then you blink and you're a widowed, single parent and your world goes dark.

Then you meet an understanding man, who, with his teenage son, has also experienced a painful loss. You fall in love, get married, come together as a blended family and you see light again.

Grace turned to her husband, John Marshall, behind the wheel of their RV as they traveled north on Interstate 15, a few hours south of Las Vegas.

He's a good guy.

We may not be a perfect family, if such a thing exists, but we're doing our best.

Now, after two years of marriage, Grace and John, along with her daughter and his son, were facing a new challenge together: moving across the country to Pennsylvania.

It wasn't easy, especially for Riley, her fourteen-year-old daughter, who had just broken up with her boyfriend at Grace's insistence.

Ever since they left San Diego that morning at dawn, Riley had sobbed softly, her face welded to her phone as she exchanged messages nonstop with her friends. With each mile Grace still grappled with whether their move from California, where she and Riley had always lived, was the right one.

But that decision was behind them.

After discussing it with Grace, John had accepted a new job as communications director with a Fortune 500 retail company in Pittsburgh. It meant more money than what he was earning as public relations manager at the clothing chain in San Diego, where things had not been going well for him. Grace would leave her job at the University of California, San Diego Medical Center, transfer her RN license and, because of her qualifications, stood a good chance at getting a position at the University of Pittsburgh Medical Center.

"This will be a new start for us," John had said.

The idea excited Grace and despite her uncertainties, she agreed, reasoning that it was best to take control of their future.

At the outset the move meant a new, fully furnished house in Pittsburgh that John's company would lease to them for a year, giving them time to find a home, or renew. For John and his son, Blake, it meant the Steelers, the Pirates and the Penguins. Grace had only been to Pittsburgh once, years ago for a conference, and she'd liked the Carnegie and Warhol museums.

For the kids the move meant new schools, which was why they were making the trek now, to get them enrolled.

It also meant leaving mild Southern California winters for snow and cold.

It meant severing ties with San Diego, leaving good friends, selling their beautiful home in Mission Hills where Grace had lived with Tim, her first husband, the home in which Riley grew up.

For Riley, the move was an emotional amputation of everything she'd known in her life, and in a sense, for her, it was a betrayal of her father's memory.

Grace got that. John got that.

This move was hard for all of them.

For Blake, it meant leaving the life he'd known in California where his mother and sister had died tragically together. But if Blake had concerns about moving he never voiced them. At seventeen, after all the adversity he'd endured, Blake was patient and uncomplaining. At times he could be quiet, withdrawn, as if he had something on his mind.

Like now, Blake, like Riley, was also lost to his phone.

Grace and John exchanged glances.

So far this trip was not what they'd envisioned.

"Come on guys," John said, "you haven't looked away from your phones since we left."

No one responded.

"We're all sad to leave San Diego," John said. "We got this RV to see America as a family, not to watch your screens. Come on, guys, get with the program."

No answer.

John continued. "So like we planned, we'll stop in Vegas for a bit then we'll see the Grand Canyon. What do you think?"

Silence.

John let out a long breath, glanced in the mirror. Blake was at the dinette, Riley at the sofa. Both were indifferent.

"Guys—" Grace turned to the kids "—this is our chance to make some memories. You're missing the mountains and the valleys. It's majestic."

"It's pretty boring," Riley said to her phone.

"Look—" John pointed to the pencil-like tower ahead of them "—we're coming up to Baker with the World's Tallest Thermometer. We can stop, take pictures. It'll be fun. What do you say?"

"Whatever," Blake said.

"Don't care," Riley said.

Grace got out of her seat, went to Riley and Blake and snatched their phones.

"Hey!" Blake said.

"What the hell, Mom?" Riley said.

The air tensed.

"Your dad and I are trying hard to make something of this trip with you, but you've shut us out. You're being rude." Grace dropped back into her seat, turned off each phone. She thrust them into the glove compartment, fished keys from her bag and locked it. "Now, we'll spend the rest of the drive to Las Vegas enjoying the views."

"This sucks!" Riley said.

Minutes later, they passed Baker without stopping or speaking.

Riley folded her arms across her chest, pondered her new moon and stars bracelet, then said, "You've lost your freaking mind, Mom. Give me my phone!"

"No, we're going to enjoy this trip."

"*Enjoy?* Seriously?" Riley's voice quavered. "You made me break up with Caleb. You made me leave Sherry and all my friends, all the people I love! I'll never see them again! How am I supposed to *'enjoy'* that?"

"I'm sorry, honey," Grace said. "You'll make new friends, I promise."

"Riley, it'll be better once we get settled in Pittsburgh," John said.

"No, it won't. You're tearing me away from my life. You're both so cold and heartless!"

"Riley, stop," Grace said. "We've been over all of this."

Brushing at her tears, Riley caught Blake looking at her, narrowed her eyes and flipped him her middle finger.

"Screw this!" Riley stood. "Why'd we leave so freaking early, like farmers? I'm going to sleep."

She stomped into the bedroom at the rear, slamming the privacy door behind.

"Riley!" John called.

"Let her go." Grace turned to her window, massaged her temple while looking at nothing.

John looked at the road ahead.

Blake stared into the desert.

The tires hummed.

An hour later, they crossed into Nevada at Primm, a cluster of casinos, restaurants and hotels.

Depending on your direction on the I-15, it offered your first chance, or last, to test your gambling luck in Nevada.

"Want to stop here?" Grace asked.

"Let's keep going. There's a new place I read about a couple miles ahead," John said.

A few miles north of Primm they pulled into the Silver Sagebrush, a truck stop busy with rigs wheeling in and out from the interstate, gears grinding, air brakes hissing. Dozens more filled the lot while other vehicles parked in different sections.

"This is massive," Grace said.

"Wow, it's wild," Blake said.

John found a spot in a far corner, partially shaded by palms. He parked and turned off the engine.

"Blake, wake up Riley," John said.

"No. Let her sleep." Grace reached for her bag. "I'll leave a note. We'll get her something and bring it back."

John rubbed his chin as if ready to challenge his wife's decision, but yielded. Grace jotted down a note, stuck it to the inside door handle, then she left with Blake and John, who locked the RV's door. They walked across the immense lot to the main building, a colossal glass and glazed brick structure in an art deco motif. The Stars and Stripes, county, state and corporate flags flapped from poles that reached high above the entrance, which was landscaped with cacti, violets and pink roses.

About a half hour later, they returned.

"I can't get over how big the place is," Grace said.

"It's epic," Blake said.

"It's something all right," John said before he entered the four-digit PIN on the RV's keypad. They got in and prepared to leave.

"Blake," Grace said, buckling her seat belt, "would you go back and check on Riley, please?"

Blake went to the back then returned, just as John started the engine.

"She's fine." Blake flopped back into his place at the dinette.

John shifted the transmission and they resumed heading north on the interstate.

"We're not far from Vegas." John bit into an apple.

Grace nodded, resumed watching the sweeping views. Sipping her diet soda, anticipating how trying life was going to be for Riley in Pittsburgh. Grace then thought of her friend Sherry, Tim's former colleague at work, and how good she had been to Grace and Riley in the time after Tim's death. Already missing her, Grace thought how she could use Sherry's help now.

I've got to be more patient with Riley. She's got a lot to deal with.

They'd gone less than ten miles past Jean, Nevada, when Blake, sitting alone at the window of the dinette, had finished his bag of chips and Coke.

"Grace, do you think I could have my phone back?"

"Just hang tough, son," John said. "We'll be in Vegas soon."

"Would you go get Riley?" Grace asked, pulling Riley's favorite drink and snack, pecan tarts, out of the bag from the truck stop.

Blake hesitated but then got up from the dinette, went to the back and knocked softly on the privacy door to the bedroom.

"Riley?"

He knocked again, louder.

There was no response.

He tried the door, expecting it to be locked but to his surprise he slid it open to reveal an empty room.

Cursing to himself, he knocked on the adjoining bathroom door and it swung open.

Empty.

"She's not here!"

Two

"What do you mean she's not there? You just saw her!"

Grace hurried to the back, looked at the empty bedroom and bathroom then checked the bunk over the cab.

Empty.

Grace glared at Blake, his face reddening as she raised her voice to him: *"You said she was fine!"*

"I'm sorry, Grace—I lied."

"Why?"

"I figured she was sleeping. I didn't want to wake her and piss her off more!" Tears stood in his eyes. "I'm sorry."

"Oh my God! She must've gotten out at the truck stop. John! Didn't you lock the door?"

"You can get out from the inside—she's not there?"

"Go back to the truck stop. Turn around!"

"Okay, okay!"

He searched the interstate's three lanes of north-bound traffic, scanning the concrete barrier dividing three lanes of southbound traffic, failing to find a safe place to reverse their direction.

"I'm so sorry," Blake said.

Grace flashed her palm at Blake. "Why didn't we see her in the truck stop?" she shouted to John.

"It's a huge crowded place," John said. "We could've easily missed her."

"Oh God." Grace's stomach tightened. She rushed to her seat and reached for her phone. "I'll call her!"

"You can't," Blake said. "You took our phones."

Grace unlocked the glove compartment. Sure enough, the phones were there. She banged it shut then spotted her own handwriting on the note she'd left Riley. It had fallen to the floor.

Did she even see it?

"Turn around, John! We have to go back now!"

"I know. I'm looking for a spot to turn!"

John searched for an exit ramp, an overpass, but saw nothing but six lanes of traffic cutting a straight line across the desert.

"Why doesn't she call us?" Grace said. "She could get to a phone and call me!"

"She's probably mad at us," John said.

Grace plunged her face into her hands and swore to herself. Then she rummaged through the bag of snacks until she found a receipt for the Silver Sagebrush. The telephone number was on the top. She punched it into her phone.

After several rings an automated voice mail greeting answered: "You've reached the Silver Sagebrush, Nevada's largest..." Grace bit her bottom lip as the emptiness rolled by. This call was her best way to contact her daughter. "For directions, press '1'... For hours of operation, press '2'... For fuel sales and truck services, press '3'..."

"Oh please!" Grace said as the message tortured her.

"...the casino, press '4'..."

Grace squeezed her phone.

"For restaurants, press '5'... For the motel, press '6.' To repeat this message, press the pound key. For a Silver Sagebrush customer agent, press '0.'"

Grace jabbed the 0 key. It rang twice.

"Silver Sagebrush," a female voice sounding no older than Riley's said, "this is Brandy, how can I help you?"

"Brandy, we were at the Sagebrush a little while ago and we're on our way back because we accidently left without my daughter. Her name is Riley Jarrett, she's fourteen."

"Oh my."

"Do you have a public address system?"

"Yes, ma'am, we do."

"Could you please page her, ask her to come wherever you are, so I can talk to her?"

"Hold on a moment."

"Don't hang up!"

"I won't, just hold on."

Brandy didn't put her on hold. She placed the

receiver down and Grace could hear her talking with someone then a moment later she heard the echo of Riley being paged.

"Hello, ma'am?" Brandy was back on the line. "We've just paged her so give it a moment."

"Thank you so much, Brandy." Grace exhaled a measure of relief. Then she pointed with her free hand. "There! There!"

"I see it," John said.

Ahead in the distance they saw an opening in the dividing barrier where it was possible to make a U-turn.

John switched on the flashing hazard lights. Slowing the RV, checking his mirrors and traffic, he cut across two more northbound lanes triggering horn blasts as he came to a stop at the U-turn's opening.

Traffic rushed by them in both directions as John read the signs posted at the opening, warning that only authorized vehicles could execute a turn there.

"Hurry, John!"

"I know!"

Grace was still holding, hoping to hear Riley's voice, expecting her to be upset at them for leaving without her.

After waiting for a safe gap, John entered the stream of southbound traffic to the blare of a semi's air horn, then another burst from a charter bus. Cursing, keeping his hazard lights flashing, John pressed down on the accelerator and made his way to the far right lane.

"Brandy?" Grace feared she'd lost her connection.

"We keep paging her, ma'am. We're still waiting for her to come to the desk."

"Maybe she went outside. She's wearing a white T-shirt with the *Friends* TV show logo on it."

"We'll get Security on it, ma'am."

Exceeding the speed limit, John passed slower vehicles for about a mile when out of nowhere a car blurred by the RV's left side before swerving into their lane cutting too close in front of them.

"What the hell!" John shouted.

To avoid colliding he stomped on the brake pedal and twisted the wheel. The RV swayed, lurched wildly to one side. John wrenched the wheel to correct it but the RV veered violently the opposite way, weight shifting, tilting the vehicle, lifting the wheels from the road.

"John!" Grace grabbed a side handle.

"Dad!" Blake gripped the dinette table.

The RV left the road, tipping, throwing everything into a maelstrom hammering the vehicle to the ground as it crashed on its side.

Grace screamed.

The driver and front passenger airbags deployed, the windshield blossomed with fractures. The front dash separated, spewing components in an explosion of wires, cables and plastic shards. The interior broke apart, the sink, the fridge and counters fragmented, doors flew off, shelving fell out and ejected food and kitchenware as Blake tumbled through it all.

The RV slid along the paved shoulder at high speed, trailing a plume of sparks before stopping.

Dust settled amid the acrid smells of burning rubber and melting plastic. Fluids dripped everywhere, hissing on the hot engine.

Buried in the heap, a small voice called from Grace's phone.

"Hello? Ma'am? We've made several announcements. I'm sorry, we can't find your daughter."

Three

The RV's shattered windshield crackled as it was peeled away, then a man's face appeared in the opening silhouetted against the sun.

"Everybody okay in there?"

"I think so," John grunted. "I can't move."

John and Grace were still buckled in as the RV had come to a rest on its side. But the front dash had shifted, trapping them in their seats. Reaching down, John found Grace's hand under the deflated airbag and gave it a gentle squeeze.

She squeezed back.

"I'm okay," she responded to the man. "Help us please—our daughter—where's my phone?"

"Blake!" John called out.

"I'm all right, Dad. I landed on the cushions."

They could hear Blake moving through the interior's wreckage, maneuvering his way toward them while the sweet, maple smell of vaporizing engine coolant battled the sewer stench of the leaking black water tank.

"Try to relax, folks," the man said. "Help's coming."

"Are you hurt bad, Grace?" John asked.

"I'm okay, just stuck, and bleeding a little. Are you hurt?"

"I'm okay. I'm stuck, too. I'm sorry this happened."

"It's not your fault." Grace fought tears then pulled her hand away to feel around. "Where's my phone? They were paging Riley—I've got to talk to her—"

"We'll get to her," John said.

"That truck stop is so big, John! How will we ever find her there?" Grace fought her sobs.

"Hang in there, Grace," John said. "Blake, can you look for Grace's phone back there?"

"Okay."

John wedged his hand into his pocket in an effort to reach his phone, but it didn't work. They could hear Blake lifting loose and broken things. At the windshield they could hear tense, adrenaline-pumped snippets of multiple conversations:

"…see what happened?"

"They got cut off."

"Road rager maybe after they pulled a U-turn."

"Lost control, rolled to the side."

"I called 9-1-1…"

"Should go help those guys clear debris off the freeway…"

Amid the destruction, through the RV's broken rear window, Blake, his shoulder throbbing, saw several motorists who'd stopped to help. People were kicking and carrying pieces of wreckage from the highway to the shoulder, while others waved away slowing cars and trucks.

Somewhere in the hum of passing traffic came the sound of sirens as the yellow emergency trucks from Clark County Fire Department and units from the Nevada Highway Patrol began arriving. First responders got to work. One of them stuck his head inside the RV.

"Everybody's conscious?"

"Yes," John said.

"Anyone in pain?"

"No, I don't think so, but we're pinned in here," John said.

"Don't worry, folks. We'll get you out ASAP. I'm Mark Cook. I'm a paramedic. Don't move at all. I see you back there, son, are you okay?"

"Yes," Blake said. "But I can't get out. I'm blocked."

"No, you hang tough until we get your folks out first," Cook said.

"But our daughter's—" Grace started to cry. "Our daughter—"

There was a loud series of radio dispatches.

"How many people are in the vehicle?" Cook asked.

"Three," Grace said. "We left our daughter,

Riley, behind by mistake at the Silver Sagebrush. She's fourteen. She's alone. We need to locate her."

More static popping with radio dispatches.

"Sorry," Cook said, "where's your daughter?"

"She's alone at the Sagebrush truck stop. Please send someone to find her! Her name is Riley Jarrett, she's from San Diego. She's wearing a white *Friends* T-shirt!"

"Okay, we'll alert Metro Police, just hang on."

What followed was a spurt of conversations, radio dispatches, the thump and clink of equipment.

"We've got to go through the dash here to get to you," Cook said. "We've got to hose things down first because of leaking engine fluids, then it's going to get noisy. Whatever you do don't move."

Some water sprayed into the cabin, then with a deafening roar rescuers used a hydraulic cutter to work through the RV and in short time they cleared through the wreckage and extricated Grace, John and then Blake. They helped them to the back of an ambulance. All three were shaken and bleeding from cuts and abrasions. Cook and another paramedic, Laura Farrow, cleaned and bandaged their wounds while assessing them for other injuries.

"Any pain in your chest?" Farrow asked Grace, who shook her head.

"It's my daughter I'm worried about."

"I know. Let us take care of you first." Farrow continued working.

"Take a deep breath for me," Cook told John

while listening with a stethoscope. "Do you remember what happened?"

"We were cut off, I swerved to avoid a crash and we rolled," John said.

When Farrow finished with Grace, she moved on to Blake, checking his breathing, his overall condition.

"You folks are lucky," Cook said while he and Farrow evaluated the family's level of consciousness, signs and responses. "You got bashed around pretty good, but you don't appear to have any serious injuries. Still, to be safe, we'll take you to the medical center in Las Vegas for further assessment."

"No," Grace said. "We need to go back to the Sagebrush to get our daughter."

Cook and Farrow exchanged glances.

"We advise that you be transported to the hospital for assessment for any underlying injuries," Cook said.

"I'm an RN. I know the protocol. We're not seriously hurt, and you can see by our mental condition that we're competent to refuse further treatment and leave the scene."

After a moment, Cook said, "All right, then you'll need to sign a release."

"We will and we need someone to take us to the Sagebrush right away."

As Farrow went to the front of the ambulance for the documents, a Nevada Highway Patrol trooper, who'd been observing, spoke into his radio: "Vehicle's been searched. We've got three. No other occupants." Then, with his notebook in his hand, he approached them.

"Excuse me, I'm Michael Hicks, Highway Patrol. Looks like you're wrapping up here. Everyone okay to talk?"

"We need your help finding our daughter at the Sagebrush," Grace said.

"Yes, ma'am, I understand we've alerted Las Vegas Metro and they're responding."

"Thank God! We need someone to take us there now, please!" Grace said.

"We'll look into that, but first, we have to take care of things here. I need names and IDs of the occupants, driver's license, registration and proof of insurance."

"I'm John Marshall." Wincing, he reached for his wallet. "My wife, Grace Jarrett, our son, Blake Marshall and our daughter is Riley Jarrett. Most everything's in the RV. It's a rental."

"My purse is in there with my phone. Blake's and Riley's phones are in the glove compartment and we need everything."

Hicks nodded, reached for his shoulder microphone and spoke into it, then turned back.

"We'll have someone retrieve those items," Hicks said. "Now, who was operating the RV?"

"I was," John said.

"Sir—" Hicks stared hard into John's eyes "—have you been drinking, or using cannabis, or illicit drugs, or are you under any medication?"

"No."

"Were there any mechanical problems with the RV?"

"No."

"Tell me what happened."

After John gave Hicks his account of the crash, a second trooper emerged with the items from the RV. Grace seized her phone, sent Hicks her most recent photo of Riley and gave him a detailed description of her. Then Hicks relayed the information to his dispatcher. As Hicks completed his preliminary work, Grace, John and Blake signed the medical statements for Cook and Farrow.

"All right." Hicks had finished. "No charges at this time, but we'll continue to investigate. Your RV's going to be taken to our on-call tow yard in Las Vegas. You can get any other belongings from there later. Looks like it's a write-off, so you better alert your rental company, check your policy, make arrangements for transportation. All the contact information you need is here. You folks are lucky. This could've been much worse."

Hicks gave John his copy of his preliminary report.

"Can you please take us to the Sagebrush to get Riley?" Grace asked.

"Stand by. I'll get someone." Hicks reached for his radio microphone.

At that moment, she and John noticed that Blake was no longer with them. He'd stepped away to take a closer look at the RV, as if in awe of the crash that they'd survived. No gas had leaked out, but he watched firefighters continue hosing the wreck as a precaution. Blake looked to the south then north. An army of emergency vehicles, their lights flashing, had responded to the accident. Troopers had closed the far right lane backing up traffic, crawling bumper-to-bumper lines for as far as he could see.

Traffic in the northbound lanes slowed and people gawked.

He walked around the RV, studying the undercarriage, looking at it in silence. He glanced at chunks of the RV that had been scattered to the shoulder until he heard Grace call him.

"Come on, Blake, we're going to the truck stop to get Riley!"

Four

Riley Jarrett smiled at Officer Nate Rogan of the Las Vegas Metropolitan Police.

After studying her photo on his phone, he turned it to Carl Aldrich, operations manager for the Silver Sagebrush.

"Just got this," Rogan said. "I'm sending it to you."

Seconds later Aldrich's phone pinged. He tapped a message to go with Riley's photo and description then sent it to every staff member and every affiliate working at the Sagebrush.

"Like I was telling you," Aldrich said as they resumed walking briskly through the complex. "We started searching after we got her mother's call. I put people on all the doors looking for any girl wearing a *Friends* T-shirt and fitting her description. This picture will help. And, we're paging her every five minutes."

Rogan nodded, absorbing the info.

He'd been a few miles away in Primm following up a vehicle break-in and the theft of a cell phone when he was dispatched to a possible missing person case involving a fourteen-year-old girl at the Silver Sagebrush.

Given her age and the location, they had to act fast.

As a resident officer working from Metro's Jean substation, he'd been to the Sagebrush countless times after it opened a year ago. Still, Rogan never ceased to be amazed by its scale, surpassing all casinos, hotels and roadhouses in the area, like Whiskey Pete's, Terrible's and Buffalo Bill's.

The Silver Sagebrush was one of the largest truck stops in the country.

The new sprawling complex had seven hundred truck parking spaces and another thousand for general vehicles. It had truck service bays, scales, inspection zones and truck washing facilities. It had sixty commercial diesel pumps, 160 gasoline pumps, fifty car charging stations and over twenty RV dump stations.

Aldrich and Rogan moved through its huge main building. It was noisy and active with hundreds of travelers. It housed four table-service restaurants and a food court with ten major fast-food outlets. The aroma of deep-fried food swept through the air. The complex also had a huge gift store, grocery store, convenience store, an arcade, ATMs and a pet area. There was a drivers' lounge, auto parts supply store, a barber shop, a chapel, a public laundry, a fitness room, showers, major courier outlets and an adjoining two-hundred-room motel.

Rogan and Aldrich walked across the huge main lobby with its information desk and massive floor-to-ceiling maps and murals celebrating grand American landmarks. The chimes and jangle music of a couple of hundred slot machines spilled from the casino as they passed it.

Staring at the travelers walking through the Sagebrush, Rogan checked the time. It was about an hour since Riley Jarrett's family stopped here, plenty of time for anything to happen to a fourteen-year-old girl at a big, busy truck stop. No one knew how this case would play out. As the first responding officer, Rogan was responsible for the preliminary investigation, and there were key steps he needed to take because anything and everything could be evidence.

"I want to see your security footage."

"Sure, Nate, that's where we're headed."

"Save all the recorded security footage you have. Depending on how this goes, we may need it."

"Of course," Aldrich said. "I'll check with legal, but we'll cooperate fully."

"And no trash gets thrown out. And request everyone on shift stay so we can talk to them. This may take some time, but it could be crucial. At worst it's an inconvenience, but we're talking about a child here."

"Certainly," Aldrich said.

"And you still have people searching—what about all the restrooms?"

"We have a total of one hundred and sixty stalls," Aldrich said. "We've got staff checking each one. We also have people looking inside and outside, checking the parking lots for her. It's a big area to cover."

"And that doesn't include the desert around us," Rogan said.

"You know fifty thousand people pass through our area along the interstate every day," Aldrich said. "And of that, we get ten thousand visitors a day here at the Silver Sagebrush. We're a twenty-four-seven operation."

Rogan nodded. The figures were sobering, and it was overwhelming to consider the possibilities of what may have happened to Riley Jarrett. Rogan needed to organize a more comprehensive search but couldn't do it alone. He reached for his phone to request more specialized units to assist and hand it off to detectives with the Missing Persons Detail.

As they continued across the complex, a woman's voice announced a message through the Sagebrush's public address system: "Riley Jarrett, please come to the information desk in the main lobby... Riley Jarrett, please..."

Minutes later, down the hall of a far section, they came to a door identified as "Security." Aldrich opened it to a windowless room with toned-down lighting and the ambient glow of control panels, buttons, switches, keyboards and dozens of video monitors, each rolling different streams of images from inside and outside the Sagebrush.

A man in his twenties, with a shaved head and round glasses, sat at the controls.

"Travis, Officer Nate Rogan. Nate, Travis Quinn, our new surveillance chief."

They shook hands and Quinn continued working at his keyboard, the banks of video monitors reflecting in his glasses.

Rogan's focus went to the screens and footage rolling from all the facilities inside the complex, the motel, all the truck pumps, the gas pumps, the expansive parking lots, the continuous stream of traffic coming and going.

"Do you have her on camera, Travis?" Rogan asked.

Quinn took a breath as he scratched the stubble on his chin.

"I've got good news and bad news."

Five

Nevada

Phone pressed to her ear, Grace's mind raced as the Nevada Highway Patrol's SUV threaded southbound traffic on Interstate 15 and she reconnected with Brandy at the Silver Sagebrush.

"Yes, ma'am, we're still paging her and the police are here searching."

"Please have her call me the moment you find her! We'll be there soon!"

"I will."

When Blake saw that the call had ended he said, "I'm sorry I lied about checking on her."

"Don't, Blake. Not now."

Grace ignored the stiffness in her shoulders, her arms and her bandaged hands. She concentrated on the two phones on her lap, keeping an eye on hers, hoping that Riley had found a way to send her a message.

None had come.

She turned on Riley's phone, desperate to find

a clue as to who she might've been talking to before she'd confiscated it.

Grace knew Riley's password because ever since Grace got Riley her first phone she had insisted that she would have access to it to make spot checks. As Riley got older she grew resistant to what she considered an invasion of her privacy and lack of her mother's trust. Grace had promised not to be intrusive, but there were predators online; Riley was fourteen and those were Grace's rules.

But right now all she found were a few older exchanges with friends about music and clothes.

Grace sagged.

"Blake, I can't find any of her messages from this morning."

Without looking from his phone he said, "That's because she uses apps with messages that delete themselves after a few minutes, or longer, whatever she sets it to."

"What?"

"I thought you knew," Blake said. "You see only what Riley wants you to see on her phone."

How could I be so naive? Believing all the mundane stuff I saw was everything when for all I know, she could've been sexting with Caleb, or anyone.

What else don't I know about her?

At that moment Riley's phone pinged with a notification, a text from her friend Dakota: You there? What's up? You lose service? Get back to me.

Grace caught her breath then began typing.

Dakota, this is Riley's mom. I have her phone. We're in Nevada. If you hear from her, please tell her to call me ASAP!

A few seconds passed before Dakota answered.

Good one, Ri. Seriously why'd you stop talking to me? What's up?

Grace typed: It's not Riley. And it's no joke. I'm Riley's mom and I need her to call me now.

A moment passed then Grace sent another text.

Dakota, please tell all Riley's friends that if they hear from her, I need her to call me now, please.

Another moment passed.

This for real? You're her mom?

Yes.

What's wrong? She all right? Is everything OK?

Grace glanced at her bandages. No need to go into everything, she thought before typing: Yes. I just need her to call me, please.

This for sure is real?

YES IT'S REAL DAKOTA!!!

Sorry OK I'll pass the message round.

Grace let out a breath. She may have embarrassed Riley, but she didn't care. She turned to Blake, who was seated beside her in the back of the SUV, pushing back her anger at him for the lie because she needed his help.

"Can you reach any of her friends? Maybe she borrowed a phone at the truck stop and contacted them to complain about us leaving her? Maybe you could get a message to her?"

"I'm on it, and I'm checking her social media accounts in case she got online and posted something for friends there."

Grace looked at Blake's bandages, grappling with her emotions, facing the fact they'd survived a crash.

"How are you doing?"

"I'm fine, Grace." He glanced from his phone, offering her a little smile. "I'm okay."

Blake had messed up but he was a good kid. Like his dad, she thought. The two of them had endured so much and now this. Grace was thankful no one had been hurt badly. She looked to the front. Trooper Gwen Sanchez was at the wheel and talking softy into her radio. John was beside her, on his phone, preliminary police accident report in his hand, sorting crash and insurance matters with the RV rental company.

Grace looked to the desert, silent and beautiful moments ago; now she saw its yawning emptiness as she grappled with Riley's absence.

Is she so angry with me for Caleb and the move

that she's punishing me? No, she wouldn't deliberately do something like this. Would she? Riley's not perfect but she's not like that.

It's my fault. Why didn't I wake her? I was angry, too. But I'm her mother. I'm the adult. I didn't handle things well. I was hard on her, not giving enough consideration to her state of mind about all the changes in her life. She screamed them at me: breaking up with Caleb, moving across the country, leaving her friends, leaving Sherry. And those changes had compounded the earlier ones, my marriage to John, becoming a new family, even going back to the most horrible change: her dad's death.

The circumstances over how Tim died began to rise, forcing Grace to grapple with her guilt. It was always there, in an unhealed, guarded corner of her heart. Blinking back tears, she fought against letting it overwhelm her now as the Sagebrush came into view.

Sanchez guided the SUV to the main entrance where two highway patrol and two Las Vegas Metro Ford pickups were parked, giving Grace a sense of relief and unease because the police presence underscored the seriousness of Riley's case.

"Ten-four," Sanchez said into her radio. "They want us to go to the security room."

"Did they find her?" Grace asked.

"No," Sanchez said.

Grace's stomach knotted as they walked quickly through the complex, amid the bustle of hundreds of travelers. John took her hand and they cut through the crowds, searching faces, praying for this to be over.

Nate Rogan and Carl Aldrich were with a group of police and staff waiting in the hall outside the room as the family approached. Grace tried to read their faces while the officers and staff made notice of the family's bandages and torn clothes.

There were quick greetings and introductions.

"I don't see her," Grace said. "Did you find her?"

"Not yet," Rogan said. "We've got people doing a sweep of the complex and detectives from our Missing Persons Detail are on their way."

"Oh God." Grace struggled to hold herself together.

"But she has to be here. Right?" John said.

"Come inside," Rogan said.

Six

Grace, John and Blake were taken into the dimly lit control room.

Working at the control panels, Travis Quinn greeted them then indicated the banks of monitors.

"Please look at number nineteen."

In slow motion, amid crisp clear images of people shopping in the convenience store, they saw a girl in a white T-shirt. At one point she faced the camera, revealing the stylized *Friends* graphic on her shirt. Then the girl's face was clear as she stared in the direction of the camera before walking out of the frame.

Grace's hand flew to her mouth.

"Oh my God, that's her! That's Riley!"

"We can confirm she was here and the time," Rogan said.

"So where is she now?" Grace asked. "Where'd she go?"

"We don't know," Quinn said.

"But you must know!" John indicated the banks of monitors covering every corner of the truck stop. "You got dozens of cameras here. Track her through the building."

"We can't," Quinn said.

"Why not?"

"There's a glitch," Aldrich said.

"We have cameras everywhere," Quinn said, "inside and outside, for liability and security. Two days ago while updating our software, we experienced problems."

"What problems?" John asked.

"We're not sure why yet, but we discovered most of our surveillance points were not storing recordings. They're all live streaming," Quinn said, "but most of them are not recording. So we don't know where Riley went after the store."

John swore, then added: "I don't believe this!"

"We're working on fixing it, but that won't help us right now." Rogan thought a moment, then turned to Aldrich. "What about your motel?"

"We don't have cameras inside the motel," Aldrich said.

"I'm talking about the exterior. Are they recording?"

"Yes, they're on a different network," Quinn said. "We already checked the motel footage for the time period from when the family arrived."

"Run through it again," Rogan said.

Quinn operated the controls for the cameras covering the exterior front, rear and walkways of the Sagebrush motel, cueing up the images. He ran the footage. They studied the sprinkling of people, couples, families and individuals coming and going, moved in fast motion. But no one in the series fit Riley Jarrett's description.

"We have to keep searching for her!" Grace said. "She has to be here!"

"We're doing all we can. Carl's got people searching the complex," Rogan said. "Right now we're going to need individual, preliminary statements. To expedite this, my colleagues will take you into separate offices here. Grace, you'll go with Officer Kilroy and Blake, you go with Officer Jenkins. John, we'll go to the table in the corner here."

"But we're wasting time," John said. "We should all be out there looking for her."

"Sir," Rogan said, "I assure you we have people doing that and more people coming. Your statements will help us."

Once separated, Grace, John and Blake each related their account of events surrounding Riley's disappearance. When they finished, Grace and Blake returned to the control room where John had grown impatient.

"It's now nearly two hours since we stopped here," John said. "You should've set up roadblocks."

Rogan said: "We'd do that if it was clear she had been abducted—"

"Abducted?" Grace's eyes widened.

"—and so far it's unclear what's happened," Rogan continued.

"Can you put out an Amber Alert, or something?" Grace asked.

"Unfortunately—or perhaps fortunately this case doesn't meet the criteria at this time. We'll consider it but we have no confirmation of an abduction, or a suspect, or a vehicle. Maybe she wandered off, or is lost?" Rogan said. "But we've alerted all of our people and the NHP, and we'll expand our search."

At that moment John saw that Blake, who'd been scrutinizing the monitors, stepped closer to one.

"Dad. There." Blake pointed. "Number twenty-six."

All eyes went to the monitor at one of the gas pump lines.

Aldrich told Quinn: "Pull in tighter."

The camera closed in on a white SUV, bringing the passenger side into focus.

"I see her!" Grace turned to John.

But John wasn't there.

He'd flown out of the control room.

Seven

Nevada

John ran outside to the gas pumps toward the white SUV he'd seen in the security monitor.

A person was in the rear passenger seat wrapped in a blanket, head leaning against the closed window.

"Riley!" John shouted.

The bearded man fueling the SUV had on a tank top, his arms sleeved with tattoos. He didn't distinguish John's voice above the noise of cars and trucks arriving and leaving. He didn't turn from watching the digits blur on the display of the self-serve pump.

As John got to the SUV, the blanket shifted below the window frame but not before he saw flashes of a white shirt and brown hair—*Riley's hair*—spilling from it.

John slapped his palms on the glass.

The head lifted weakly, long hair curtained in front of the face of a young girl who appeared groggy.

"Riley!"

John tried the door handle. It was locked. Over his shoulder he glimpsed Grace and the others approaching. Some of the officers were reaching for radios just as the man at the pump grasped that John was attempting to open the door of his SUV.

"Hey, hey, hey!" The man replaced the nozzle. "What the hell! Back off!"

John tried the front passenger door handle.

The man moved around his vehicle drawing his holstered handgun, extending his muscled arms to point it at John.

"Hey! Asshole! I said back off now!"

"That's my daughter!" John pointed to the girl. Witnessing the drama unfolding, other customers moved away, some crouched for cover, others reached for phones. A woman screamed: "He's going to shoot!" One man went into his car for his handgun.

Rogan and other officers, their weapons drawn, radios crackling, had taken positions around the gun holder. "Put your weapon on the ground, sir! Get on your knees, twine your fingers behind your head! Now!"

The gunman didn't move. "Tell the asshole to back off!"

"Back away, John!" Rogan shouted. Then to the gunman: "Put your weapon down, now!" Rogan repeated. "John! Raise your hands, step back and sit on the ground now!"

NHP units roared to the pumps, blocking the

SUV. John backed away. Seeing few options, the man slowly placed his gun on the ground and officers moved quickly to place him and John in handcuffs and recover his gun, defusing the situation and ordering others to stay away.

Rogan went to the rear passenger door and peered at the girl.

"Open the door for me," Rogan told her, holding up his badge.

A few seconds passed, locks clicked and Rogan opened the door. The girl appeared to be in her midteens. She brushed her hair aside, blinking as if not fully awake. Rogan turned and indicated for Grace to approach.

Hands covering her mouth, eyes brimming with tears, Grace moved closer shaking her head slowly.

"It's not her. It's not Riley."

"What's your name, sweetheart?" Rogan asked.

"Olivia Vaughan," she slurred.

"How old are you?"

"Sizzzteen."

"She's my niece," the handcuffed man said. "She's sedated because she just had her wisdom teeth taken out in Vegas. I'm taking her home to her mom, my sister, in Primm. I'm with the Guard. I got a permit for my gun and paperwork from the dentist for Olivia."

After assessing the circumstances, Rogan made several radio dispatches then nodded to the other officers.

"We've got paramedics coming to check the girl. Remove the cuffs, we'll sort this out."

Rogan then took John, Grace and Blake aside.

"I get that this is an emotionally intense time," he said, "but it's dangerous to take matters into your own hands. You've got to let us do our job."

"And what're you doing?" John said.

"We're continuing to search the complex for her. Detectives from our Missing Persons Detail will be here soon. We'll likely bring in our Search and Rescue Unit. We'll expand the search to increase our efforts to find your daughter."

Helpless and sore, Grace, John and Blake surveyed the huge truck stop, with its gas lines, parking lots and traffic, and nodded.

Forty-five minutes later, after talking with the paramedics, the girl, Olivia Vaughan, and her uncle, Darryl Hecker; and after verifying their identifications, their documents and making calls, Rogan had determined Hecker had no record and no outstanding warrants. He was a sergeant with the Nevada National Guard's 72nd Military Police Company. His license and permit were in order and his story checked out.

They were free to leave.

But not Grace and her family.

They were hostage to growing fears about Riley.

Grace and Brandy, the young staff member, went through every restroom inside the complex, looking in empty stalls, calling for Riley over those that were in use. Grace's heart rose each time her phone or Riley's chimed with a notification for a text.

It was never Riley.

It was Dakota, or one of Riley's other friends, Claire or Ashley, asking if there was any news on where she was.

We haven't heard from her.

Is she all right?

Is something wrong?

Her body aching, her mind numb with worry, Grace went from bathroom to bathroom with a patient Brandy, listening to the public address echo as the truck stop continued paging Riley.

This can't be real.

It was as if Grace were walking through a horrible dream.

Riley, where are you? Why didn't I wake you up? Why didn't I check on you before we left? This is my fault.

The surroundings blurred and Grace sat on a bench and sobbed.

Brandy sat next to her, put her arm around her.

"It's going to be okay." She passed her tissues. "We'll find her."

Even though Rogan and Aldrich had said the entire Sagebrush had been searched, John looked for Riley in the drivers' lounge, the fitness room, the showers, the arcade and the pet area.

It was futile.

I should've paid more attention. I should've insisted Blake wake Riley when we stopped. From the time we left San Diego, this morning was strained. Everyone was on edge. I should've taken that into account when we stopped here. I knew there was a risk, leaving her in the RV after she'd argued with us...

At that moment, John's memory pulled him back. But he fought it because he didn't want to remember.

He continued searching for Riley in the barber shop, then the public library. Then the chapel.

That's where he could no longer keep the past from tormenting him as he remembered the knifing wind, the whipping rain and the ocean rising and falling.

Eight

Detective Michelle McDowell of the Missing Persons Detail tapped her fingers on the steering wheel of the unmarked Chevrolet.

She had a tendency to do it each time she and her partner were called out on a new case. Tapping helped her anticipate all they had to do. The twist in this one was the crash. McDowell turned to her partner to gauge his thoughts.

Good luck with that.

Dan Elsen's face was as impassive as the presidents on Mount Rushmore. He rarely smiled. He'd lost his wife two years ago after she overdosed on opioids while mourning her parents who'd been killed by a drunk driver. Elsen was at her hospital bedside, holding her, when she took her last breath.

Since his wife's death, McDowell was one of the few people Elsen tolerated. He'd once confided to her that his job and his dog were the only things keeping him upright.

Now, after swiping through his tablet and reading updates, Elsen looked at the road ahead. They took the Boulevard south because 15 was still backed up with traffic.

"Got some video of her; and a false sighting by the family leading to an altercation between the father and a guardsman at the pumps," he said. "Nothing beyond that, yet."

"What's your take so far, Dan?"

"We'll talk to the sub then the parents, and we'll ascertain the possibility of a criminal act. We'll enhance search efforts. We'll assume nothing."

"I know the drill." McDowell reached for her Raiders coffee cup, a gift from Jack, her ten-year-old son. She shared custody with her ex and his new girlfriend. "I want your thoughts."

"You want me to speculate?"

"What do you think of the situation, leaving the girl, the crash?"

"At this stage there's nothing to be gained by speculating. We work with facts and evidence," he said. "I'm curious. What does your gut tell you?"

McDowell let out a breath.

"In most cases we find people."

"But not every time."

"No. Not every time."

She looked out at the desert without having to say more.

They both knew.

Rhythmic ticktocking sounded as McDowell signaled for the exit to the Silver Sagebrush.

* * *

Officer Nate Rogan greeted the detectives and walked them through the truck stop to the section with security and admin offices. They went straight to the control room to see the video of Riley Jarrett in the convenience store.

Rogan then took McDowell and Elsen into an empty office and closed the door. His deep-set eyes grew intense as he read from his notes, briefing them for several minutes. He assured them that search efforts were ongoing with Metro officers, NHP and employees before closing his notebook and handing off the investigation.

"Aldrich is holding staff," Rogan said. "Shifts have ended for some and they want to go."

"They need to be patient," Elsen said. "And if any staff have left recently, or their shift ended, call them back so we can talk to them."

"We'll request more people from the detail for interviews," McDowell said. "We'll likely set up a command post and call in the SAR unit."

"Let's put out an Amber Alert," Elsen said.

"But the key factors aren't there," Rogan said. "Was she abducted, taken against her will? Is she in danger? We have no suspect vehicle."

"We know, but taking everything into consideration, let's move on it. You can direct any pushback to me," Elsen said. "And, I saw the electronic advertising signs. Can you get Aldrich to get her face and details up there, too?"

"Sure," Rogan said.

"We need someone to follow the RV to the tow yard for potential evidence. Michelle and I will get a warrant," Elsen said.

"We'll get someone on the RV," Rogan said. "Management cleared some offices for us. I've separated the family so you can take their formal statements." Rogan reached for the door. "I'll let you get to it."

"This is going to be a challenge," Elsen said.

Rogan and McDowell waited for him to elaborate.

"We've got malfunctioning cameras in a location that is second in the state only to McCarran for its volume of travelers. We're coming up on two and a half hours since the family says they first stopped here. Time's working against us."

Nine

Nevada

Grace sat alone in the empty office, helpless, waiting at someone's desk as if trespassing on their work space and their life.

To the right of the monitor and keyboard was a coffee mug with Best Mom Ever printed on it. To the left, a tiny plush velour teddy bear next to a framed photo showing an adolescent boy and girl, a woman and a man, all beaming in front of a sign that read Nova Scotia. Clipped to the half wall above it was a calendar with dates noting, "Billie/Dentist" and "Report Due" and "Trevor's BDay!" circled in red.

It was as if she'd been inserted into someone's happy, ordered life, while hers spun out of control.

Grace set the two phones on the desk, covered her face with her bandaged hands, sliding her shaking fingers into her hair, stifling a scream.

Where are you, Riley?

Why are they making me sit here when I need to keep searching?

Riley's phone vibrated. Grace snatched it up. It was a text from Dakota.

Hi Mrs. Jarrett. No one's heard from her still. What's going on?

Grace began typing a response. Her chin crumpled and she deleted what she'd started, clenched her eyes shut, opened them and looked to the ceiling. She just couldn't do it. She couldn't lie to Riley's friends that everything was fine, or everything was going to be fine.

Not knowing was unbearable, filling her with fear for what they faced: the size of the Silver Sagebrush, so many people, so many cars and big trucks coming and going out here in the middle of the desert.

Grace pressed Riley's phone to her heart and prayed.

Please, Riley. Please. Just materialize. Just show up with a stupid explanation—any explanation. If you're angry with me then let's have it out. But please, please, don't punish me like this. Not after all we've been through. Come back to me! I can't go through this again.

In an instant Grace was back in her living room, on that night, wondering what was taking Tim so long, wondering why he wasn't answering his phone. Then she saw headlights. But it wasn't Tim.

A police car had stopped in front of their house. Through the window she saw two uniformed officers get out, a male and a female. Her doorbell rang. She opened the door and saw it in their sober faces, saw it in their eyes, and she knew, knew it before they spoke the words.

"Ma'am, is this the home of Timothy Phillip Jarrett?"

The office door opened.

Grace's thoughts shifted to the man and woman who'd entered.

She guessed the man was just over six feet, wearing a dark sport coat, white shirt and green checkered tie. He was bald with short salt-and-pepper hair on the sides. He looked to be in his early fifties. His craggy face held a world-weary expression while his eyes held a measure of sadness.

The woman appeared to be on either side of forty and was about five-five. She had a pin-striped navy blazer over a white shirt and jeans. She had blond hair, brushing her shoulders, sharp, pretty eyes, a sincere smile and a warm, firm grip.

"I'm Detective Michelle McDowell, this is Detective Dan Elsen. We're with Las Vegas Metro's Missing Persons Detail. We're going to help you find your daughter, but we need your help."

"Yes, anything."

Taking inventory of Grace's bandages and scrapes, Elsen asked: "You're okay to talk?"

"Yes."

"We want you to know that in most cases, we are able to locate missing people," McDowell said.

Grace nodded, embracing the encouragement.

"And we're going to do all we can to ensure Riley's reunited with her family."

"Yes, thank you."

"We need to ask you some questions to help us."

"But we've already told Officer Rogan everything."

"We've spoken with him and have his preliminary report, but because this is now a missing person matter we're taking responsibility."

Grace's eyes widened slightly, and she swallowed as McDowell unfolded the keyboard case of her tablet and positioned it on the desk.

"If it's all right with you, we'll record this so we have all the information accurately?"

"Sure, but people are still out there looking for her, right?"

"Yes," said Elsen, who'd been watching Grace closely.

McDowell began by stating who was present, the location, the date, the time, the case and number assigned to it. Then she took out her notebook and continued by having Grace provide details of Riley's date of birth, physical description and detailing the clothing Riley was wearing.

"Now, for the record, we'll go over a few things. Some questions may be difficult but we need to ask them, okay?" McDowell said.

"Okay."

"Why don't you start by telling us what happened."

Grace related how they were in the process of moving from San Diego to Pittsburgh and had rented an RV for a cross-country family vacation, leaving that morning planning to make Las Vegas their first stop before going on to the Grand Canyon. She recounted how Riley and Blake kept their faces in their screens, frustrating her to the point she confiscated their phones and locked them in the glove compartment.

"That's when Riley and I argued and she stomped off to sleep in the back bedroom."

"This was when you were at or near Baker?" McDowell said.

"Yes."

"But you didn't stop there and your only Nevada stop was here?"

"That's right."

"Riley was angry you'd taken her phone?" Elsen asked.

"Not just that, she was angry about moving, leaving her friends and because I pushed her to break up with her boyfriend, Caleb Clarke."

"Why did you do that?" McDowell asked.

"Caleb was seventeen, almost eighteen. He was too old for her. I didn't think it was appropriate."

"How long had they been dating?" McDowell asked.

"About five months. I was against it the whole time, but it was hard to keep them apart."

"Did Riley often defy you?" Elsen asked.

"No, just with Caleb."

"Do you think Riley was in contact with Caleb all morning?" McDowell asked.

"Maybe but I can't be certain. Blake said she uses self-destructing messages."

"Could Riley have arranged to secretly meet Caleb here?"

"No, he's not even in the country because he was flying to Africa with his dad around the time we left," Grace said. "And, our stop here was not planned. Besides, she was asleep in the back."

"And she was still sleeping when you stopped here?" McDowell said.

"Yes, in the back bedroom with the door closed."

"Why didn't you wake her?" Elsen asked.

"Because of her mood, because she'd been up so early, because I knew we wouldn't be long. So I left her a note."

"But you can't be sure she saw it?" Elsen said.

"No, I can't."

"So she leaves the RV without a phone and her family drives away thinking she's asleep in the back. That's what happened?" Elsen said.

"Not exactly. I mean, yes, she must've gone inside looking for us. We didn't see her but we assumed she was in the back because—"

"Excuse me, why didn't you check on her before leaving the truck stop?" Elsen asked.

"That's just it. I asked Blake to check and he said she was fine."

"So was she there, or not there?" Elsen said.

"No, Blake lied about checking—"

"Why?"

"—because we were all still upset about the fight. And I—I—" Grace thrust her face into her hands. "I should've checked myself. I should have, but—" Grace took a teary breath "—for the same reasons we didn't wake her before. I was mad at her. I wanted her to sleep. Oh God, I was wrong! I should've checked on her!"

"All right, so you'd gone a few miles past Jean when you realized what had happened and turned around?" McDowell said.

"Yes, that's when we crashed."

"And in all this time Riley's never got to a phone, never contacted you?"

"No." Grace held up Riley's phone. "Her friends haven't heard anything from her either."

"Will you give Riley's phone to us so we can check who she's been in contact with, what sites she's visited?" McDowell asked.

Grace hesitated before handing the phone to her.

"Thank you. We will obtain a warrant for it."

"A warrant?"

"It's a routine matter," McDowell said. "We'll also need any other devices she has."

"There's her tablet but it's in the RV."

"We'll look through it at the tow yard," McDowell said. "To see if anything was left behind that might indicate where Riley went. We'll get a warrant for the RV, too."

"This sounds so serious."

"We're just following procedure," McDowell said.

"And no one has contacted your family claiming to have kidnapped Riley, or demanding a ransom?" Elsen asked.

"No."

"Grace." Elsen leaned closer to her. "If they warned you not to talk to police, you should tell us."

Grace swallowed and shook her head. "No one's contacted us."

"Has Riley been to Nevada before?" McDowell asked.

"No."

"Do you have relatives or friends here, anyone she may have tried to contact?"

"No."

McDowell continued the questions. Had Riley ever been missing before? Had she ever missed school, appointments? Does she have any medical issues requiring medication? Does she have any mental illness, or physical impairments, any suicidal thoughts?

Grace answered no to each of them.

"Has she ever run away in the past?" McDowell asked.

"No."

"To be safe, we'll get San Diego police to watch your house there in case she went back," Elsen said.

"Is she undergoing any therapy or psychiatric care?" McDowell asked.

"No, not anymore."

"Not anymore?" Elsen repeated.

Grace took a moment then said, "When her father, my first husband, died, we both received grief counseling."

McDowell exchanged a subtle glance with Elsen then resumed the questions. Does Riley abuse alcohol or drugs? Had she ever been charged with any offense?

Grace answered no.

"You are Riley's biological mother?" McDowell asked.

"Yes."

"How is your relationship with her?"

Grace blinked away tears, half smiling, shrugging.

"Typical mother–teen daughter. Aside from Caleb, we argue about friends, clothes, tattoos, makeup, screen time."

"Would you say you are close?"

"Yes. After her dad died, it was just the two of us. We needed each other. Then I met John."

"How did your first husband die?"

"In a car accident."

McDowell nodded and let a moment pass before continuing.

"How's Riley's relationship with John and his son—" she glanced at her notes "—Blake?"

"Good. It's good. We've been married for two

years now, adjusting to being a blended family. I guess you could say we're a work in progress."

"Are there any stress points in Riley's relationships with others in the family?"

"No. I mean, we're each finding our way." Grace got a tissue and touched it to her eyes. "John lost his wife and daughter, too. So we're survivors, hanging on to each other, doing the best we can."

"How did John lose his wife and daughter?"

"It was a boating accident. They drowned in a storm when their boat capsized near San Diego." Grace paused and looked to the detectives. "What does any of this have to do with Riley? We need to be searching for her."

"We've put out alerts, we've got people looking for your daughter," Elsen said. "These questions are relevant, so bear with us."

McDowell resumed. "You're a registered nurse?"

"Yes."

"You would be familiar with child abuse cases and how they're investigated?"

Grace eyed both of the detectives. "Why?"

"Has your daughter ever told you, or have you ever suspected, that she'd been abused sexually, physically, or otherwise, by someone in the family?"

Shock and hurt creased Grace's face. "What? No!"

"By anyone outside your family?"

"No!"

"Do you know of anyone who would want to harm your daughter?"

"No."

"Has your husband or son ever struck her?"

"No, why're you—"

"Have you ever struck her?"

Grace swallowed. "God, no. I can't believe you would ask me this!"

"Are you involved in your daughter's disappearance?"

"No!"

"Do you believe your husband, or son, are involved?"

"No! My God! We left her behind by mistake and you're talking to me like we're a family of monsters!"

"Mrs. Jarrett," Elsen said. "People lie to us all the time. We take the case of a missing fourteen-year-old very seriously."

"Is Riley sexually active?" McDowell asked.

Pushing back tears, she didn't answer.

"Grace," McDowell said, "do you think she's sexually active, given her relationship with Caleb?"

"I don't know."

"Would she have confided that to you?"

She looked into her hands. "Maybe not."

"Do you think she's ever sexted, sent explicit photos of herself?" McDowell asked.

Grace looked away. "It's possible."

"Could she have connected with someone online and arranged to meet them?" Elsen said.

"But how? We stopped here on impulse and I had her phone."

"Maybe she had a burner phone, one that you weren't aware of," he said.

Grace stared at Elsen.

"It happens," he said. "Kids are good at keeping secrets from their parents."

"No, I don't think so."

"Grace, do you or your husband have drug or gambling debts, financial pressures?" McDowell asked.

"No."

"Can you think of anyone who would want to harm Riley for any reason?"

"I can't."

"Has your family been threatened?"

"No."

"Has anything strange happened to your family in the time leading up to your trip?" she asked. "Any strange calls, wrong numbers, emails, deliveries, visits to your house, people following you?"

"No."

The detectives leaned back, suggesting they were done, but something unsettling telegraphed between them.

"One last thing," McDowell said. "Please don't read anything into this, but it's something we have to ask."

The air in the room tensed.

"Would Riley know or have any familiarity with a girl by the name of Eva Marie Garcia?"

Staring at McDowell and Elsen, Grace's mind raced but the name didn't ring a bell.

"No. Why?"

"Again, we have nothing to say there's any relation to Riley," McDowell said, "but about a year ago, seventeen-year-old Eva Marie Garcia was on a group trip to Las Vegas. She and her friends were returning to Riverside, California, when they stopped at Primm, not far from here. They reported her missing. Searches yielded nothing."

"Did they ever find her?"

McDowell shot a glance to Elsen before she answered.

"Forty-four days after she'd disappeared, her body was found in the desert a few hundred yards from Interstate 15 near the California border, a few miles from here."

"The case remains unsolved," Elsen said.

Grace covered her face with her hands as warm tears rolled over her bandages and her fingers.

"This can't be happening."

McDowell touched her shoulder.

"I'm sorry, Grace, but we had to ask you about any possible connection. We've found nothing to suggest Riley's been hurt. We're searching. We can still find her. You've got to believe that."

Grace nodded but her heart was flooded with fear.

Ten

In a room across the hall from where detectives were questioning his wife, John Marshall paced.

He hated waiting alone in here, unable to search for Riley, not knowing if they'd found her.

His pulse still thudding from the crash and the standoff at the pumps, he stared at his phone hoping that maybe, just maybe, Riley would contact him if she could.

But nothing showed on his phone.

John rubbed his forehead.

She could be anywhere. Anything could've happened.

This whole thing was unbelievable and he blamed himself for it, for uprooting his family, tearing them away from their lives in San Diego. He'd expected some resistance to moving to Pittsburgh, especially from Riley, but he'd underestimated how much. Riley's painful accusations from the argument in the RV echoed in his head.

Did her blowup with Grace set events in motion?

He should've done more. He should've gotten Riley up when they stopped but he didn't. He yielded to Grace. Maybe because it was easy, because deep down John sensed that in addition to Riley's continuing struggle adjusting to their new family, she didn't like him because in her eyes he could never measure up to her father.

And maybe on some level he gave Riley the same impression; that he was always measuring her—her behavior, her attitude and her appearance—against his beloved daughter, Courtney.

Like the time he went to the movie theater to pick up Riley and her three girlfriends. Her friends, all about fourteen, were wearing T-shirts, shorts or jeans. But Riley was wearing a low-cut top, a skirt that was way too short and lots of makeup. All of this in addition to the fact she'd started dating Caleb Clarke, a boy much too old for her.

John was so upset he barely spoke while driving Riley and her friends home because he was thinking of Courtney. In his heart he knew that, even at sixteen, Courtney would never have dressed like that. He'd mentioned Riley's appearance to Grace when she came home from the hospital. Grace talked to Riley privately, and John never saw her wear that skirt again. But she was cooler to him for the next few days.

Was he being unfair comparing Riley with Courtney? Or was he being a concerned dad? He didn't know. He'd made so many mistakes in his life. He should've done more in the RV, should've insisted they got Riley out of the back before driving off. Blake lying about checking on her only made things worse.

Maybe their move, the breakup with Caleb, the meltdown in the RV, was connected to Riley being missing? Maybe she was pulling a stunt to get back at them?

He hoped so because the alternative terrified him.

He'd already lost one daughter. He couldn't lose another.

God, I've made so many mistakes, grave mistakes.

John stopped pacing. He kneaded the knot in the back of his neck, and in an instant he was reliving the deaths of his wife and daughter…the whipping wind, the heaving waves, the terrible rolling…then—the door opened.

A man and a woman entered the room.

John's eyes went to their badges, then to their faces.

Detective McDowell and Detective Elsen introduced themselves.

"Did you find her?" John asked.

"No."

At a loss, John absorbed the fact that Riley had now been missing for three hours.

"Mr. Marshall," McDowell said. "Please have a seat so we can talk."

John refused. "Tell me what you're doing to find

her. Time's slipping away! Why isn't every truck and car being searched? Why aren't there road-blocks, an Amber Alert or search teams?"

"Mr. Marshall," Elsen said. "We're putting out an Amber Alert. Keep in mind, we're still in the process of determining what may or may not have transpired but we are taking action."

"We told you what happened! She's been miss-ing for almost three hours!"

"John—" McDowell was calm "—we've got people looking for Riley, we've circulated her pic-ture, her details to all police units and we're ex-panding our efforts. Search and rescue people are on their way. We understand this is an anxious time, but we need your help."

Blinking quickly, John took a breath.

"Please, John. Sit down and cooperate with us so we can find Riley."

Releasing some of his anger, he sat. McDowell set her tablet to record, and for the next several minutes John recounted events with the detectives asking questions.

"So after the argument, Riley went to the back to sleep?" McDowell asked.

"Yes, that was around Baker. Later when we got to Nevada, I wanted to stop here because I'd read how this new complex was one of the larg-est truck stops in the world and thought the kids might like it."

"If that was the case, then why didn't you wake Riley?" Elsen asked.

"I wanted to, but Grace wanted her to sleep because we'd been up so early, and she was in a mood. Grace left her a note."

"How long were you away from the RV?" Elsen asked.

"Twenty minutes, give or take."

"Was she locked in the RV?" Elsen asked.

"No. It was locked from the outside, but she could get out."

"It has a keypad lock and you need a PIN to unlock it, correct?" Elsen said.

"Yes. I created our PIN for this trip. The rental company instructed me," John said.

"Who else has the PIN?" Elsen asked.

"Grace, Blake and Riley."

"Why didn't you wake her before you drove away from here?" McDowell asked.

Staring at the floor, John shook his head. His haggard, whiskered face bore scrapes from the crash.

"We just assumed she was there sleeping. My son said he checked on her."

The detectives let a moment pass.

"Did you, Grace and Blake stay together when you came inside?"

"Except for using the bathrooms, yes. We went to the store for food and things, that's it."

"Then what?" Elsen said.

"We left, heading for Las Vegas, for our hotel, the Golden Nugget. We were five, maybe seven miles past Jean when Grace asked Blake to wake

Riley and that's when we realized what had happened, that she was gone and didn't have her phone. Grace called here for help and I turned around at the first U-turn, then we crashed."

"Tell us about the crash," Elsen said.

"After the U-turn we'd gone less than two miles when this car came out of nowhere on my left and cut us off."

"Any chance you got the plate number, or state, make or model?"

"No, it happened so fast. It was a sedan, that's all I know."

"Did it hit you?"

"No, it blurred by, shocking me. I had to brake then we swerved and crashed."

"Was it a dark or light colored car?"

John shook his head. "I don't know."

"Did the RV have a dash cam?"

"No," John said, "but you've got cameras along the interstate, right?"

"We'll check with Transportation," McDowell said. "It could be a case of road rage arising from your U-turn."

"Take us back to the argument you and your wife had with Riley," Elsen said. "It sounds like your daughter was very upset?"

"Yes, she was."

"Did she at any time give any indication that she would leave, or run away? Maybe go back to San Diego, or try to reconnect with her boyfriend?"

"No. Caleb left the country with his family.

Riley was upset about the move, but she gave us no sign that she was going to run away."

"Has she ever run away in the past?" McDowell asked.

"No, not since I've known Grace."

"All right, can you give us a timeline of the day?" Elsen said.

For the next few minutes John recounted how they'd left San Diego just before sunrise then detailed their route and how once they cleared all the Greater Los Angeles traffic they kept going, stopping in Fontana.

"Did you ever get a sense you were followed?" Elsen asked.

"No."

"When you stopped in Fontana were there any altercations or incidents there, or anywhere else along the trip?"

"No."

"Who else knew the route you took?"

John gave it some thought: "A few days before we left we had a farewell party at our house in San Diego, and I mentioned to friends that we planned to take 215 past San Bernardino then 15."

"We may need a list of people who attended the party," McDowell said.

John nodded.

"Have you ever driven this route before?" Elsen asked.

"Years ago when I was in college, with friends for a weekend in Las Vegas."

"Nothing more recent?" Elsen asked.

"I flew to Las Vegas about two years ago for a conference."

John watched Elsen make notes.

Another twenty minutes passed with the detectives asking John a number of questions, covering a range of areas before McDowell said: "Can you tell us again, why you're moving to Pittsburgh?"

"I have a new opportunity there in corporate communications with a large company. It's a promotion with a bigger salary."

"Have you ever been in trouble with the law, John?" Elsen asked.

John stared at him, then McDowell at the sudden change in questioning.

"No. Unless you count a speeding ticket a few years ago."

"Prior to marrying Grace, you lost your wife and daughter in an accident?" Elsen said.

John hesitated at another abrupt shift in questioning. "Yes."

"How old was your daughter when she died?"

An uncomfortable silence passed before John said: "Sixteen."

"What happened?"

"I don't see what this has to do with any—"

"Please, John," Elsen said. "It's important we have as much background as possible, and we'd appreciate your cooperation."

John swallowed and blinked several times, recounting the tragedy.

"We'd gone sailing when late in the day the water got rough. There was a storm surge. We were trying to get home. The wind and rain were relentless. We were in San Diego Bay, off the tip of Point Loma, trying to get to Buoy One, when our boat capsized and we ended up in the water clinging to the overturned hull. My wife and daughter got swept away and they drowned."

"I'm sorry for your loss," Elsen said. "So you and Grace have been married two years, now?"

"Yes."

"How would you describe your relationship with Riley?"

John inhaled then released a slow breath.

"Good, but I can't replace Tim, her biological father, and she lets me know it. I think she's having a hard time accepting me as her stepdad and Blake as her stepbrother. I think our moving is a challenge for her, leaving friends, you know?"

McDowell nodded.

"John—" Elsen leaned closer to him "—have you ever struck Riley or abused her in any way?"

"What?"

"Have you?"

John stared hard at Elsen: "No."

"Do you think Blake or Grace have abused Riley?"

"No!"

"Are you involved in any way in Riley's disappearance?"

"No. What is this?"

"Do you think your wife or son may be involved?"

"Absolutely not."

A tense moment passed with the detectives taking note of John's reaction. McDowell then asked if he was familiar with the name Eva Marie Garcia.

"No, why?"

"She's the victim of an unsolved homicide that happened near here a year ago," McDowell said.

John's face turned white. "A homicide? And you think it's related to Riley being missing?"

"No," Elsen said. "But these are questions we need to ask."

John let out a long breath.

"We know this is difficult and we thank you for cooperating." McDowell patted John's shoulder. "We understand that you have volunteered to let us search your RV for anything that might help us locate Riley."

John nodded.

"We'll go to the tow yard after we talk to your son."

John swallowed and raised his head. "Do you think Riley's dead?"

Elsen and McDowell exchanged glances.

"John," McDowell said. "We have nothing to suggest she's been harmed in any way. We consider her a missing person, and we're doing all we can to locate her as soon as possible."

Eleven

Blake Marshall kept rubbing his legs and checking for messages on his phone.

Nothing.

This was out of control: Riley missing; the crash; that girl at the pumps who looked like her; that guy pointing a gun at his dad, all the cops with their guns out.

The saliva in Blake's mouth dried up. He tried to stay calm.

What's the real reason the police put me alone here in this room?

Voices in the hall. His heart beat faster. A woman and man came in.

"Sorry to keep you waiting, Blake," the woman said, closing the door. "I'm Detective Michelle McDowell and this is Detective Dan Elsen. We're with the Missing Persons Detail of Las Vegas Metro Police."

"Are you all right?" Elsen took stock of Blake as the woman set up her tablet.

Blake swallowed. "I'm worried. Did you find Riley?"

"Not yet, but listen," McDowell said, smiling. "We're doing everything we can to find her. More people are arriving to search. Right now we need your help, okay?"

Blake nodded.

"Let's start with you telling us what was happening in the RV in the time before Riley went missing," Elsen said.

For several minutes Blake told the detectives everything he could remember about the drive.

"So why lie about checking on her?" Elsen asked.

Blake took a long breath and let it out slowly. "She was so pissed off after the fight she flipped me the finger. I had nothing to do with it. I didn't want her awake and sitting with me, you know? Not when she was so bitchy." He swallowed, blinking back tears. "I know it's stupid but that's the truth."

The detectives let a long moment pass.

"So it was clear," McDowell said, "Riley didn't want to move."

"Real clear."

"Blake," Elsen said, "did Riley at any time prior to the trip or during the trip confide or indicate to you that she was going to run away, or meet up with Caleb or anyone else?"

"No."

"Who was she talking to on her phone all morning?" McDowell asked.

"Her friends, likely, I don't know."

"Can you give us the names of some of her friends and any contact information?"

"Three I know are Dakota Lawson, Claire Nakamura and Ashley Hernandez. They all go to school together."

With Blake guessing at the spellings, McDowell noted the information.

"What do you think happened to Riley?" Elsen asked.

"Well, from the security video, she got out of the RV and was in a store looking for us, probably pretty pissed that we drove off. After that, I don't know."

"Do you think it's possible she's hiding, or tried to get a ride to San Diego as a way of getting back at you guys for leaving her?" Elsen asked. "Maybe meet up with Caleb."

"No, first because I think Riley would be too scared to try to do anything like that. And second, Caleb and his father went to Algeria."

"On your way here, your dad said you made a stop in California," Elsen said. "Where was that?"

"Fontana, at a Chevron."

"Did Riley stay in the RV?"

"We all went in, used the bathroom, got something to eat. I got a burrito, Riley got yogurt."

"Did you notice anything unusual like someone watching you, or following you, or trying to talk to Riley?"

Blake shook his head.

"How would you say everyone in your family has been getting along lately?" Elsen asked.

"Okay. All things considered. I think we're all nervous about the move. Riley didn't want to leave San Diego, that's for sure."

"And how're you with the move?"

"I'm like, whatever, Dad's got a big new job, so we have to move. That's it."

"And how do you get along with your mom?" McDowell asked.

"With Grace? I don't call her my mom. I call her Grace."

"Yes, how do you get along with Grace?"

"Okay."

"Does she have a temper? Have you ever seen her use physical punishment on Riley?" McDowell asked.

"No, no way. Grace is actually pretty nice. Once I came into our kitchen and Grace was alone crying. She seemed embarrassed. She was sad about her first husband who died. I told her it was okay. I get sad sometimes about my mom and sister. We all understand about losing someone close to you and what it does to you."

"What about your dad?" Elsen said.

"What about him?"

"Does he have a temper? Does he get angry? I

understand he lost it at the pumps when he thought he saw Riley."

"I wouldn't say he has a temper." Blake thought a moment. "I know he'll always be angry at himself over the accident when we went sailing and got caught in the storm. I know he'll never forgive himself for that." Blake brushed a tear from his face.

"Do Grace and your dad ever argue about anything?" McDowell asked.

"No, not really."

"They have any stress about finances, bills, debt?"

"I don't think so."

"Any issues with drinking too much or using illegal drugs, or gambling, or having affairs?"

"I don't think so, nothing that I would know, except the issue with Caleb Clarke."

"Tell us more about that," McDowell said.

"They didn't like the idea of him dating Riley, especially Grace. She didn't like that Caleb was my age and too old for Riley and they kept pressuring Riley to break it off. Grace even tried calling Caleb's father. He's divorced and Caleb lives with him."

"What happened?"

"Not sure. I heard Grace tell my dad that Caleb's dad said he would talk to Caleb about it, but I don't know if he did." Blake shrugged.

"And Riley's reaction to it all?" Elsen asked.

"She hated the idea of Grace trying to get her to break up with Caleb."

"She kept seeing him."

"Yes."

"She was defiant?" Elsen asked.

"Yes."

"So Caleb's nearly eighteen and he's dating your fourteen-year-old stepsister," Elsen said. "How'd that sit with you?"

"Not well."

"You ever meet or confront him?"

"A couple of times. I said, 'Dude, find someone your own age. Riley's too young for you.' And he goes, 'Riley and I are in love.'"

"So with the move to Pittsburgh, the relationship was going to end?" McDowell said.

"That's right," Blake said. "A couple of days before we left San Diego, my folks threw a big farewell party at our house, invited all their friends. Riley and I invited all of our friends. Grace wasn't happy that Caleb came, but since Riley was supposed to break it off with him that night, she kind of went with it. I mean we were set to drive across the country, and he and his dad were flying off to Algiers."

"So how did it go for Riley and Caleb at the party?"

"I saw them in a corner of the yard, hugging and kissing, crying, too. I think they were both upset about it."

The detectives let a moment pass before Elsen resumed.

"How do you get along with Riley?"

"Maybe not as good as I should. Maybe I should try harder. Dad, too."

"What do you mean by that?" Elsen crossed his arms.

"I know Dad expects her to be more like Courtney, my older sister, which doesn't go over well."

"What do you mean?"

"Riley misses her dad and will never accept my dad as her father."

"So there's a little tension there?" Elsen said.

"A little but it's getting better over time, in my opinion."

"And you? How's your relationship with Riley?"

"Okay. I guess I'm still having a hard time adjusting to our new family and having her as my sister because I miss Courtney."

"Do you argue with Riley?"

"Not really. If she argues, it's with Grace about clothes, curfews, Caleb, mom-daughter stuff like that."

"Has Riley ever run away before?"

"No, not since we've all been together."

Elsen leaned closer to Blake. "I'm going to ask you something and I want you to be honest, Blake."

"Okay," Blake said.

"Ever look at porn?"

Blake swallowed, his face reddened and he

shrugged. "Sure, who hasn't? It's online every-where."

"Do you know if Riley's ever looked at it?"

"I don't know, but likely."

"Has she ever sexted?"

"I don't know."

"Do you suspect she's sexted with Caleb?"

"Likely."

"Had sex with him?"

"Probably."

"She ever tell you any of her secrets?"

Blake shook his head.

"Does she use drugs, alcohol, anything like that?"

"Maybe she'd tried stuff at parties, like most kids do."

"Does she have a burner phone?"

Blake shifted in his seat. "I don't think so. I know she lets Grace see her phone, but she uses self-deleting apps because once she had some kind of problem with her phone and asked me to help her fix it. I saw she hid some apps, or tried to hide them in a folder."

Elsen drew even closer to Blake. "You ever strike Riley or abuse her?"

"No!"

"Do you know what happened to her? Where she is?"

"No."

"Tell us the truth, are you in any way involved in her being missing?"

Feeling the full weight of two unsmiling detectives on him, a sweat droplet webbed down Blake's back before he answered.

"No."

Twelve

Nevada

After interviewing the family, McDowell and Elsen set out to talk to the staff member who had seen Riley Jarrett just before her shift ended.

Walking through the busy complex, McDowell said: "What's your read on Grace, John and Blake?"

"They're anxious. But we never get the whole picture first time around."

"Maybe. I don't know," McDowell said. "I've got a bad feeling."

"We're too early into this to know what we have."

The detectives saw Riley's face and information displayed on the big advertising screens. The public address call for her continued, echoing in the air that carried the aroma from the food outlets along with the pings and whirs of slot machines in the casino. All the while, they scanned the crowds for a young girl in a white *Friends* T-shirt until they arrived at the store where Riley was last seen in the footage recorded by a security camera.

The Silverado convenience store.

Carl Aldrich, the operations manager, met them there with an update on his security people's search of the truck stop.

"Nothing so far but we all know she was here and we're actively looking for her." Aldrich led them to a woman behind the counter at one of the registers. She was about twenty and wore a Silver Sagebrush golf shirt. She had a silver nose ring and was looking at her phone. Her name tag read "Skylar Brown."

"Skylar," Aldrich said. "This is Detective Mc-Dowell and Detective Elsen. Skylar's shift ended but we called her back."

McDowell flipped to a new page in her notebook. "Thanks for coming back, Skylar."

"No problem."

"Go ahead. Tell us what you know."

"That's definitely her." Skylar raised her phone and pointed to Riley's picture on it. "And she was definitely here walking around the store, came right by me at the counter then she left."

"Did she speak to you?"

"No."

"Was she with anyone?"

"No one. But a little while later, say five or ten minutes, she was back walking around as if she was looking for someone. Then she left a second time and I never saw her again."

"Did it appear as if anyone followed her?" Elsen asked.

"Not that I could tell."

"So she entered and left alone?"

"From what I could tell, yes."

"Did you see her talk to anyone?"

"No."

"What was her demeanor?"

"Like she was a little scared and a little ticked off, I guess."

"Did she buy anything?"

"No."

"Approximately what time was it when she walked out the second time?"

Skylar thought. "I know it was right when a woman bought a lucky dice key ring. I'll check the receipts." She began tapping on the register's keyboard. A moment later, Skylar gave McDowell and Elsen the time and they finished by taking down Skylar's name, address and contact information.

"Thanks," McDowell said. "Carl, I think the family will want to talk to Skylar then resume searching with your people. Can you help with that?"

"Absolutely."

In an effort to retrace Riley's steps, the detectives then followed the most likely route through the complex to the nearest exit. They talked to staff in every outlet along the way before leaving and taking the most direct path across the huge lot to the spot by the palms where John Marshall said he'd parked the RV. While the detectives assessed the lot and heavy volume of traffic flowing in and out of the truck stop, McDowell's phone vibrated with a message.

"Okay," she told Elsen while looking at her phone, "they're sending the mobile command center with more bodies. They'll set up an incident command post. They're also bringing in the Search and Rescue Unit."

"Things are ramping up," Elsen said.

"Yup." McDowell scrolled through her phone. "Aldrich and Nate Rogan will keep us posted on the family."

"Have we got gloves and shoe covers in the trunk?"

"I put more in yesterday."

"Let's go take a look in the RV to see if anything was left behind to indicate where Riley Jarrett went."

Driving to Las Vegas through the desert and mountains, McDowell glanced at Elsen.

"Dan, if it's an abduction, then we know what the numbers tell us."

Elsen looked ahead at nothing. "She'd be killed within hours."

"She could've met someone who gave her a ride to the city, to the Nugget."

"We'll call Nugget's security and send them info," Elsen said.

"The Silver Sagebrush is a mega truck stop, and

you said it yourself—it's got high-volume traffic second only to McCarran. There's the possibility of human trafficking, and we can't forget the Garcia case," McDowell said.

"We can't rule anything out. But right now, we have no evidence connecting this to Garcia, nothing at all pointing to a criminal act."

McDowell said nothing as the road rushed under them.

"What we have," Elsen said, "are statements, a few facts and circumstances. All indications are that, in the time leading up to Riley Jarrett going missing, there was tension in that RV."

"I just don't know." McDowell tapped her fingers on the wheel.

"The family's upset. They had a lot going on before this happened," Elsen said. "But there's no evidence of a crime, nothing to suggest the family are bad people. Right now, nothing about them seems off to me. They volunteered their daughter's phone, and that's valuable to us. We'll get our tech team to see what they can extract from it. And the family's signed off on letting us search their vehicle. They're cooperating. We need to maintain good relations with them. In case things take a turn."

McDowell exhaled and nodded.

"And we'll run background on the family in San Diego," Elsen said. "We're just getting started."

McDowell looked to the desert, thinking of Eva Marie Garcia as they neared Las Vegas.

Thirteen

Las Vegas, Nevada

Willing & Able Towing was at the southern edge of Las Vegas in a light industrial section along with Arkall's Golden Storage facility, Sonik Zebra Electronics Warehouse and a tack shop.

A Las Vegas Metro marked unit sat in front of the tow yard.

In keeping with procedure—should the RV become evidence—Metro Police Officer Silvia Lopez had observed and followed the on-call tow operator, Lee Solano, who'd loaded the RV on a flatbed, covered it and transported it from the crash scene to the yard.

"As you'd instructed, Mr. Solano secured it in the locked Quonset hut over there. Nobody's been near it," Lopez told McDowell and Elsen as she consulted her notes. "I logged one NHP trooper and two Clark County responders who'd gone inside the RV at the scene. I have the names for you."

A dog was barking from somewhere.

"And the rental agency wants to have their guy look at the RV. The thing's a write-off," Lopez said.

"The rental guy can wait." Elsen looked at the four-acre lot. It held damaged vehicles within ten-foot-high chain-link fencing, topped with strands of barbed wire. Visitors were alerted to several large No Trespassing signs clipped to the fencing. The locked hut was inside the yard, a teenage boy with a dog on a leash near it. The dog barked again. "Can we open things up so we can access the RV?" Elsen said.

Lopez turned, waved and a man wearing a Raiders ball cap, a Springsteen T-shirt and grease-stained jeans emerged from the office.

"Lee Solano," he said, shaking hands with the detectives before entering the code on the keypad, opening the electronic gate and leading them into the yard to the hut were he began unlocking the chain.

"Who do we have here?" Elsen nodded to the boy and the dog.

"This is Craig Willing," Solano said. "His dad started the business."

"You two standing guard?" McDowell smiled.

"Yeah, I work here part-time after school and stuff. I hope to join the Marines or be a cop."

Elsen looked at the dog with its beautiful fawn coat and black mask.

"Who's your partner, son?" Elsen asked.

"Ranger."

"That's a good-looking animal. Is Ranger a Belgian?" Elsen asked.

"Malinois."

Solano removed the lock and chain, rolled open the hut door, revealing the RV. Then he removed his ball cap and wiped his forearm across his brow. Ranger's leash jingled as he pulled against it while barking.

"Ranger's sure excited," McDowell said. "Keep a good grip on him for us, okay?"

"Yes, ma'am."

After stepping inside Elsen and McDowell slipped on shoe covers and tugged on gloves. The hut was clean. The RV rested alone inside, upright, a crumpled hulk. Crouching, Elsen and McDowell entered through the front. Maneuvering along the passage where the windshield and dash had been removed to extricate the family, they were hit with the sewer smell of the ruptured black water tank.

"Very fragrant," McDowell said. "Police work is so glamorous."

The inside of the RV was a stew of webbed and tangled cables, cascading insulation, jutting spears of framework, molding and plastic. They stepped carefully around heaps of broken items and furniture.

The dog continued barking as they took photos and video for their own records.

"You go through the front," Elsen said. "I'll take the back."

For the next twenty minutes they poked through spilled food, scattered debris and luggage for anything that might point to where Riley Jarrett went. The sound of the detectives shifting fragments and pieces of material was accompanied by Ranger's barking.

Nothing in the way of a lead surfaced until McDowell noticed a patch of bright yellow near the front passenger seat. She took a photo, then reached down to retrieve a piece of lined notepaper. It bore handwriting in blue ink, some of it blurred because it appeared liquid had spilled on it. The note read: "Honey I didn't want to wake you. We went inside to get some food. I'll get tarts for you. Stay here. We'll be right back. Love you, Mom."

McDowell photographed the message thinking how the note, discovered in the wreck, supported some of Grace Jarrett's account leading up to Riley's disappearance.

The dog barked.

"Hey, Dan," McDowell said. "I got something here, the mother's note."

Elsen didn't respond. He was sifting through the rear, choosing his steps with care. They continued searching for several more minutes with the dog barking the whole time.

"All right, I think we're just about done here," McDowell said. "What do you think is up with Ranger?"

Elsen thought for a moment.

Then they worked their way out of the RV, and he went to Craig Willing.

"Son," he said, "tell me about your dog."

Fourteen

Nevada

Grace peered into a Ford Escape with Utah plates and an I Love USA decal in the rear window. It was empty.

Beside it was a Toyota Corolla with a Jesus fish symbol bumper sticker, also empty.

"Riley!" Grace called out while threading her way through the Silver Sagebrush parking lot, her face still burning from the questions McDowell and Elsen had asked and what had followed.

After the detectives had finished, Grace, John and Blake went with Aldrich to the Silverado to talk to the clerk who had seen Riley.

"Which way did Riley go?" Grace began. "Who was she with? Did she talk to you?" Grace's demands quickly became desperate, evolving into accusations as she shrugged off John's attempts to calm her. "Why didn't you let her use your phone? Couldn't you see she needed help? My God, you're the last person to see my daughter!"

"I'm sorry, it wasn't like that," the clerk said, tears filling her eyes.

Grace froze. Realizing she'd lost it, she apologized.

Aldrich had intervened, suggesting that the family join the searchers.

Now, moving through the lot, Grace looked a few rows over to Jodi Hartell, a Sagebrush employee accompanying her. She was wearing a lime-yellow safety vest and carrying a two-way radio.

Grace, John and Blake had split up to join truck stop staff in the search. Grace and Jodi were in the southeast corner lot going from car to car, looking inside, checking and calling for Riley.

The lot seemed to go on forever.

And stretching beyond the complex was the desert.

Heat radiated from the pavement, parked cars and trucks. Grace wiped her brow with the back of her hand. To the drone of the interstate, she looked at the traffic coming and going at the Sagebrush. She saw security people, also in fluorescent vests, stationed at exits, waving down each vehicle, even the big rigs, showing drivers Riley's picture and looking closely inside.

But we could be too late.

Now, with the sun slipping nearer to the mountains, Grace struggled to control her rising panic as police vehicles continued arriving, one of them a truck resembling a big white motor home with the words, "Las Vegas Metropolitan Police Mobile Command" on the side. Its emergency lights wigwagging, its diesel engine roaring, the truck moved across the lot before stopping and parking in the same area where, hours before, Grace and her family had parked their RV.

Staring at the truck and the other Metro Police vehicles nearby, at more officers gathering there, the bursts of radio transmissions, Grace was overcome with the gravity of what was unfolding.

I'm not dreaming—this is real. And it's my fault...just like with Tim.

Grace looked at Riley's smiling face on her phone, praying for a message from her, or even a friend, to say she's safe, to say where she was. No messages came.

An idea flashed in her mind. She could contact Caleb to see if he'd heard from her.

Aware of the ill feelings arising from Caleb's relationship with Riley, and her own dislike of him, Grace hesitated. She glanced at the police vehicles, the growing search. She had no choice.

She scrolled through her contacts coming to the number she had for Caleb and began typing a message.

Caleb this is Grace Jarrett, Riley's mom. Please get back to me as soon as possible. It's about Riley. It's important.

After sending the text and waiting, Grace remembered that Caleb was on a plane to Africa with his father, or was already there.

Would he get my message? Would he respond if he did?

Several minutes passed without an answer. Grace felt utterly alone, at the edge of an abyss. Like the night Tim died.

She really needed Sherry Penmark now. Grace would never forget how they'd become friends after Tim's death, how Sherry had helped her and Riley through the most horrible time in their lives. They wouldn't have survived without their friends, especially Sherry.

Blinking back tears, Grace cued up Sherry's number, was poised to send her a text but stopped. Sherry was in Salt Lake City now, to be with her aunt, who'd practically raised her, and was now terminal with a brain tumor.

I can't call Sherry now, not with all she's facing.

Grace then thought of Jazmin Reyna, her friend and fellow nurse at UCSD Medical Center, who'd recently separated from her husband. Grace thought of all they'd seen, all the heartbreak they'd been through while caring for patients in the pandemic. Then Jazmin had tested positive for COVID-19. But while recovering at home, Jazmin lost her mother to the virus. It was a horrible time, and Grace had helped her through it as they prayed for this pandemic to end. Jazmin had friends at the University of Pittsburgh Medical Center and was helping her get a job there.

What would she say to Jazmin? *I lost Riley at a truck stop? I left her there because of an argument?*

Shame, guilt and fear washed over Grace and she lowered her phone.

Riley was all Grace had in this world. Yes, John and Blake were in her life but... But Riley *was* her life.

Grace brushed at her tears.

Why didn't I check on her? It's not Blake's fault. I'm her mother. I'm the one who should have checked on her. Why didn't I do it?

Grace met the truth in a far corner of her heart.

It's my fault, just like it was my fault Tim was on the road the night he was killed.

Because of what I was planning to do.

Fifteen

Nevada

Beeps and spurts of jangly celebratory music filled the air of the Silver Sagebrush's darkened casino.

After leaving the Silverado convenience store, John and Carl Aldrich were searching the rows of digital slot machines and video card games.

"No one under the age of twenty-one is permitted in this area." Aldrich nodded to the posted signs.

"It wouldn't stop Riley," John said, "especially if she was angry. She can be strong-willed."

"Our staff has been through here."

"But not her family. I have to look, Carl."

Aldrich understood, and they moved deeper into the huge room.

John studied the people perched before the machines. All types: young, old, middle-aged, slender, average and overweight. Nicely dressed, poorly dressed, inappropriately dressed, bejeweled and tattooed. Smokers, gum chewers, nail biters, beer drinkers and soda sippers. He knew some gamblers could play for hours, that some developed relationships with their chosen machines as they followed betting strategies. Their faces were portraits of concentration. Occasionally there'd be the dinging of a jackpot.

Would any of them even notice if Riley was here? Could any of them be involved in her disappearance?

He began by approaching a woman at a slot machine, waiting until she was between plays.

"Excuse me?"

She was in her fifties, wearing heavy makeup. Her earrings, dangling musical notes, swayed when she faced John, who held out his phone. Riley's picture glowed in the dim light.

"I'm looking for my daughter. Have you seen her?"

She took his phone, blew out cigarette smoke from the side of her mouth.

"What a sweetheart. Sorry, no, hon, I haven't."

John thanked her and moved to a man in his fifties with a ball cap with a US flag. He was unshaven, had a toothpick in the corner of his mouth. His checkered shirt was straining the buttons. He barely looked at John's phone when he asked him about Riley before shaking his head.

"I ain't seen nothin' but bad luck, buddy."

Next, he approached a man who looked to be in his thirties but had slicked-back white hair and blinding white teeth. He was dancing in his seat to music only he heard as he took gulps of an energy drink in a can.

"Let me look," he said without interrupting his dancing. "No, sorry, man. But good luck."

John continued approaching player after player, not giving up, like these gamblers.

Life is a risk. It boils down to calculation and chance.

Again, he glanced at Riley on his phone.

I'm not going to lose another person in my life. Not like this.

He took stock of the players at their machines, the reels spinning, landing on bars, on cherries, diamonds, sevens or lemons. Players at the video poker games were dealt and discarded cards.

Everyone had a strategy.

John swallowed. He had a strategy, too, a big plan. It was how he landed his new position in Pittsburgh, working his way toward a better life. He took a calculated risk. If anyone found out why he left his job in San Diego, it would destroy him.

We can get through this if I just hold on.

If we just find Riley.

Sixteen

Nevada

"Everybody, listen up for your assignments."

Metro Police Lieutenant Shanice Jackson stood outside the mobile command center, next to its exterior forty-inch LED TV displaying Riley Jarrett's face. More than a dozen officers had gathered around it in the shade of the vehicle's extended awning.

Jackson turned, ensuring she had their attention.

"We're looking for a missing juvenile, female. Riley Jarrett, age fourteen, from San Diego, California, last seen here inside the Silver Sagebrush."

In briefing the group, she confirmed they all had been sent photos, the security video clip of Riley, a detailed description and key information from the detectives' interviews with her family and statements from Sagebrush personnel.

"Your job is to get whatever intel, surveillance videos, any potential lead you can for the detectives. Now before you get your assignments, are there questions?"

"Did we grab her phone?" one officer asked.

"The family volunteered it," Jackson said.

"Are we searching the family's RV?"

"The detectives are doing that as we speak."

"Are we bringing in SAR people to check the area?"

"Yes. Anyone else?" After a brief silence, Jackson said, "All right, let's get rolling."

Lining up for their tasks, which were logged in the system, officers were dispatched to Primm, to check places like Whiskey Pete's, Buffalo Bill's, the Primm Valley Resort, gas stations, retail and fast-food outlets. Others were sent to Jean, to check the Ramada, the Cholla Sun Trail Hotel and Terrible's locations, along with gas stations and fast-food outlets there.

Jackson also sent officers to check with the Nevada Department of Corrections at the minimum-security women's prison at Jean's eastern edge. And she tasked some officers to stay at the Silver Sagebrush to enhance search efforts at the complex.

Marked and unmarked units headed out in an ever-widening search.

Jackson went inside the mobile unit.

Two other officers were at workstations using laptops, cataloging tasks and creating a spreadsheet to track all leads and tips. In supporting the investigation, they ensured details of the Jarrett case were submitted to local, county, state and national police databases, like the National Crime Information Center, giving every law enforcement agency in the country access to it.

Calls were made to the California Highway Patrol in Barstow, the sheriff's department in San Bernardino and Riverside counties. A specific request was made to the PD in Fontana, California, to obtain any security video and to interview staff on duty at the Chevron station when the family had stopped there.

Jackson checked her phone for the latest texts from Officer Rogan and Carl Aldrich. They had Silver Sagebrush staff with the family who were helping search the complex. She then turned to the notes bulleted on the dry-erase board.

They'd alerted security at McCarran, the bus station; all transportation, taxi, shared ride and shuttle services. They'd alerted the FBI-led Child Exploitation Task Force to Metro's new missing juvenile case, which alerted casinos in Las Vegas and throughout the state that were part of the task force security program. They'd also advised other county and state agencies with eyes on and off the road, like the Nevada Department of Wildlife.

She was studying her tablet when her phone rang.

"Lieutenant Jackson."

"Les Perrins, Department of Transportation, getting back to you on our traffic cameras."

"Go ahead, Les."

"We're only responsible for cameras on highways and interstates."

"Right."

"So at this time, along Interstate 15, starting from St. Rose Parkway south, we've got five cameras, but there are gaps."

"Did you pick up anything linked to the RV crash for us?"

"No. I double-checked with our road operations command center. Our cameras are live. They don't record."

"I thought so but we needed to confirm."

"We don't have the capacity and resources to hold recordings."

"So definitely nothing from DOT?"

"Correct. Nothing from us. Maybe you'll get lucky with some business or citizen footage?"

"Maybe. Thanks, Les."

We could use some luck, Jackson thought, checking the time and how long Riley Jarrett had now been missing. *Time is working against us.*

Jackson concentrated on the LED wall monitor displaying maps of the area and recalled the times in her career she'd filled in for vacationing subs working the area surrounding what some still call State Line. She was fearful if Riley Jarrett had somehow wandered off, because the 100-degree heat and desert terrain could exact a toll.

A radio crackled with a dispatch from the Metro Search and Rescue Unit a few moments in advance of the helicopter thumping, beginning an aerial search. Relieved, Jackson then contacted Metro dispatch to put Silver Sky Search and Rescue, the volunteer organization, on standby for a call to assist.

Her phone rang. "Lieutenant Jackson."

"Detective Elsen."

"Hi, Dan, what's up?"

"Where's the family now?"

Jackson put the call on speaker and checked her phone for any updates from Rogan or Aldrich. Nothing had changed.

"The family's searching alongside Sagebrush staff."

"Okay, we need to keep a visual on them."

"Why?"

"We may have a lead."

Seventeen

Nevada

Blake Marshall couldn't shake his fear that the detectives knew something about Riley's disappearance.

What do they know that they're not telling us?

His gut was still knotted from their brutal questions—*You ever strike Riley or abuse her?... Do you know where she is?... Are you in any way involved?*—then seeing Grace losing it with the clerk at the store, and everything escalating.

Blake's attention returned to the woman walking with him, in her twenties and kind of pretty. Lindy Hudson, one of the workers helping him search.

"We'll go in here next," she said. "I'm sure it's all been searched but let's still try."

It was called the Silver Tortoise Emporium. Its long storefront had floor-to-ceiling windows displaying shelves, cases, racks and bins of artwork, collectibles, clothing, shoes and an array of souvenirs, from salt and pepper shakers to back scratchers. Before they entered, Blake's phone vibrated and he stopped to check the message.

Hi Blake: It's Claire Nakamura, Riley's friend. Got your number from Dakota Lawson, who said something weird is going on with Riley. Is everything OK?

Blake responded: We're just trying to reach her. If you talk to her tell her to call me or Grace, please.

OK but what's going on? Isn't she with you? Aren't you guys driving across the country right now?

It's complicated. Were you talking to her today?

Yes. Then she suddenly stopped texting and nobody can reach her.

How was she? What did she say?

That's kinda private.

Please, Claire, I'm her stepbrother, and it's urgent.

You're scaring me.

Please just tell me what she said to you today.

She was pretty broken up leaving SD, Caleb, and was thinking her life was ruined.

Anything else?

Not really. Did she run away or something? This sounds ominous.

Just let me know if you hear from her, please Claire?

I will.

Blake lowered his phone and took a breath.

"You okay, Blake?" Hudson asked.

"I just want to find my sister."

"Was that message helpful?"

"It was one of Riley's friends wanting to help us."

Hudson took stock of Blake, noticing how he averted his gaze. "Well, let's go in here. It's one of our largest stores. It's near the Silverado. Maybe Riley stopped here to look for you guys, or to browse while thinking you'd find her here?"

Blake nodded and went with Hudson.

"What does she like to shop for?" Hudson asked. "Clothes? Shoes?"

Blake thought, then noticed the jewelry section and nodded to it.

They stopped at a display of Southwest-style jewelry with Blake looking at a bracelet made up of tiny turquoise-and-silver beads.

"She likes stuff like this. I saw her wearing similar things," Blake said.

Hudson asked the sales clerk about Riley, showing her photos on her phone.

"Yes," the clerk said. "We've had security here and police asking about her." The clerk turned to Blake. "I'm sorry, but I don't think she was here looking at jewelry."

Nodding, Blake noticed the sign across the store for the electronics section and headed there with Hudson following him.

He went to the display of prepaid phones— burner phones.

Hudson stood next to him, glancing at the display then at Blake.

"Do you think she might've bought one of these to call you?" Hudson asked.

Blake took a moment as he looked over the phones. "It's possible. She had some cash and a credit card."

"Let's check."

Hudson went to the nearest clerk. "Brad," according to his tag. Showing Riley's picture, she asked Brad whether he'd seen her in here.

"We had cops in asking us about that earlier." Brad shook his head. "Nobody saw her here. Sorry."

As they left the counter, Hudson's phone rang. She answered and listened while walking. "Yes." She looked at Blake. "He's with me right now in the Emporium." Hudson listened a moment longer before her call ended.

"What is it?" Blake asked her.

"I don't know, but they want you at the security office right now."

Eighteen

Nevada

A transmission crackled over Jodi Hartell's two-way radio in the parking lot, then she waved at Grace.

"They want you inside at security now," Jodi said.

"Did they find her?"

"I don't know. They just said for us to come in now."

Nearly trotting to the entrance, Grace's mind whirled with hope and dread.

Moving through the complex, weaving around travelers, Grace glanced up at Riley looking down from the information alert displayed on one of the large advertising screens. Grace pushed back tears. She couldn't stop hoping that they'd found her; that she was moments away from taking her into her arms, screaming at her while crushing her to her heart and never letting go.

They left the retail area, hurrying into the administrative section of the Silver Sagebrush, moving swiftly down the hall toward the security office.

That's when Grace's pace slowed at the scene.

Several uniformed officers and security people were there, John and Blake among them. They'd turned to her, their faces sober. There was no sign of Riley.

Grace tensed. *Something's wrong.*

She saw McDowell and Elsen wearing hardened expressions as she joined the group.

"Did you find her?" Grace asked. "What's happening?"

Elsen looked at her then said, "Grace, John, Blake, would you each place your hands in front of you please."

Confused for a moment, no one moved.

"Why?" John looked at the unsmiling faces of the Metro officers circled around them.

"Please," McDowell said, "do as we request."

Slowly, Grace, John and Blake extended their hands. Elsen nodded, then, with soft metallic clicks and snaps, handcuffed each of them.

"What the hell's this?" John's eyes widened, staring at his wrists, then at Elsen and McDowell.

"We're placing all of you under arrest," Elsen said.

"Under arrest? Why?" Grace's voice broke.

"You're each facing charges of conspiracy to possess narcotics with intent to distribute," Elsen said.

"What?" John said. "This is ridiculous!"

"You have the right to remain silent..." McDowell read them their rights.

Staring at his wrists, Blake, on the verge of tears, shook his head in silence.

"Oh my God!" Grace repeated as officers began escorting them separately back into the same rooms where earlier they'd been questioned.

"We'll be in to talk to each of you shortly," Mc-Dowell said.

"This is wrong!" Grace shouted.

"You don't know what you're doing!" John yelled.

Blake remained silent.

Grace sat at the same desk in the same chair.

Her eyes swept over the same Best Mom Ever mug, the same framed photo of a happy family in Nova Scotia, the same calendar.

Only this time Grace wasn't alone.

A uniformed female officer sat at a desk across the room, watching her.

"This is wrong," Grace said. "We need to be looking for Riley!"

The officer said nothing.

"Drug charges? Drug charges. I don't get it! Are they trying to frame us for something?"

The officer looked away before looking back. "Ma'am, I'm sorry I can't say anything. It's best if you don't talk to me."

"I can't believe what's happening!"

Feeling the weight of the metal around her wrists, Grace brushed at the tears rolling down her face, her bandages scraping against her skin.

Stressed, exhausted, trembling, her thoughts

pulled her back to the start of her day, how she was anxious yet excited about moving, about a new chapter of their lives. Hours later, Riley goes missing, they crash and now she's sitting here.

In handcuffs.

Facing criminal charges.

Not believing this was real.

Going numb.

Just like the day she sat beside Tim's casket.

"This is bullshit!"

Nostrils flaring, chest heaving, John glared at the officer sitting in the corner of the room watching him.

"You've got to remain calm, sir."

"Calm?" John lifted his handcuffed wrists. "My daughter's missing and this is what you do to us?"

"The detectives will be here soon. Just hold on, sir."

Hold on.

Blinking back his rage, lifting his head to the ceiling as his world continued to fracture, he was catapulted back to that night.

…the water roiling, waves and wind gnashing at the overturned hull, struggling to breathe. "Hold on! We can make it if we just hold on…"

They must know something.

Blake looked around the room then at the officer in the chair nearby, staring at her phone.

He looked at his wrists, encircled in metal. He'd never been handcuffed before. His throat was scratchy, and it hurt a little when he tried to swallow.

They definitely know something. Drug charges. This is freaking serious.

Nineteen

Anita Wells looked at the setting sun painting the sky coral as the lights of the Strip and the city twinkled below.

"You guys celebrating anything tonight?" their server asked while pouring their wine.

Anita turned to Jeff, her husband.

"Freedom," he said, smiling. "We haven't been out in a while. Swamped at work."

"Well, enjoy," their server said and left.

Anita and Jeff toasted their view from some eight hundred feet up at the Top of the World restaurant in the Stratosphere.

The wine was a dry, mildly fruity merlot from Napa.

"Good," Anita said after a taste. "We haven't been here in a long time."

"I feel like we're tourists." Jeff took in the city lights and the mountains. "Almost forgot what a spectacular view this is. It feels good to get out.

I was thinking this would be a good time to talk about things."

"What would you like to talk about?" She smiled and took another sip.

"Starting a family."

"Oh, well, that sounds—"

A cell phone vibrated. Jeff felt his jacket.

"No, it's mine." Anita set her glass down and reached for her purse.

"Can't you let it go?" Jeff said.

"I wish. Sorry."

She didn't recognize the number when she answered. "Hello."

"Anita Wells?"

"Yes, who's calling?"

"Dan Elsen, Metro. We got something happening concerning a missing fourteen-year-old girl and a possible drug transport vehicle you should know about."

"All right, hang on." Anita reached for her purse and stood. "I need to take this over there." She nodded to the bar. "I'm so sorry, sweetheart. I'll be as quick as I can."

They were both busy professionals. Jeff was a surgeon. And, as the chief deputy district attorney for Clark County, who led the DA's High Intensity Drug Trafficking Area team, Anita was always on call, too. Her team was part of a federally funded enforcement effort involving other agencies such as the FBI, the DEA. She found an empty stool at one end of the bar, out of earshot, took out her notebook and pen.

"Missing child. Go ahead, Dan."

Elsen brought her up to speed on Riley Jarrett's case, up to the tow yard and the dog's relentless barking and focus on the RV.

"Turns out," Elsen said, "Ranger's a retired DEA drug detection dog that a friend's dad gave to the kid. So we let Ranger investigate, and he reacted to the presence of drugs in the undercarriage of the RV."

"Did you find any drugs?"

"No, but we found a couple heavy-duty bungee cords connected to the rear crossmembers and frame assembly that could've supported bundles."

"Dan, the dog's retired. He's not certified."

"We know. We called in a dog with the Narcotics Detail and our dog reacted the same way. We have detected the presence of drugs. So we've Mirandized the family. We're holding them now."

"Holding them for what? Where are you, exactly?"

"The Silver Sagebrush near Jean. My partner and I are calling from our car. We've got you on speaker."

"But you found no drugs in the RV?"

"Correct but we're checking with NHP to possibly track down who was present at the scene, and to search the scene, the debris and—"

"Hold on, Dan. You know you don't have enough to hold or detain the family—not even on conspiracy. No cause for an arrest or charges based solely on your narcotics dog alerting to the possibility of drugs in a rented RV."

"We know. But there are aspects we need to discuss. We know we can't proceed with charges, but we want to use this as leverage because it raises suspicions about the family, about them being truthful about the circumstances concerning a missing juvenile."

"Didn't you run background on them?"

"We did. There are no criminal histories, no warrants and no complaints. We need to do more checking."

"What's the issue? You're Missing Persons. You need to find the girl and from what you're telling me, this family's committed no crime."

"Like I said, Anita, the drug thing leads us to believe that the family's not being truthful, like they're concealing something from us. Maybe they're covering something up. We wanted to alert you and get your input."

Tapping her pen on the bar, Anita let out a breath.

"Okay, I get it. As you are well aware, the volume of narcotics coming up from Mexico specifically through San Diego is heavy, wildly heavy. And you may have a case of a transnational shipment. Or not."

"Right."

"But with criminal drug organizations, if someone involved, someone working for a cartel, loses their drugs, then it's common for a family member to go missing and be held for return of the drugs, or for monetary value."

"Ransom."

"Yes. I'm not saying that's the case here. These are just scenarios to consider. But based on what you've told me, you cannot charge this family with anything yet. It's your call if you choose to use the drug factor to employ a strategy for questioning, but it sounds like you're unsure of what you have at this stage and you have no grounds to hold them."

"Correct."

"It could also be a human trafficking situation. You'd mentioned the boyfriend—she could be a runaway. There's that case of the murdered California girl who was found last year near State Line. You've got a world of possibilities. Above all, you've got a missing fourteen-year-old to find and one thing is certain."

"What's that?"

"You need to know more about this family, so you need them to open up and cooperate."

Twenty

Nevada

"We don't think you're telling us the whole truth." McDowell looked Grace directly in the eye.

Grace held her gaze then shifted to Elsen. He drew close, invading Grace's space, forcing her to lean back, making her chair creak.

His voice soft, he asked: "Why were narcotics hidden in the RV?"

She didn't respond.

Then he asked: "How are they linked to Riley?"

Her eyes gleaming with tears, Grace's jaw began working but her words were delayed until she started slowly moving her head from side to side. "I don't know anything about—"

"Grace," McDowell said. "Are you transporting drugs for someone?"

"No!"

"Do these people have Riley?"

"I don't know where she is! Why're you doing this?"

"Did they threaten to harm her if you told police about the drugs?"

"Oh God, what's happening? None of this is real!"

The handcuffs jingled as Grace raised her hands to her face.

"We're just a family. My daughter's missing, and all you do is keep asking me horrible questions!"

"We're doing all we can to find Riley," McDowell said.

"But we need you to tell us the truth," Elsen said.

"I'm telling you the truth!"

"Are you?" he said.

Her nerves tightening, Grace brushed at the tears trickling down her face as McDowell and Elsen stared at her.

The detectives finished talking to Grace then entered John's room and dismissed the observing officer.

"This is nuts!" John stood with his handcuffed hands before him. "I want lawyers for all of us!"

"Please sit down," McDowell said. "You don't need a lawyer."

"You've read us our rights."

"John," Elsen said, "you haven't been formally charged with anything. Sit down. Please."

Hesitating, trying in vain to discern deceit, John sat.

"Why were drugs in your RV?" Elsen asked.

"I don't know anything about that. It's not *our* RV, it's a rental. Maybe you should question the rental agency in San Diego, or the people who rented the thing before we did."

"Are you transporting drugs for someone?" McDowell said. "Are they holding Riley? Who're you delivering to in Pittsburgh? Or are there drop-offs along the way across the country?"

"Now is the time to tell us the truth, John," Elsen said. "So we can find Riley."

John shook his head. "I don't know what the hell this is. We told you the truth. We made a mistake. We accidentally left Riley behind and now we can't find her."

"Do you owe drug people a debt?" Elsen asked.

"Are you listening to me?" John took a breath and shook his head. "I know nothing about drugs in the RV. We stopped in Fontana, we parked here. A lot of people could have had access to the RV."

Tears filled his eyes.

"I've told you the truth." He struggled to keep from breaking down, shaking his head. "Our daughter's missing and you waste time with this BS."

John stared at the wall for a long moment before turning to the detectives.

"If she ends up dead, it'll be your fault!"

"Do you think we'll find Riley?"

Blake waited for McDowell and Elsen to answer.

"We find nearly everyone we look for, son," Elsen said.

"What about the people you don't find?"

"Some people don't want to be found," Elsen said. "Not every case ends happily, like in the movies."

"But how do you know Riley's not dead?"

Elsen and McDowell traded a glance.

"Because we've found no evidence to even suggest she's been hurt," McDowell said. "What we need is the truth about why drugs were in the RV."

Blake nodded.

"Will you tell us the truth?" Elsen said. "Because if you don't, you could be spending the night in the Clark County Juvenile Detention Center."

"It's not a nice place," McDowell said. "Tell us about the drugs, Blake."

"There's nothing to tell. I don't know anything about that."

"This is not the time to lie, son," Elsen said.

"I'm not lying. The RV's a rental. I don't know anything about drugs."

"Blake—" McDowell moved closer to him "—is someone holding Riley? Are they threatening to hurt her if you tell us your family is shipping drugs?"

Blake looked at his handcuffs.

"No." His voice was teary and he sniffed. "We just need to find her."

After the detectives had finished questioning Grace, John and Blake, they removed their handcuffs. No drugs had been found; they were not being charged.

"You're free to go," Elsen said. "Carl Aldrich will make arrangements for you to stay here, if you like. Get some rest. People will be searching through the night. We'll update you as soon as new information arises."

John glared at them in stunned silence as Grace wiped at her tears. Blake looked at his parents then the detectives.

Twenty-One

Nevada

The warm night air carried the drone of interstate traffic across the parking lot as McDowell and Elsen walked to the mobile command center.

Lieutenant Shanice Jackson was waiting outside for them. "There's coffee; we've got drinks and sandwiches in the fridge."

Inside, the other officers continued coordinating the investigation at their workstations to the clicking of keyboards and soft, static-filled radio dispatches, undistracted as the detectives selected refreshments and left.

"Anything on the Amber?" McDowell asked.

"A lot of tips that went nowhere, like a woman arguing with a teenage girl at a mall in Henderson. Not even close to being Riley Jarrett. Then someone spotted a girl with a *Friends* T-shirt at McCarran but she was twenty years old and from Peru."

McDowell and Elsen nodded wearily.

"So what's your lead?" Jackson asked.

"Our dog picked up the smell of narcotics in the RV's undercarriage, but we found no drugs." Elsen bit into his ham and cheese sandwich.

"What's the family say?" Jackson said.

"They deny it. We couldn't hold them on anything, never really intended to. We released them." McDowell started on a bagel and egg salad. "But we don't think we're getting the full story from them."

"You think they're covering up?" Jackson said.

"Could be a drugs-ransom thing." Elsen took another bite. "Could be a runaway, an abduction. Could be anything at this stage."

"What else you got?"

"Not much. We'll keep digging into their background. We'll get the Digital Forensic Lab to work on the girl's phone. It could be the most valuable piece of the puzzle." Elsen took the last few bites. His water bottle swished as he drank.

"And the family?" Jackson asked. "After you released them, where'd they go?"

"They'll stay at the Sagebrush motel," McDowell said. "Rogan and Aldrich are helping them."

"You got any intel or video for us?" Elsen asked.

"Nothing yet. A couple of unfounded sightings that went nowhere. But the canvass continues. Ready?"

Jackson logged into the case file through the exterior forty-inch LED TV and point by point she updated the detectives on all that had been done, was being done, and was going to be done before wrapping up.

"So in addition to all of that, we've blasted her info everywhere on social media, coordinated with the FBI's task force," Jackson said. "We're making a full-court press. We'll keep going through the night. Silver Sky Search and Rescue will be here at dawn. We've already had media calls. By morning this search will get a whole lot bigger."

As Elsen and McDowell drove back to Las Vegas on Interstate 15, the night sky thudded.

They looked up to the array of low-flying colored lights of the Metro Police Search and Rescue helicopter heading to the truck stop to resume combing the desert with its infrared camera and powerful searchlight.

McDowell's face then glowed in the light of her tablet as she cued up files, reports and statements.

"Let's run things down," she said.

Elsen sipped coffee, concentrating on the highway. "Go."

"We'll get the girl's phone to our people in the digital lab."

"That's key," Elsen said.

"I'll try contacting her friends to see who she was talking to, what she was saying before this happened."

"Good," Elsen said.

"We'll follow up with Narcotics and the RV rental agency, and keep in touch with the Nugget in case she went there, and San Diego in case she went home."

"And, we've got to go deeper on the family's background, see if John's got anything more than a speeding ticket," Elsen said. "He lost his wife and daughter in a boating accident and Grace's first husband was a traffic fatality. We need to keep that stuff in mind."

"Yes, and we'll reach out to San Diego, to Child Protective Services." McDowell swiped and typed. "We'll look at their jobs, financial situation and their history, coworkers, friends, neighbors."

"We need to get the family to give us a list of everyone who was at their farewell party," Elsen said. "Some of that can't be done until tomorrow. What about the traffic cameras posted along here? They capture anything?" Elsen nodded to the highway.

"Zip. Jackson confirmed with DOT."

"What about Fontana?"

"The log says Fontana PD's taken action on the Chevron to interview staff and check for video of the family. That's still pending. Nothing from California Highway Patrol, San Bernardino or Riverside."

McDowell's tablet pinged.

"Just got a message from security at the Nugget. No sightings of Riley Jarrett there. They'll remain on alert for her."

"What about the casinos, McCarran, all of that?"

McDowell swiped and shook her head. "Other than the Amber stuff, nothing from them, or any of the transportation services." She reached for her coffee. "This drug angle complicates things, Dan."

"I know. It could be the critical factor. Maybe Narcotics will have something." Elsen thought for a moment. "Let's assume the family's truthful and we look at the situation leading up to Riley's disappearance."

"She's having a fit about the move, about missing the love of her life," McDowell said.

Elsen continued. "So when she finds out they've left her at the truck stop, she's furious. Maybe she had some sort of plan to run away and join her boyfriend?"

"Even though he's out of the country?" McDowell said.

Elsen rubbed his chin. "Yeah, we'll look into that."

"Then we've got Garcia, unsolved," McDowell said. "And look at the size of the Silver Sagebrush, the volume of people in an out of the place. It's perfect for human traffickers and she's a perfect target—she's upset, someone notices, agrees to help, maybe offers her a ride."

"I know." Elsen turned to the darkness for a moment. "I know."

The next few miles passed in silence.

They'd planned to return to headquarters. As they neared the city's edge, McDowell made a phone call.

"Hi, Cathy," she said. "Is he still awake? No, no, don't wake him. Listen, it looks like I'll be working late then up early in the morning…can you keep him for a bit longer? I'm really sorry… Okay thanks so much." She ended her call.

"You're lucky to have someone like that," Elsen said.

"I am. She's a good friend."

"Forgive me for prying, partner, but how's custody working with your ex—what's his name again? Cheating Bastard?"

McDowell smiled and shook her head. "He consistently breaches the terms, and I think he's going to marry Lolita and she'll want to adopt Jack."

"Oh no."

"I anticipate future court appearances," McDowell said. "And what about you? It's been two years. You seeing anyone?"

"Me? Naw. I'm happy with Daisy. She's a good listener."

"Just you and your retriever?"

"And memories of my wife."

"That's sweet, but you can't live like that forever. You gotta find a girl, reconnect with the world."

"The world." Elsen dipped the word in bitterness. "I've got issues with the world."

He stared ahead at the emerging skyline, the interstate elevated as it paralleled the Strip, offering a view of the casinos. The forty-three-story Mandalay Bay hotel rose to the right.

Elsen looked at it, blinking several times.

They both knew what was churning inside him.

McDowell had been out of town on October 1,

2017. Elsen was in the city that day, off duty when a friend had called him at home.

"My buddy called and said we've got an active shooter at Mandalay Bay." Elsen had recounted the night for McDowell, opening up about it sometime later, over coffee at a Del Taco outlet on Charleston. "I called dispatch, was on hold for nearly a minute. That never happens. I turned on my radio and I could hear guys, the intense emotion in their voices. I could hear bursts of gunfire. I drove down there. All you could see and hear were lights and sirens on the freeway. The sirens going nonstop, like one prolonged scream. Everybody responded. Had to be a thousand cops down there. It was a war zone, the victims, the blood, the sirens. I'll never forget that night for as long as I live."

Tonight, as they passed Mandalay Bay, Elsen said nothing as he turned his eyes forward, focusing on their destination a few miles away, the exit that would get them to Martin Luther King Boulevard and headquarters.

They planned to do more work, then go home, grab some sleep then get back on the case.

"Look," McDowell said.

The FBI-led Child Exploitation Task Force had access to digital billboards across the city and was supporting the investigation. The display was one of the actions they'd taken.

Riley Jarrett's face smiled down at them from a large billboard.

Staring hard at it as they passed, McDowell prayed that they would find her.

Alive.

Not like Eva Marie Garcia.

Twenty-Two

Nevada

The Desert Cloud Motel took up much of the northeast section of the Silver Sagebrush, evoking an art deco style with its glass brick and ceramic tile face.

Aldrich led Grace, John and Blake to room 157 on the ground floor then swiped the key card through the lock.

The room had two queen beds and was spacious. The interior door was open to an identical connecting room with two more beds.

"You have a suite with adjoining rooms." Aldrich gestured. "We're sorry police would not release your luggage from the RV."

"Why not?" John asked.

"I can't answer that," Aldrich said. "But we took the liberty of guessing approximate sizes of each of you and provided these items, donated by some of our outlets."

T-shirts, sweats, shorts and underwear neatly

folded with the tags still on, and toiletries in bags, lay on the bed in four separate piles. Grace touched her hand to the one for Riley.

"Food is on the way. Everything is being taken care of. You're our guests," Aldrich said.

He gave them keys, and for a moment held Grace's hand in his, squeezing it with encouragement.

"We'll find her," he said.

A soft knock sounded at the door. Aldrich answered and directed a woman wearing a Sagebrush shirt and carrying a large pizza box and two brown paper bags to set them on the table.

"Thank you, Melinda." Then to the family, Aldrich said: "Please, eat, get some rest. The search will go through the night. If there's news, we'll alert you. You have my numbers. You have everyone's numbers. If there's anything you need, call me."

"Thank you." Grace managed a teary smile.

Aldrich closed the door behind him, leaving them with their nightmare, finding a degree of comfort in the fact the detectives freed them without charges.

They stood in the quiet without speaking.

Blake's stomach yowled. They hadn't eaten a meal all day, and the aroma of baked onions, cheese and pepperoni proved too much for him. He lifted the lid of the pizza box, tugged out a slice and bit into it. John did the same.

Grace lowered herself slowly, sitting on the edge

of the nearest bed, bandaged hands in her lap, holding her phone, turning the day over and over in her mind. She looked at John and Blake, at their bandages, their scrapes; their heads bowed, eating silently, reverently, like mourners at a funeral reception.

John looked back at Grace, seeing fear in her eyes.

She detected shame and guilt in his for needing to eat. Recognizing her uneasiness, he put a slice of pizza on a paper plate then offered it to her. "You should eat, Grace."

She refused the plate. John set it on the bed beside her.

"I can't do this," she said. "My God—drugs! How could they think we're involved with drugs?"

"Grace." John's voice was soft.

"Do you know anything about drugs?" She glared at them. "Does that have something to do with Riley? You tell me the truth! Blake?"

"Me?" He stopped eating. "No!"

"Why should I believe you?" she said. "None of this would've happened if you'd checked on her when I asked you to instead of lying about it!"

Blake set his half-eaten slice on the table and looked away.

"Grace, he made a stupid mistake," John said. "He's apologized."

"And what about you?" she said. "What do you know about drugs?"

"Grace, stop." John remained calm. "It's all a

mistake. It's got nothing to do with us. A lot of people rented the RV before us."

She was breathing fast.

"Please," John said, "eat something and get some rest."

"No." Shaking her head, she said: "I can't do this. I can't sit here eating, not knowing where she is. We need to keep looking for her."

"Yes, but right now you need to eat and rest. You can't help when you're exhausted." John noticed something in his clear plastic toiletry bag. He opened it, took out a vial of over-the-counter sleeping pills, shook out two for Grace. "Take these. Get some sleep, then we'll look for her in the morning."

Grace stared at the pills in her palm.

Blake was watching.

Grace went into the bathroom, leaving the door open. While running the cold water she looked into the mirror, at the bandages on her temple and cheek, the dried, bloodied abrasions, the creases worry had carved into her face, her messed hair and her glistening eyes.

Riley.

She had to find Riley.

Grace was about to take the pills when a phone rang. It was John's.

She went to him, catching her breath, listening, her hopes soaring.

"Yes," John told the caller. "We're doing our best...yes... Really?"

"Did they find her?" Grace asked.

John shook his head, held up his hand, continuing with the call. "You don't have to—well, yes… Right. The Silver Sagebrush on 15 just north of Primm. We're here at the motel. Thank you, Norm. Thank everyone for us."

Ending the call, he looked at Grace. "That was Norm Hollister," he said.

"Norm, our old neighbor? The retired police officer?"

"Yeah, he saw a story about Riley on a San Diego TV station. And it's on social media. Norm and his wife volunteer with the San Diego Police, and they're coordinating a group to come here from San Diego to help search."

Grace put her hands over her mouth.

"Some are driving," John said. "Some will fly at their own expense. They want to be here as early as possible to start tomorrow."

"Oh, that's so—I can't believe it!" Grace said.

John ran a hand over his haggard, unshaven face.

"That's good, right?" Blake said.

"It's good," John said, glancing around the room. Then, rubbing his upper arm and the back of his neck, as if recalling the crash and other horrors of the day, he said: "Grace, we really need to rest so we can be ready to do whatever we need to do in the morning."

Blake indicated the next room. "I guess I'll take that one." Then, nodding to the piles, he said: "Want me to take Riley's stuff in there, too?"

"No! Leave it!" Grace burst with alarm, her restraint fracturing. "Where's Riley going to sleep tonight?" Grace sobbed and screamed, "Riley!"

John wrapped his arms around her, holding her, soothing her as she buried her face into his chest and cried. He nodded to Blake to dim the lights. He did. Then Blake retreated to his room with his bag, as John continued to comfort Grace.

"Take it easy, take a breath, you're drained." He held her, rocking her. "Let the pills do their work and rest, just rest."

They stayed that way for the longest time.

When her sobbing subsided, John tenderly removed only her shoes before laying her back on the bed, covering her with the blankets and kissing her.

Then he switched off the lights.

Grace hadn't taken the pills John had given her. Still, she'd sunk to the edge of sleep. For how long, she didn't know.

Coming out of it, her sluggish brain thudded like a hammer against an anvil, pounding reality into her.

My daughter's missing!

Get up! Find her!

Grace opened her eyes. A night-light spilled from the open bathroom door.

John was in the other bed, atop the sheets, dressed, breathing hard, dead asleep.

Blake's door was closed. She saw a seam of light along the floor and guessed he was awake.

Turning her head aggravated the stiffness in her neck and shoulders. The aftermath of the crash, she thought as her nightstand vibrated where her phone was charging. Her pulse skipped as she seized it, swiping to check who the message was from.

Jazmin Reyna.

Just heard about Riley! So sorry! A bunch of us from the hospital are coming to the truck stop ASAP to help! Keep the faith! Praying hard!

Grace's screen blurred as tears rolled down her face and she typed, It's the Silver Sagebrush. Thank you!

Holding her phone to her heart, she wiped her cheeks.

Again, she saw Riley's items piled neatly at the foot of her bed like a headstone to her absence.

Like an accusation of Grace's failings.

Why didn't you check on her? Why did you leave her?

Screaming inside, Grace put on her shoes and left the room to search for her daughter.

Twenty-Three

Nevada

The moment Grace entered the main building, she texted John and Blake. Couldn't sleep. Looking for Riley.

It was 1:30 a.m. Every outlet and restaurant was open, and while it was not as busy as it was during the day, a number of all-night travelers were moving through the complex. The casino's ringing, beeping and flashing lights were unrelenting. In the main lobby, she looked up at one of the large electronic advertising signs.

Riley's face was there. Haunting her.

Grace was pulled back to the day she'd taken Riley to the supermarket. Riley was three and didn't want to sit in the baby seat. She wanted to walk holding the cart. Grace was taking her time reading ingredients, comparing two brands of food. When she'd finished and looked down, her stomach lurched.

Riley was gone.

Grace looked up and down the aisle.

No Riley.

She called out for her, running to the next aisle, her throat dry, her heart racing, panic webbing through her until she found Riley, alone at a display for pet food tapping a life-size cutout of kittens.

Now, staring at her face, Grace pleaded. *Let me find you again.*

Needing to form a plan, Grace went to the Silverado store where Riley was last seen. A new shift was on staff. She approached a man in his forties restocking shelves, showing him photos on her phone.

"No, ma'am. I haven't seen her. I'm sorry." He shook his head and resumed working.

Grace went to the counter, to the young woman there who studied the pictures, too.

"You're her mother? They told us to watch out for her." The woman hadn't seen her. "I just started today and this is my first shift."

Grace made the same inquiry with every person in the store before she moved to the food court and restaurants, approaching strangers, stopping them.

"Excuse me…excuse me…" Grace would begin, thrusting her phone at them, desperation in her voice. "I'm looking for my daughter—have you seen her?"

Women, themselves mothers, met her appeal with concern, even empathy. A few younger men were indifferent, suspicious her request was a pretext to a scam.

No one had seen Riley.

As Grace continued, she noticed that the announcements paging Riley had ceased. But she kept moving, inspecting the bathrooms, checking every stall, crouching, calling for Riley. She scrutinized the casino, interrupting gamblers, imploring them to help.

As she passed The Long Haul Bar & Grill she stopped in her tracks.

Riley was looking out from one of the rows of big screens flickering above the bar. One of them was showing an all-news channel. Grace was too far away to hear the story. Riley's face filled the top corner of the screen, while images of the Silver Sagebrush played above the news crawler, which read: **Search For Missing California Teen Near Las Vegas.**

More images of their crash on the interstate, flashing lights on emergency vehicles, traffic backed up, the truck stop, the police command post and the police helicopter flying over the desert.

Grace's stomach knotted.

Then the report displayed the face of another teen next to Riley's. Eva Marie Garcia, age seventeen, of Riverside, California. The images, flagged as *File: One Year Ago*, showed yellow crime scene tape, investigators in white jumpsuits moving a body bag. The ticker read, **Is New Case Linked To California Teen's Unsolved Murder In Area?**

Shaking her head slowly, Grace's scalp tingled. She began walking, then half trotting toward the exit. Stepping into the night, she ran.

Twenty-Four

Nevada

D*AD!*

The cold water...the heaving waves...a hand breaking the surface...trying to reach her...the rolling swells taking her deeper into the blackness...a gurgled horrifying scream. HELP ME, DAD!

"...Dad?"

Half-asleep, John wondered why he was dry, why he was shaking and why Blake was talking to him now.

Then another jolt woke him.

"Dad. Wake up. She's gone."

Grunting, he sat up and Blake held his phone to his father's face.

John squinted in the motel-room light, momentarily disoriented before focusing, reading Grace's text.

"This isn't good. We've got to find her." He got up. "I need a second."

Wincing and rubbing the soreness in his shoulders, John went to the bathroom, splashed water on his face, dried off, grabbed the room key then unplugged his phone from its charger.

"Let's go."

They left their room, hurried down the long breezeway connected to the main building and started looking for her.

"She should be sleeping," John said. "She must not have taken the pills."

"Where do you think she went?"

"Could be anywhere. We'll split up. I'll take the casino, the bars and food places. You take the Silverado store and everything in that section."

"Okay."

"Let's keep each other posted. Be safe."

Blake strode in the direction of the store, leaving his father alone in the middle of the main lobby.

John took a breath and let it out. As he started for the casino, his phone rang. Seeing the number, he tensed before answering.

"Apologies for the late call, but I've just learned the terrible news."

"What do you want?"

"Let me say, I'm very sorry your daughter's missing, and I hope it will all be resolved happily."

"Thank you. Goodbye."

"Wait, John. I need to remind you."

"Of what?"

"The agreement."

"Why?"

"To stress that you cannot disclose it, under any circumstances, even to the police in this time of crisis."

A silent moment passed between them.

"Did you disclose it to police, John?"

John was silent.

"You understand, John, this is a critical time and disclosing it will have a negative impact for you and all parties involved."

Another moment passed. Then, through gritted teeth John said, "I didn't tell anyone."

He hung up and wiped his shaking hand over his face.

Blake did not go to the Silverado.

Careful that his father, or Grace, wherever she was, didn't see him, he went to the store near it, the large retail outlet that had the jewelry he thought Riley would like.

Few people were shopping there when he walked through it, searching for Grace, his dad, anyone who might know him.

He didn't see them here.

Relieved that the staff had changed, he went to the electronics section and the area displaying prepaid phones.

A guy with frizzy red hair tied into a ponytail emerged behind the counter.

"Need some help?"

"I'll take that one." Blake tapped the glass, pointed at a phone. "With that plan."

"Sure." The clerk began ringing it up. It was less than fifty dollars.

"I'll pay cash."

After purchasing the phone, Blake went to the nearest bathroom, entered a stall where he unboxed the phone and began setting it up.

Switching it on, he heard the welcoming jingle. Then he went through various steps, setting up a number, paying for the plan with the refill card. He received a message that activation would take a few minutes. A chime indicated he had internet access.

He skipped setting up accounts, secured the phone with a strong PIN, skipped various apps he didn't need, scrolled through and accepted the privacy statement and a few minutes later, the phone indicated he was good to go.

Tossing the packaging in the trash, Blake left the bathroom and found an alcove that offered a degree of privacy. Keeping his back to a wall, ensuring no one was within earshot, he tapped in a number he'd memorized and called it.

It began ringing. And ringing.

Come on. Come on. Answer.

A connection was made but no one spoke.

Waiting a moment, adjusting his hold on the phone, he spoke. "This is Blake from San Diego."

Then a barely audible male voice said, "Wait."

A long moment later a new male voice was on the line. "You were told never to call this number."

Blake swallowed. "This is an emergency—my sister—"

"We know what happened. The whole world knows what happened."

"It wasn't my fault."

"You fucked up, bro."

"No, it wasn't my fault! Do you know where Riley is? Do you have her?"

The line went dead, sending fear slithering up Blake's spine.

Tears stood in his eyes. *What have I done?*

Lowering the phone, he looked around, helpless as the night his mother and sister drowned.

Grace ran through the parking lot. She had to find Riley.

Her attention went to the far reaches of the lot where they had stopped their rented RV and got out.

It was only hours ago but it felt like a lifetime.

Again she took in the police command post that occupied the same spot, but now there were additional emergency vehicles beside it, as if Riley's disappearance had become a growth industry. Grace debated going to the command post, thinking police there might know something, might tell her something.

No, if they'd found her, I'd know.

She avoided the command post because she couldn't bear to hear police telling her for the millionth time: "We're doing all we can. We're searching everywhere." All the while their suspicions about them bubbled below the surface.

Have you ever struck her, or abused her? Are you involved in her being missing? Where is she?

And now they found the RV had drugs in it. They'd put them in handcuffs!

Grace's mind raced. Eclipsing it all were her failures, and her guilt for being angry at Riley and not waking her.

Because I didn't want to deal with her, I left her here and now she's gone.

Grace's phone vibrated with a text from John. Where are you?

She tapped her answer: Did they find her?

No. Please come back and rest. Where are you? I'll come get you.

I can't sleep. I'm looking for her. Talk to you later.

Grace, tell me where you are. Please.

She didn't respond.

Heart aching, mind racing, she moved across the road and into the desert east of the Silver Sagebrush. The darkness beyond was dotted by searchers in the distance looking for Riley, their flashlights sweeping the ground.

Grace turned on her phone's light and, finding a gap in the low-lying barbed-wire fence that paralleled the interstate for miles, she headed farther into the night. She was slowed by the uneven sand and stone terrain, stumbling at times. But she kept going.

She brushed against cacti and the tug of waist-high shrubs but continued, combing the ground with her light, searching for Riley, her panic and guilt shooting her back...

Back to the night Tim flew home from Chicago without telling her, surprising her. He was so happy, kissing her, wanting to talk about a decision he'd made.

But before they could talk, she'd sent him out. Sent him to his death.

Grace's heart beat faster. She was being punished for what she did to Tim.

Grace heard the thumping of the police helicopter, on the other side of the interstate, far off to the west, its powerful searchlight probing the desert for Riley.

Grace screamed out for her daughter. "RILEY!"

Her phone rang.

Weak with relief, she answered the call from her friend Sherry Penmark.

"Grace! I just heard the news about Riley. I'm coming!"

"Sherry, oh God!" Grace sobbed. "No, no, your aunt is sick."

"It'll be okay. I'm getting on an early-morning flight. I'll be there."

Grace let her tears flow, and with it, the truth.

"It's my fault."

"What're you talking about?"

"She was asleep. We argued. I was so mad at her. I didn't wake her and we drove off without her."

"Don't beat yourself up—"

"How could I leave her? I lost her! It's my fault, like with Tim!"

"Stop. I'll be there as fast as I can and we're going to find her."

After the call Grace remained rooted in the night as the helicopter passed overhead, its blazing light piercing the night, the beginnings of downwash stirring sand and dust around her. In the raging fury and chaos she thought of Eva Marie Garcia, the images of a body bag being transferred from the desert on a gurney.

She fell to her knees.

Please, let me find Riley.

DAY 2

Twenty-Five

Jean, Nevada

The next morning Margot Winton took out her phone while waiting in line to check out of the Cholla Sun Trail Hotel.

She'd left Las Vegas yesterday, stopping in Jean for the night. She'd wanted to get an early start this morning on the two-hour drive home to Barstow, California. But the people checking out ahead of her had an issue with their bill and there was only one clerk on duty.

Not a problem for Margot.

Waiting patiently, she made use of the time by reviewing the pictures she'd taken of her friend's visit, smiling at the first one she'd swiped to.

My goodness, she hasn't changed a bit.

As beautiful as ever, Margot thought, admiring her sixty-eight-year-old girlfriend, Julie Frahan, by the pool.

They'd met when they were in their late twenties, working side by side as copy editors at the now-defunct *Los Angeles Morning Post*.

Where did the years go?

Under impossible deadlines, they turned raw copy into strong, clear news stories, both of them sharp-eyed experts on grammar and the paper's style. Julie had taped a quote to her work space from Robert Louis Stevenson: "Do not write merely to be understood. Write so you cannot possibly be misunderstood."

Eventually, Julie left to join the *Boston Globe*, where she'd retired. And after the *Morning Post* folded, Margot found a part-time job at the *Desert Dispatch* in Barstow before retiring. They remained lifelong friends, visiting each other two or three times a year.

Their most recent visit ended yesterday, when Margot had driven Julie from her house in Barstow to catch her return flight in Las Vegas, where they squeezed in some fun and took pictures.

Margot continued swiping.

Here they were out front of Caesars Palace and here at the fountains of the Bellagio.

"No, no, that's not correct! Check again!" The woman ahead of her was stabbing the paper copy of her bill on the counter with her finger as the clerk tapped on his keyboard, maintaining his professional composure.

That's when Margot noticed that the flat screen above the reception desk was not only displaying hotel features but the picture and security video of a young girl. A missing teenage girl from California.

Studying the young girl's face and scanning the information, Margot recalled the tragic case of another California teen, also missing before her body was found in the region a year ago.

The name of the young white girl on the screen was Riley Jarrett from San Diego.

How distressing for her family, Margot thought, wishing a happy reunion for them before going back to her phone, and the video she'd recorded.

Here were Julie and Margot at the Statue of Liberty, now here they were at the Gateway Arch in St. Louis. They were posing at the huge murals of landmarks in the lobby of the Silver Sagebrush, where they'd stopped yesterday on the way to Las Vegas.

It wasn't far from Jean.

Julie had an appetite for kitsch, garish, out-of-this-world stuff, and had insisted they stop at what was billed as one of America's largest truck plazas. It was mind-bogglingly huge.

Next, she played a video she'd taken of the Hoover Dam mural, then Julie laughing and waving in front of the Golden Gate Bridge mural among other travelers in the lobby.

Something caught Margot's eye.

Wait a minute. Is that— What was that?

She replayed her video.

Then she looked up at the flat screen and the appeal for help finding the missing San Diego girl.

Margot examined Riley Jarrett's face and re-played her video.

Her head snapped back and forth between the screen and the images on her phone.

Oh my Lord.

Twenty-Six

Las Vegas, Nevada

Elsen got little sleep and was up before the sun.

He fed Daisy. It was still dark when he walked her to the park, and mourned his wife. Some days her death wasn't real to him; he'd go back home expecting to find her there. But the house was empty, and it took everything he had to keep going, to put one foot in front of the other and step into another day.

In the twilight, a distant siren evoked memories of the Mandalay Bay shootings as he took Daisy home then drove to headquarters, asking fate to give them a break in Riley Jarrett's case before he went to the Digital Forensic Lab.

Fortunately, Officer Sue Watson was an early riser. I bike to work. I'll be in at 5:30, she'd said in response to his text last night.

And Watson was there on time this morning. Elsen gave her Riley Jarrett's phone, along with the password volunteered by Grace Jarrett, a copy of the emailed warrant and other documentation.

"We need you to pull everything you can, who she contacted, what sites she visited. Everything," Elsen said.

Watson gave it all a preliminary inspection.

"It'll take time," she said. "All depends on the technology and if we have to subpoena the creators of the apps she's used for access to their servers. We'll work as fast as we can, Dan."

Elsen took the elevator to the Missing Persons Unit, went to the kitchen and made fresh coffee. It was 5:45 a.m.

On his way to his desk he saw that McDowell had arrived and was on the phone. He pointed to his mug, indicating an offer to get her a coffee. She smiled, holding up her Raiders coffee cup. A moment later she ended her call.

"That was Jackson at the command center," she said. "Grace Jarrett was near hysterical, wandering in the desert last night before they got her back in her room."

Elsen thought. "Maybe we should get eyes on the family."

"You're sure you want to go that way?" McDowell said. "We can't charge them with anything that will stick."

"But have we ruled them out?"

"No, but—"

"But we're not confident they've been truthful," he said. "What if the mom's hysterics was an act?

What if she was hiding evidence or meeting some-one out there?"

"Then we go out and find it. But you said we need to keep an open door with them, and we've already played hard on the drug issue."

"I'm not talking full-bore surveillance," Elsen said. "We should just keep an eye on them."

"All right. I'll tell Jackson and Rogan to get a dog team and follow the mom's path for anything, and to keep a friendly watch on the family."

"Right. Did Jackson have anything new for us?" Elsen asked.

"Not much. What've you got?"

"The phone's with the lab, I've updated the DA and I talked to Narcotics. They'll reach out to their sources for any leads," Elsen said.

"I started working on warrants on the rental his-tory of the RV."

"We keep coming back to the drugs." Elsen took a hit of coffee. "She could've been taken if the family failed to deliver drugs, you know, a cartel-ransom-for-debt thing."

"That's still a possibility, but what if this Caleb Clarke, the boyfriend, is in a gang?" McDowell said. "Or ran up a debt, or was approached to offer Riley up for trafficking?"

Elsen nodded at her theory. "Something he might do, if she dumped him and was moving away."

"An act of vengeance against the mom. And,

being out of the country makes him look clean," McDowell said.

"I'll reach out to the FBI, get their legal attaché office that covers Algeria to locate Caleb Clarke for a phone interview and we'll run down his background."

McDowell made a note. "It's chilling. When I was on the task force, I worked some trafficking cases. Girls Riley's age are never on the Strip. They're in the back rooms of massage parlors. Traffickers change their appearance radically and so fast, they almost vanish."

Elsen shook his head.

"And we've got the unsolved Garcia case not far from the Sagebrush. Homicide is looking for any connection to ours," he said. "And since we have the warrants we'll get CSI to process the RV."

As time passed, the detectives worked solidly, going back over everything again, rechecking the tip lines, checking with security at McCarran, the Golden Nugget, other casinos, all transportation outlets. They checked with police in California, in San Bernardino and in Riverside for updates, and the status of the request for security video from the Chevron in Fontana where the family stopped.

McDowell called the twenty-four-hour hotline for San Diego County's Child Protective Services and was put in touch with an investigator to handle her inquiry for any reports of abuse, any investigations concerning Riley Jarrett. The investigator said she would get back to McDowell.

At the same time, Elsen continued querying law enforcement databases for any criminal history for Riley Jarrett, Grace Jarrett, John Marshall, Blake Marshall and Caleb Clarke.

All he could find was a speeding ticket for John.

They called the San Diego hospital where Grace had worked and the clothing chain in San Diego where John had worked, *SoCal SoYou*, to inquire about their background or any issues that may have a bearing on the case. They also made calls to Riley's and Blake's schools.

Between calls, McDowell turned to Elsen. "I'm going back," she said, "to her breakup with Caleb, the move, being pissed at her mom, who grabbed her phone. She could've simply run off."

Elsen, studying his phone, nodded. "We've seen cases like that. Her friends might know."

McDowell flipped through her notebook. "I called the parents of her friends last night and spoke with some of the girls—Claire, Ashley and Dakota. They've not had contact with Riley since her disappearance. All said she was upset about her breakup and the move and were sure she was texting with Caleb before disappearing."

"Her phone is key," Elsen said.

"Then there's the farewell party," she said. "We still need the family to give us a list of everyone who attended." McDowell's cup was empty. "I need more coffee, how about you?"

Elsen was concentrating on his phone.

"What is it?" McDowell came over to him.

"Well, John and Grace each lost someone tragically before they married."

"Are you saying that's a consideration?"

Elsen slid his phone into his pocket, got his cup and stood. "I don't know."

They started for the kitchen when McDowell's phone rang.

"Michelle, this is Shanice Jackson at the command center. We need you down here. We've got something."

Twenty-Seven

Jean, Nevada

Some forty minutes later, Elsen and McDowell entered the lobby of the Cholla Sun Trail Hotel.

"This way," Tracy Harris said upon greeting them.

Harris, a former US Marshal, now hotel security manager, was all business leading them through the main floor.

"One of our guests alerted us to information potentially significant to your case," Harris said.

She brought them to the Gold Miner, a small, dark-paneled, white-tablecloth restaurant, now empty because it only served dinner. They came to a booth occupied by a woman and Metro Police Officer Nate Rogan, who had briefed the detectives over the phone during their drive down.

"This is Margot Winton of Barstow," Rogan said, making introductions.

Then Harris said: "Anybody want anything, coffee?"

"I'm fine, thank you," Margot said.

"We're good." McDowell smiled.

"We'll leave you to it." Harris left with Rogan.

Even though they'd received Rogan's summary concerning Margot Winton's report, Elsen and McDowell requested her account. As she related the circumstances, Elsen took in her white cropped hair, high cheekbones and blue eyes behind her glasses. She struck him as a strong, credible witness as she cued up the video she'd recorded on her phone.

Margot sent it to McDowell, who pulled it up on her tablet, giving them an enlarged view. Angling the screen, she played the video in slow motion.

It began with Margot and her friend Julie at the huge murals in the busy Silver Sagebrush, where they'd stopped on their way to Las Vegas the previous day. They were standing before the Golden Gate Bridge mural when in the far left corner there was a glimpse of a girl in a white T-shirt.

"See?" Margot said. "I couldn't believe it. It's the missing girl!"

McDowell replayed the scene, freezing it on a small but clear image of a teenage girl wearing a shirt with the stylized *Friends* logo from the TV show. From the photo Grace Jarrett had given them, and footage from the security camera in the Silverado store, there was no doubt.

"Yes, that's her," Elsen said. "Keep going."

In slow motion the video continued to the Gateway Arch in St. Louis, only now a man had emerged among the people; out of a corner of the frame. When he was in, he could be seen briefly but clearly: a white man in his late forties, early fifties. He was holding a phone, taking photos or making a video of the murals. His other hand was out of the frame, but positioned as if he was holding something.

"Replay it," Elsen said. "And stop on every frame."

A closer look revealed how the focus of the man's recording had subtly shifted to Riley Jarrett.

Margot's video of the Hoover Dam showed flashes in the corner of Riley and the stranger recording her. Other travelers and Riley were oblivious to what the man was doing and just before Margot's sequence of the Hoover Dam ended, something happened.

"Wait!" Elsen said.

"I got it."

McDowell replayed the frames carefully.

The end of the Hoover Dam sequence showed the man holding a bag with something in it and walking right up to Riley in front of the Golden Gate Bridge mural before they both vanished from the video. Suddenly, Riley and the stranger surfaced again, in the corner.

McDowell slowed then froze images.

Riley appeared worried and the man appeared to be talking to her, putting a hand on her shoulder. Riley brushed it away before they both vanished from the recording as it ended.

Elsen and McDowell traded a quick, knowing glance.

They thanked Margot Winton and after taking her statement and formally initiating a warrant for her video, they thanked Harris and Rogan and set to work in their car.

Reviewing the video again, they detailed the man's description, estimating hair color, age, height, weight. He was wearing light khakis, a navy-colored polo shirt with a small yellow crest over his heart. Paging through notes, they aligned the time of the recording, determining it was not long after Riley had left the Silverado store.

"Let's start there," Elsen said. "What's he got in that bag? Did he buy something from the store?"

With McDowell on the phone to Carl Aldrich and Elsen at the wheel, they drove to the Silver Sagebrush.

Skylar Brown, the clerk who'd been working when Riley Jarrett was in the Silverado, shook her head after watching the video of Riley and the stranger for the fourth time.

"No, he doesn't look familiar."

Elsen and McDowell asked her about the bag he was holding.

"Look at the logo. Is it from here?" McDowell asked.

"I can't see it clearly. It could be ours." Skylar bit her bottom lip. "Oh! I forgot to tell you something yesterday. You gotta check with Bick."

"Bick?"

"Chad Bickerstaff."

"What about him?"

"Yesterday, right after I saw the girl, I stepped away to go to the bathroom for like, five minutes. Bick covered for me before he left for the day. He's in the back now." Skylar reached for her phone and texted. "I'll get him to come out."

"Did we miss interviewing him?" Elsen said.

McDowell checked her notes. "He was one of the staff who'd left before the case broke. He never got back to us," she said.

A moment later, a lanky man in his twenties with a mop of curly hair arrived at the counter, his eyes flicking to Skylar and the detectives, who, after explaining, asked if he could identify the stranger in the video.

Bick leaned his slim frame into the screen, giving the request his full concentration. McDowell offered to play it a second time but Bick was nodding, keeping his eyes on the images.

"I remember him," Bick said. "All smiles but kinda creepy."

"Why do you say that?" Elsen said.

"Just gave me a bad vibe. I remember he bought duct tape and scissors."

"Really? Did he pay with cash, or a card?" Elsen asked.

Bick thought. "Cash."

"Cash?"

"No, wait. I remember, he opened his wallet for cash but had none. He seemed ticked at himself for not having cash and having to pay with plastic."

"Can you show us the record of his purchase?"

"I'll have to ask because, I mean, I don't know if that's legal and all."

"That's all right. We'll get warrants," Elsen said.

"Whoa, am I in some kind of trouble?" Bick said.

"No, you're not. Don't worry."

In the next few moments calls were made and emails sent with McDowell informing a judge of the facts in Riley Jarrett's case, the new exigent circumstances and that more warrants would likely be needed. The judge agreed that probable cause existed to issue the warrant.

In that time, Aldrich arrived at the Silverado, and management continued cooperating. Receipts were searched and the credit card number used in the purchase was obtained by the detectives.

They reached out to security at the credit card company.

The man's name was Frayer Ront Rykhirt, aged forty-eight, of Riverside, California.

McDowell looked at Elsen. "Riverside, Dan."

"Yeah, I know."

That was where Eva Marie Garcia was from.

Twenty-Eight

Nevada

Elsen got on the phone to Jackson at the mobile command center.

"It's a concrete lead, Lieutenant. Where's the family now?"

"Talking with the Silver Sky Search and Rescue people, marshaling beside us."

"Can you pull them aside? We're on our way to you."

"Will do."

As they walked through the complex, McDowell, phone to her ear, had reached dispatch with a request to run Frayer Ront Rykhirt's name through law enforcement databases for any criminal history or outstanding warrants. They were in the lobby when McDowell's tablet pinged with the first piece of information.

It was from the California DMV. Rykhirt's driver's license loaded onto her screen. She stopped, copied his photo and cropped it, making a separate image of his headshot, along with a cropped headshot of him from Margot Winton's video.

"We'll go with these, Dan."

They continued walking across the Sagebrush's parking lot to the command center and vehicles where the Silver Sky people were clustered.

At the command center, the detectives had Grace, John and Blake take turns individually looking at the photos. Not knowing which way their investigation would go, and needing to protect its integrity, Jackson, McDowell and Elsen provided no name or details about Rykhirt.

They watched the family's reactions, starting with Blake's.

"Do you know this man? Is he familiar in any way?" Elsen said.

After examining the man's face, Blake shook his head. "I don't know him."

"Take a good look, son."

"I did. I don't know him."

"You're sure?"

"I'm sure. Why're you asking me?"

"That's all we need for now."

Blake left and they brought John inside to see the photos.

"No idea," John said. "Why're you asking if we know him?"

"We'd like to talk to him. That's all we can say," McDowell said.

"Seriously?" John said. "Tell me what you know."

"John, we'll keep you posted."

John left, barely masking his frustration, which Grace noticed when she entered to view the photo. Fear stood in her bloodshot eyes as she scrutinized the man's face.

"I've never seen him before. Who is he? Why're you showing us these pictures? Does he have something to do with Riley? What's happened?"

"Grace, take it easy." McDowell and Jackson helped her to a seat inside the vehicle while Elsen brought in John and Blake so they could now speak to all of them.

"We showed you this man's pictures," Elsen said, "because we have to know if he has any connection to Riley or your family."

"Why?" John asked. "Does he have Riley? One of those photos looked like it was taken in the Sagebrush. Who is he?"

Elsen held up his palms. "We think he may have information we need."

"What kind of information?" Grace asked.

"We don't know."

"Why would he have information about Riley?" Grace's voice rose. "Was he in the truck stop?"

Elsen waited a moment. "We're going to issue an appeal to locate him. He's what we call a person of interest."

"What? Oh God!" Grace groaned. "You think he has Riley!"

McDowell's phone, then Elsen's vibrated but they continued with the family.

"We've confirmed nothing. We need to keep investigating," Elsen said, nodding to Jackson who then opened the door.

"Folks," Jackson said. "Your friends from San Diego are arriving. Let's go back to the search and rescue van and let the detectives work."

Grace stood and stepped closer to Elsen and McDowell.

"You asked me about the girl who was murdered near here a year ago. Now you're asking me about this stranger." Grace's voice broke. "You tell me the truth right now. Is my daughter dead? You tell me!"

In that moment, McDowell's armor as a detective was pierced. Her professional distance evaporated and she was a mother meeting pain in another mother's eyes.

"Grace," McDowell said, "we have no evidence to suggest Riley's been hurt. All we know right now is that she's missing and we want to talk to this man who may or may not have information to help us."

Grace searched McDowell's face until she was satisfied she had heard the truth—or as much of it as they were going to tell her. Then John put his arm around his wife and after a long moment the family left.

In the time that followed, Elsen and McDowell remained in the command center checking messages and making calls.

Within minutes more crucial information reached them, including key facts that put a knot in McDowell's stomach.

Frayer Ront Rykhirt, aged forty-eight, of Riverside, California, was a convicted sex offender whose crimes and acts involved young girls.

Twenty-Nine

Nevada

A thirteen-year-old girl had been riding her bicycle through a park in Riverside, California, when she fell and hurt her knee and hand.

Frayer Ront Rykhirt, who was in the park taking pictures of birds, came to her aid, offering to drive her home a few blocks away. Bleeding and upset, the girl agreed. But Rykhirt didn't drive her home. He drove out of the neighborhood, taking the girl to an abandoned shed at the edge of the city where he touched her inappropriately while trying to remove her jeans.

The girl struck him with a piece of brick, escaped and flagged down a car, driven by a retired judge and her husband who got a description and partial plate of Rykhirt's vehicle when he tried to leave the area.

He was arrested and charged.

Riverside detectives investigating Rykhirt also linked him to another complaint from six months earlier. In that case, a man had lured a twelve-year-old girl from a suburban Riverside mall to the parking lot and into his car where he touched her inappropriately before she escaped. Packing tape, rope and a pillowcase were found under the front passenger seat of his car.

Rykhirt was convicted and served eight years in prison for his crimes. He'd now been free for nearly three years and worked at odd jobs.

McDowell shook her head as she finished reading Rykhirt's history, while Elsen's poker face twisted into the beginnings of a scowl.

They were in the mobile command center, working fast, continuing their pursuit of Rykhirt on several fronts.

He was five feet ten inches tall, weighed 175 pounds had brown hair, brown eyes and a small scar on his left temple where he was struck with the brick. His vehicle was a 2015 Nissan Versa, four-door hatchback, metallic blue with a valid California plate.

They'd submitted the new information, including photos and a description of Rykhirt's clothing, to all databases, including NCIC. They alerted California Highway Patrol, San Bernardino and Riverside counties, and Nevada Highway Patrol that Rykhirt was wanted as a person of interest in the case of Riley Jarrett. They'd requested Riverside PD pick him up at his address if they located him there, or sit on it with unmarked cars.

Elsen also alerted Homicide to the new information concerning Rykhirt to run against what they had about Eva Marie Garcia's unsolved murder.

McDowell got a text advising that police efforts to locate Rykhirt through his cell phone GPS had so far been fruitless.

"Let's huddle up," Lieutenant Jackson said. "I've been on the line with the AMBER coordinator to issue an updated alert, as well."

"Thanks, Lieutenant," McDowell said.

"Once it's out, we'll manage calls to the tip lines and determine leads," Jackson said. "We'll keep our search and canvass operations going full bore here now that we have more volunteers. And we'll give the heads-up to our public info people to manage the expected increase in media inquiries and coverage."

As they continued working, the detectives checked with the security people at the credit card companies and bank Rykhirt used for the most recent activity. It was a lucky break that Rykhirt had used the card instead of cash when he did, the detectives thought, because it enabled them to identify him as the suspect in Riley's disappearance.

But now there was no new activity showing for his cards, nothing since he purchased duct tape and scissors at the Silverado.

Duct tape and scissors.

Now, staring at Rykhirt's photos, rereading his criminal history, McDowell could only imagine why he bought those items at the time he saw Riley.

And the fact he'd ceased using his plastic.

He's stopped leaving a trail.

She looked at his face, knowing what he did, or tried to do, to those other girls.

Then she swiped to the photos of Riley Jarrett.

We've got to find you before it's too late.

Thirty

Las Vegas, Nevada

At that time, some thirty miles north of the command center, Metro patrol officers George Sike and Renee Bonnar wheeled into a Rebel Oil gas station near the south end of the Strip.

They'd already responded to the new ATL/BOLO on their car's terminal. It was an alert to "Be On The Lookout" and "Attempt To Locate" Frayer Ront Rykhirt, believed to be driving a blue 2015 Nissan Versa. They'd searched for the Nissan at several hotels in their zone while responding to other calls.

Now, taking a break, they stepped into the Rebel outlet.

"Lock into your vacation yet?" Bonnar secured the lid after refilling her reusable coffee mug.

"Yup, I'm going fishing in British Columbia." Sike got a can of Diet Coke and a chicken chipotle wrap from the cooler. "What about you, Ren?"

"Going to my girlfriend's wedding in Dallas."

"You might meet a fella there." Sike winked.

"No chance. I'm a bridesmaid and the dresses are hideous, a cowgirl theme with boots."

"Yeehaw." Sike grinned, shaking his head.

"I'm not joking, George. Cowgirl."

They returned to their car.

Sike had bit into his wrap and opened his soda. Bonnar got behind the wheel and took another look at the BOLO on their terminal. She stared at photos of Rykhirt, descriptions of him and his car, a summary of his link to Riley Jarrett's case and his criminal history.

The officers already had two new calls waiting; someone had smashed the windshield of a Ferrari GTB at the Excalibur. The other call was a report of a stolen commercial dumpster from the Hooters off Duke Ellington Way.

"You know what I'm thinking?" Bonnar said.

"You don't want to be a cowgirl bridesmaid." Sike took a sip of soda.

"Ha ha." She nodded to the place across the street.

Their marked patrol car was parked in the gas station's lot at the busy intersection of Koval Lane and Tropicana Avenue, in the shadow of the MGM Grand. Across the street was the Dreamy Breeze Motor Inn.

"On the way to our calls we can scan the Dreamy lot for the Nissan Versa and the subject."

Sike crumpled his wrapper and downed his Coke. "One more won't hurt. Let's do it."

* * *

The Dreamy Breeze was a low-budget motel with five hundred units in two large two-story structures shaped like the letter *E*. The motel stretched across a quarter of a block and had eight zones that all looked the same. In each zone, most vehicles were parked a few feet from the doors to the rooms.

For tourists the Dreamy Breeze was relatively clean. Occasionally guests found spiders, used towels in the sink, cigarette burns in the floor, gum smeared on the wall, hair in the shower, and some claimed they could see outside through the cracks in the door frame. But it had a nice pool in a palm-shaded courtyard, and without resort fees and other charges, it was affordable and a short walk from the Strip.

Police were familiar with the inn for other reasons.

Bonnar and Sike started in Zone 8. They slow-rolled by sedans, vans, pickups and motorcycles, searching for the blue Versa from California. They found a white one from Utah that was the wrong year. Moving on to the next zone, they saw a man and woman with towels, morning swimmers, heading to the pool.

No Versa was parked in the zone's lot.

It was tedious work as they cruised through the next zone and struck out. They cut through a laneway to the other zones.

Crawling along, checking vehicles, they saw

an older woman walking a leashed white poodle. Bending to pick up her dog, she waved to them and came to Bonnar's window.

"There are so many discarded needles around here," she said, cradling her dog. "It's not safe for pets, or children."

"We know, ma'am," Bonnar said.

"Can't you arrest somebody?"

"We're looking into it, ma'am."

"I'm on my way to complain to the manager."

"Have a good day, ma'am."

They moved on to the next zone and struck out again. As they continued on to the next zone, Sike began humming, "Deep in the Heart of Texas," until Bonnar punched his shoulder.

Turning into the second-last zone, it appeared no blue 2015 Nissan Versas were parked in the lot. They were leaving the zone when Sike glimpsed something blue.

"Hold up, Renee."

"What?"

"That big Ford F-150. Look, something blue's parked on the other side of it. Get us closer."

Bonnar pulled up their patrol car, stopping broadside at the rear bumper of the small blue car, blocking it.

"A metallic blue Nissan Versa," Sike said. "Looks like a 2015, four-door hatch with a California tag."

Bonnar tapped on the keyboard, checked the ATL/BOLO. "That's the plate. That's him," she said.

With a surge of adrenaline, Sike took up the

radio microphone, alerted dispatch that they'd located the subject's vehicle.

"How do you want to do this?" Bonnar asked.

"Wait for backup, take things from there."

"But he could have her in there with him."

Sike considered this.

"George, we need to grab him now." Bonnar was calling the front desk on her phone.

"What're you doing, Ren? We should wait."

After a quick conversation with the manager, Bonnar confirmed Rykhirt's room number.

"He's got one-forty-nine."

Sike absorbed the information as time ticked by.

"George," Bonnar said, "could you live with yourself if you knew he was in there hurting her while we're sitting here?"

Sike rubbed his chin hard, reached for the radio, updated dispatch.

"Let's go," he said.

They went to 149, taking tactical positions at the side of the door, weapons drawn. They could hear voices inside. Bonnar knocked on the door. No answer.

An older man in the next room opened his door, eyes widening when he saw the officers.

"Get back in your room, sir and get on the floor," Sike said.

The man's door closed.

Waiting a long moment, Bonnar knocked again louder. "Las Vegas Police! Open the door now!"

No response.

Sike and Bonnar exchanged glances, tightened their grips on their guns.

They heard a girl's scream from inside—facing an emergency situation, Sike kicked the door, splintering the frame, rushing in with Bonnar, their guns sweeping an empty room. Two empty beds, one unmade as if recently slept in—nothing under them. The bathroom and shower were empty, save for an open suitcase, clothing on chairs and toiletries on shelves.

The TV was on, tuned to a horror movie.

Take-out food wrappers and cups were on the small table next to an open laptop.

Sike took his pen and tapped the space bar; the screen came to life.

"Cripes."

The monitor filled with a gallery of images of naked young girls, some blindfolded and in bondage. Among the photos were frames of Riley Jarrett, taken of her in the lobby at the Silver Sagebrush complex.

"My God, George!" Bonnar said from behind him. She was looking at the pictures.

"All right," Sike said. "We need to seal this room for processing and alert our sergeant."

Closing the damaged door behind them, the officers stepped outside and holstered their weapons.

While catching their breath, preparing to make calls and get crime scene tape from their car, glass smashed to the ground nearby. Sike's and Bonnar's heads snapped toward the sound.

A man had just rounded the corner of the zone and dropped a bag from a liquor store where it had shattered on the sidewalk.

It was an instant of recognition.

Frayer Ront Rykhirt stood there, mouth open, shocked at the sight of police.

"Stay right there!" Sike shouted.

Rykhirt vanished around the corner with Bonnar running after him, followed by Sike, who'd reached for his radio to alert dispatch.

Rykhirt fled down the lane with Bonnar gaining. Ahead, Bonnar saw the woman walking toward them with her white poodle in her arms and in the direct path of Rykhirt just as approaching sirens could be heard.

Despite being weighed down by her utility belt, her vest and gun, Bonnar was closing the gap on Rykhirt but she was too late. Striking like a cobra, he seized the woman, sliding an arm around her chest, another around her neck, sending her dog squealing to the ground. Metal flashed as he twisted so Bonnar could see the knife pressed against her throat.

"No, please!" the woman screamed.

"Back off, bitch!" Rykhirt shouted.

Bonnar stopped, held up her palms. "Let her go. Don't do this." She took slow steps toward him. "Don't make this worse."

The little dog yipped at Rykhirt's ankles, and the woman sobbed as Rykhirt continued moving backward, keeping her locked in front of him as a shield, keeping the knife at her throat.

"Please! You're hurting me!"

The sirens grew louder, and Bonnar glanced around wondering where Sike was.

"Let her go."

"I'm not going back to prison," Rykhirt said.

"Let her go and we can talk."

Bonnar glimpsed Sike ahead of them, crouching behind a van as Rykhirt backed closer and closer to it.

"Frayer—" Bonnar softened her voice, keeping her palms out "—we can talk. Let this lady go."

"I can't. I can't go back."

Rykhirt continued moving backward with the poodle yipping at his ankles, distracting him, when Sike lunged at him with rocket force, taking him— and the woman—down, slamming him hard to the ground and sending the knife flying, rolling him to his stomach and handcuffing him.

Bonnar comforted the woman, who was bleeding, crying and holding her poodle as it licked her face. Paramedics were called and two patrol cars arrived, sirens wailing, lights wigwagging. Motel guests were watching the scene from the ground and the upper deck.

When Sike read Rykhirt his rights, he began mumbling.

"It's so messed up. I just wanted to be her friend."

Thirty-One

Nevada

Grace Jarrett struggled to pay attention.

Silver Sky Search and Rescue's incident commander, Warren Taylor, was briefing the volunteers at the group's command post in the Sagebrush parking lot. Upward of sixty women and men of all ages, wearing fluorescent orange vests, T-shirts, hats and backpacks with radios clipped to the straps had stopped their lives, left their jobs, to rush down here and help in the search for Riley.

Grace stood among them with John and Blake. She was dressed in donated sweatpants, and a T-shirt with "Nevada" arched across it and fighting to concentrate on what Taylor was saying, but all she could think of was the detectives showing them photos of a strange man who may know something about Riley and then that poor girl murdered nearby last year. It was all too much.

Am I losing my hold on reality? Wandering and

collapsing in the desert last night and now I can't
stop fearing Riley was taken by a stranger.

Grace struggled to focus on the search, but she'd lost track of time. Was it twenty minutes or over an hour since McDowell and Elsen had asked her about the strange man, saying they had no evidence Riley had been hurt? How could they be sure? Seeing those photos of the man had shaken her, and she was still reeling. Now, Grace battled to grasp what Taylor was telling the group about the next stage of the search as he pointed to a large map affixed to the side of the command vehicle.

"We're liaising with Metro Missing Persons. We'll deploy teams to scout prime areas," he said. "We'll assign others to work with Silver Sagebrush security to again comb the facility and search surrounding areas."

He moved onto technical aspects, making a 360-degree circle with his hand over the map, taking into account Riley's height, weight, her condition, estimating a pace of three to five miles an hour in any direction.

"We've calculated these search parameters, which should put us in close proximity of where Riley could be." He paused as a police helicopter passed overhead then said: "As the sun climbs, we're looking at desert temps of up to one-ten, one-fifteen. She could be dehydrated. There are snakes, coyotes, mountain lions; a lot of factors." He pointed to the distant west side of the interstate, noting some searchers would be transported to search areas there.

"We'll never quit searching until we find her," Taylor, a retired US Marine major, told the group, concluding by directing people to line up to receive assignments and form teams. Grace looked at John. His face, still bearing abrasions from the crash, was taut, barely masking his stress, having endured tragedy in the past, and now this with Riley.

And there was Blake beside her. His stoicism had given way to worry, evident in his sober expression. He was her son. She knew she had to get past her anger at him for lying to her about checking on Riley.

"How are you holding up?" she asked him.

He looked at her, his eyes glistening, heavy with concern and something else behind them, as if he were wrestling with a force buried deep inside, something Grace couldn't identify.

"Do you want to talk?" she asked.

Blake looked to the desert and said: "I'm scared."

"I'm scared, too."

"We've got to find her." He looked back to her, tears standing in his eyes. "I don't want to lose her. I know what that's like. We can't lose her."

Grace brushed his hair. "I know," she said. "I know."

Blake swallowed then looked at his phone. "Look, some friends have started an online fundraiser for a reward for information that leads to us finding Riley."

Grace looked at the site on his phone.

"See, donations are up to four thousand with more coming."

Nodding, she almost smiled, then she heard her name spoken by a familiar voice, turned and saw her friend from the hospital in San Diego.

"Jazmin!"

Jazmin Reyna took Grace into a long, crushing hug. Jazmin's beaming eyes and warm, strong smile lifted Grace.

"Oh, thank you!" Grace said. "Thank you so much for coming."

"You couldn't keep us away."

Jazmin gestured to more than a dozen people nearby, Grace's friends and coworkers from the University of California, San Diego Medical Center. Like Jazmin they were wearing T-shirts, shorts, backpacks and holding walking sticks and bottled water.

"A caravan of us left San Diego super early this morning," Jazmin said. "More people are coming. You're not alone, Grace. We're going to find Riley."

Grace moved to give each of them her heartfelt thanks. Not long after, a man approached John.

"Norm Hollister, John."

"Yes, Norm. You made it."

"Our team just got here. Left when it was still dark, made good time. One of the churches donated a bus. A couple folks flew. They should be here."

"I don't know what to say," John said.

"No need to say anything. In times like this, we pull together."

Blake then recognized some of Riley's friends—Dakota, Claire and Ashley, who'd arrived with their parents to join the search. They went to Blake to offer support.

Awed by the small army of Californians who had come to help them, John, Blake and Grace moved among the people, embracing their consolation. Grace felt their love, for here they were, in the process of moving away from San Diego, yet their friends and neighbors had traveled hundreds of miles across the state to come to their aid. It meant so much to her. She went from person to person, thanking them when suddenly she stopped and cupped her hands to her face.

Sherry Penmark had just arrived and was talking with one of the search officials.

A sob was rising in Grace's throat, emotion swirling in her heart.

Sherry.

Grace could never repay her for all that she'd done for her and Riley over the years; for helping them cope with Tim's death; for helping Riley deal with losing her dad; for becoming a member of their family. Sherry, who had worked with Tim and was also devastated by his death, had stepped up, helped them heal, helped Grace find the courage to keep going, becoming a friend, a nanny, a housekeeper, you name it, encouraging her to date again, helping her meet John and start over. And when they'd decided to move to Pittsburgh, Grace was convinced that despite all the promises they'd made to keep in touch, they would inevitably fade from each other's lives.

But here she is. I'm so blessed to still have her in my life.

Grace went to her with open arms. "Sherry, you really came."

The two women hugged. Holding Sherry was balm for Grace.

Like the others, Sherry was prepared, wearing jeans, T-shirt, a backpack and hiking boots. "I got an early flight from Salt Lake, grabbed the stuff I needed."

"But your aunt, shouldn't you be with her?"

"I talked it over with her doctor and my uncle. My aunt's fairly stable, for now. I told them I needed to be here to do whatever I can. They'll keep me updated but they said it would be good for me to be here."

Grace blinked back tears of gratitude.

"How're John and Blake doing?" Sherry asked.

"They're pretty shaken, but they're doing the best they can."

Sherry studied her face, the scrapes, her bandages, her anguish, then took her aside. "I want you to tell me how this happened." She nodded to Hollister. "Norm got the word out last night to your network of friends. They say that the security video here failed. One of the lawyers said you guys could sue."

Grace shook her head and through her tears detailed how events had unfolded, described the breakup with Caleb, the argument, driving off, the crash, the drugs, being arrested, the unsolved murder, photos of the strange man. While listening, Sherry nodded, passed her a tissue and asked a few gentle questions.

When Grace finished Sherry took her hands. "Listen to me, Grace. You're going to survive this because we're going to find her. Okay?"

"I hope that's true."

"You've survived bad things before."

"But…"

"But what?"

Grace pulled away, searched around for nothing.

"What is it?" Sherry asked.

"Don't you see? This is my fault."

"No, stop."

"I left her! I didn't check on her myself! What kind of a mother does that?"

Grace began sobbing and Sherry pulled her close, holding her, calming her, soothing her and assuring her that they would find Riley.

"This isn't your fault," Sherry said. "Stop blaming yourself. You're going to get through this. Do you hear me? You're going to find her."

Eventually Grace regained much of her composure. Brushing away tears, she thanked Sherry for restoring hope and giving her strength. "I'm so glad you're here."

Sherry smiled.

Grace's phone rang and she answered.

"Grace, this is Detective McDow—" Static filled the connection.

"Sorry, what did you say?"

"...development...... Ry... Las Veg..."

"I'm sorry, I can't hear—"

The call ended and Grace clutched at her phone. What if there had been a development?

"What was that?" Sherry asked.

"One of the detectives was trying to tell me something."

Sherry looked over Grace's shoulder, and Grace turned to follow her focus. A man with a TV news camera and a woman holding a microphone were talking with Lieutenant Jackson at the mobile command center. Another news crew was arriving. The operator pointed the camera skyward as the police search helicopter made a loud pass. Nearby, a man with a camera around his neck was focusing for still shots of volunteer searchers.

"Excuse me."

Another man approached, holding a microphone. He was tanned, wearing sunglasses, had well-coiffed hair, brilliant white teeth. With him was another man in a Las Vegas Golden Knights T-shirt, camera on his shoulder, lens aimed at Grace.

"Are you Grace Jarrett, Riley's mother?"

"Yes."

"Kirk Keating with KLKZ. Can you give us a sec? We'd like to get your reaction."

"Reaction? To the search?"

"The arrest."

"What arrest?"

"Metro just arrested a man in Las Vegas in connection with the case, a convicted sex offender from California."

His words hung in the air as if Grace had witnessed an explosion. Her chest tightened; she fought to breathe.

Thirty-Two

Nevada

A sex offender had taken Riley?

The TV reporter's revelation was a gut punch, staggering Grace.

"This can't be," she said to him.

"He was arrested a short time ago at the Dreamy Breeze Motor Inn near the Strip." Kirk Keating produced his phone and showed her. "Our desk got this video from a guest."

Grace and Sherry viewed shaky footage of a chaotic, dramatic scene taken from a balcony of two officers confronting a man holding a woman at knifepoint, tackling him to the pavement, handcuffing him.

"Oh my God! Where's Riley?" Grace demanded.

"She was not with him, according to our sources." Keating glanced at the camera operator. Eagerly taking advantage, they both stepped closer to her. Keating inched his microphone nearer as Grace called out for John and Blake.

Within seconds other news people crowded around the family and began firing off questions.

"Can you explain how your daughter went missing?" a reporter asked.

Grace provided basic facts about driving off thinking Riley was asleep in the RV. "It was all a mistake—it was—then there was an accident."

Another reporter asked: "Does your daughter know Frayer Ront Rykhirt?"

"Who?" Grace asked.

"The man police just arrested?"

"No, she wouldn't know him—"

"Did you know he's a registered sex offender in California?"

"We don't know anything about him." Grace shook her head.

"Does your family have any connection to Rykhirt?" another reporter asked.

"Please." John held his hand up. "We really don't know—"

"Did your daughter know Eva Marie Garcia, the Riverside teen who was murdered in the area last year?"

"No," John said.

"We understand police found evidence of illegal drugs in your RV?"

"No," John said. "That's got nothing to do with us—"

"Is there a drug connection to the case?"

"What?" John said. "No! The RV's not ours. We rented it."

"Have you been questioned by police?" Keating asked.

"We've been helping them," John said, "but we really don't have—"

"Sir, what's your line of work in San Diego?" Keating asked.

"I'm in corporate communications and Grace is a nurse."

"Where were you heading and why?"

"We're preparing to move to Pittsburgh because of a new opportunity," John said. "What's this got to do with…"

"Who're you?" A reporter nodded to Blake.

"He's our son," Grace said.

"Can we get the spelling of your names and your ages?"

"But why?" Grace asked.

"News stories may help locate your daughter. The more people know, the more they care," a female reporter said. The sympathy in her blue eyes seemed sincere to Grace, and she gave them the information.

"And can we get your phone numbers, so we can update you if we learn anything?"

Grace and John provided their numbers.

"Thank you." The woman smiled. "One important question, as a mother myself, Grace, could you tell me, if there's one thing you could say to Frayer Rykhirt right now, what would that be?" She extended her microphone. The station flag on it read KV 99 FirstFront News.

"I just—I just—I just want my daughter back." Tears flowed as Grace broke down, her world spinning with John and Blake steadying her as Sherry returned, the family unaware that she'd left to bring back two Metro officers with her.

"Okay, people," Lieutenant Jackson said to the press as she and Officer Rogan collected the family, moving them toward the police command center. "We'll issue an updated statement for you very soon. So let's give these folks some space. We'll let you know whatever we can when we can. Meantime our search operations are ongoing."

Once they were all inside the center John said, "We've got to go to Las Vegas, to talk to this man you arrested."

"I understand," Jackson said. "That's all being taken care of. This is a police matter. I know it's not easy, but the best thing you can do is stay here and hold tight."

Grace sat down and sobbed. John moved to comfort her as Blake looked out the open door to the desert, the search activity, biting back his tears, saying nothing.

Glancing around the small center, John noticed something.

"Where're Elsen and McDowell?"

Jackson didn't answer.

"Lieutenant, earlier when they showed us photos of a man, they said he may know something about Riley. McDowell tried to call Grace. Please tell us.

We deserve to know. Why are we now being updated by reporters?"

"The detectives have gone to Las Vegas to talk
to Frayer Rykhirt, the man in the photos. Things
are moving very fast. I know it's upsetting, I'm
sorry. That's all I can tell you right now."

Thirty-Three

Las Vegas, Nevada

In the minutes after Frayer Ront Rykhirt's arrest, more Metro Police converged on the Dreamy Breeze Motor Inn.

Marked patrol units took up points at every entrance and exit, sealing the entire facility.

A command post was established; Elsen and McDowell conferred with ranking officers determining actions to be taken as more investigative and support details and vehicles arrived.

Taking quick, coordinated steps, police ordered all housekeeping to be halted. All laundry and trash pickup was stopped, dumpsters searched for potential evidence linked to Riley. Elsen and McDowell questioned the clerks at the reception desk to learn whether Rykhirt was alone when he had checked in, his demeanor, if he made calls from his room phone, any requests, or received any deliveries.

Records were checked, security camera footage reviewed.

At the same time, K-9 teams went through every zone in an effort to track Rykhirt's travels as other officers went door-to-door searching rooms, questioning guests, showing them Rykhirt's and Riley Jarrett's photos. Still other officers canvassed surrounding businesses.

Media crews and curious bystanders watched from the other side of yellow tape stretched across entrances. Some sharp-eyed news photographers moved around the street, finding angles in landscaped areas that afforded them a sliver view of room 149.

They zoomed in tight to the activities, capturing Rykhirt's blue Nissan Versa being loaded onto a flatbed and covered before it was transported off-site for further processing.

The TV guys got video and the newspaper guys captured frame after frame of the crime scene van parked in front of 149. Analysts wearing moon suits came and went as they processed Rykhirt's room.

Inside, forensic experts took photos, made sketches and copious notes while methodically collecting and preserving physical evidence.

Concentrating on her job, Lisa Faber, who'd been with the Crime Scene Detail for nearly ten years, was working in Rykhirt's room with surgical care. She came to a grease-stained paper fast-food take-out bag. It had been flattened, but she noticed images and lettering that were apart from the chain's logo.

One side had a crude drawing made with blue ink, a jaggedly sketched stick person—a girl, her eyes huge with terror, a strip indicating her mouth was bound. Her arms were up over her head, suspended by a rope, her hands clasped with a strip indicating binding on her wrists.

The drawing had been titled. Above the figure, something scrawled in a creepy, frenetic style as if done in a state of delirium.

One word.

"Riley"

Thirty-Four

Las Vegas, Nevada

Michelle McDowell felt the hot breath of a malignant force on the back of her neck.

The case had taken a dark turn.

After leaving the Dreamy Breeze motel, where the investigative work was winding down, she and Elsen had gone to headquarters and huddled with supervisors in preparing to interview Frayer Ront Rykhirt.

McDowell studied her new notes, preliminary reports and images of the evidence collected. *That chilling sketch.* With each swipe and tap on her tablet, she felt the dawning dread that Rykhirt had killed Riley Jarrett.

McDowell and Elsen stood with their sergeant and people from Homicide behind one-way glass watching an officer escort Rykhirt into the adjoining interview room.

"Did he really waive his right to an attorney?"

Gabe Delwood, a gravel-voiced homicide detective asked while at the glass staring at Rykhirt.

"Got his signature, right here." Elsen tapped a folder with the document.

They watched as the escorting officer fastened a chain from Rykhirt's wrists to the handcuff loop on the table.

Delwood sucked air through his teeth. "Hope his waiver doesn't come back to bite you. Seems a little off."

"We've connected dots," Melody Reeves, Elsen's sergeant, said. "But not all of them. Not yet. Let's see how this goes. This is our first shot at him."

Reeves nodded to Elsen and McDowell.

It was time.

The interview room was small, with white walls, black carpet and a light gray table where Rykhirt sat in one chair with his handcuffed hands clasped in front of him.

Elsen and McDowell set their folders and tablets on the table before taking the two chairs across from him.

The soft hum of the air-conditioning was the only sound as they assessed him.

Forty-eight, five-ten, with a build on the slender side. He had long messy dark hair, streaked with gray. Cheerless eyes stared from a doleful, pasty face, drooping from his skull as if all the trouble in this world was pushing down on his shoulders.

"Mr. Rykhirt," McDowell began, "given your

history, you're aware our conversations in this room are videotaped and audiotaped?"

Rykhirt stared at her.

"I am aware."

Rykhirt's voice was a rasping whisper. McDowell thought of those young girls he abused, and the words "gentle fiend" flicked like a snake's tongue through her mind.

"Frayer." Elsen slid a sheet of paper from a folder to him. "You're still Mirandized, but waived your right to an attorney." Elsen tapped the signature line. "Keeping that in mind, do you wish to proceed without a lawyer?"

"I understand. Yes, we can proceed."

Elsen collected the paper. "Let's get to it, then. Where's Riley Jarrett?"

Rykhirt shut his eyes, sinking deep into thought as if remembering. Whether it was something pleasant, or something beyond comprehension, remained caged in his mind. He didn't answer.

"Mr. Rykhirt, she's a missing minor," McDowell said. "And you're the last person to be seen with her. What do you say to that?"

He didn't answer.

"She was missing from the Silver Sagebrush, a truck stop on Interstate 15, a few miles north of Primm."

Rykhirt was silent.

"We have proof you were there, Frayer." Elsen nodded to McDowell.

She tapped her tablet to Margot Winton's video

showing Rykhirt with Riley, touching her shoulder and Riley recoiling.

"Why did you approach her? What did you say to her? Why did you touch her?" Elsen asked.

Rykhirt said nothing.

"We know you also purchased duct tape and scissors at the Silverado store," Elsen said. "Why?"

When Rykhirt didn't respond, McDowell produced more images.

"We found these photos on your laptop that you took of Riley Jarrett at the truck stop," Elsen said. "And we found this in your motel room." Elsen nodded to the sketch. "What did you do with Riley Jarrett, Frayer?"

He closed his eyes again, lifted his tired face to the ceiling and remained silent.

"Frayer," Elsen said, "you spent eight years in prison. How did that go for you? Did the other inmates hold you in high regard? We know they segregated you, but, well, it's prison, and things happen."

"Mr. Rykhirt, you're facing a harsh reality as a repeat offender," McDowell said. "You're going back inside."

His eyes remained closed as he lowered his head, shaking it slowly, his voice grating but eerily soft. "No, I can't go back."

"You're going back," Elsen said.

"You're a registered offender who has made contact with a minor, is in possession of child pornography, and much worse," McDowell said. "It's time you unburdened yourself. Tell us where Riley Jarrett is. We know you need help. Help us help you."

"What did you do to her, Frayer?" Elsen said. "Did you leave her in the desert?"

He remained silent.

For nearly an hour, Elsen and McDowell questioned him about Riley Jarrett, going back and around, hammering at the same points without progress, until there was a knock on the door.

Sergeant Reeves was there. She signaled for them to step out to the hall, closing the door behind them.

Thirty-Five

Nevada

Grace's fingers trembled while scrolling on her phone. Her attempts to reconnect with McDowell after the dropped call had failed.

Nerves shredded, Grace looked out at the teams of searchers moving over the desert at a funereal pace, heads bowed like mourners. Seeing them spread around now as she scoured the desolate terrain for Riley drew Grace back to the day she'd stood at her husband's grave.

Her world had stopped. Trapped in a maelstrom as Tim's casket was lowered into the ground. How could she go on living? While accepting condolences she battled her agony and culpability for his death, yet there were bursts of clarity in that raw, dark time.

Tim was loved by everyone, and like the searchers today, people had come from all over for the service, to share her pain. A large group had come from the Chicago branch where Tim had been working, having accepted a temporary promotion, commuting back to San Diego whenever he could.

Sherry had come with the Chicago group. That's when Grace first met her, at Tim's funeral. She was so warm, so giving and so concerned for her and Riley. Soon after, Sherry was transferred to the San Diego branch. Not knowing many people in the city, she grew close to Grace, helping her and Riley struggle through their grief.

It's how they had become friends.

Grace wiped her moist brow, drank from her water bottle and looked at Sherry in the distance, talking with John, at times placing her hand on his shoulder. Sherry then moved on to Blake, who was with some of Riley's friends. Grace heard snippets of the girls' conversations, unable to distinguish words but picking up on their worried tone. She suspected that, while upset, the girls also enjoyed being with Blake, given he was older, nice and a good-looking kid. Grace's heart went out to Blake, knowing how he'd be more comfortable searching alone, like her. He likely welcomed Sherry when she took him aside from the girls to talk to him.

That Sherry had left her sick aunt to fly here, to help her, was a testament to their friendship. Grace was blessed that Sherry and Jazmin Reyna were part of her life.

There was Jazmin, far ahead with the others from San Diego.

Jazmin was a beautiful strong woman, an excellent nurse with a caring heart. Her recent separation from her husband, Miguel, had saddened Grace. She and Jazmin had lived through some of the worst moments of their lives together. They'd supported each other through the pandemic, easing the pain of families then sobbing together in private later after losing friends, terrified of testing positive.

When Jazmin got infected, she was unable to be in the hospital where her mother was on a ventilator losing her battle to the virus. Grace was there and held Jazmin's mother's hand when she died, something Jazmin would never forget.

They were close in so many other ways.

Tim and Jazmin's husband, Miguel, had coached their daughter Cleo's soccer team. Grace and Jazmin would sit in lawn chairs and talk on the sidelines while watching the games. Jazmin had been there for her too, when Tim died, helping her cope, taking phone calls in the middle of the night, helping her hang on through the darkness.

Like Sherry, Jazmin had come to help find Riley and had brought everyone with her.

Then there was their neighbors, Norm Hollister and his wife and all the other volunteers from San Diego.

All of them here looking.

Looking for what?

Grace stopped in her tracks, feeling the heat and sudden confusion of her thoughts.

What are we looking for? My daughter's grave?

Staring at the brush, the sandy rocks, the great lonely emptiness, Grace could not take another step.

Her phone rang. She didn't recognize the number. "Hello?"

"Is this Grace Jarrett, Riley Jarrett's mother?"

"Yes, who's calling?"

"Elliott Downey, I'm a reporter with the *Press-Enterprise* in Riverside. I got your number from our stringer in Las Vegas. I think she was with the media who spoke to you a little while ago."

"I don't know, there were a lot of reporters."

"Can I ask you a few more questions for the story we're doing?"

"What story?"

"Frayer Rykhirt's arrest. You know he's from Riverside, California?"

Grace changed her hold on her phone. "I'll talk to you on one condition."

"What's that?"

"You have your sources, police sources, there in Riverside?"

"Yes."

"You tell me everything you know about this Rykhirt and my daughter."

"Well, I might know some but I'm not sure—"

"Don't do this, Elliott. Don't call me up like this and play games when my daughter's life's on the line—"

"No, I'm not, I never would—"

"You sound like a decent person, so just listen. I don't care how much or how little you know or how bad it sounds. I want to hear it. I deserve to hear it. Give me your word you'll tell everything you know."

Silence passed between them.

"Do I hang up or do we have a deal, Elliott?"

"I'll tell you what I know."

"All right. Go ahead."

Downey first went through a summary of Riley's case with Grace pausing to breathe, to keep from crying as once more she recounted events leading up to the disappearance.

Then she pressed Downey on Rykhirt.

Reading from his paper's older stories, Downey began telling her about Rykhirt. From coverage of Rykhirt's trial—and from what he knew from police that had not been reported—Downey described in detail Rykhirt's crimes against the two Riverside girls.

Grace took a moment to steady herself, then she pressed him to tell her everything he knew concerning Riley.

"Okay—" Downey dropped his voice a little "—but you can never say I told you this. I just got this from my sources who are working with Las Vegas police."

"Tell me, Elliott."

"They have video of Rykhirt approaching your daughter in the Silver Sagebrush."

"Go on."

"When they arrested him in Las Vegas, he had pictures of your daughter on his laptop."

Grace covered her mouth with her hand.

"As I understand it, those pictures were taken when she was in the truck stop," Downey said.

"Go on."

Downey swallowed. "In his room, they also found a sketch of her, bound."

"A sketch? Bound? Like tied up?" She could barely get the words out.

"Yes."

Grace took a shaky breath. She had to press on. "What else do you know?"

"That's pretty much it."

"Elliott, don't hold back. Is she dead? Do they think he killed her?"

He coughed, cleared his throat. "I don't know."

"Elliott, please!"

"I really don't know. What I can tell you is that they're looking hard at him for the murder of a Riverside girl whose body was found in the desert near Prlmm, a year ago."

"Eva Marie Garcia?"

"Yes. They suspect him of her murder."

Grace released a small, anguished groan. A moment passed.

"I'm sorry, Mrs. Jarrett, I told you all I know."

"Yes, Elliott, I needed to know." Her voice weakened. "Thank you."

Ending the call, Grace lowered her phone.

Rooted in place, she stood there gazing at her shadow on the ground as if gazing into a grave.

Thirty-Six

An RV rolled up to the pumps at the Chevron station in Fontana, California.

John Marshall got out and started fueling it.

When John finished, he, Grace, Blake and Riley walked into the ExtraMile store.

"This was put together for us by Fontana PD," Sergeant Reeves said. "It just came in. Keep watching."

Elsen and McDowell stared at the security video playing on the laptop in the viewing room as the recording's perspective shifted from the islands to inside the store. The family was now browsing, selecting drinks and food.

"Watch the girl."

McDowell watched Riley, an everyday California teen living her life. For a heartbeat McDowell wasn't a cop, but a mother, stabbed with the urge to reach into the screen and grab Riley, to keep her safe.

The recording showed Riley moving away from her family and down an aisle where she picked up a granola bar and was reading the label. A man, who'd already paid for gas with his credit card, was on his way out when he glimpsed her. Instead of leaving the man began browsing shelves near her. The man had long dark hair. He turned his head, looking at Riley until she walked away with the granola bar, not noticing him.

"That's Rykhirt," McDowell said.

"Fontana confirmed it with his credit card purchase of gas," Reeves said.

The family left the store and the perspective shifted to the pumps as they returned to the RV then drove off. The footage changed again showing Rykhirt exiting the store. Then it shifted to Rykhirt getting into a blue Nissan Versa, four-door hatchback and leaving the station in the same direction as the family.

"They got this next sequence from city and commercial cameras," Reeves said.

New footage showed the RV turning onto the on-ramp for Interstate 15, north.

A moment later, Rykhirt's blue Versa turned onto the ramp for Interstate 15, north. He was not far behind.

"He followed them to the Sagebrush," Elsen said.

"Bingo," Reeves said.

McDowell turned to the one-way window, looking at Rykhirt sitting there.

"He was hunting," she said.

* * *

Leaving Rykhirt alone in the interview room was also a tactical move, giving the detectives the chance to observe his reaction to their first round of questioning.

Stock-still, eyes closed, he appeared placid.

Elsen and McDowell also used the time to follow up with Fontana and Riverside PDs, and the Crime Scene Detail, securing new crucial elements.

"Time to push," Elsen said. "He's got to tell us where she is."

An hour after they'd left Rykhirt, they returned to the interview room to resume questioning him.

Rykhirt looked at them as they were seated.

"I'm hungry. May I have something to eat?"

Elsen stuck out his bottom lip. "Sure, we can get you something." He tapped and scrolled on the tablet, turning it, showing Rykhirt a take-out and delivery menu, with tantalizing photos of cheeseburgers, salads, souvlaki, pizza, tacos, club sandwiches, chicken platters and more.

"Look good?" Elsen said.

"I like chicken," Rykhirt said.

"Okay." Elsen turned the tablet back. "Here's the deal. We'll get food for you after you tell us where Riley is and what you did to her."

Rykhirt's jaw tensed and ever so slightly his nostrils flared. He swallowed then raised his chin in defiance.

"Oh and here's something else on the menu," Elsen said.

McDowell cued up the video from Fontana and played it for Rykhirt.

He watched in silence as the detectives watched him.

Then they replayed it.

Then they replayed the video taken at the Silver Sagebrush showing Rykhirt touching Riley. Then they showed him the evidence photos of his gruesome sketch, titled "Riley."

Rykhirt's face was blank.

"We know you stalked her, that you followed them, looking for the right moment to strike," Elsen said. "They stopped at the Sagebrush and the opportunity presented itself, a golden opportunity."

Rykhirt closed his eyes.

"There's no way out for you," Elsen said. "You're going back to prison."

"Now's the time to help yourself," McDowell said. "Either we tell the district attorney that you cooperated, or we tell her you didn't. It could make a difference at sentencing."

"Frayer," Elsen said. "Where is Riley Jarrett?"

Rykhirt took in a long breath, released it slowly then opened his eyes.

"I know what you're attempting," Rykhirt said. "It's an exercise in futility."

"We just want you to admit the truth," McDowell said.

"It's too late."

A chill shot up McDowell's spine.

"Did you hurt her?" Elsen asked.

Rykhirt was silent.

"Maybe," McDowell said, "you didn't mean to hurt her, maybe something went wrong; maybe it was an accident."

He stared hard at McDowell and repeated: "An accident?" He smiled. "You want the truth?"

Blinking, Rykhirt stared off as if watching a movie playing on the wall.

"She was beautiful. Incandescent," he said. "I was awestruck when I first saw her."

"Where was this?"

"Fontana." Eyes on the wall, remembering, he swallowed. "The urge to possess her was instant and overwhelming. It burned inside me."

"So you followed the RV?"

"In my heart we were meant to be together."

"What happened?" Elsen asked.

"When they got to Nevada, I parked near them at the truck stop, watched them all get out of the RV, but not her. I was surprised, unsure of what to do. I was weighing my options when eventually she got out."

"Did you approach her in the parking lot?"

"No, I followed her inside. I needed to buy some things."

"Did she notice you?"

"No. She was looking for the others but she never saw them, and I never saw them. When she returned to the lot, the RV was gone. I was shocked that they'd left her. She returned inside, understandably upset—then—" Rykhirt stopped, his eyes to the wall, his drooping face, crumpling, awash with sadness.

"Then what?" Elsen said.

"You won't understand."

"Help us understand," McDowell said.

"I wanted to help her. I wanted to be her friend, her everything. I wanted to date her."

"Date her?" Elsen repeated. "Is that what you call it?"

Rykhirt's head snapped up, his face reddening. "You two think you know everything," he said.

"No," McDowell said.

He began shaking his head, tears rolling down his face. "You can't possibly know what it's like for me." Rykhirt was silent for a long moment.

"Listen good, Frayer. Because here's what we do know," Elsen said. "You bought duct tape and scissors to bind her."

Rykhirt stared at Elsen. "The driver's side mirror on my car came off its mounting," he said. "I needed to secure it."

"We found the sketch of Riley in your motel room," Elsen said.

"I saw the TV news reporting that she was missing and I fantasized with a doodle."

"Stop lying." Elsen tapped and swiped the tablet, turning it. "Look at these pictures of what our crime scene people found in your car."

Rykhirt glanced at the photos of a tarp, a pick and shovel.

"I'm a part-time cemetery worker in Riverside. I dig graves."

"The officers who arrested you at the Dreamy Breeze motel report that while Mirandizing you, you stated 'It's so messed up. I just wanted to be her friend.'"

"I told you—I—"

"I'm not finished," Elsen said. "Riverside Homicide says you live ten blocks from the home of Eva Marie Garcia, the seventeen-year-old girl whose body was found in a shallow grave near Primm, not far from the Sagebrush where you were the last to see Riley Jarrett."

Rykhirt's jaw muscles pulsed.

"Did you stalk Riley Jarrett like you stalked Eva Marie Garcia?"

Rykhirt said nothing.

"As we speak our forensic experts are studying all the evidence," McDowell said.

"Frayer, stop lying to us," Elsen said.

Rykhirt stared at his handcuffs, his raspy voice devolving into a groan of anguished rage. "I ached for her."

"Tell us the truth," Elsen said. "Where is Riley Jarrett?"

Rykhirt's face stretched into a feral grin. "She's with me. She'll always be with me."

Thirty-Seven

Nevada

John scanned the desert, sweating under the sun and boiling with anger about the stranger in the photos the detectives had shown them.

Rykhirt.

No one had told John anything more about him and he wanted to rush to Las Vegas, find where Rykhirt was in custody and demand answers about Riley.

John's stomach churned with chilling images. He swiped his hand over his face to blot them out, his fingers brushing over his scrapes and stubble.

This was not supposed to happen. This isn't what I planned.

For a moment, John was alone with his thoughts while he searched in the desert with the others, then his phone rang with a blocked number. He answered.

"Is this John Marshall?"

"Yes."

John didn't recognize the caller's voice.

Fourteen-year-old Claire Nakamura was scared for Riley.

She had come from San Diego with her friends, Dakota and Ashley, their parents and other friends to help search for her. This was so serious.

Last night, and again this morning, while on their way here, Claire, like Dakota and Ash, had talked to the detective on the phone, telling her that she'd been talking to Riley just before she went missing. Claire didn't have the texts because they were using apps with self-deleting messages, but she told the detective how Riley was livid, really angry at her parents for forcing her to break up with Caleb and move away. It was pretty much all Riley talked about before she just went silent. At first Claire figured Riley was in a dead zone, but then she got worried when she couldn't reach her.

Then the police called and things got worse.

The girls had heard all the rumors; like how some creep got arrested after he was in the truck stop the same time as Riley; like how a girl was also murdered around here; about drugs in Riley's RV.

With all those things going on, Claire didn't know what to believe.

It was frightening.

The main thing was they had to find Ri.

Claire, considered the most mature among her

girlfriends, the one who could easily talk to adults, was thinking how Riley's mom and dad were so freaked out. She wanted to tell them to be strong, that they were going to find Riley.

Spotting Mr. Marshall by himself in the desert and not far away, Claire headed toward him, trotting down a narrow gully. Stepping from it and approaching him, she heard him talking on the phone. His back was turned. She was within a few yards but could hear him, upset with whoever he was talking to.

"What're you saying to me? I don't have that kind of money. What you're demanding is crazy! We're not going to pay that—"

At that moment John, phone to his ear, turned, surprised to see Claire, her mouth open in astonishment before she said: "Sorry!"

Embarrassed, she turned and fled.

John's hands were shaking when the call ended. Rippling through him were his anger at the caller, and the fact that the end of his side of the conversation was overheard.

He'd tried to wave Claire Nakamura back, but it was too late. She'd run off to join the others. He wasn't sure of how much, or what, she'd heard.

He looked around in an effort to think. But the call had left him at a loss. Then, something he'd overlooked, a new set of circumstances flared from the allegations by the police that their rented RV was used to transport drugs.

What's going to happen when his new employer in Pittsburgh learns about the drug accusations?

Pittsburgh's our lifeline, our way out. If I lose Pittsburgh, we lose everything.

Again he cast around, feeling insignificant, powerless in the emptiness.

Grace is not aware of what I did, of what's at stake.

His mind swirled just as new voices carried on a breeze tumbling over the desert, jerking him from his thoughts.

Far off, up ahead amid the scrub, several yards from the paved shoulder of the interstate, a few people were clustered in excitement.

They'd discovered something.

Thirty-Eight

Nevada

Blake checked his burner phone for some sort of answer. Nothing.

It was hopeless. He wanted to talk to them again, demand the truth, not caring if they'd warned him never to call.

This is life and death for Riley.

But he couldn't call, not now with Ashley and Dakota walking so close to him, consumed with their own fears, going on about how devastating it was for Riley to break up with Caleb.

There were way more important things to think about, Blake thought. Like the creep.

When the detectives had shown his family the guy's picture, they were so grim. And now, with the focus shifting to this Rykhirt perv, it changed everything.

Did he take Riley out here somewhere?

Did he take that other girl the police and press people had talked about, the one who was killed out here a year ago? A thousand scenarios blazed across Blake's mind, like those he knew from video games and movies.

But this was not a game.

He thought of Riley then his mother and sister. And how they'd died.

Biting back on the images and swallowing hard, he resumed examining the ground, golden tan under the hot sun. Its sandy, rocky texture crunched under his shoes as he checked it and the randomly spaced shrubs for any trace of Riley.

"Hey, Claire," Ashley said.

Panting, Claire Nakamura had trotted up to them.

"What is it?" Dakota said. "You look weird."

Claire swallowed water from her bottle, wiped her mouth. "I went to talk to Mr. Marshall but something's going on."

"Like what?" Blake looked past her at his father in the distance.

"I went to give him our support, to tell him to stay strong, but he was on the phone with someone."

"So?" Blake said.

"It's like I surprised him, interrupted him. Anyway your dad sounded angry, practically yelling at whoever was on the line."

"Who was it?" Blake asked.

"I don't know but it was a pretty heated conversation."

"What'd he say?" Blake asked.

"Something like, 'I don't have that kind of

money, what you're demanding is crazy, we're not going to pay that!' That's what I heard before I realized I shouldn't be there, so I left."

"Whoa, that is weird," Dakota said.

"Yeah, like a ransom call or something?" Ashley said.

"Ransom?" Blake said, staring back at his father with puzzled concern, trying to decipher what Claire had just reported.

"What do you think, Blake?" Claire asked him.

"I don't know. He's under a lot of pressure. I don't know." Blake looked at Claire. "Did you tell anybody?"

"No, it just happened. I'm telling you."

"Okay, keep it to yourself, all of you. Leave it with me. I'll talk to him."

Some searchers in the distance started shouting. Up ahead a group was gathering in the scrub not far from the interstate. Some were waving and calling with urgency. Some were squatting, or bending over at a shrub, all focused on the ground.

Two Silver Sky searchers in fluorescent orange vests joined them with one of them talking quickly into her radio.

Thirty-Nine

No one will ever understand.

Frayer Ront Rykhirt could only guess at how long he'd been alone with his thoughts in the interview room. He stared into his hands then closed his eyes, lifting his face to embrace the vision seared in his memory.

She was standing before him.

Radiant. Celestial.

Stirring his hunger.

He'd employed all of his skills to possess her. But he'd lost control, made mistakes—like not having cash at the truck stop. He thought he had cash until he opened his wallet and saw that he didn't and was forced to use his credit card or lose her— and now he grieved that things had ended the way they did.

The door opened. The detectives took their seats across from him, their faces stone-cold.

"Have you considered your situation?" Elsen said. "Are you ready to cooperate?"

They hadn't brought food. He was beyond hungry but didn't care. They played games, but he had the upper hand and was a better player.

Rykhirt closed his eyes. "It's not what you think," he said.

"Make it clear to us," McDowell said. "What did you do to Riley Jarrett?"

He took in a breath and let it out. "You would not, or could not, possibly comprehend."

Elsen's palm slammed on the table. McDowell flinched but not Rykhirt.

"Stop the bullshit!" Elsen said.

Rykhirt's jaw muscles bunched as he glared back, his mouth trembling and twisting with burning emotion, working to form words.

"You don't know my pain!" Rykhirt's voice was a phlegmy cry. "I ached for her!" He dropped his head, burying his face in his arms, sobbing.

"Did you kill Riley Jarrett?" Elsen asked. "Did you kill Eva Marie Garcia?"

He didn't answer for the longest time, then, his voice barely audible, he said: "You're going to feel my pain for all the years I suffered, just for loving them."

Rykhirt then wept for several minutes before collecting himself and raising his tearstained face to the detectives. "I have to go to the bathroom," he said.

Elsen and McDowell looked at him while deciding.

"All right," Elsen said.

A moment later the door opened. An officer entered. The chain clinked as he unfastened it from the metal loop on the table, then Rykhirt stood with his handcuffed hands in front of him, eyeing both of the detectives before leaving the room.

In the hall, the officer took a firm grip of Rykhirt's upper arm.

"This way, to the left, at the end," the officer said. "I'll be with you the entire time. Don't give me any trouble and this will go smoothly for you."

Relieved at being freed from the confines of the interview room, Rykhirt took stock of the surroundings. The hall was empty. They passed doors to offices, a water fountain, then the elevators and more office doors. He could feel the officer adjust his grip on his arm when he indicated the sign for the bathroom just ahead on the right.

A few paces farther, Rykhirt saw the sign for the emergency exit.

He began turning for the bathroom door but broke free of the officer's grip, bolting for the emergency exit.

The startled officer's curses echoed behind him as Rykhirt thrust his palms against the exit door's push bar, bursting into the stairwell. Without hesitation he hefted himself over the metal railing into the vertical shaft that was clear to the bottom, plunging five floors, his body bouncing and thudding against the steel railing and concrete edges, level after level, as he fell to the ground floor.

Forty

Catching on to the activity near the interstate ahead of her, Grace began moving toward it.

Her heart beat faster as she neared the group that had huddled around a patch of brush some twenty yards from the paved shoulder at the bank of desert wash.

Some people were crouched. Others were leaning over them to look.

Oh God, what did they find?

Jazmin and Sherry were there, on their knees.

"Grace!" Jazmin's face creased with concern when she saw her coming. She nudged Sherry, who turned.

"Oh, Grace!" Sherry said.

People were clustered around a shrub, a desert senna. The round bush was about two feet tall, two feet wide, leafless and dead looking.

Embedded in the base of the bush was a sneaker.

Its aquamarine color was brilliant against the

brown scrub, rocketing Grace back to six months earlier at the mall with Riley.

These are so cute, Mom. They were laceless slip-ons, lightweight canvas mesh with thick foam padding and white soles... Riley pulled them on, loved them. *Like I'm walking on marshmallows! Can I get them please?*

It was Riley's left sneaker.

Amid tense cross talk on walkie-talkies Grace got on her knees, picked up the shoe, traced her fingers over it then held it to her cheek.

"Ma'am, please," one of the vested searchers, a man, said between dispatches on his radio. "You have to refrain from—" A static burst on his walkie-talkie interrupted him.

"He's saying you have to put it back." Sherry clasped her hand on the shoe.

Two Las Vegas officers arrived, taking quick stock of the discovery

"Everyone please. Leave the item where it was found," an officer said.

Tenderly Grace set the shoe in the bush, keeping her eyes locked on it.

"Who found it?" the officer asked.

"I did. It was in the bottom of the bush," Sherry said.

"Did you touch it?" The officer pulled out his notebook.

"Yes. I picked it up."

"I did, too," Jazmin said, "when she called me over."

"I'll need your names and information," the officer said.

"Then Grace here, she held it," Jazmin said.

The other officer took pictures of the shoe with his phone then checked description details on the initial missing person report. Then to Grace: "Mrs. Jarrett, can you confirm that this item appears to belong to your daughter?"

"It's Riley's," Grace said through her tears.

"All right," the picture-taking officer said, "we need everyone to please back away using the same steps you used to enter this area. The people who touched it will need to be fingerprinted."

The officers began making calls, requesting the Crime Scene Detail, talking urgently about sealing the area.

Grace stared at her daughter's shoe until something inside her broke and the ground, the mountains and sky began spinning.

Forty-One

Las Vegas, Nevada

Cactus Springs Medical Center was a sleek, new six-story building with tinted blue exterior glass.

The intensive care unit was on the fourth floor. McDowell thought the soft tones of its blue mosaic wall tile brightened the place. She welcomed anything positive because any hope they'd held for finding Riley Jarrett had dimmed a short time ago when Rykhirt tried to kill himself.

McDowell took another deep breath, digesting what had transpired.

She and Elsen had been in the interview room when they'd heard the outburst in the hall. They'd rushed to the stairwell, encountering the distraught escorting officer, then they'd spotted Rykhirt's contorted, bleeding body on the bottom floor.

Another officer was with Rykhirt, checking for signs of life.

"What the hell happened?" Elsen said.

"He broke away, threw himself over the railing," the distressed officer said.

McDowell flew down the stairs to Rykhirt and bent over him.

"Frayer! Can you hear me? Frayer!"

He was unconscious but alive, the paramedics had said when they'd brought him here to Cactus Springs, which was less than five minutes from police headquarters. McDowell and Elsen had rushed to the hospital determined to get an admission from him. After Rykhirt had undergone emergency surgery, a tall woman wearing a white coat found them in the cafeteria.

"Dr. Christine Grady," she said. "They told me to look for you here."

"How bad is it for our guy?" Elsen asked.

She removed her glasses, folded them.

"He's got multiple skull fractures, a spinal fracture, ruptured abdominal organs, internal hemorrhaging. It's unlikely he'll regain consciousness or survive."

"You're aware of our situation, Doctor?" Elsen said.

"I was told he was being questioned while in custody."

"We need to be at his bedside if he does wake up."

Grady nodded then slipped her glasses into her pocket.

"You can wait in the ICU waiting room on the fourth. I'll take you there."

* * *

The room had bright-colored cushioned chairs with generous armrests. Artwork featuring calming landscapes and nature scenes hung on the walls. Floor-to-ceiling windows opened to vistas of the mountains in the distance.

"If you need privacy, you can use this." Grady opened the door to a small, welcoming room. "This is our room of solace for families to use after a patient is deceased."

The walls were papered with cards and children's artwork thanking staff. One said: "Thank You For Being With My Grandma So She Didn't Die All By Herself." Taking in the messages, Elsen nodded and McDowell thanked Grady.

In the time they waited, the detectives grew accustomed to the smells and sounds of the hospital as they worked. There would be an investigation into how Rykhirt escaped, but right now their priority was to extract the truth from him.

And as long as he was still drawing breath, there was hope he could lead them to Riley. McDowell and Elsen were busy on their tablets and phones following up on other elements of the case with other investigators when McDowell's phone pinged. It was a notification from the search people at the incident command center. As she read the message, she caught her breath.

"Whoa, did you see this from Lieutenant Jackson?"

Elsen's eyes were on his phone. "Looking at it now."

"This is something solid."

They swiped through color photos of an aquamarine, canvas mesh sneaker. In her accompanying message, detailing the time and location of the discovery by searchers, Jackson said it appeared the shoe belonged to Riley Jarrett. Jackson advised that Crime Scene was processing the new evidence while she directed sectors to be searched.

Tapping on her tablet, McDowell called up Grace Jarrett's statement and report on her missing daughter, going to the detailed description of her clothing and the footwear Riley was wearing at the time of her disappearance.

"The shoe matches the mother's description."

McDowell then replayed the video showing Riley being approached and touched by Rykhirt near the murals in the Sagebrush lobby. She froze it on the brief, unobscured sequence, showing Riley head to toe. McDowell enlarged the image to study Riley's sneakers.

"Look, Dan." McDowell tilted the screen. "It's her shoe."

Elsen studied it. "Another piece of the puzzle, Michelle."

Suddenly the quiet was broken by the rush of nurses into Rykhirt's room. The bleating of monitors spilled into the hall as they pushed the door. Dr. Grady materialized, uncollaring a stethoscope as she entered seconds behind them.

The detectives moved to the door where another nurse stopped them from going any farther.

"You must wait outside. Please."

The detectives returned to their seats and twenty minutes later, Grady approached them. "He took a turn," she said.

"Is he dead?" Elsen asked.

"No, Detective, we've stabilized him. He's conscious."

"We need to talk to him."

Grady blinked as she weighed matters. "He may not be lucid, or coherent, but this may be your only window," she said. "I'll allow five minutes, no more."

"Let's go," Elsen said.

"First," Grady said, "I want you in gowns, gloves, masks, hair covering. He's in ICU, and we'll adhere to procedures for patient safety."

Once they were properly gowned, their hands, feet, face and hair covered, Grady took the detectives into Rykhirt's room.

The softly lit unit, with the rhythmic hum and subdued beeping of the equipment, gave it an air of calm.

Rykhirt's face was swollen and bruised, his eyes closed.

A clear oxygen tube looped under his nostrils, a sensor was clipped on his right index finger, the cable meandering to a monitor. An IV line ran from his left arm.

A nurse stood near Rykhirt, reading and adjusting some of the equipment next to his bed. Grady gestured, and the nurse moved the IV pole so the detectives could move to the head of the bed with McDowell on Rykhirt's left side and Elsen on his right.

The detectives looked to Grady who nodded for them to proceed.

"Mr. Rykhirt," McDowell said. "I'm Detective Michelle McDowell here with Detective Dan Elsen. Can you hear us?"

A moment passed and Rykhirt's eyes opened, glassy as he took in the detectives.

"Can you acknowledge us?" Elsen said.

Rykhirt's eyes fluttered, and he gave an almost imperceptible nod.

"We need your help," McDowell said. "We need you to make a declaration—a true statement to help us."

Rykhirt's eyes fluttered.

"We found Riley's shoe in the desert, Frayer," Elsen said. "Where is she and what did you do to her?"

Rykhirt shut his eyes and the monitor bleeped.

"Frayer, think of her family," Elsen said. "If you truly care for her, now is the time to do the right thing. Unburden yourself and tell us the truth."

Rykhirt clenched his eyes tighter and his mouth began moving, his raspy voice barely rising above a whisper.

"Not…going…back…to prison…"

"Mr. Rykhirt, where is Riley? What happened to Riley?"

The monitor's beeping kicked up.

"You…never…find…her…"

"Frayer, tell us where she is," Elsen said.

The nurse, who had been watching Rykhirt's signs and numbers on the display screens, shot Grady a glance of concern.

"Frayer," Elsen said. "Tell us where she is."

"She'll…always…be…with…me…"

Rykhirt's head lolled to the side, triggering high-pitched alerts from the monitors. The nurse and Grady stepped into action. McDowell, who'd been recording Rykhirt on her phone, cleared the way. More staff arrived, forcing the detectives out of the room with urgency as the tracking lines on Rykhirt's monitors flattened.

Nearly half an hour later, Grady came out of the room, her face flushed, moist with perspiration.

"He went into cardiac arrest," she told the detectives. "We did all we could."

McDowell and Elsen exchanged glances.

"He's deceased," Grady said, observing the two enlarged images filling McDowell's tablet.

A brilliant, aquamarine sneaker in the desert and next to it, the Silver Sagebrush lobby with a man's hand on a girl's shoulder.

Forty-Two

Nevada

*B*ut *maybe finding Riley's sneaker was a good thing?*

Scenarios ripped through Grace's mind, at times encouraging her.

Maybe Riley escaped from Rykhirt, was frightened and hiding somewhere in the desert. Or maybe Riley was so angry with Grace she ran from the truck stop, got hurt and was out here praying to be found.

Grace scanned the horizon, unable to stop her imagination from stabbing her with the darkest possibility of all.

Rykhirt brought her out here and killed her.

That fear had consumed Grace when she first saw her daughter's shoe then nearly collapsed. Jazmin, Sherry, then John and Blake, had come to her aid. Though she'd since recovered somewhat, her scalp was prickling and she'd slipped into a state of numbed reality while watching the sun sinking lower and lower, like her hope.

A dog yipped, giving her a modicum of comfort.

Despite the odds, every effort to find Riley continued.

In the distance a police K-9 unit, having scented off of Riley's shoe, worked to detect a possible trail, while crime scene analysts wearing protective gear methodically processed the sneaker and the area around the bush. They took samples of the branches and sifted the soil for any trace evidence.

Police had also refocused their search of the surrounding area, combing it shoulder-to-shoulder while a helicopter crisscrossed overhead.

John touched Grace's shoulder, indicating a message on his phone. "They want us to go back to the command center."

"We continue to hope for the best," McDowell said, "but you must be prepared for all possibilities."

John and Grace exchanged looks. "What the hell does that mean?" John said.

"And why didn't you keep us updated?" Grace said. "Why are we learning everything from the press?"

"I'm sorry," McDowell said. "I did call but the connection was weak and we got cut off, then we got busy."

"We had our hands full at the time," Elsen said. "We have to protect the integrity of the investigation," McDowell said. "That said; we should've done better."

McDowell glanced at Elsen; their sober expressions signaled that things had deteriorated in the case. The family stood alone inside the mobile command center with the two investigators.

"What is it you want us to be prepared for?" John said.

McDowell's eyes threw John's question to Elsen.

"Rykhirt is dead," Elsen said.

"What?" John said.

"During a bathroom break while being questioned, he escaped custody, flung himself down a stairwell and died of his injuries. We wanted you to hear it from us first."

Grace's hand found a counter to steady herself while staring at the detectives.

"But you talked to him?" John said. "What did he tell you about Riley?"

"We know he was involved," Elsen said.

"We all know that!" Grace said. "What does his death mean now?"

"We're still investigating, working on evidence," Elsen said.

"Didn't he tell you anything?" John said. "We know he was with Riley. Where is she? Did he hurt her?"

Searching their faces, Grace gave her head a shake. "You don't know, do you?" she said.

"We have nothing to confirm she's been hurt," Elsen said.

"That's wrong. We found her shoe out there," Grace shouted. "We found it, not you!"

"Mrs. Jarrett, we know this is difficult," McDowell said.

"Difficult? He was a sex offender who liked young girls! We know he touched my daughter! She's gone and now he's dead!" She closed her hands into fists and pounded her knees. "From the start you accused us of hurting her, being drug dealers and liars. Then you find the man who took my daughter and you won't tell us the truth. Why are you torturing me? Tell me the truth!"

"We're telling you the truth," Elsen said.

"You're not!" Grace shook her head wildly, tears flowing. "It's just like that other girl, Eva. My daughter Riley's buried out there somewhere, isn't she? Isn't that what you want me to brace for?"

"Grace," McDowell said.

"Riley's dead, isn't she?" she screamed.

Blake put his hands on her shoulders to comfort her as she dropped her head and sobbed.

McDowell lowered herself before Grace and placed her hands on her knees.

"I know this is hard and nothing we say helps," McDowell said. "But until we know for certain, we can't lose hope."

Grace stared at the floor, her tears falling.

A moment passed then the detectives left.

Forty-Three

Nevada

Grace looked out at the miles and miles of scrub.

It was late, long after Elsen and McDowell had returned to Las Vegas; long after the sun had set, streaking the sky in peach and pink coral before it dissolved into darkness and an eternity of stars.

Sweeping her flashlight she found a large rock, sat, and tried to swallow her pain.

How could she go on? She and the others had continually searched the truck stop, the desert all in vain but for Riley's shoe, leaving Grace to grapple with her anguish.

It seems like only hours ago we'd set out to start a new chapter of our lives. It can't end this way. I know you're punishing me, but please God, don't let it end this way. I'm begging you.

But Grace was familiar with unwanted endings, with death and her role in it.

A light raked over her, the ground crunched, then John emerged to be with her. They sat, silent in the quiet, watching the lights of searchers dotting every corner of the desert, combing and probing for as far as they could see, the interstate traffic humming in the distance.

"It's my fault," Grace said to the night. "For arguing with her then leaving her." Her voice broke. "How could I leave her?"

"Stop." John put his arm around her, pulled her to him and she sobbed on his chest. "We don't know anything, until we have proof. But one thing I do know is that this is not your fault. It's mine."

"Yours?"

"We wouldn't be here if it wasn't for me moving us all to Pittsburgh. You and Riley had a life in San Diego."

"So did you and Blake. We all did."

"I didn't think this through. I was thinking of myself."

She pulled away from his chest, brushing her face. "But you have this great job and a better salary waiting."

"Yes."

"You said things were terrible at *SoCal SoYou*. You'd put in hard years working your way up, then management changed and they began treating you so badly you had to get out. You said you had no choice."

"I never told you how bad it got, what was at stake," he said.

"Why not?"

John didn't respond. Grace saw his profile silhouetted against the night sky as if now, in the darkness, in this moment, he was ready to lay bare, to confess, his deepest feelings.

"So much was going on at work, at home," he said. "We—mostly you—had your hands full with Riley and Caleb. I was no help. Blake was withdrawn and my relationship with Riley needed work. These aren't excuses, but I let you down."

Grace said nothing because it was true.

"I was focused on getting the Pittsburgh job," he said. "To give our new family a new start, a journey we'd take together."

"And I agreed. And when you got the job, I was so proud of you."

"Now I'm afraid we could lose Pittsburgh."

"Lose it? Why?"

"The allegation that we're involved with drugs—it's in the press, online, it's everywhere."

"But we rented the RV, we weren't charged. Police were just being thorough."

"But once you're accused of something, it's like a permanent stain."

"The drug allegations are wrong. *Aren't* they, John?"

A moment passed and Grace saw John's Adam's apple rise and fall. "They're wrong."

"Then what're you trying to tell me?"

John was silent.

"John?"

"That maybe we shouldn't've moved from San Diego, that I should've looked harder to find another position there. I don't know." He ran a hand through his hair. "I gambled moving us to Pittsburgh, I gambled with our lives and I lost, just like I did with Lana and Courtney."

"I don't understand what you're saying."

"I never told you this, but that day we went sailing the forecast had called for a chance of a storm. Lana was nervous. She suggested we not go, but I said she was being too cautious and dismissed her concerns. I said I was willing to bet the weather would be fine."

John paused for a moment.

"Then you know what I said? I said, 'besides, if we lose the boat, we're insured.' Can you believe it, Grace? I gambled with our lives, and it cost me my wife and my daughter. And Blake? Blake's irreparably damaged, withdrawn into himself. He'll never be the same after that night."

John stopped. Grace could hear him crying softly. She rubbed his shoulders.

"I took a risk, Grace. After that night I swore I'd never take another risk again, but look at us. Look what I did. I take risks with peoples' lives. And I lose."

After considering what he'd told her, Grace took a breath.

"No, don't do this to yourself. You can't be blamed for tragic circumstances. If anyone is to blame for causing deaths, it's me." Grace's voice weakened. "I've done unforgivable things, horrible things," she said. "I'm not the person you think I am."

John took her into his arms.

"Honey, you're distraught, you haven't slept, you've haven't eaten, you're exhausted. Let's go back to our room, get some rest."

"No," she said.

"Just for a few hours, then we'll come right back and keep looking."

"No, I want to tell you about the night Tim died. I listened to you, now you listen to me."

It took a moment for John to realize she needed to talk. "Okay."

John already knew much of what Grace related about Tim. How he was an IT systems manager and had accepted a promotion, a big secondment job with his company's operations in Chicago that paid well at a time when they needed the money. But Tim didn't want to uproot his family and disrupt their lives in California, so he decided to travel back and forth when he could.

Their commuter marriage worked well. They had video calls. Tim flew home every couple of weeks, making the best of their time together. Grace and Riley visited Tim at his Chicago apartment and saw the sights.

"The night he died, he flew home without telling me, took an Uber from the airport. Turned out he was not going to renew his secondment because he missed us and wanted us to return to a normal life in San Diego. But I didn't know at the time."

"He didn't tell you?"

"No, he came home that night without telling me anything, wanting to surprise me and Riley with the news—but I..." Grace's voice faded.

"You what?"

It took a long time to find her words. "I wasn't feeling well. I had a bad head cold. We talked just a bit, but not long after he came through the door, I sent him back out to a CVS to get me cold medicine." Grace hesitated. "Tim was tired after a long flight, but he was such a kind man, such a good husband, he got in the car and went out into the night, and drove to the CVS in a rainstorm for me. That's when he crashed. Police said that he likely lost control when he swerved to miss a dog and his car rolled over. But I'll always know that Tim's death is my fault."

John put his arm around her. "Grace, you can't feel guilty because it's just like you told me, a set of tragic circumstances that were out of your control. If we could go back in time, we'd change things, but that's not how life works."

Minutes passed in silence with the interstate humming in the distance.

Watching the searchers, Grace and John retreated into their thoughts, each knowing that while they'd both made revelations, they had not told the other the whole truth about their pasts.

Forty-Four

Nevada

Grace and John were trapped in an intense beam of white. Behind it came the crunch of footsteps.

"Dad? Grace?" Blake lowered his flashlight.

"Oh." Grace stood and hugged him.

"How're you doing, Grace?" he asked.

"The best we can, honey. Are you okay?"

"Now that the creep's dead, I'm more afraid than ever for Riley."

"We can't give up hope, son," John said.

"That's right." Grace rubbed Blake's shoulders. "We can't stop praying and looking."

"Um, I need to talk to you, Dad."

"Sure," John said.

"In private?" Blake said.

Grace stopped rubbing his shoulders.

"What is it, Blake?" John said. "You can tell us both."

"It's no big deal, but I just wanted to talk to you alone, Dad. I'm sorry, Grace," Blake said.

"It's okay," Grace said. She squeezed Blake's shoulders then dropped her hands, as if releasing him.

As Blake and John moved away, she thought she'd overheard Blake say: "Dad, Claire overheard you talking about money…" but was uncertain as she watched them vanish in two circles of light gliding over the scrub.

The thing was, Grace *did* mind that Blake wouldn't talk to both of them.

Blake was usually quiet, internalizing his feelings. There were times he talked alone with John, and Grace respected that. But now? Under these circumstances?

Maybe I mistake his reticence for him being okay. I haven't been the best mother to him, and he doesn't trust me to understand him. Is there something going on with him that I should know about?

"Grace." Jazmin's light brushed over her before she joined her on the rock. "What're you doing here all alone?"

"Asking for forgiveness."

"Oh, sweetie, why would you need to be forgiven?"

"For leaving my daughter behind."

"No, you don't need to be forgiven for anything. You need to keep the faith and stay strong because we're going to find Riley."

"I want to believe that, but it's just so hard."

"That's because you haven't slept or eaten. We

need to get some food in you and you need to go back to the motel and rest."

"I can't, Jazmin, not when she could be…"

"Shh, shh, stop. You've got an army on your side to take the burden from you. We're going to win this. We're going to find her, you'll see."

Grace took a moment. "Thank you, Jazmin. Thank you for coming."

"No thanks needed, not after all you've done for me."

"After all we've done for each other."

"You know," Jazmin said, "there's something I've wanted to confess to you but I could never—" She stopped.

"What is it?"

Grace heard Jazmin take in a long breath. "What you did for my mom in the last minutes of her life. You were there, you held her hand. What you did was kind, merciful."

"It's what nurses around the world do every day."

"I know, but this was us. This was personal. I couldn't be there with her but you were. And after it happened, this sounds awful, but at first, I secretly resented you for it."

"Resented me?"

"It was like with you being there with her, instead of me, you took something from me. Something that was mine, that I had a right to. And it hurt, it really hurt. Some days I hated you for it."

"Jazmin, I never knew."

"Look, I know it's a totally irrational feeling, a

reaction to my loss, the grief, and being sick and scared at the time. Then after I got through the choking fog of it all, I saw things in a clearer light, saw what really mattered and I realized that if I couldn't be there with her, there was no one else in the world I would've chosen to take my place but you. And I loved you for it, for what you did for me."

"You would've done the same for me."

"I don't know why I'm telling you this now. I guess because even though that feeling is gone, I wanted to be honest with you. I wanted you to know the truth."

For a moment, Grace stared in her direction, trying to find Jazmin's face. They found each other's hands and squeezed. They stayed that way for a few minutes as Jazmin tried to convince Grace to go back to the Sagebrush and get some rest. But Grace refused to give up searching.

"One thing," Grace said. "The detectives need the names of all the people who attended our farewell party. Would you and Sherry help me with the list?"

"Absolutely."

The two women hugged before Jazmin set off to get Grace a sandwich from the command post, knowing she likely wouldn't eat it.

Jazmin stepped away, leaving Grace alone.

Not long after, Grace began sobbing in the torment of a second night without knowing if her daughter was alive.

DAY 3

Forty-Five

Las Vegas, Nevada

It was 6:30 a.m. Lieutenant Moe Holland turned his neck slightly while reading an email on his phone.

He didn't speak. He didn't have to. The muscles bunched in his jawline conveyed his displeasure to his detectives, Elsen and McDowell, after he and the upper ranks had demanded to know why they had used an unsealed floor to interview a suspect.

Their emailed response stated they'd been advised that the section on the secured floor they had wanted was temporarily closed for upgrades to the alarm and sprinkler systems and that the floor they were assigned was secure.

Holland had more questions about Rykhirt's death in custody, but they'd be addressed by Internal Oversight's probe of the incident.

Holland took a breath, set his phone down then took inventory of the nearly two dozen people who'd settled around the table. Investigators from several Metro units and outside agencies, including the FBI, the DEA, Nevada Highway Patrol and others on the line, had convened in the second-floor meeting room at Las Vegas police headquarters. Phones, tablets, laptops and notebooks covered the table's edge.

The air was a mix of fresh coffee and tension.

Holland started the case-status meeting with quick introductions before nodding to the detectives to begin.

"You all have our case summary," Elsen said. "Frayer Ront Rykhirt died last night. We've issued a statement, and you can't miss the media reports." He cleared his throat and continued. "The evidence we have leads us to believe that Rykhirt abducted Riley Jarrett from the Silver Sagebrush truck stop, near Jean. For those who haven't seen it, we'll share some of it now. Watch the screen at the end of the room and, for those on the line, Detective McDowell is sending the link."

The videos from Fontana and the Sagebrush played, along with photos of Rykhirt's chilling sketch of Riley; the scissors, tape, the tarp, pick and shovel that were found in his car.

Elsen also pointed to Rykhirt's criminal history and strong suspicions of his involvement in the homicide of Eva Marie Garcia, who'd lived ten blocks from Rykhirt's address in Riverside, California.

"The stats tell us that children abducted by predatory pedophiles are killed within hours of being taken. Officially this is a missing person case. At this time we don't yet have solid evidence Riley Jarrett is a homicide victim. Until we find it we work and live in hope that she isn't. Our priority is to locate her as we continue to follow every avenue of this investigation. Now, I'll pass this to my partner."

McDowell continued with a rundown of key aspects. "As of this morning, with the exception of the shoe, the search in and around the Sagebrush has yielded nothing new but continues with an intense focus on areas of probability arising from the discovery of the sneaker," she said. "We're continuing to run background on all people employed, or recently employed, at the facility."

In Las Vegas, more Metro officers had been sent to recanvass the area around the Dreamy Breeze Motor Inn. Homicide was using Rykhirt's credit and bank cards and, where possible, security cameras to establish a timeline and travel history for Rykhirt. Riverside PD continued reexamining and comparing Jarrett with the Garcia case for potential leads.

Updates from forensic results arising from the RV, Riley's phone, Rykhirt's Nissan, phone, computer, his belongings, his motel room, were still forthcoming. Results from the area where Riley Jarrett's sneaker was recovered were not yet available.

"However, indications are that they may only get partial latents at best from the shoe because of the uneven surface," McDowell said.

No solid leads to date from the FBI-led Child Exploitation Task Force and the casinos in the security program. The detectives continued checking with the airport, bus depot and other transportation outlets, the tip lines, then other county and state agencies.

"While Frayer is our primary suspect, he's not a sure thing. Work continues on other avenues," McDowell said.

They were still following up on the family's background and queries with San Diego County's Child Protective Services, their employment, school and financial history, as well as compiling a list of everyone who attended the family's farewell party.

"And, we just got this bit of encouraging news. Our people in the Digital Forensic Lab working with IT people at the Silver Sagebrush report that while there is no guarantee, they're working on possibly recovering additional video of areas where Riley Jarrett may have been present around the time her family was at the truck stop."

When McDowell reached the end of their item-by-item status report, Holland shifted the meeting into a Q and A brainstorming session.

"Let's set Rykhirt aside," Holland said. "What other roads of investigation are you considering?"

The detectives exchanged glances.

"Every piece of evidence points to him," McDowell said.

"We haven't nailed this shut yet," Holland said.

"So we can't get tunnel vision. Let's hear some other theories, things we can consider or rule out based on what we know."

"Rykhirt could've brought her to town and sold her to traffickers," said Special Agent Barry Caffrey, a member of the Child Exploitation Task Force. "Last month, here in Las Vegas, we rescued two dozen sex trafficking victims, all young girls, and arrested ten adult traffickers in an operation to take down a global human trafficking network."

"Is the FBI hearing something further on that?" Elsen said.

"We're following up on a tip from an informant that Rykhirt may have been working with traffickers and may have sold her," Caffrey said.

"That could fit. Thanks," Holland said. "Anyone got anything else to consider?"

"We've been pursuing a lead, but nothing's panned out yet," said Audrey Haberfeld, a DEA agent with the High Intensity Drug Trafficking Area team.

"Go ahead," Elsen said.

"The dogs give us a strong indication that drugs were present in the RV, right?" Haberfeld said.

"Yes, but none were found and our people are still checking with their drug sources, as well as the rental history of the vehicle," Elsen said. "What've you got?"

"We're hearing that the family may have delivered a shipment to a contact at the truck stop. Then the contact discovered they were shorted and took the daughter in retaliation and is holding her for ransom."

"But we have video of Rykhirt stalking the family, touching her, sketching her," Elsen said.

"Could all be coincidental, part of his fantasy," Haberfeld said.

"I can't buy the drug connection." A tin-sounding voice crackled over the telecom speaker. "Del Burton, Riverside Homicide."

"Why's that, Del?" Holland said.

"It just doesn't align with the evidence you have on Rykhirt," Burton said. "I mean look. Rykhirt's pattern here, and in the Garcia case, is so strong. He's a hunter. Just look at the discovery of Riley Jarrett's shoe. How did it get there? Maybe she fought him, or ran. It was found north of the Sagebrush, just east of the interstate's northbound lanes. She could've walked that far, or it could've been tossed from a car headed for Las Vegas. He could've driven her up into the mountains and buried her there. What I'm saying is you have compelling evidence that points to him. Rykhirt has to be the correct path to clearing the case."

The investigators continued debating scenarios for several minutes before the meeting wrapped up. People collected their phones, tablets, laptops and notebooks and headed out of the room, leaving Holland, Elsen and McDowell alone for a post-meeting huddle.

But before Holland spoke to the detectives, he

nodded to the two FBI agents at the opposite end of the table. Both were examining their phones.

"What's up?" Elsen asked.

Caffrey got up and shut the door. "We just got something that you need to know," he said.

"A lead from the trafficking task force?"

Before answering, the two FBI agents took seats beside Elsen, McDowell and Holland joining them at their end of the table.

"No," Caffrey said. "Dan, you had requested the Bureau locate Riley Jarrett's boyfriend, or rather, ex-boyfriend, Caleb Clarke for a phone interview."

"Yeah. He flew with his father to Algeria. His father had a short engineering consulting contract for several weeks," Elsen said.

"My partner here, Agent Stacy Brooks," Caffrey said, everyone nodding at her reintroduction, "has been in contact with our legal attaché in Tunisia, which covers Algeria."

"Caleb Clarke did not arrive in Algeria with his father," Brooks said.

Forty-Six

Las Vegas, Nevada

Elsen stared at the agents, then at McDowell and Holland, then back at the agents.

"He didn't arrive? What, did his dad cancel the trip?"

"No, his father arrived but Caleb didn't. He never got on the plane," Brooks said.

"Where is he?" McDowell asked.

Brooks looked at her phone. "Here's what we know from our legal attaché at our embassy in Tunis. He spoke with Algerian authorities; and we also had our Los Angeles office consult with the TSA at LAX and the Algerian embassy in Washington. Caleb was denied boarding because he'd misplaced, or lost, critical travel documents. His father boarded because he was contractually committed and bound to a schedule in the city of Algiers."

"He left without him?" Holland said.

"He had to, but before departure, and on the

flight, Caleb's father managed to make emergency arrangements with the assistance of his contacts at the Algerian embassy and the airline. Approved documents would be reissued and provided for Caleb so he could leave alone the next day," Brooks said.

"And?" Elsen said.

"Caleb was not on the later flight," Brooks said.

"Where is he?"

"Unknown at this point," Caffrey said.

"His father had arranged for Caleb to stay in the Hilton, one of the airport hotels, with the understanding he was to board the flight the next day," Brooks said. "Airport security and the LAPD have Caleb Clarke in their systems but so far he can't be located."

"Was he at the Hilton?" McDowell asked.

"No," Brooks said.

The investigators had begun processing the meaning of the development when Brooks's phone pinged.

"That's Martin Clarke, Caleb's father in Algiers. We reached out to him and he'll take a call." She began tapping numbers. "It's later there. They're about eight hours ahead."

Brooks turned up the volume and switched to speaker, setting her phone on the table. The line rang several times.

"Hello?"

"Martin Clarke?"

"Yes."

"Agent Stacy Brooks in Las Vegas."

"Yes, hi."

"I've got you on speaker with Agent Barry Caffrey, and from Las Vegas police, Lieutenant Moe Holland and detectives Michelle McDowell and Dan Elsen. Sir, have you heard from Caleb?"

"No, nothing. Once I learned he didn't get on his plane, I started texting and calling nonstop since I arrived. Have you learned anything?"

"Not at this time but we've got people looking," Brooks said. "Mr. Clarke, are you aware of the situation here, that your son's former girlfriend, Riley Jarrett, has been reported missing by her family?"

"Friends have sent me news stories. It's terrible. My heart goes out to her family."

"Sir, Detective Dan Elsen, Las Vegas Metro. Do you think there could be a possible connection to Caleb missing his flights and Riley being missing?"

"In what way? I don't understand."

"We're told that just before she left San Diego with her family she ended her relationship with your son," Elsen said. "Do you think he may have tried to somehow reunite with her?"

A static-filled moment passed. "I know he was crushed by their breakup and her moving away. It's why I thought this trip to Africa would help him," Clarke said, "but no, she was moving across the country. We're scheduled to be here for six weeks."

"Has Caleb ever done anything like this before, or run off in the past?" Elsen asked.

"No," Clarke said. "Nothing like this, ever."

"What reason might there be for your son missing his flights?" Elsen asked.

"Look, I don't—he was devastated about the breakup. It could be that, but we don't know—my ex-wife's texting me. She hasn't heard from him. He's not responded to her calls and texts. We're worried."

"Agent Brooks here, sir. In the wake of the situation with Caleb, have you received any communication, any suggestion of a threat or ransom demand concerning your son?"

"My God, no!" Clarke said, followed by muffled voices at his end. "Why do you ask? Is there something we don't know? You're scaring me with these questions."

"I'm sorry, but given the nature of your work in that region of the world and the way events have been unfolding here, it's something we need to know."

"Agent Brooks. My son failed to get on a plane. Let's keep things in perspective. This is not some spy thriller movie."

"We have to ask these questions, Mr. Clarke," Brooks said.

"The answer is no."

"Mr. Clarke, Detective McDowell. Is it possible your son returned to San Diego?"

"From LA?"

"Through a ride share or a ride from a friend?"

"There's no one home in San Diego. Our house

is being managed by a property service for insurance purposes."

"Is it possible he could go home by himself, or stay with friends?" McDowell said.

"I suppose anything's possible. We could contact them."

"Sir," McDowell said, "could you send us names and contact information for anyone who might know his whereabouts. We'll get San Diego police to make some checks."

"Yes, I'll do that."

"Thank you, Mr. Clarke," Brooks said. "I'm sure this will get cleared up and we'll see Caleb united with you. We'll keep you posted. Meantime, if you hear anything please alert us."

"Yes, yes. Thank you."

The call ended with the investigators assessing matters.

"That was interesting," Holland said, then to Brooks: "You mentioned the nature of Clarke's work in that region, can you elaborate?"

"His work is at a new semiconductor plant, helping design integrated circuits. His contract is a lucrative one. In the past he's worked on US defense contracts. We know there are factions interested in acquiring the technological ideas, innovations and intelligence capabilities of the US government. We know organized crime and terror groups have been involved in stealing that information through kidnap-ransom schemes in various regions of the world."

"Is that what's going on here with Clarke?" Holland asked.

"We have nothing concrete to suggest that," Brooks said. "Our Counterintelligence Division is investigating that aspect, and we have nothing so far. We've confirmed that prior to accepting his contract in Algeria, Clarke and his family were vetted by US national security and he was cleared to work there. But this intelligence theft possibility is something that we can't rule out."

Elsen rubbed his chin while looking at photos of Rykhirt on his phone. "This kidnap-ransom scheme and the possibility Caleb abandoned the flight to find Riley are plausible theories. But we have nothing hard that puts Caleb with Riley after her disappearance. We have proof she was in the Sagebrush with Rykhirt, we have her shoe in the desert, his sketch, his record. Everything points to Rykhirt."

"Yes," McDowell said, "but we can't rule out Caleb Clarke until we locate and question him."

Forty-Seven

Nevada

Was there any chance they'd still find Riley alive?

It was the question trapped in Claire Nakamura's heart, the question no one dared ask aloud among those who'd gathered in the early morning at the Silver Sky Search and Rescue command post in the Sagebrush parking lot.

The number of volunteers had doubled.

"An item belonging to Riley Jarrett was discovered yesterday," Warren Taylor said during his first briefing of the day. "We can draw hope from it."

As of that morning, more than one hundred people had now deployed to the site. Wearing ball caps, sunglasses, shorts, T-shirts, fluorescent vests, equipped with backpacks, gear and radios, they listened to Taylor's updates.

"Working with Metro's Missing Persons Detail and the Metro Police SAR unit, we'll be expanding our effort today and targeting new areas of probability," said Taylor, incident commander for the volunteer group.

Teams would be transported on ATVs to outlying areas, following old desert pathways and desert roads, then they would be searched on foot. As well, drones would be used for further searches of outlying areas.

"The line starts here for your assignments," Taylor said.

Taking her place among the others with Dakota and Ashley, Claire's skin tingled with worry as if she were going to burst.

"Oh my God," Dakota whispered to her friends. "I can't believe they just don't say what everyone's thinking."

"What?" Ashley asked.

"Everyone knows they found Ri's shoe, right?" Dakota said.

"Yeah," Ashley said.

"I heard people saying that the creep likely murdered her and buried her out there, and he probably murdered that other girl last year," Dakota said.

"Stop," Claire said. "We don't know that's true."

"Well, I heard two guys talking and they said this is not really a search anymore, but a recovery, meaning they're looking for a body. One of them said he heard they have a body bag ready."

"Oh my God, no." Ashley's hands flew to her face and she started crying. "No."

"Dakota! Stop right now." Claire put her arm around Ashley. "You're spreading stupid rumors."

"I'm telling you guys what I heard," Dakota said. "Speaking of that, Claire, you should tell police what you heard Riley's stepdad saying."

Claire didn't respond.

Then Ashley, regaining some composure, looked at her. "She's right. You should, Claire."

Weighed down with concern, Claire looked among the crowd until she'd spotted Riley's step-father and stepbrother in the distance. They were with Riley's mom and her friends, talking.

"I don't know," Claire said. "Blake told me not to. He said he would take care of it."

"Did he?" Dakota said. "I bet he didn't. I bet he won't. He'd want to protect his dad."

"What if something's really going on," Ashley said, "and no one knows what you heard?"

"Yeah," Dakota said. "You said he sounded angry on the phone and thought no one was around to hear, but you said you heard him saying things that sound like they're related to a ransom. You should tell police, Claire."

"What if I did tell and somehow I messed things up?" she said.

"Claire," Ashley said. "What if you didn't and then learned that Riley got killed or something because you kept your mouth shut? You'd have to live with that for the rest of your life."

Paralyzed with indecision, Claire's breathing quickened. "Maybe I should tell my parents first," she said.

"No," Dakota said. "They'd tell Riley's dad and

he'd likely deny it or something. Tell the police. You've got to."

"I'm so scared."

"Claire," Dakota said, "if you don't tell, then we will and police will come to you anyway."

Claire's mind raced as Dakota and Ashley scanned the group.

"Where's the detective we talked to on the phone, Michelle?" Dakota said.

"Look." Ashley nodded toward the police mobile command vehicle where some officers had gathered. "There's that Lieutenant Jackson. She's nice. Go to her, tell her in private. She'll know what to do."

Claire looked at the lieutenant. She was nice. "Okay. But you guys walk over there with me."

"No." Dakota was nearly whispering. "You go alone, it'll be less conspicuous."

"But what if someone asks what I'm doing talking to police?"

"Just say you're worried, which we are, and you were asking if they had anything new they could tell you, that kinda thing," Dakota said.

Claire hesitated until she could summon the courage. She nodded, steeled herself then went to the police command center. When she got there, she waited at the periphery. When the lieutenant finished talking to the officers, she noticed Claire.

"Can I help you with something?" Lieutenant Jackson had a warm smile.

"Um."

"What is it?"

Claire let out a breath. "I have something to tell you—to report. It might be important."

Blinking and thinking, Jackson said, "You're one of Riley Jarrett's friends from San Diego, aren't you?"

"Yes, ma'am."

Jackson held out her arm, gesturing to a door. "Why don't you come inside and we'll talk there."

As Claire entered, she looked over her shoulder. Dakota and Ashley nodded their encouragement. Claire glanced beyond them.

John and Blake were watching her.

Forty-Eight

Nevada

"Come in, John, have a seat," Lieutenant Shanice Jackson said.

"What's this about?"

It was midmorning. Immediately after listening to what Riley Jarrett's friend Claire had told her, Jackson had contacted McDowell and Elsen, alerting them to new information that needed pursuing. Jackson had related much of what she knew over the phone as the detectives made their way to the Silver Sagebrush. Then she'd requested John Marshall come to the mobile command center.

Now, sitting inside, John looked to the far end of the vehicle, to the officers coordinating search efforts at their workstations amid the soft radio cross talk, the pinging of notifications on laptops and phones. Jackson read the dread written in John's eyes, as if he was bracing for the worst news a father could hear.

"Did you find something?" he asked.

"No, I'm sorry, it's nothing like that."

"Then why am I here?"

"We need to follow up on some information."

"What information?"

"Let's wait for the detectives to arrive. Shouldn't be long," Jackson said. "Can I get you anything, John, water, coffee?"

He declined and Jackson moved off to work quietly with the officers, leaving him alone. John sorted his thoughts, uncertain if making him wait was a police tactic. Drawing his hand over his unshaven face, he glimpsed a scene through the door window.

Outside, he saw Elsen and McDowell next to their parked sedan, talking to Claire Nakamura with her parents. The detectives were taking notes, listening, nodding. Realization was dawning on John, but he was interrupted when his phone rang.

It was Cynthia Litchfield, his new boss in Pittsburgh.

He stared at the phone as it rang. This was her first call since Riley's disappearance. He hadn't informed her of what had happened. She must've seen the news, the media reports. It rang again. John swallowed.

Jackson turned to him. "Why don't you answer it?"

"It's a colleague, job related." John silenced the call. "This isn't a good time. I'll call back later."

John watched the call go to his voice mail, looked up to Jackson holding him in her focus for a moment before she nodded to the door, which had opened.

Elsen and McDowell were ready for him.

The detectives didn't enter the command center. They stood outside under the shade of the extended canopy.

"Sorry to keep you waiting, John," McDowell said.

"What's going on?"

"Let's talk out here," Elsen said.

John stepped outside and Jackson ensured they were left alone, posting an officer to keep others away, giving them privacy in the shade.

"Last time we spoke, you told us to be ready to face the worst," John said. "What is it?"

"We're following up, John," Elsen said. "Have you told us everything we should know?"

John saw that he was recording their conversation on his phone. "I don't know what you're asking," he said. "Get to the point."

"John," Elsen said. "We can get a judge to give us access to your phone and digital communication, but it would be better if you cooperated with us."

John seethed. "We've done nothing but cooperate!"

"Are you being extorted? Is someone holding Riley for ransom?" Elsen said.

"No! What's going on? I thought you—with all

the news stories—that Rykhirt was your suspect. What's this?"

"John, you have to tell us if you're being extorted," McDowell said. "Is this connected to the drug issue with the RV?"

"We understand you made statements on a call about a demand for payment," Elsen said.

Lack of sleep and anxiety delayed John's coming to a conclusion but when he reached it, he knew.

"It's about Claire, isn't it, what she thought she heard me saying yesterday?"

"John, we can't help you if you don't help us. Think of Riley."

His face strained, he rubbed his stubbled chin and shook his head.

"Brad Vardy. Two hundred thousand," he said.

McDowell looked to Elsen who said: "Keep going."

"He's with legal for the RV rental company. He said their claims guy, the one I'd talked to after the accident who said the RV was a write-off, had been looking at news coverage and heard the police allegations, and that if, he stressed if, it was used in criminal activity, to transport illegal drugs, the insurance policy is voided and I have to pay the cost of replacement—two hundred thousand dollars."

The detectives said nothing.

"He called to tell me that now, at this time. With all we're facing," John said. "I thought he was being a prick. I lost it with him on the phone. I shouted at him that I didn't have that kind of money; that what he was suggesting was crazy and I was not going to pay. It was a rental, we have nothing to do with any drugs, but thanks to you guys, this is what I faced."

The detectives said nothing.

"That's when Claire overheard me. I'm sure it scared her but she misinterpreted it. I wanted to explain it to her but I never got the chance."

"Brad Vardy?" McDowell said.

"Yes."

"Do you have his spelling?" McDowell said.

"No. Do you want his number?"

"No. We'll contact him. We have the rental policy."

Elsen looked at John for a long moment. "You know, it's a crime to lie to us," he said.

John stared at him.

"John, have you got debts that are off the books? Do you owe someone? Does this have anything to do with the drugs? Or are you covering up another crime?"

John's face tightened. "No."

"Think of Riley, your family."

"I swear to God, I'm telling you the truth."

Elsen stared at John for a long moment before he slowly nodded. "All right, thank you. We'll verify your account of the call with Vardy. I hope it's true. For everyone's sake."

"It is," John said.

"Good." Elsen stared at John. "But if there's

anything else that you know and we don't, it would be advisable for you to tell us now."

John's face reddened as he stared back. "There's nothing."

Forty-Nine

Nevada

After talking with John Marshall, Elsen and Mc-Dowell went inside the police command vehicle. They got coffee and muffins, then found a place to work.

McDowell searched their contact files. After a series of calls, and by the time he'd finished his pecan muffin, Elsen had reached Brad Vardy, a lawyer with American Unified Underwriters. Elsen put the call on speakerphone so McDowell could participate.

"Yes, the RV rented in John Marshall's name is with Rolling Republic Rentals, one of our major clients," Vardy told them from Hartford, Connecticut.

Elsen then asked Vardy to confirm a call with John.

"Yes, I spoke with John Marshall in Nevada. We're following up on his claim."

Vardy then recounted the nature and specifics

of his conversation with John, relating as much detail as he could.

"Basically, I reviewed the terms of the policy with the aim of making sure he understood that if the allegations concerning the RV being a transport vehicle were true, we'd be seeking replacement and administrative costs for the unit. One moment, I have it all here."

They heard a keyboard clicking.

"Mr. Marshall rented a late model, upscale luxury unit," Vardy said. "Class C RV, with low mileage, so that cost with processing fees is upward of two hundred thousand dollars, maybe two twenty. We're still finalizing estimates. I also offered to discuss a payment schedule with him, once a determination was made by law enforcement. Look, I didn't want him to be hit with any unpleasant surprises so I alerted him to the possibility of replacement costs."

"And how would you characterize his reaction?" Elsen asked.

"Oh, he was angry. Had a few choice words for me but quite understandable given his situation."

"All right," Elsen said. "Thank you, you've been very helpful, Mr. Vardy."

"A couple things while I have you, if you don't mind?"

"What's that?"

"You do believe the family used the RV in criminal activity, correct?"

"We don't discuss such matters in an ongoing case," Elsen said.

"I understand. Lastly, I'm curious, but I expect in the course of your investigation you're going to take a look at the other tragedy Mr. Marshall experienced?"

"And what would that be?" Elsen said.

"The deaths of his wife and daughter while sailing near San Diego."

"We're aware," Elsen said.

"Good."

"Mr. Vardy," McDowell said, "why do you ask?"

"Well, in our research we conduct due diligence to guard against fraudulent claims," Vardy said. "From what I learned, it seems before a large payout was made to John Marshall on life insurance policies for his wife and daughter, questions were raised about their deaths."

"What questions?" Elsen asked.

"It's not for me to say. I had nothing to do with the case. It was another company and we have no affiliation with it. The benefit was paid, so it was resolved."

"Mr. Vardy, what questions? What are you suggesting?"

"Well, from what I'd heard on the insurance grapevine, there was some question as to whether or not the deaths of John Marshall's first wife and their daughter were accidental."

Elsen and McDowell exchanged looks.

"It might be something to keep in mind, Detectives," Vardy said.

Fifty

Nevada

John seemed frazzled after he'd finished with the detectives, giving Grace a sickening feeling that something dreadful was emerging.

Determined not to be left in the dark, she went to him. "Did they find her?"

John wearily shook his head. "No. Nothing like that."

"What did Elsen and McDowell say?"

John appeared to be looking for someone in the parking lot among the searchers who'd not yet been dispatched to the desert.

Grace grabbed his shoulders. "John! Why did they talk to you?"

"It's about our insurance for the RV."

"The insurance?"

John repeated what he'd told the detectives about his call from Brad Vardy and how they might have to pay two hundred thousand dollars for the RV.

"*What?* Why would he call about a thing like

that now? You never told me about this call," Grace said.

"I'm sorry. I wasn't thinking clearly," he said. "I told Vardy I wasn't going to pay. Riley's friend Claire must've overheard me, mistook it for a ransom call and told police. That's what happened."

Grace looked at him, trying to process what he was saying.

"Is that what really happened, Dad?" Blake said. He'd been standing near them unnoticed while listening. "Because Claire told me you sounded pretty freaked out. Was that call really about insurance?"

John looked at his son. "We've had this conversation, Blake. Is there something else we should talk about?"

"Was it really about insurance, Dad?"

"Yes, it was."

Blake studied his father's face for any trace of deceit while John looked at his son with worry. Struggling to decipher the exchange, Grace's attention shot back and forth between them, until Blake walked away to join the searchers.

Grace turned to John: "What was that? Why would he think the call was not about insurance?"

"Grace, I don't know. Because he's not sleeping, not eating, anguish, we're all stressed out. You're a nurse, you tell me."

Concerned, Grace watched Blake.

Running his hand through his hair, John then stared at his phone, at the notice for the voice mail.

"I need to call Cynthia Litchfield in Pittsburgh," he said. "She called me a little while ago."

Unsettled, Grace looked at John for a tense moment, processing things, thinking.

"All right," she said.

Then she turned to watch Blake as he moved farther away from them.

Claire, Dakota and Ashley were across the parking lot with other searchers waiting for the bus that would take them to the desert on the far west side of the interstate.

Blake joined them suddenly, seizing Claire's wrist. "Come with me. I want to talk to you."

He walked quickly with her well out of earshot of the others, stopping in the shade of a palm tree. "I told you not to tell," Blake said.

Claire's face whitened and she took a breath.

"I had to, Blake. Dakota and Ashley were going to tell."

"My dad's call was about insurance. The company wants us to pay for the RV."

"What?"

"You don't know what you've done."

"What? I don't understand. I wanted to help."

He shook his head.

"Blake," she pleaded, "there's the creep, there's Riley shoe. We're so afraid. I had to tell."

"I told you not to tell. You don't know what you've done, sticking your nose in things, talking about ransom when you don't know a damned thing."

"Blake, you're kind of scaring me."

"You don't understand. I've been through this before."

Claire looked at Blake. He was trembling. Grasping to understand, to make sense of the way he was acting, Claire landed on a reason.

"You've been through this before with your sister, Courtney. Riley told us. Do you want to talk about it?"

Blake didn't answer. His eyes were shiny, glazed over.

"Just go, Claire."

"Blake, you're so worn out, you need sleep."

"Just go, Claire. I'll be fine."

A motor growled.

A yellow school bus had rolled into the lot. Its brakes creaked when it stopped to pick up the searchers. Claire's friends were waving for her, then she looked to Blake.

"I can stay with you, if you want—"

"No, go."

Reluctantly, Claire left.

When she was far enough away, Blake took out his burner phone and dialed the number he'd memorized. It rang and rang before the connection was made. "It's me, Blake."

After a long moment and muffled sounds, a male voice said: "Stop calling."

"Did you demand money from my dad?"

A long silence without an answer.

"Why did you do that?"

Another silence.

"I told you it's not my fault!" Blake said.

Another long, tense silence passed.

The voice said: "You fucked up."

"No, I did everything you wanted. What happened is not my fault!"

"You fucked up and this is not over."

The line went dead, leaving Blake to stare at his phone.

"Blake?"

He turned to see Grace approaching.

"Are you okay?" Grace said. "You were so upset with your dad. Want to talk?"

He shrugged. "It's all right."

"Who were you just talking to?" She indicated his phone. "What's not your fault?"

He shoved his phone in his pocket. "One of my stupid friends—it's stupid—I just—" Tears filled his eyes and he stared off. "I'm so sorry I lied to you about checking on her, Grace."

"What's done is done."

"I should've been—I could've been—more like a big brother to her, watching out for her. It's just that—" His shoulders shook, he lowered his head and his voice broke. "When Courtney and Mom drowned—I just—I just don't know how much more of this I can take. You know?"

Blake took a great gasping breath and Grace

took him into her arms. They stood there alone for several minutes, a mother holding her son. A portrait of grief.

For one moment, before ending their embrace, Grace searched the distance and saw John on his phone. Then she lifted her face to the sky, believing that secrets were being kept from her.

Fifty-One

That afternoon Felicia Keane was checking messages on her phone behind the wheel of her octane-red Dodge Durango when a marked San Diego police car pulled up behind her.

Looking up into her rearview mirror, Keane gave a little wave before stepping from her SUV to greet Patrol Officer Ron Holcomb from Western Division.

"Thanks for helping us out," Holcomb said.

"Not a problem, anything we can do."

The house was a single-level hacienda-style home in peach-coral stucco, with an orange clay tile roof, a two-car garage and queen palms in the yard. It sat on a quiet street where Mission Hills bordered Hillcrest.

"Did you receive your copy from us of permission from the owner?" Holcomb asked.

"I did, yes."

"Okay, so this is like a welfare check. Ready?"

"I'll just get my tablet, for any questions." Keane retrieved it from her car, and they went to the front door. The handle was equipped with a lockbox.

"So your company looks after the house while the family's in Africa?" Holcomb said.

"That's right. Diamond Palm Property Management takes care of properties for absent owners including American expats abroad."

The keypad on the lockbox beeped as Keane entered the code, and they entered.

The home was tastefully furnished. It had an open floor plan with hardwood floors, high ceilings and an abundance of natural light. They walked through the living room with Holcomb scrutinizing everything.

The house smelled of polish and cleaner.

Holcomb and Keane went to the kitchen where he opened the fridge. It was empty. He checked the ovens. The trash was empty. The place was spotless.

They moved on to the bathrooms. Again. Clean. Spotless. No toilet tissue, no indication the showers had been used, nothing unusual in the medicine cabinets. Nothing in the trash.

In the bedrooms, Holcomb inspected the beds, closets and dressers. Nothing out of order. Then they stepped out onto the rear deck. As they took in the private fenced yard, Keane asked a question.

"So, the son somehow missed his flight and the thinking is he might've come home here?"

"Something like that. Let's check the garage then we're done."

Taking the steps from the deck along the side of the house, they came to the front of the double garage with the lockbox on the frame. Keane swiped her tablet. "I've got the code here."

"They have two vehicles, correct?"

"Um, yes." Keane concentrated on her tablet. "They have a BMW M3 and a new Ford Explorer SUV. Now, that door code. Ah, here it is."

The keypad beeped as Keane tapped the sequence.

The automatic door came to life with an electronic rattle and slowly began rising.

Holcomb saw tires and a rear bumper, but as the door rose he saw only one vehicle. The BMW.

He looked at Keane. "Where's the SUV?"

"I don't—that's odd." Keane consulted her tablet. "Our people were not scheduled to take them."

"Check."

Keane shifted the tablet, got out her phone and pressed a number.

"Mitch Cooper, our operations chief, will know," she said, nodding. "Mitch? Hi. Felicia. I'm at the Clarke property with Officer Holcomb... Right. Did your people pick up one of their vehicles for any reason—the Ford Explorer?" A silence passed. "No?" Felicia shot Holcomb a worried look as she continued on the phone. "That's what I have... Right. It's gone, Mitch... Yes, I'm sure! We're standing in the driveway looking in the garage and it's gone."

Holcomb reached for his phone.

Fifty-Two

Riley Jarrett's phone sat on the counter of Officer Sue Watson's workstation in the Digital Forensic Lab at Las Vegas police headquarters.

On a far corner, bearing evidence tags, sat the phone and laptop that had belonged to Frayer Ront Rykhirt.

Watson, along with her colleagues in the lab, analyzed computers, phones and other electronic devices, including drones, computerized systems in vehicles and videos to produce evidence for criminal investigations.

Their caseload was overwhelming.

In fact, Watson was not the only analyst on the Jarrett case. One of her unit's forensic specialists had been dispatched to the Silver Sagebrush to help work on its security camera system for potential recovery of archived recordings.

And at headquarters, since receiving Riley Jarrett's phone from Dan Elsen, Watson had been working on it steadily.

Watson embraced the challenge. As a kid growing up in Henderson, she'd had an aptitude for puzzles and problem solving. In her teens she tore apart computers and phones then reassembled them to study how they worked. She got a degree in computer science, passed the police exam, worked on patrol before getting her dream job in the Digital Forensic Lab.

She stared at Riley Jarrett's phone as if it was a puzzle. One way or another Watson would solve it.

A cable connected the phone to a state-of-the-art digital extraction device. Another cable ran from the device to Watson's computer, transferring data, enabling her to see the inner workings of the phone on one of her two large monitors.

Again and again she reviewed Riley Jarrett's call logs, web browsing history, device notifications, cookies, emails, videos, images, various text and instant messages. In some cases she could see and recover deleted conversations. Most were mundane.

Watson then checked to see if any of the messaging apps Riley used had a third party archiving feature, but there was nothing with cloud providers that she could find.

Most challenging were the apps with messages that delete themselves because Watson had trouble accessing them. She knew that the longer it had been since data was deleted, the less chance there was of recovering it. Deleting data sends it to memory that can be overwritten, like when a message written in pencil is erased and you write over it. It can be recovered, but recovery's a long shot.

Watson made repeated attempts but could not gain access to the deleted messages. She was forced to write warrants for the creators of the apps to give the Las Vegas police access to their servers.

While waiting for them to comply, Watson initiated work on Frayer Ront Rykhirt's phone and laptop.

It didn't take long before she found disturbing pornographic images on both of his devices. Watson also found the photos Rykhirt had taken of Riley at the Sagebrush. Watson was digging deeper into hidden folders when her official police email pinged with a notification.

It was a response to the warrants. Critical information had arrived from the creators of the self-deleting apps Riley had used, essentially a map to finding the messages on their servers. They had not yet been overwritten.

Watson sat up. Checking the timeline provided by the detectives, Watson, before expanding, began reviewing messages created on the day Riley Jarrett left San Diego with her family in their rented RV.

Messages that were supposed to be deleted emerged in Watson's monitor. She began reading conversations Riley was having with her friends Dakota, Claire and Ashley.

It appeared Riley was angry about having to "get up so early, to climb into this stupid RV where you basically drive around with your own toilet water. Gross!"

She went on complaining about how "devastated" she was over breaking up with Caleb, being uprooted from San Diego, "and taken like a hostage to freaking Pittsburgh."

You should jump out and come back, Dakota said.

I should, Riley said.

Just kidding, Dakota said. No, I'm not. Yes, I am.

Then Riley began a conversation with Caleb.

Where are you now? Riley asked.

Security line at LAX. Phone going off soon.

I miss you so much it hurts, she said.

I miss you too.

My parents are evil for doing this, she said.

I'll love you forever.

They're going to regret making us break up.

You're the love of my life, he said.

Time went by, then Riley resumed talking with her friends, telling them her "prison van" was coming up to Baker.

John wants us to look at the World's Tallest

Thermometer. Please kill me now! Riley wrote to her friends.

Then nothing.

Watson checked the timeline. This had to be around the time Grace Jarrett said she'd seized the phones of her daughter and stepson.

Watson thought, then clicked on the drafts folder. Sure enough, there was a message Riley had crafted but never sent.

Reading it once, twice, three times, Watson checked and double-checked. The draft was the last thing Riley wrote. It was never sent.

She reviewed the message, reflecting on it, copying it.

Wow.

She swallowed and her keyboard clicked as she began typing a preliminary report for Elsen and McDowell.

Fifty-Three

San Diego, California

Nolan Pace wheeled into the Mobil station, his Silverado pickup rumbling and clunking before he shut off the engine.

"You gotta fix that muffler, pal," said the man walking by his driver's window, giving the truck a once-over. "Your ride's lookin' mighty ancient."

Pace, who had parked at the side of the convenience store, nodded. *Yes, genius, I'm aware my twenty-one-year-old truck needs repairs*.

The master of the obvious walked off.

Pace groaned with fatigue. He'd just finished another shift as a security guard at a downtown high-rise complex. Ten hours of dealing with addicts, homeless people, drunks, idiots and millionaires who thought you were put on this earth to serve them for minimum wage. Now with Carmen six months pregnant and unsure how much longer she could stay at her job making up rooms at the Holiday Inn, he worried. They were barely scraping by as it was. How were they gonna survive with a baby?

Pace picked up his phone, rechecked her text. Bread and milk, peanut butter cookies and butterscotch ice cream.

He got out of the truck. The gas station was at Washington Street and San Diego Avenue, which led to an on-ramp for I-5, making for a heavily trafficked area.

Inside it was the late-day rush with people everywhere in the store, picking things up and queuing at the counter to pay. Pace got the bread and cookies, went to the dairy case for milk and ice cream.

A young woman with oversize sunglasses perched on top of her head was reaching for chocolate milk. As Pace waited she glanced at him. He smiled. She didn't. *Whatever*, he thought.

Before she was done, she gave him a furtive look of unease then lowered the oversize sunglasses over her eyes.

It gave Pace pause but he shrugged it off, got his things and got in line.

The same girl was ahead of him, holding her chocolate milk, potato chips, tarts and a couple sticks of jerky, one of which slipped from her grip to the floor. She didn't notice.

Pace tapped her shoulder. She turned to him, tense, as if she were gripped with trouble. She appeared to be fourteen, maybe fifteen. She looked at Pace as if she were afraid.

"You dropped the jerky." He pointed to the floor. Her hands were full. So were his, but he adjusted things, bent over and picked it up, noticing her sneakers were so new they glowed.

"Thanks," she said when he handed it to her. She paid for her stuff with crumpled bills.

After he paid and headed outside, he noticed her look back at him, anxious as she climbed into the front passenger seat of an SUV. A guy, another teenager, stared at him from behind the wheel.

Pace gave the SUV a hard look before it drove off.

When Pace got home, he heard Carmen in the kitchen, closing the door to the microwave. Leftovers again. That was fine. He loved leftovers. He put the bag on the counter, kissed her then washed up.

A few minutes later, she put a plate of beans, rice and enchiladas before him, joining him at the table with a plate for herself. They talked and watched TV, catching the tail end of a rerun of *The Office*. Carmen liked the show; it made her laugh.

"So how you doing, babe?" he asked.

"My ankles hurt."

"I'll rub them for you later. So what's new?" he asked as he ate.

"We might have to move in five months. Yolanda's breaking up with her boyfriend. She called me. I don't know what we're going to do."

"We'll figure it out."

"That's just after the baby comes, Nolan."

"Don't worry. I'll talk to her."

The show ended with a block of commercials. Then the local evening news began. Pace was a consumer of news, old-school and online, to stay informed for his job.

The top story was about the discovery of another illicit tunnel at the border, then something on local politics and zoning.

"So I called my mother, to tell her," Carmen said. "Know what she said?"

Nolan had eaten much of his meal when the third story came on, an update on a fourteen-year-old San Diego girl who was missing near Las Vegas. The girl's face popped up on the screen.

Carmen was talking but Pace had ceased eating, he was fixated on the anchor. Vera Henderson was throwing to a reporter in Nevada.

"We go now to Drake DeKarlow with our Top Story News Team on the scene near Las Vegas," Henderson said.

"Vera, mystery continues to surround the disappearance of Riley Jarrett of San Diego and now involves police in Nevada, California, and the FBI…" DeKarlow began as more photos of Riley Jarrett filled a quarter of the screen, along with footage of an RV crash, a huge truck stop, the Las Vegas Strip, and search activities.

"…last seen at this massive truck plaza, the Silver Sagebrush, located off Interstate 15 south of Las Vegas. Investigators suspect she was approached by Frayer Ront Rykhirt, a convicted sex offender from Riverside, California, who died in an attempt to escape police custody while being questioned…"

Footage of Rykhirt's arrest and his mug shot were shown.

"…police will not confirm or deny theories that the Jarrett case may be connected to the murder of Eva Marie Garcia of Riverside, California, and if Rykhirt was a suspect in that case as well. The seventeen-year-old's body was found a year ago in the Nevada desert not far from where I'm standing. Police have also refused to confirm reports that the family's rented RV was being used to transport illicit drugs."

Pace watched as footage of search teams and helicopters ran.

"Exhaustive searches of the area are increasing and expanding after a single sneaker, said to belong to Riley Jarrett, was discovered in the desert a few miles from where she went missing.

"Warrants and subpoenas have been issued in the case. Police say the family has been cooperating and detectives have not ruled out anything or anyone as their investigation continues.

"Meanwhile, the reward for information leading directly to Riley Jarrett's safe return, raised through online donations and supporters in San Diego, now stands at twenty-five thousand dollars."

Pace's eyebrows climbed a little.

"Las Vegas investigators ask that anyone who has any information on the case call them."

Photos of Riley Jarrett and a detailed description filled the screen for a few seconds.

"Nolan?" Carmen said. "Did you hear me tell you what my mother said?"

Pace grabbed the remote and froze the screen on Riley Jarrett's face and written description.

"Nolan, what is it?"

"I saw that girl, the missing San Diego girl. I saw her today at the Mobil station before I got home."

Fifty-Four

Las Vegas, Nevada

The sun had set over Las Vegas, silhouetting the mountains, turning the sky into a sea of burning red.

At Metro headquarters working at her desk, McDowell texted Jack saying she wouldn't be home for pizza with him and Cathy.

"I'm sorry, honey."

"It's okay. We're going to watch *Ghostbusters* number one. Love you."

"Love you, too."

She downed the last of her tepid coffee from her cherished Raiders cup, continued following up on leads when she came to a new report from Sue Watson in the Digital Forensic Lab.

Watson had finally gained full access to Riley Jarrett's phone.

After reading her analysis and the attached pages of Riley's conversations with her friends and her ex-boyfriend, realization pinged in McDowell's mind.

This is definitely something.

Seeing Elsen was still talking on his phone, she reread the report until he ended his call.

"That was San Diego PD—" Elsen started.

"Dan, did you see Sue Watson's report? We just got it."

"No, I was on the phone."

"Look at it now before you tell me anything."

Observing the enthusiasm in her face, Elsen turned to his keyboard, opened Watson's email and read. McDowell came around, leaning behind him, pointing her capped pen, nearly touching the messages.

"Look. Here. Caleb's at LAX security and she says her parents are evil and will regret making them break up."

Elsen nodded, scrolling down.

"And here," McDowell said, "she begs Caleb not to go."

"He doesn't respond," Elsen said.

"Right, he likely switched his phone off at security."

They reread more of Watson's analysis on the timing.

"Then this," McDowell said, pointing. "The draft Riley never sent. The last thing she wrote before her mother took her phone. In her report, Sue wrote she thinks Riley was going to send this to one of her friends but never did."

They both read: I should just escape the first chance I get, go back home and wait for Caleb.

"Go home and wait for Caleb," McDowell repeated.

Elsen let out a soft, low whistle.

"This is a strong indicator," McDowell said. "It goes back to one of your theories, that Riley was incensed and had some kind of plan to run away and join her boyfriend."

Elsen was shaking his head.

"What is it?" McDowell asked.

"The call I just finished was with San Diego PD. They did a check at the Clarke residence. One of the family's vehicles is missing, a Ford SUV."

"Caleb?"

"Could be."

"I'm thinking if we find him, we find her."

"Could be."

A silence passed between them while they sent messages updating their supervisors. For the next fifteen minutes, Elsen and McDowell weighed more theories when they noticed Lieutenant Holland approaching from across the empty squad room.

"Did you read Sue Watson's report?" McDowell asked him.

"I did."

"And you know about the missing Clarke vehicle?" Elsen asked.

"I do." Holland loosened his tie and leaned on

McDowell's desk. "I just got off the phone with the captain, the FBI and San Diego PD."

"Where do you see this going?" Elsen asked.

"I see it going to California," Holland said.

Elsen and McDowell exchanged glances.

"Listen," Holland said. "San Diego just got tipped that a girl fitting Riley Jarrett's description was spotted at a Mobil station getting into an SUV driven by a male teen. They shot out a BOLO for the vehicle and alerted the border. The FBI still has nothing on the boy's phone. They're going for warrants on the Clarkes' vehicle, try to track its GPS. San Diego PD will go after security video. Everything's in NCIC. Things are getting hot."

The detectives listened.

"We want you to go to San Diego, follow this through. We're booking you on the first flight out in the morning."

"Tomorrow?" Elsen said. "So we just drop the Rykhirt aspect?"

"Not drop. Pause," Holland said. "The evidence pointing to Rykhirt, the video, his photos of her, the sketch, her shoe, the shovel and pick in his car, is very strong and we're not ruling him out. But we've got to eliminate all other aspects. The Rykhirt evidence can wait. It's not going anywhere, and our desert search for Riley won't stop. But right now we've got fresh developments that cannot be denied. We must act on this now."

"We still have other considerations that have not been put to rest," Elsen said.

"The suspicion of drugs in the RV?" Holland said.

"The drugs, the kidnap-ransom possibility," Elsen said.

"Right," Holland said.

"And the family history. We were told that the drowning deaths of John Marshall's first wife and daughter were thought to be suspicious."

"Yes, I saw your notes on that," Holland said.

"And we get the sense that the family's not been entirely truthful with us," McDowell said.

Holland nodded then stuck out his bottom lip. "We know these cases are not like TV," he said. "When you delve into people's lives, you find a lot of complications and uncover a lot of ugly things they want to keep secret."

"Happens all the time," Elsen said. "We keep that stuff in our back pocket. And, we won't alert the family about San Diego just yet."

"Right. If they, or someone close to them, are involved in any way, it would tip our hand," McDowell said. "They won't like it, but we have to protect the investigation as best we can for now."

"Absolutely," Holland said. "Our job is the safe return of Riley Jarrett to her family and to determine if a crime's been committed. With the exception of Rykhirt's actions, we have no evidence of a crime. Riley's shoe in the desert is troubling but not a crime, but it may point to one. So far we have no evidence the family's involved in drugs or being extorted, or concealing another crime. What we have is a missing juvenile, disturbing circumstances and hearsay. Until we clear this case, nothing's ruled out."

"Got it," Elsen said.

"You've got the list of people who attended the family's farewell party, right?" Holland said.

"Yes," McDowell said.

"Use it when you're in San Diego. Follow up on everything you can while you're there, and we'll keep things rolling here."

"All right, boss," Elsen said.

"San Diego PD and the FBI are standing by to assist you in California," Holland said. "Get some sleep. You've got an early flight."

It was dark when Elsen got home.

He called Wendy Davis, his neighbor, a professional pet photographer who owned a lab called Sheeba. Elsen asked her if he could leave his dog with her while he was out of town.

"I love having Daisy. Drop her off in the morning, Dan. I'll be up."

Elsen fed Daisy then made himself a ham and cheese sandwich with some coleslaw. Then with Daisy watching he packed.

Enough for a few days, he figured.

It was late when he took Daisy to the park. They had it to themselves. The peace was nice and Elsen thought of his wife, his memories not as painful with the passing of time.

When he got home, he set the alarm on his clock

radio and on his phone, charging on his night table. Then he got into bed.

But he couldn't sleep. Riley Jarrett haunted him.

Between what his heart wanted and what his gut told him, the case was tearing him up.

McDowell left headquarters and drove north to Cathy Miller's house.

Cathy had been Jack's schoolteacher in the second grade, before she lost her five-year-old daughter to a brain tumor. Then Cathy's husband, a card dealer at Caesars, divorced her.

McDowell had reached out to her to offer support. Later, Cathy offered a shoulder when McDowell's marriage ended. In those dark times they'd forged a friendship.

Cathy liked looking after Jack and he liked staying with her. It was never stated, it didn't have to be, but in some way having Jack in her life filled a void for Cathy.

"I'll be happy to watch him for you while you're away. I'm taking an online course at home, so it works out," she told McDowell when she stopped to check on her son.

It was late. Jack was asleep in Cathy's daughter's room. Her picture was on the wall. McDowell looked in on him, kissed his cheek.

Rather than wake him only to bring him back in the morning, they decided he would spend the night.

"I'll drop a bag of his things at your door on my

way to the airport. I can't thank you enough for this, Cathy," McDowell said.

That night, at home in her bed, McDowell swiped through her tablet looking at pictures of Jack.

Then she played the video of Riley Jarrett and Rykhirt in the Sagebrush, studying the worry on Riley's face, how he put his hand on her shoulder before she brushed it away.

McDowell swiped to the evidence photos, Rykhirt's crude bondage sketch and the photos of Riley's shoe in the desert.

Then she looked at the texts Watson had extracted from Riley's phone, then the photos, swiping through those of Riley with Caleb, smiling.

Teen bliss. The love of her life.

Was Riley alive and in San Diego, her mind fogged with hormones and emotion? Was she taken in some sort of kidnap-ransom, possibly involving drugs? Was the family covering up another crime?

Or was she buried in the desert?

McDowell put away her tablet. But she remained awake, staring into the cool darkness for a long time before sleep came for her.

DAY 4

Fifty-Five

Nevada

While the detectives contemplated Riley Jarrett's death, south of Las Vegas Grace lay awake before sunrise in her motel room at the Silver Sagebrush remembering Riley's birth.

In the delivery room...the rhythm of her contractions...pacing her breaths... Tim clasping her hand...staring up, the lights so bright...the doctor telling her...deep breaths...push, Grace...you're doing fine...squeezing Tim's hand, her knuckles whitening...pushing and pushing...here we are... her baby's first cry...her tiny, scrunched face... Tim's laugh...his kiss...love, joy and tears...never knowing she could be this happy...holding her daughter...

Grace ached to hold Riley now.

But as the morning sky began growing light, the dark reality settled upon her with chilling images of Rykhirt and Riley. And her shoe. Like a piece of her in the desert.

Please, God, it can't be true.

She sat up, taking stock of her life and her new family in the stillness. After searching much of the night, they'd all tried to get a couple of hours of rest. John snored beside her, and through the half-opened door to the adjoining room, Blake.

Both asleep.

With their secrets.

It troubled her how they'd acted after John was questioned alone by the detectives with Blake casting doubt on his explanation. Were they hiding something from her? She didn't know what to believe because she couldn't think anymore.

Grace plunged her hands into her hair. Her head throbbed, her stomach was roiling. She got up, showered, dressed then checked her phone again, finding no new messages. Unplugging the charge cord, sliding her phone into her pocket, she left the room.

Starting her fourth day without Riley, Grace walked across the big Sagebrush parking lot, believing nothing was real.

But it's all real.

She prayed Riley had run away—but remembered Rykhirt and her shoe. Grace knew the statistics for child abductions, knew that with every passing minute the likelihood increased that Riley was dead.

The interstate traffic hummed. The hissing, growl and grind of the big rigs coming and going underscored for her that this was one of the country's biggest truck stops where anything could happen to a fourteen-year-old girl. Grace had seen the signs posted on the bathroom stall doors in four languages: "If you are a victim of human trafficking, call this number..."

Coming to the police mobile command center, she didn't see McDowell and Elsen. She went to Lieutenant Shanice Jackson.

"Did you get some rest, Grace?"

"Some. Are we any closer to finding her?"

Jackson's eyes softened, then she offered her coffee. "I'm sorry, nothing new so far, but we're not letting up with the search."

"Where are McDowell and Elsen?"

"Working, following every possible lead."

At a loss, Grace looked to the desert. "It's so hard. It hurts so much."

Jackson touched her shoulder. "I know. Don't lose faith."

"Thank you." Grace accepted her encouragement and coffee before walking over to the Silver Sky Search and Rescue command post.

Upward of fifty volunteers had already gathered. Grace threaded through the group thanking each person, receiving hugs and hope.

"We'll never stop searching," Warren Taylor told her.

Grace continued, meeting with friends and supporters who'd joined them from California until someone tugged her wrist. She turned to her neighbor Norm Hollister, the retired police officer who'd organized one of the first volunteer groups.

"Oh, Norm." Grace hugged him. "Thank you."

"We're going to find her," he said.

John and Blake were up now and talking with the searchers. Sherry and Jazmin were there with backpacks loaded, prepared for another day in the desert. Upon seeing Grace they came to her.

"You got some rest?" Jazmin asked.

"A little. Did you guys sleep?"

"A bit," Jazmin said.

"I didn't sleep much. I searched as long as I could," Sherry said.

John and Blake joined them. "Taylor says they're expanding things today, going out farther," John said.

"Excuse me," said a man with a rich, baritone voice.

He had a familiar face, well-coiffed hair, was tanned with bright teeth and was wearing a navy polo shirt and khakis.

"Sorry to interrupt, but you are Grace Jarrett and John Marshall, Riley's parents?"

"Yes," Grace said.

"Drake DeKarlow, Top Story News, San Diego." He extended his free hand while gripping a microphone with his other hand. "Can we get your reaction to information we've learned in the search for your daughter?"

"What information?" John asked.

DeKarlow threw a glance to the camera operator behind him, a woman in a faded Bob Dylan T-shirt and cargo shorts, aiming her lens at the family. DeKarlow took a notebook from his back pocket then raised his microphone.

"There's been a possible sighting of Riley in San Diego."

"What?" Grace looked at DeKarlow, then to family and friends. Jazmin's and Sherry's faces registered shocked, teary hope.

"Riley's in San Diego?" Jazmin said.

"This is fantastic!" Sherry said.

"Is this for real?" Blake asked.

"Is this credible?" John said. "We've had false alarms before."

"Our sources are rock-solid that someone fitting her description was spotted at a gas station," DeKarlow said. "We understand that Riley's boyfriend—" DeKarlow looked at his notebook "—Caleb—"

"Caleb Clarke, yes!" Grace was breathing faster.

"Right, that Caleb Clarke was supposed to leave the country but didn't get on the flight."

Grace gasped.

"And that a teenage girl fitting Riley's description was spotted at a gas station near Old Town getting into a vehicle like one reported missing from the Clarke family home in San Diego."

"Oh my God!" Grace's voice trembled. "What else do you know?"

DeKarlow glanced at his notes. "Two Las Vegas detectives flew to San Diego this morning."

Her heart racing, her hands shaking, Grace

pulled out her phone and made a call that was answered on the fourth ring.

"McDowell."

"It's Grace. Is Riley in San Diego?"

"Grace."

There was a rush of air, traffic noise. It sounded like McDowell was walking outside.

"Where are you right now?" Grace asked.

"Grace, slow down."

"Tell me."

"San Diego but listen—"

"Why didn't you tell us about the break? Do you have her?"

"No, it's not like that. Hold on."

The sound on McDowell's end was muffled like she was talking to someone. Likely Elsen, Grace thought, running her hand over her face.

DeKarlow nodded to the camera operator to ensure she was getting everything.

McDowell came back. "Grace, we're here following up on new information. I'm sorry but we can't discuss it at the moment."

"I'm her mother! I deserve to know what's happening—"

"Grace."

"We're coming to San Diego!"

"Grace, we suggest you hold tight. We know this is difficult, but what's going on here could amount to nothing."

"And it could be everything. We're coming right now!"

Fifty-Six

Nevada

The road blurred under them as Sherry drove her rented Chrysler well over the speed limit north on Interstate 15 to Las Vegas.

Hope had swelled in Grace's heart, her skin tingling at the chance—the unconfirmed report—that Riley was alive in San Diego.

It had been less than an hour since they'd learned about the sighting, and from that moment everything had moved in swift, ordered chaos.

The news had spread among the searchers. Other reporters had converged on them. John and Blake brushed them off while searching for flights on their phones. Friends gathered protectively around them as they made their way back to the motel.

"It's fantastic news, honey, but are you sure rushing back to San Diego is the right thing to do now?" Jazmin asked Grace. "Wouldn't it be better to wait here until police know for sure?"

Grace took Jazmin's concern to heart. Leaving now—if it turned out to be the wrong decision—would be like abandoning Riley again. But not going home to find her if she was there would be more than she could bear.

"I have to go," Grace said without breaking her stride. "I have to believe she's alive."

"Okay," Jazmin said, keeping pace, shifting her backpack on her shoulders. "But you need people who are close to you to stay. I'll stay and keep looking."

"Our team will stay too and keep searching with the others," Norm Hollister said. "So you'll have everything covered in both places because we don't know until we know."

"There are flights every couple of hours," Blake said, his face in his phone.

"I'll get tickets for the flight that gets us home in the shortest time," John said.

"We can get an Uber or Lyft to the airport," Blake said.

"No, I'll drive you in my rental," Sherry said. "It'll be the fastest way to get you there."

At the motel, they'd packed their few items into tote bags while Carl Aldrich, operations manager for the Sagebrush, offered to hold their rooms for them in case they returned.

"But I'm hoping you won't need them again," he said, wishing them well.

Now, as the miles rolled by, they passed the spot where they'd crashed the RV.

It seemed like a lifetime ago for Grace.

Nothing was there to mark it. *Like it never happened.*

They shot by it in silence, the air in the car tightening with anxiety as everyone retreated into their thoughts. John and Blake punctuated the quiet, typing on their phones, responding to concerned friends while from time to time Sherry patted Grace's knee.

"It's going to be okay," Sherry said. "Trust me."

Grace gave her a weak smile, gripping her phone in her shaky hands, staring at pictures of Riley, hoping against hope for a message from her. Or news from McDowell or Elsen. Soon huge casino signs promoting famous acts greeted them at the city's edge, then the beginnings of the skyline rose in the haze as they neared the exit for McCarran.

"What's your flight and terminal?" Sherry asked.

John read the details from his phone then said: "Terminal One."

Sherry followed the airport signs, bringing them to the departure curb for their airline. She helped them unload before exchanging hugs.

"I'm praying with my fingers crossed," Sherry said.

"I don't know what to say except thank you," Grace said.

Blinking back tears, Sherry looked hard into Grace's eyes then started to say: "I was just thinking—"

"What?"

"No."

"What is it?"

"Just have a safe flight."

Sherry got into her rental, waved then drove away.

They got in line for security screening and Blake, careful that no one noticed, reached into his pocket as his lane approached a trash bin.

While some people got rid of bottled waters, he took a take-out food wrapper he'd picked up and surreptitiously used it to drop his burner phone into the garbage.

They moved smoothly through security, arriving at the preboarding area for their gate with time to spare, using it to study their phones, send messages and make calls.

"The reward fund is over twenty thousand now," Blake said.

Grace reached Jocelyn Robertson, the real estate agent selling their San Diego home.

"I don't know if you're aware of what's happened to our family, Jocelyn."

"Yes, everyone here's praying for you."

"We're coming home. We need our house."

Grace asked that Robertson not have any more showings and requested that she take the house off the market until further notice.

"Yes, we can do that. All your furniture and material we used for staging's in place. Whatever you need. I'll send you the code for the lockbox."

* * *

Ever since she'd first called, John had been exchanging voice messages with Cynthia Litchfield in Pittsburgh. This time when he called her she answered.

"Thank you for calling me back, John. How're you and your family holding up? Is there anything we can do to help?"

John looked back to Grace and Blake after stepping away for the call.

"Thank you. We're doing the best we can. I take it you've seen the news reports about our situation, Ms. Litchfield?"

"Cynthia, please. I've seen the news. If there's anything we can do…"

"Given the circumstances, our arrival might be delayed."

"Don't worry about that for now. Is there anything else?"

Unsure what kind of news reports she may have seen, he hesitated while determining the best way to frame his next request.

"I just want you to know that not all of the reporting is accurate."

"I'm sorry, I don't understand?"

"The accusations about us."

"Oh?"

"The RV was a rental and whatever the media may be reporting is not true. I want to be clear, and police have acknowledged this, many other people rented the vehicle before us."

"You're referring to the question of transporting drugs?"

"Yes." John cleared his throat. "It's a matter of geography really, with San Diego being on the border. Police have to be thorough. But we're not involved in any way, and I hope that has no bearing on your impression—this is a difficult time—you understand, Cynthia?"

A second passed. Then two more.

"Absolutely. It must be devastating for you. Again, John, if there's anything we can do to help. As a matter of fact, the company made a contribution just this morning to the online reward fund."

John swallowed as flight information echoed over the public address.

"Thank you."

"Are you at an airport?"

"Yes, we've learned Riley may be in San Diego. Police received a tip."

"That's positive, John," she said as another airport announcement echoed. "I better not keep you. Please know that you're in our thoughts, and we look forward to you being reunited with Riley and settling here. You're going to love our company and Pittsburgh."

"Thank you, Cynthia."

John ended the call, clenched his eyes shut, convinced he'd detected an undercurrent of skepticism in Litchfield's tone. His gut telling him that his new job was hanging by a thread.

* * *

Grace gazed out the window at jets taxiing, landing and lifting off.

Clutching her phone, she looked at her favorite pictures of Riley, praying that she had run off with Caleb.

I can deal with that because she'd be alive.

Then she began scrolling through the news stories she'd saved about Rykhirt, stopped and looked away.

If he killed her and buried her in the desert, I'll never forgive myself.

Grace prayed for McDowell or Elsen to call and end her nightmare. Glancing at John and Blake, she chided herself for her suspicions that they'd been secretive, for not realizing that this crisis had ripped open the wounds of their tragedy.

The light diffused.

"Grace?" Sherry stood before her, purse and a small bag over her shoulder. "I'm going to San Diego with you."

Grace leaped up and threw open her arms, hugging her as John and Blake stood near them in surprise.

"You didn't have to do this. You've already done so much," Grace said, wiping the corners of her eyes.

"What about your aunt in Salt Lake?" John said.

"I checked with my uncle. There's no change. He's been watching the news—he knows what's happening. He urged me to keep helping. He said that I'm only a flight away from Salt Lake. I want to be with you."

"I don't know what to say," Grace said.

"Listen, my car's at the airport in San Diego. When we land, I can drive you wherever you need to go. It's the fastest way."

"Thank you, Sherry," John said. "Let us reimburse you for your flight."

"Don't even think about it. I wanted to be with you when you find Riley, and you're *going* to find her."

Grace took hold of Sherry's hand and studied her face.

"I wouldn't have survived this long without you," Grace said. "Having you with us means the world to me."

At that moment the public address system called the preboarding announcement for their flight.

Fifty-Seven

Nevada / California

The landing gear rumbled up, tucking into the belly of the Airbus A320 as it lifted off from McCarran with John gripping Grace's hand.

The jetliner climbed over Las Vegas. He scanned the mountains and the desert below. He thought he'd spotted Lake Mead, Hoover Dam, maybe the Grand Canyon in the distance and then the Mojave. Grace gave his hand a squeeze. He smiled at her and said: "Just hold on."

Hold on.

That's what he'd told Lana and Courtney. They never wanted to go sailing that day. He made them go, assuring them it would be fine. Just like he knew Grace, and certainly Riley, never wanted to leave San Diego.

John's jaw tightened remembering the months after his wife and daughter died. After the autopsies, the questions, after strangers combing through their personal lives. "It's required," the insurance people said, "to establish the circumstances of their deaths, sir."

Then one afternoon it all ended when a sober-faced insurance agent placed a check on his kitchen table. As the agent explained the accidental death benefit in the policies, and the boat, John stared at the check.

It was an astounding amount of money. But it never silenced their screams or...

...the wild wind... "Hold on!" Waves curling...swallowing Lana...foaming crests...taking Courtney into the darkness...the terror in her last words... HELP ME, DAD!

He fought so hard to save them. They could've all made it if they could've just held on.

Then it became John's turn to hold on. He went through the motions of living while he and Blake received counseling. John stumbled in his private darkness trying to find a way to go on. Then he found Grace and together they found the light again.

But secretly, as he'd done on that day he went sailing knowing but never accepting that a storm was possible, John began taking risks; huge risks that Grace didn't know about. That *nobody* knew about. Before long it got out of control; things began disintegrating, forcing John to take even greater risks without Grace knowing the truth.

Now they had to leave San Diego because of what he'd done. Pittsburgh was another risk, but it was their lifeline. They had to find Riley or it would all fall apart and they'd lose everything.

What if we don't find her? Will I bury another daughter?

Cash another check?

Is that what I've become?

Fifty-Eight

Nevada / California

Crushing John's hand, Grace prayed with all of her heart that Riley was in San Diego. *Will I hold her in my arms today? Will I ever hold her again?*

The flight would take less than an hour, but it might as well be an eternity.

Grace looked at her hand in John's. Hold on, he'd said. But she didn't know how much longer she could endure not knowing if Riley was alive, or if Rykhirt— No she couldn't think about that.

Stay positive. Have faith. Be thankful.

And she was thankful, for the searchers, their friends, Norm, the volunteers, everyone coming to Nevada. She didn't deserve their kindness.

She was thankful for Sherry and Jazmin, rushing to her side with all they'd been through over the years. Without them she couldn't go on.

She looked toward Blake in the seat in front, then to Sherry sitting across the aisle a couple of rows ahead, thinking how fortunate she was that

Sherry came into her life when she did, because in the wake of Tim's death Grace was fighting to survive on every level.

Losing Tim had brought her world to a stop while the rest of the world continued turning with indifference. They hadn't been good managing their money. Even with Tim's higher salary, the cold fact was they had been living beyond their means. That left Grace facing huge bills for renovations to the house, the installation of the new pool, landscaping, loans, medical and dental bills, payments for vacations, the two cars, credit cards, an IRS bill for a tax screwup and Tim's funeral. Even with Tim's insurance and benefits, Grace was struggling.

Jazmin and Miguel had offered her money but she couldn't take it, for all sorts of reasons. And another bank loan was out of the question for her.

Grace's situation forced her to make financial adjustments and go back to full-time, round-the-clock nursing shifts. But she vowed not to make Riley a latchkey kid, coming home to an empty house while still mourning her dad.

Again Jazmin offered to help but she had her hands full with her family, and Grace knew that things between Jazmin and Miguel were strained. Grace knew in her heart she couldn't go to her.

She searched for a nanny—one she could afford—but it didn't go well. After one week, the first one showed up intoxicated, the second stole Grace's jewelry, the third couldn't complete a sentence without swearing and criticizing Grace. All this was happening while Grace had not gotten control of her finances. She sat up nights aching, sobbing for Tim and weighing selling their home, their dream home, the only home Riley had known.

This was when Sherry, who'd had her fill of Chicago winters, transferred to San Diego. She worked from home writing company reports so may as well do it from a warmer climate, possibly even on a beach. One day she had coffee with Grace to see how she was doing and Grace, trying to make light of it, revealed her challenge finding a nanny.

Sherry offered to help because she didn't know many people in San Diego.

"I was a nanny in college. I'd be happy to do it for free. It would get me out of my place. Besides, I can work anywhere."

After some coaxing, Grace accepted and depending on schedules, Sherry would come to the house for a few hours when Riley came home from school. Or Sherry would stay overnight, helping with breakfast or dinner, a few chores and appointments. Riley loved her. "She's like a cool big sister," she'd say. And Grace, seeing that she was good for Riley, loved her, too. Sometimes they'd visit Sherry when she moved from her apartment into her new town house in Mission Valley. It wasn't far and it had the best places to shop.

As the jet's engines droned, Grace pushed back her tears, thinking how Sherry held a special place in her heart for all she'd done for her and Riley. It was largely because of Sherry that Grace was able to keep the house.

Then one night, Sherry, who was a few years younger than Grace, told her that she'd been engaged to a law student in Chicago. But when they'd learned that it was unlikely that Sherry could have children, he left her.

"I've learned that in this life people make promises they can't keep, and that no matter how long it takes you have to find a way to not let it destroy you," Sherry said.

It broke Grace's heart and she grew protective of her.

Some two years after Tim's death, Jazmin and Sherry encouraged her to date again.

"You're a beautiful woman with a lot to offer," Sherry said.

"You could test the waters," Jazmin said. "You'll know when it's right."

The truth was, Grace was lonely but nervous and conflicted about her guilt over Tim's death as Sherry introduced her to online dating sites where eventually she helped her find John Marshall.

"Look at this guy. He checks all the boxes, and he's handsome, too. It wouldn't hurt to have coffee with him."

Despite being terrified of dating again, she had coffee with John. Then they made a date for another coffee, then a date for dinner. Grace found John understanding and compassionate because he'd also suffered a tragedy. Over time they fell in love and got married, creating a new blended family, moving into Grace's house with Sherry remaining a part of their lives.

"You're so blessed to have two great loves in your life," Sherry told Grace at her wedding.

Now, looking at the rows ahead in the jet at Sherry's shoulder, Grace drew strength from having her near, helping her in the most difficult times of her life. Like this one.

Grace clasped John's hand, clinging to hope as the plane's public address crackled.

"Ladies and gentlemen, if you could make your way back to your seats, we'll be starting our descent into San Diego. Please secure your carry-on items, stow your tray table…"

At that moment an older man came down the aisle, returning from the bathroom. His foot somehow hooked the strap of Sherry's bag, sending it down the aisle toward Grace, spilling its contents over the floor.

The plane then hit some rough air and the man almost lost his balance, bending to recover the bag and contents with Sherry standing behind him.

"I'll get it, sir," Grace said, unbuckling her seat belt. "It's my friend's. Go to your seat, it's okay."

"Sorry," the man said.

Collecting Sherry's wallet and hairbrush, Grace noticed the glint of a chain half out of the bag. She picked it up, studying it in her palm.

A bracelet with double gold chains, one with a

small half-moon charm and the other half filled with star charms that came together.

The small hairs at the back of her neck stood up.

Grace turned to Sherry. "Why do you have Riley's new bracelet?"

Sherry smiled, reaching down for her bag. "It's mine."

"But you gave Riley this bracelet as a gift at the party. She was wearing it when we were in the RV."

Sherry put her hand on Grace's shoulder. "Didn't she tell you? I got one, too."

"What?"

"Here." Sherry got her phone, swiped through photos to a selfie of her and Riley at the party, wrists up, each showing their moon and stars bracelet. "See?" Sherry showed Grace the picture. "I got one, too. I told her that we'd always be friends."

"Ladies, please return to your seats," an attendant told them.

Grace stared at Sherry until she understood, nodded and smiled.

At that moment, Blake turned to look at Grace then Sherry. "Everything all right?" he asked.

"Yes," Grace said.

"Please return to your seats now," the attendant said. "Fasten your seat belts. We're preparing to land."

Fifty-Nine

San Diego, California

Blake heard the hydraulic groan of the landing gear dropping and locking. Greater San Diego grew closer until his stomach lifted and they touched down smoothly. As the jet trundled to their gate, his thoughts pinballed. *Why did Sherry have to come? Does she know something? Why did the detectives really need a list of people who were at the party? Will they talk to my friends in San Diego?*

He glanced out the window at the city, fear twisting his gut.

Sixty

San Diego, California

The girl enters the Mobil station store wearing large sunglasses. Images of her shift in jump cuts as she walks to the dairy case where she adjusts her glasses to the top of her head before replacing them, then selects other items. Her shoes are fluorescent pink. She drops an item. The customer behind her retrieves it. She pays with cash, leaves, gets into a late-model blue Ford Explorer driven by a male. Traffic at the station is heavy. The Ford's plate is obscured.

"Want me to run it again?" said Detective Emery Moore, with San Diego's Juvenile Missing Persons Unit.

"Please," McDowell said.

Upon landing and getting a rental car, McDowell and Elsen had gone straight to San Diego police headquarters on Broadway and met Moore. He took them up to a third-floor room where they were joined by FBI Special Agent Laurie Price from the San Diego field office. They began by studying the gas station video. It was challenging. The girl looked like Riley, but the sunglasses hid much of her face. The SUV was a Ford Explorer. The plate contained the letter *G*, like the plate on the Clarke's missing Explorer.

Now, after replaying the footage, the sequence finished.

"The footage doesn't give us the full plate," Moore said. "We haven't yet confirmed this is Riley Jarrett and Caleb Clarke, but this video and your information makes it a near certainty."

"The shoes," Price said. "You found one of Riley's sneakers in Nevada, and in the video the girl appears to be wearing new sneakers."

Elsen looked at his notes: "And according to the tipster, the girl was anxious, as if she didn't want to be seen."

"Since Riley and Caleb were reported missing," Moore said, "they've not used social media and there's been no activity on any bank accounts or credit cards."

"Have you considered a new Amber now that Caleb and the missing SUV are in the mix?" McDowell said.

"The key factors aren't there for us," Moore said. "Was Riley abducted, or taken against her will? Is she in danger?"

"We don't know for certain," Elsen said. "There's her shoe."

"Yes, but that's not enough to meet our criteria

for an Amber," Moore said. "Both were reported as missing juveniles, and your latest information from her phone points to her being a runaway. If that plays out, then you charge Caleb with contributing to delinquency of a minor."

"But we need to get the word out here," McDowell said.

"Oh, it's out. We'll find the SUV," Moore said. "Local press is reporting on the case. We've got BOLOs everywhere, all the counties, California Highway Patrol, toll roads with plate readers, all ports of entry and border people. We've updated all our social media."

"And we've updated everything," Price said. "The National Center for Missing and Exploited Children, NCIC, other state and federal agencies, with the latest info and photos."

"Good," McDowell said.

"One more thing," Price said. "If it's working, we'll try to track the SUV through its onboard GPS system."

"What about Caleb's phone?" McDowell asked.

"We've got nothing on his phone so far," Price said. "He might've disabled or tossed it."

"And background history?" Elsen said.

"We followed up on local checks for you on both kids," Moore said. "We ran them through ARJIS, our Automated Regional Justice Information System. If they were ever a victim, a witness or a suspect in a crime, they'd be in there."

"And?" Elsen said.

"Negative," Moore said. "We also ran the parents' background history. Nothing but the speeding ticket for John Marshall. Nothing with Child Protective Services. No calls, no previous history of running away."

"And," Price said, "the FBI's still working on the possibility of a kidnap scheme linked to Caleb's father's work overseas."

"Anything there?" McDowell said.

"Not yet, but let's back it up a bit," Price said. "We understand you were looking hard at a convicted sex offender, Frayer Ront Rykhirt from Riverside for this, that you had evidence pointing to him."

"Strong evidence. We haven't ruled him out," Elsen said. "But this new San Diego lead, coupled with the other intel, is strong and live. So we're moving on it."

Price nodded, then asked: "What about the drug angle? You know the volume of narcotics coming up through Mexico then through here at the border is just wild. And if someone loses a shipment, it's common for a family member to be taken and held for ransom to replace the monetary value of the drugs."

"Yeah, we know," Elsen said.

"It's also common," Price said, "for the family, out of fear, to never disclose this."

"Yes," Elsen said.

"Look," Price said, "the family has an online reward for information going, and last I looked it was close to thirty thousand. What if that were part of what's happened? Maybe Caleb was involved? Or it's a money-making fraud of some sort?"

"But we don't have anything pointing to that," McDowell said. "We've consulted with the DA on the HIDTA team. We found no drugs, so no charges."

"The family could be covering up something," Price said. "Keep it in mind."

"Something else to keep in mind," Moore said. "You know that Grace Jarrett lost her first husband in a car accident, and John Marshall lost his first wife and teenage daughter in a sailing accident in San Diego Bay?"

"We know," Elsen said.

"There was some suspicion about the Marshall drownings because of a large insurance benefit," Moore said. "Denny Winslow's our homicide guy who looked into it. He's retired but I reached out to him, to get him to shed any light on it. I'll keep you posted."

"We also have a list of potential witnesses," McDowell said.

"Witnesses?" Moore said.

"Arising from a party the family gave just before they left San Diego. They might shed some light," she said. "So, depending on how things go, we'll be talking to people while we're here in your yard."

Moore consulted his notes for the family's address. "Sure, they live in Mission Hills. Let us know if we can help on that."

A knock sounded at the door, then it opened to a female officer. "Sorry to interrupt, Emery, but dispatch said you'd want to know."

"What's that?"

"Northeastern Division's got a good sighting of a Ford Explorer and descriptions fitting your two juveniles in Rancho Bernardo."

Sixty-One

San Diego, California

Nearly trotting through the terminal forcing the others to keep up, Grace began making calls as soon as they landed. She tried McDowell and got her voice mail. She tried Elsen and got his, too. She left messages.

On the escalator John scoured his phone for the latest local news stories for any updates.

"Blake," Grace said, "can you reach any of Caleb's friends? Maybe they know something."

As she and the others hurried to the parking lot, Grace gave her bag to John so she was free to begin calling the reporters whose numbers she'd kept, leaving messages asking for the latest information on Riley's sighting in San Diego.

Finding Sherry's white Chevrolet Traverse, they tossed their luggage in the back. With Blake and John in the rear seat, Grace in the front passenger seat, Sherry got behind the wheel and started out of the lot.

"I got the gas station from a *Trib* story," John said. "It's a Mobil at San Diego Avenue and Washington. That's near here."

"Want me to head there?" Sherry said.

"Yes, we'll ask around," Grace said.

Sherry threaded through the lot to the pay station then began navigating their way out.

They got onto North Harbor Drive. Jets whined overhead as Grace took in the palms, expressways, the hills and skyline. She dropped her window to take a breath and make a plea. *God, please let her be here alive and safe.* They stopped at a traffic light.

"None of Caleb's friends know anything," Blake said.

"Keep trying," Grace said. "Ask them if they know other friends."

Before the light changed, Grace's phone rang with a San Diego number. "Yes," she answered.

"Is this Grace Jarrett, Riley Jarrett's mother?" a woman asked.

"Yes, who's calling?"

"Rhonda Carter, I'm with Top Story News in San Diego. I got your number from Drake De-Karlow."

"Yes."

"Drake said you were coming back to San Diego and looking for updates?"

"We just arrived."

"Have police told you what's happening with the sighting of your daughter?"

"No, I mean she was seen at a gas station near Old Town, that's all we know. Why, what's happening?"

"This is incredible timing, but they think they may have located her."

"What? Where?" Then to the others: "They might have her!" Then into her phone to Carter: "Do they have her? Is she okay?"

"We don't know. It's breaking on our newsroom police scanners now," Carter said.

"Where? Where's this happening?" Grace said.

"It's up in Rancho Bernardo, near or on Matinal Road—"

"Rancho Bernardo, Matinal Road," Grace said to Sherry. "Go there now!"

"Hang on, we'll pinpoint the address," Carter said. "We've got a news team heading there, and we'd like to secure an exclusive inter—"

Blake worked fast on his phone. "We're thirty minutes away. Take the 163 north then take northbound I-15."

"Yes, yes, Rhonda," Grace said, "whatever you'd like! Thank you. Please keep us posted. We're on our way there now!"

Sherry pushed her foot down on the accelerator.

Sixty-Two

Rancho Bernardo, San Diego, California

The automatic garage door was half closed, nearly concealing the blue Ford Explorer inside as a male and female walked around the rear bumper.

The photo was taken surreptitiously on an older phone. Grainy, most of the content was dimmed in shade but with enough clarity to see the female's bright pink sneakers as she blocked the plate, allowing only the digit "3" to be seen.

"I took it yesterday while walking Ollie," Celia Donovan told San Diego Officer Manny Perez, standing in her kitchen studying the picture and checking his information on Clarke and Jarrett.

A key fact was that the plate of the Clarke SUV was 2GAT123.

"That's the Fowlers' home," Donovan said, her collie resting at her feet. "Natalie and Brian left last week with the kids for a vacation in Canada. No one should be home. Those two trespassed, squatted, or invaded, whatever you call it. Lord knows what they're doing in there."

Turning his radio down, Perez nodded for her to continue.

"Then I saw the story on the news about the missing girl and her boyfriend and the missing car. I used to be with our neighborhood watch. That's why I called. The missing car's license plate is just like the letters and numbers of the one in the Fowlers' garage."

"Do you know if the occupants are in the house now?" Perez asked.

"Yes. I've been keeping my eye on it all morning. Come here." She went to the window. "You can see their house from mine around the corner on Matinal right there. I saw the blue car go out and come back. They're in there. Can only imagine what's going on." She continued watching the house from her window as Perez followed her gaze.

"And how do you know the Fowlers, Mrs. Donovan?"

"I'm a retired music teacher. I taught Jen and Clinton Fowler piano. I know the family."

"Would you have a phone number for them?"

"I have Natalie and Brian's numbers. I'll get them. Want some coffee?"

Perez declined and thanked her for the numbers.

In the time that followed he returned to his car, which he'd parked far from the Fowler house but at an angle that allowed him to see it.

He liked Rancho Bernardo. It was in the northern reaches of San Diego, amid canyons and rolling hills, a sprawling suburb of schools, trails, shopping centers, office parks and golf courses. Matinal Road meandered through a beautiful, tranquil section of a terraced neighborhood. A good place to raise a family, he thought as he got to work.

First, he updated his dispatcher and commander on what was emerging. Then, using his mobile computer he confirmed Brian and Natalie Fowler were the residents, ran a call history of the Fowlers' address, checked for any registered guns, ran their registered vehicles. He also ran the family names in several databases for criminal history or outstanding warrants. Nothing. The family and address were clear.

Perez then reached the Fowlers who were visiting relatives in Vancouver, British Columbia. They were alarmed at a call from San Diego police, asking if anyone should be in their home—friends, relatives, service calls.

"Absolutely not," Brian Fowler said after Perez explained. "I can't believe this! We just had our home security repaired before this trip. It was working fine and should've been activated."

"People find ways to bypass them," Perez said. "Are there any firearms of any kind in the house?"

"No."

"We'll check things out and keep you posted."

Perez updated his sergeant. SWAT was not needed, but more units were dispatched to contain the area and choke off all possible exits.

"And Manny, a heads-up," the sergeant said. "This case has profile. One of our detectives, two from Las Vegas, and an FBI agent are on the way."

"Copy that."

Soon marked units, careful not to use lights or sirens, quietly began taking points on Matinal, the street above it and the two nearest cross streets. The detectives joined them as news crews were arriving. *The media guys don't miss much*, Perez thought.

Neighbors were kept back to gawk from lawns and driveways in the distance, guessing at what was happening.

Perez spoke into his radio. "All set."

With everyone in place Perez and Kelly Cardona, another officer, went to the Fowlers' front door and rang the bell.

They heard voices inside then sudden movement. Shielding his eyes at a window, Perez glimpsed figures running and reached for his radio.

"They're coming your way, Denny!"

The rear door to the house burst open, ejecting two people, a young male and female. Officer Denny Hong tackled the male on a patch of grass, got him on his stomach, smoothly handcuffing him.

The female broke free of Officer Jan Lymon's grip and escaped over a fence. Lymon got on her radio as she pursued the female with Perez and Cardona joining. From the front sidewalk they glimpsed the suspect busting through hedges, scaling fences, darting around pools as dogs barked and a car alarm sounded.

Coming to the last house on the block with Lymon behind her and now three officers blocking her way, the female dropped to her knees on the front lawn, breathless, her shirt torn.

"Get on your stomach, hands behind your back!" Cardona said.

Sobbing, the girl complied.

Cardona patted her down then handcuffed her as Perez read her Miranda rights.

Standing back behind a parked police unit, a newspaper photographer, a TV camera operator and several neighbors with phones out recorded the arrest.

Sixty-Three

Rancho Bernardo, San Diego, California

Sherry steered her SUV to the closest police car.

They'd arrived to see officers walking the hand-cuffed suspects down Matinal Road toward Perez's parked unit.

Grace bounded from Sherry's car, hurrying to them with her family and Sherry close behind.

The male suspect was nearer, and Grace called to him. "Caleb!"

The news cameras turned to her.

"Stay back, ma'am!" Perez shot out his palm.

"Caleb!"

With an officer gripping his upper arm the boy lifted his head, looked at Grace.

He wasn't Caleb Clarke.

"What's this? Who're you?" Ignoring Perez's warning, Grace moved closer down the street to where a female officer was escorting the girl whose head was bowed.

"Riley!" Grace called to her.

"Ma'am, do not come any closer!" Perez warned her.

"Riley!" Grace yelled.

The girl lifted her head to Grace.

But it wasn't Riley.

Grace froze in her tracks, tears springing to her eyes.

"Grace, come back," John said.

"Oh my God," Grace said, reeling, looking about. "Where's Riley? RILEY!" she screamed.

"Grace!" McDowell, huddled with investigators at another car, noticed the disturbance as more police and news cameras arrived at the scene. She went to Grace and took her hand.

"Michelle! Where's Riley?"

"I'm sorry. It's not them."

Grace's heart sank. McDowell, John and Blake steadied her.

"She's not here?" Sherry asked.

"No, I'm sorry," McDowell said.

John cursed. Sherry groaned. Blake's face whitened as he looked away.

"I don't understand," Grace said.

"The information pointed to them but it's not them," McDowell said. She opened the front passenger door of her rental, parked near a San Diego patrol car. "You guys wait here. I'll be back."

News cameras sprang up everywhere. The two suspects were in patrol cars being questioned, just as the garage door at the Fowlers' home opened, revealing a blue Ford Explorer. The cameras zoomed in. The plate was not 2GAT123. It was not the Clarkes' SUV. Police radios crackled.

Grace and her family heard dispatches spilling out about the suspects.

"...subject one, Patrone, Vincent, DOB—" There was static. "Subject two, Snell, Jessie Ann, DOB, stand by—" More static. "Both have outstanding warrants from Escondido...stand by..."

Sherry moved her hand up and down Grace's arm to comfort her. John had taken her hand, both of them telling her not to give up hope, that they were going to find Riley. But Grace couldn't hear them. As the scene whirled around her she sat in silence, unable to comprehend what was happening, time standing still until McDowell returned.

"All right," she said. "It appears these two have no connection to Riley. They're nineteen and seventeen from Escondido. They search social media for posts from people going on vacation then case their property and break in. They trashed this place, stole items and sold them. Nothing to do with Riley and Caleb."

"Where is she?" Grace said, her voice weak.

"Listen, Grace," McDowell said. "We have other leads here and in Nevada. I know this is difficult. Get some rest, hold tight."

"Hold tight?" Grace spat back at McDowell. "Why didn't you tell me about this when we were in Nevada? I thought you were a good person, Michelle—I thought you understood!"

McDowell had no words that would ease Grace's pain.

"Thank you," John said. "We'll be at our house. You have the address, you have our numbers."

"We do," McDowell said. Then, before leaving: "Don't lose hope."

As John, Grace, Blake and Sherry started back to Sherry's car, the media emerged. Microphones and cameras bloomed around them.

"Mrs. Jarrett, Adam Vedoe, Top Story News." His voice was urgent, excited. "Obviously police did not find your missing daughter. Can you share your thoughts at this time?"

"I want to find Riley. That's my only thought," Grace said.

"We understand the reward fund for information has now surpassed thirty thousand dollars—will that help?" another reporter asked.

"Anything will help," John said.

"If Riley or Caleb Clarke or anyone with information is watching this report, what do you want them to know?" Vedoe asked.

Grace stopped and looked into all the cameras.

"Riley, we love you. Please come home or call me. Caleb, please, if you are with her, please bring her home. Please—" Grace gasped then broke into huge sobs. "Please, please, I need you home."

Sixty-Four

Mission Hills, San Diego, California

It was a somber drive across the city to Grace and John's house. Along the way, Sherry stopped at Ralphs to get a few groceries for the family before they reached Mission Hills just north of downtown.

They lived in an upper middle-class neighborhood of beautiful homes with compact landscaped yards and vibrant gardens. Their two-story stucco house with the red tile roof was on a quiet street lined with Mexican fan and queen palms. The For Sale sign stood like a sentry on the front lawn, pulling Grace back through time.

Can we really afford to buy it? she'd said to Tim.

Can we afford not to? He'd smiled.

We were so happy here.

As Sherry parked in the driveway, Grace took stock, thinking how her dream home was now a mausoleum for a life she once lived.

"You all right?" John said.

"You know what this all means now?" Grace said. "If Riley's not here in San Diego, then Rykhirt—"

"Don't think about that now," John said. "We don't know."

"But, John…" Grace's voice broke.

"McDowell said they have other leads. We have to be strong."

Grace said nothing, tears rolling down her face.

Everyone went inside. Sherry got Grace comfortable in the family room. John and Blake got their bags and groceries while Sherry made tea and brought her half an egg salad sandwich, Grace's favorite.

Grace didn't touch the tea or the sandwich.

"You need to eat and get some rest," Sherry said.

Grace stared out the window with its view of the city and the planes lifting off and landing at San Diego International. "I should never have left her in the RV."

"Stop beating yourself up."

"It was a mistake to leave Nevada."

"Don't do this. You followed your heart. You're here. Get some rest. Stay positive. We're going to find her."

"You think so?"

"I do. Have some tea. Eat."

Grace looked at Sherry. "How's your aunt?"

"The same," Sherry said.

"You don't have to stay. I'll be okay with John and Blake."

"I don't mind, really."

"No, go. You've done so much for us." Grace hugged Sherry hard and for a long moment. "Thank you for being with me, for driving us, for everything. You and Jazmin have been my rocks."

"All right, I'll get going. I'll water my plants, but I'll be back soon and in the meantime I'm only a call away."

"Thank you."

"It's going to be okay, you'll see."

After Sherry left, Grace joined John and Blake in the kitchen. They were on the phone with neighbors and well-wishers when the doorbell rang. It was Blake's friend Arlen Dix.

"I'm going out for a bit with Arlen," Blake said.

Grace went to him. "I'd be more comfortable if you stayed here with us. Have Arlen come in."

Blake looked to his dad. "I need a break from everything," he said. "We're just going to drive down to the 7-Eleven for a Slurpee."

"Which one?" Grace asked.

"The one on Midway, I guess. Why?"

John and Blake turned to Grace for understanding. A second passed before she hugged Blake and kissed his cheek.

"Promise not to be out for long, and answer us the second we text you."

"I promise, Grace."

After Blake left, John went to his study and Grace retreated upstairs.

John closed the door to his home office then locked it.

He went to a closet, rummaged around for his backup laptop. He went to his desk and logged on, relieved that all the utilities and electricity were still switched on.

He started to call Cynthia Litchfield in Pittsburgh but aborted it. It wouldn't help. He was convinced that the thread holding his job was unraveling.

John then went to the bookshelf, took up a ceramic owl bookend. He unscrewed the owl's head and gave it a tap. A mini USB flash drive rattled from it into his palm. He inserted the drive into the laptop's port. It loaded, and he began searching backup copies he'd made of the family finances, loans and debt load as he considered the new issue of possibly paying the replacement cost for the RV. The figures staring back at him were frightening.

Then he went to the balances of his offshore investments. The grim numbers hadn't changed.

He looked at other debts he was facing, and his stomach twisted. He needed the higher salary and signing bonus of the Pittsburgh job.

He went online and clicked on the reward fund for information on Riley's disappearance. It was now $37,487.

Then he looked at the family insurance policies. He went to the one for Riley. He scrolled through the death benefit, landing on the amount that would be paid...*lightning, waves and wind raged...he was staring at the check the insurance agent had placed on his kitchen table...*

No.

John closed all the folders and dropped his face into his hands.

Blake and Arlen Dix drove in Arlen's Honda Civic, down from Mission Hills, under the freeway, to a 7-Eleven near the airport.

It was in a strip mall that included a coin laundry, a tattoo parlor, a Mexican food outlet and a place offering rush passport service.

"It really sucks about Riley," Arlen said. "You think you'll find her?"

Blake said nothing.

Inside, Arlen got a Wild Cherry Slurpee. Blake got Mountain Dew and a burner phone.

Outside in the lot they leaned against the car. Arlen worked on his Slurpee while Blake unpackaged his burner phone.

"Why d'you need a burner?" Arlen said.

Blake didn't answer.

"You know, buddy—" Arlen sucked on his Slurpee "—cops are coming to my house later today."

Blake shot Arlen a look. "What?"

"Detectives from Las Vegas want to ask me about the party."

"What about it?"

Arlen shrugged and shook his head. "But word's getting around. I heard they want to talk to Todd, Breana, Zeke and Samantha, maybe others, too."

Blake said nothing.

"I never expected to see you again," Arlen said. "With you moving away and all, then I saw the news on Riley."

Blake was quiet.

"Hey, you called me. I thought you wanted to talk? I thought you were going to pay me the two hundred you owe me."

"You'll get what I owe you."

"What I want to know," Arlen said, "is what's your deal with those two guys?"

Blake shot Arlen a look. "What guys?"

"The two guys I saw you with at the party. Who were they?"

"They were nobody."

"Musta been somebody. I saw you talking in the corner with them."

"So? We talked about sights to see driving across the country."

"Whatever." Arlen shrugged before his Slurpee splattered like blood on the pavement as it slipped from his hand. "Aw crap!"

"Don't sweat it." Blake pulled money from his

pocket. "Go back and get another drink. Here's forty of what I owe you, too."

Arlen looked at the bills. "Really?"

"Sure."

Arlen put his hand on Blake's shoulder. "Listen. It's rough. I know. But you're gonna find her." He went inside.

Blake walked a short distance away, scanning all the cars and people at the strip mall. *Are they watching me?* Seeing nothing suspicious, he called the forbidden number. This time his call was answered after three rings. "It's Blake."

Within seconds his male contact said: "Why do you call?"

"Do you have her?"

A long moment passed.

"If you have her," Blake said, "let her go, I'm begging you. None of this is her fault, or my fault. I'm working on a plan and I just need some time."

There was no response.

"Do you have her?"

"You're running out of time."

"Wait, I figured a way we can work this out—"

The line went dead.

A jetliner whined overhead. Blake turned to Arlen, who'd returned.

"You okay, Blake? You look kinda messed up."

"I need your help with something deadly serious."

Arlen sucked on his Slurpee. "Sure. Whatever."

* * *

Grace stood in the doorway of Riley's room, her heart aching. The air held the fruity floral hint of her perfume and shampoo. Lingering, the way Tim's cologne did in the weeks after his death.

Riley had been at a sleepover that night. Grace surveyed Riley's bed with the chunky knit blanket, the bright sheets and pillows; the rattan furniture, her desk which was also her vanity. There was her bookshelf holding a few classic titles and keepsakes, like the memorial shoulder patch the girls on Tim's soccer team wore on their jerseys, honoring him after his death: "CT Forever" in a heart, for their beloved Coach Tim.

And there were Riley's treasured photos of her friends and Tim, taking Grace back to days and nights of overwhelming grief spent in this room, holding Riley on this bed.

I miss Dad so much. I want our old life back.

Grace looked at Riley's framed photos of Tim, touching her finger to his face; such a good father and husband. A good man.

Riley also had pictures of her and Caleb, of course, but none of John and Blake. It saddened Grace because they were fortunate to have them in their lives, and she hoped Riley would come to accept them.

Grace glanced out the window. She was also grateful for their friends, especially Jazmin and Sherry. Sherry was so thoughtful, giving Riley that bracelet. But why didn't Riley mention to her that Sherry had one, too?

Probably because she was angry with Grace over her breakup with Caleb and the move. She hadn't exactly confided much to her in recent weeks.

And there was Jazmin, always going above and beyond, remaining in the desert to keep searching.

Grace picked up Riley's old soccer team photo with all the girls. Tim with his hands on Riley's shoulders, and near them, Cleo with her dad, Miguel. He was a good father, too.

Miguel and Jazmin's recent separation broke Grace's heart. And she was puzzled by what Jazmin had said to her the other night in the desert about her mother's death.

...you took something from me. Something that was mine...some days I hated you for it...

What did Jazmin mean by that? Was it really about me being with her mother before she died?

Grace was at a loss. Who was she kidding? Deep down she feared she knew *exactly* what Jazmin meant, but she couldn't face it.

She set the photo down then looked around the room for answers, the emptiness screaming at her—the truth screaming at her.

Grace closed the door to her bathroom and stepped into the shower. Needles of hot water pricked her skin. Steam clouds rose around her as she again recalled the night Tim died.

Riley had been at Dakota's. Grace was home. Tim never told her he was flying in from Chicago to tell her his news. He'd surprised her.

Grace scrubbed and scrubbed as if trying to wash away her guilt before convulsing with great, racking sobs, shaking so hard she crumpled to the shower floor, gasping in anguish.

She'd sent Tim out for cold medicine, sent him to his death. Only she hadn't had a cold at all.

Sixty-Five

San Diego, California

Late that afternoon, a few miles from Grace's home, Esther Webb was leaving her office downtown at One America Plaza. She stopped in the grand marble lobby, staring at her phone and listening with one earphone, gripped by a dilemma.

"Must be nice, Esther. One more week to retirement," said Fred Jennings as he passed her on his way out.

"It's nice. Thanks, Fred." Webb flashed a smile then returned to her phone.

Riley Jarrett held a deep interest for her. Webb had read every news story, every social media posting and TV news report on the case she could find, including the latest on the false sighting today in Rancho Bernardo.

Add it to all the other reports of Riley being lost in the Nevada desert, a victim of a sex offender; that another San Diego teen with ties to her was missing; that Riley's disappearance may have been related to rumors her family was involved in transporting drugs for a cartel—the factors were mounting, testing Webb's conscience.

Because she knew a secret about the family.

Police need to know, but can I tell them?

Time was ticking down. Webb realized that if Riley Jarrett was not already dead, she soon would be, if what she feared was true.

She looked to the indoor waterfall for an answer, finding it in an incident she'd buried deep in her heart for years.

Webb got back on the elevator, pressed the button for her office floor.

As it rose, she recalled when she'd started her first job after college, how a young neighbor woman in her apartment building was upset and crying in the hall. It was obvious to Webb that the woman's partner had abused her, but she begged Webb never to report anything. She didn't. A month later, the woman was dead and her husband charged with her murder. Webb was haunted by her failure every day since.

The elevator bell rang. The doors opened to the headquarters of *SoCal SoYou*, where Webb was head of accounting. She had a week left before retirement and with it her access to the company's most sensitive financial and legal records.

Most people had gone home for the day. Webb went to her office, shut the door.

If I don't do this and they find Riley Jarrett dead, I'll never forgive myself.

To strengthen her resolve she replayed on her phone news clips of John Marshall.

"...we're preparing to move to Pittsburgh because of a new opportunity..."

That wasn't true.

Webb made a phone call, and after assurances her name and that of *SoCal SoYou* would remain anonymous, she cued up critical sealed records and sent them to detectives investigating the case.

It didn't matter that *SoCal SoYou* had to remain scandal-free in advance of an upcoming IPO to take the company public. The police needed to know the truth about John Marshall.

Sixty-Six

San Diego, California

Breana Chandler touched her fingertip to the tear in the corner of her eye.

McDowell passed Breana a tissue from the box on the table in the living room of her home near Pioneer Park where she and Elsen were interviewing her.

"I wanted to go search for her in Nevada." Breana looked down at the pink cast on her right leg. "But I had this stupid wipeout on my skateboard."

"But you were at the party at Riley's house?" Elsen asked.

"Definitely, but I didn't stay long. Hard to get around and hold your drink." Breana's crutches leaned on the sofa beside her. "Oh my God this is so scary—did that guy on the news really kill her?"

"We don't know that for certain," Elsen said.

"How many days has she been missing now?"

"Four," McDowell said.

"And now Caleb's missing, too."

Elsen and McDowell each finished the last of the coffee Breana's mother had made them before closing the room's French doors and leaving them alone.

"Breana, going back—" Elsen held his notebook open, pen in hand "—do you recall anything from the party, or in the time leading up to Riley leaving in the RV with her family, anything that might be related to her being missing?"

"I saw her breaking up with Caleb. That was sad."

"You and others have told us about that. Again, have you seen or heard from her or Caleb?" Elsen asked.

"No."

"Did Riley ever talk about a plan to run away with Caleb?"

"No. I mean she always said she was in love with him and would die without him. She was pretty dramatic sometimes. But you know we never really took that too seriously."

"Is there anything else you can tell us that might help?" Elsen asked.

Breana pressed her lips together and blinked, debating with herself.

"Is there something?" McDowell said.

"Ri told me this thing about Blake."

Elsen and McDowell traded a subtle glance. "What was that?" McDowell said.

Breana puffed her cheeks and let out air. "I don't know. I don't know if I should tell you, if it's even important."

McDowell touched Breana's knee. "Tell us and we can decide."

"Do you, like, protect sources, keep things private?"

"We do. Tell us what you know, we'll take it from there," McDowell said.

Breana rubbed the tops of her legs. "Ri told me she found out Blake gambled online. A lot. And he lost a ton and ran up a big debt. Like monstrous."

"Who did he owe and how much?" Elsen said.

"I don't know. That's all she said. She was scared when she told me. She said Blake said she better be quiet about it because if anybody found out it could be dangerous, but that he had it all under control."

"Why would she tell you this?" McDowell said.

"She was really upset about moving and being forced to break up with Caleb, all while her folks thought Blake was an angel. Moment of weakness, I guess. She was pretty mad."

"When did Riley tell you this?"

"A couple of weeks before they left."

"Did you ever see him gambling?"

Breana shook her head.

"Did you ever talk to Blake about it?"

"God, no."

"Who else knows? Do Riley's parents know?"

"No, I don't think anyone knows. You can't tell anyone I told you. Please."

"We'll keep it confidential," Elsen said. "Breana, why didn't you tell police this when you first heard Riley was missing?"

"I was confused, afraid, you know? I thought maybe she ran away, that it was all a Caleb thing. She kept saying he was the love of her life. I promised to keep her secret but now…you have to swear you won't tell her I told you, please!"

"Just leave it with us," McDowell said.

The detectives closed their notebooks, thanking her as they stood to leave.

"It'd be cool if you guys signed my cast," Breana said.

Before starting the engine of their rental car, McDowell paused.

The sun had set. It had been a long day since their early-morning flight from Las Vegas. After the dead-end lead in Rancho Bernardo, they'd traveled throughout Mission Hills, North Park and Hillcrest interviewing people from the party list. None had provided them anything new until Breana Chandler.

"Blake had gambling debts," McDowell said, turning to Elsen. "Could be a debt-kidnap thing?"

"It's definitely another lead to chase down." Elsen shook his head. "This investigation is like peeling an onion. We need to reinterview Blake."

McDowell looked at her phone. "Next we got Blake's friend Zeke Mosk. You up for one more or do you want to check in to the hotel? We've still got the tip line to sort through."

"Let's do one more."

* * *

Zeke Mosk lived with his mother in an apartment complex in Montecito Point. The detectives went to the balcony, interviewing him above the lights of the community ten stories below.

Zeke wore a tattered Chargers ball cap, his arms laced with tattoos. He sipped an energy drink while answering their questions.

"I knew Blake was a player," Zeke said. "He was always up and down. I didn't know if he owed anybody, or how he kept all his activities from his folks. I think he got credit cards without them knowing. He's good at that stuff. Very skilled dude."

"And you were at the party?" Elsen said.

"Yeah, a lot of people were there. Blake and his dad were giving tours inside the RV. It was cool."

"You notice anything unusual at all?"

"Well, there were these two guys, strangers, a little older. I think they arrived late," Zeke said. "Arlen and I thought they were college guys, or friends of the parents, but they were hanging around Blake."

"You get names, anybody know them?" Elsen asked.

"No, but later the weirdest thing happened. The party ended. I left. I was a bit loaded, and I forgot my phone at Blake's house. When I went back for it everybody was gone, but Blake was in the driveway standing by the RV with one of the guys. I think Blake was kinda shocked to see me because one of the other guys was on his back on the ground under the RV, looking at it with his flashlight, like a mechanic or something."

"Where exactly under it?" Elsen said.

"Oh man." Zeke crossed his arms on his chest. "The back, definitely the rear."

"What was he doing there?"

"I don't know."

"You're sure you saw him under the RV?" Elsen said.

"Well, I was drunk. But I'm pretty sure."

"How did the strangers react to you?"

"Oh, well, like nothing. They were quiet and I just said great party, cool RV. Then Blake came out with my phone and put his arm around me and says something like those guys are thinking about renting an RV too, and I said that's cool and went home."

"Gambling and guys acting suspiciously under the RV," McDowell said from behind the wheel as she followed the GPS to the DoubleTree downtown.

"An interesting picture's emerging." Elsen watched the lights flow by.

"But does it tie in to Riley?" McDowell kept her eyes on the traffic.

"Deeper layers of the onion," Elsen said.

After checking in, dropping their bags in their rooms and making quick personal calls to Las Vegas, they went down to the hotel's restaurant.

It was nearly empty. They got a table in a far corner where McDowell ordered a hamburger, Elsen a club sandwich. They'd brought tablets and notebooks. They were making notes and discussing leads when McDowell's phone rang.

"McDowell."

"Emery Moore. I've got something new for you guys on John Marshall. Sending you both some documents now."

"It's Moore," McDowell said to Elsen as her tablet and Elsen's pinged with a notification. Back on her phone: "Got them, Emery, thanks. Anything on the search for Caleb Clarke? Or Riley?"

"Still looking. I've booked an interview room for you guys for tomorrow at our place," Moore said. "I figure after reading this, you're going to want it. Oh, and Denny Winslow got back to me. He'll come in tomorrow to talk to you about the drowning case of Marshall's wife and daughter. You set it up. I'll send you his number."

"Thanks."

The documents included a confidential, sealed nondisclosure contract between John Marshall and his former employer, *SoCal SoYou*. The other records outlined Marshall's admissions and details of his actions.

Reading through it all, McDowell bit her bottom lip knowing they wouldn't have gotten these records without a tip to generate a warrant. She lifted her head to Elsen for his reaction.

"Well," he said after reading and finishing off

the last quarter of his sandwich. "We've got a tangle of leads pointing in all directions."

"I'll call John Marshall," McDowell said, "to set up interviews with him and Blake tomorrow at San Diego police headquarters. We'll talk to Winslow first, though."

A degree of sadness rippled over Elsen as he paged through his tablet, stopping at a picture of Riley Jarrett.

"What is it, Dan?"

"I'm wondering if we haven't already lost this one, Michelle."

"What do you mean?"

"Looking at the evidence and thinking, is it Rykhirt all along? Is she dead, like the Garcia girl, or is it something entirely different that we missed, something right in front of us?"

DAY 5

Sixty-Seven

San Diego, California

The next morning McDowell and Elsen met Denny Winslow in the coffee shop at San Diego police headquarters.

With his mustache blending into his stubbled, tanned face and hair spiraling every which way, McDowell pegged him for a guy who lived at the beach. After the initial hellos and getting of coffee, Winslow slid on his glasses and got down to business.

"After Emery called I pulled together some notes for you." Winslow scrolled through his phone. "So the Marshalls go out in the bay near Point Loma when the storm hits them and their boat capsizes. They go in the water. Lana and Courtney Marshall drown. Coast Guard and Harbor Police deploy, recover the bodies." Winslow tapped his screen. "Harbor Police bring us in because of a tip about John having large policies on his family and financial problems. The medical examiner rules the cause to be accidental drowning but tells me both victims had bruising to the upper body."

"Bruising?" Elsen said. "That raises a flag."

"It did. But the ME says that while the bruises could've been blunt trauma, they were consistent with injuries both victims might have sustained being slammed against the boat in the storm, trying to hang on."

Winslow said that after investigating no evidence of a crime could be found. The case was closed and insurance was paid to Marshall.

"I'll give you all the notes I have and my insurance association contact who I worked with on the Marshall case."

"Thanks, Denny."

"You know," Winslow said. "We can always reopen the drowning investigation if there was reason."

"Is there reason?" McDowell said.

"Well, I learned this morning from my insurance guy that after John Marshall remarried, he took out policies on Grace and Riley Jarrett with even larger death benefits than those for his first wife and daughter."

The investigators took a moment absorbing that information.

"Something you guys should bear in mind when you talk to John and his son today," Winslow said.

"In fact, I suggested to Emery what room you should use for John."

"Why?"

"To gauge his reaction."

Sixty-Eight

San Diego, California

The air in the room was cold with a trace of disinfectant. Not much bigger than a jail cell, it had a single table with two chairs on one side, and one chair on the other.

McDowell motioned for John to take the single chair. Elsen closed the windowless door and they sat across from him. His chair was bolted to the floor and had a cuff bar, but he wasn't handcuffed.

John knew this room. He'd been here before when he was questioned about Lana's and Courtney's deaths.

Why bring me to this room?

"Are you going to be okay, John?" McDowell said.

He swallowed. "Did you find Riley? Did you find Caleb? Have you got something?"

"Not yet," Elsen said. "But before we go on we have to remind you that you're still under Miranda and our conversation is being recorded."

John's jaw tightened. "Am I under arrest?"

"No. We need to clear up a few things," Elsen said.

"What things?"

McDowell consulted her tablet. "John, you told us the reason you're leaving San Diego is because of a new opportunity, a better job with a bigger company in Pittsburgh."

"Yes, so?"

"But you misled us," Elsen said. "The fact is you're fleeing San Diego. You were fired from *SoCal SoYou* because over several years you had siphoned nearly a hundred thousand dollars from corporate accounts into your own."

All the blood drained from John's face.

"We have records and we've made calls to executives, John," McDowell said. "Wanting to avoid negative publicity because of an upcoming stock offering, they didn't charge you. Instead, you were fired under a secret contract you signed binding you to repay the full amount or face legal action. And they provided you with a carefully worded but positive letter of reference. Isn't that true, John?"

He ran his hand through his hair.

"The records indicate you were facing serious personal financial stress as the cause for the embezzlement," Elsen said.

John said nothing.

"Look where you are, John," Elsen said. "Look at your tragic history. We know what you do when you're under financial stress."

John looked at Elsen.

"You get desperate. You take risks, don't you? Because it comes down to a matter of survival for you, doesn't it?"

"Are you involved in Riley's disappearance for financial gain?" McDowell said.

John's eyes filled with tears.

"Because the way we see it," Elsen said, "you left San Diego because of financial problems and you needed to do something about it, didn't you?"

John's knee started bouncing in his chair.

"John," McDowell said, "is there something you want to tell us? Because if you want to cooperate, now's the time."

The stark white walls seemed to be closing in on John, and he squeezed his eyes shut.

Sixty-Nine

San Diego, California

John took a deep, quaking breath.

Elsen tilted his head, assessing him. McDowell's brow wrinkled with concern while they waited. Then John responded to what they had uncovered.

"I don't see what this has to do with Riley. My God, you should be—"

"Stop right there," Elsen said. "You were facing a large debt load before your wife and your daughter were killed. Correct?"

John said nothing.

Elsen continued. "The medical examiner said there was bruising on their bodies but could not say conclusively if the injuries were a result of blunt trauma before they went into the water, or from being slammed against the overturned boat."

John blinked.

"Your insurance policies on Lana, Courtney and your boat resulted in you receiving a total of eight hundred and fifty thousand dollars, but you lost much of it through risky investments, didn't you?"

Tears rolled down John's face.

"When you remarried," Elsen said, "you took out life insurance policies on Grace and Riley. In the event of Riley's death, you'll receive one point five million dollars."

John raised his face to the ceiling.

"Before you left San Diego," Elsen said, "you were facing huge financial stress and now Riley's missing and could be dead."

"You told us that after your family visited Las Vegas, you'd planned to stop at the Grand Canyon," McDowell said.

"Were you planning to have an accident there too, John?" Elsen said. "A tragic fall, for example? It could work out for you financially, like the last time. Couldn't it, John?"

Elsen's chair scraped as he leaned closer to John. "Are you involved in Riley's disappearance?"

Biting his bottom lip, John shook his head, the veins in his neck pulsing under his skin. "Why're you doing this? What about Rykhirt, the guy you believe abducted Riley? What about Caleb? Where is he? Why're you wasting time with these ridiculous theories?"

Elsen didn't flinch. "We're not ruling out anything. We're pursuing everything and everybody. Do you know how many times in an investigation something wild emerges then police are criticized for having missed it?"

John said nothing.

"You want us to find Riley, don't you, John?"

"You know the answer."

"Don't you want us to exhaust every avenue, leave no stone unturned in our effort to find Riley?"

"Yes, but within reason."

"Within reason?" Elsen nodded. "And who gets to decide what's within reason? You? That would be like you investigating yourself, wouldn't it?"

John didn't respond.

"Why did you lie to us, John?" McDowell asked.

"Were you planning for Grace and Riley to have an accident?" Elsen said. "The same way your first wife and daughter did? Were you planning to stage a ransom scam? Did you transport drugs? Is Blake involved? What did you do, John?"

John shook his head.

"We're going to hold you here awhile," Elsen said.

"On what grounds?"

"Possible charges for obstructing our investigation."

"This is wrong!" John covered his face with his hands, his mind speeding back to that night… *the wind, the rain, the ocean rising and falling as he cries into the dark: Hang on! God, please, hang on!*

Seventy

Nevada

Earlier that morning, with cables running from their oversize laptops to the security camera system of the Silver Sagebrush, the experts pressed on.

After Riley Jarrett had disappeared from the complex, Travis Quinn, the surveillance chief, and Cliff Lawton, a digital forensic specialist with the Las Vegas police, had been working on potential remedies to recover lost footage.

The problem appeared to have happened when Sagebrush people were updating the software at the same time they'd had a system crash. Quinn was unsure if it was a signal strength, or corruption issue, but most Sagebrush cameras were not communicating correctly. Most surveillance points had not been storing recordings.

Again and again they checked the power supply, the hardware setup and internet connectivity. They fault-checked the wiring of the entire system to determine why there was a loss during file transfer, and they looked at possible hard drive corruption. They ran various recovery programs, all without success.

Their fear was that the lost footage, which should have been archived, had been deleted. Quinn and Lawton knew that deleted files could be recovered, but if those files were overwritten and erased, then they were gone. Still, if the hard drive was not completely overwritten, then there was a slim chance they could recover footage.

This morning, Lawton proposed trying new advanced recovery software that the Las Vegas police had obtained.

"This might be our Hail Mary pass," Lawton said, referring to a last chance desperation play in football.

It took several minutes to run the recovery software before Quinn began to search for the files. He entered the same commands that had been fruitless in the past, while he and Lawton eyed the monitors. One of them came to life, then another.

"What the—?" Quinn said. "I don't believe it!"

Static-filled images appeared of people in the main lobby of the Sagebrush. Picture clarity increased and diminished, as if filtered through a snowstorm. But in patches of clarity they saw a teenage girl wearing a shirt with the stylized *Friends* logo from the TV show. The sequence showed a white man walking right up to the girl.

"That's Riley and Rykhirt," Quinn said.

The recording continued but it was indistinct.

"We've never seen this stuff before," Lawton said. "It's working. We'll have to clean it up. That'll take time. But finally we're on the right track."

"Good, good, now we'll see what really happened," Quinn said.

Seventy-One

San Diego, California

Blake's heart was beating faster. He'd never been to San Diego police headquarters and now he was on the fourth floor, sitting in a sofa chair in a carpeted room lit with lamps. It was a soft interview room used mostly for assault victims or witnesses to convey that they were safe and hadn't done anything wrong. McDowell and Elsen were in the two sofa chairs across from him.

Blake took stock of the room, the vinyl bunched in the spot where his fingers gripped the arms of his chair. The detectives noticed.

"Did you find Riley?" Blake asked. "Why do you want to talk to me?"

"No, we still haven't located her," McDowell said, "but we need your help following up on some things. Are you comfortable?"

Blake shrugged.

"We have to inform you that you're still under

Miranda and our conversation is being recorded," Elsen said.

"Are you arresting me or something? Do I need a lawyer?"

"You're not under arrest and you are not charged with anything," McDowell said. "We need to clarify a few things."

"Okay." Blake licked his lips.

A long moment passed with the detectives staring at Blake until he grew uneasy, his eyes darting between them before Elsen spoke.

"We understand that you gamble online." Another silence passed then Elsen continued. "And that you may have run up a significant debt."

Blake's eyes widened slightly and his face whitened.

"And," Elsen said, "on the night of the party you were seen with two people. One of them was looking under the RV in the same area where our dog detected the presence of narcotics."

Blake's mouth opened slightly.

"We need the truth, Blake," McDowell said.

He was silent, staring but seeing nothing. Then tiny beads of sweat formed on his forehead.

"Blake, are you in any way involved in Riley's disappearance?" McDowell asked.

His shoulders dropped. The moment he'd dreaded had come and his chin crumpled. "Yes."

Seventy-Two

San Diego, California

McDowell leaned closer to Blake. She and Elsen stared at him.

"You're involved in Riley's disappearance?" Elsen said.

"I think I am."

"You *think*?" Elsen said. "Where is she?"

"I don't know."

"Don't give us any BS. How are you involved?" Elsen said.

His lips and chin trembling, Blake stared into space. "When my mom and Courtney drowned, I couldn't deal with it. It was like, why them and not me? You know?" His voice quavered. "I didn't care about anything. I started gambling because it was the only time I felt anything."

"Did your father know?" McDowell asked.

"No, I set up online bank accounts, got debit and credit cards. There are ways around security. The online gambling I did wasn't really legal. It was on the dark web. I was up and down with winnings. But I always had it under control. I just couldn't stop."

"You were addicted?" McDowell said.

"Pretty much. Then dad married Grace and about a month before our trip, I made bigger bets, had bigger losses. I couldn't get ahead of it. One day when I went to the bathroom I left my computer on. That's when Riley saw what I was doing, how much I was losing."

"What did you do?" McDowell asked.

"I freaked out. I said that if she ever told anyone we'd be in serious trouble because it was around that time that I learned that the gambling site I used was a front operated by drug cartels."

"How much did you owe?" Elsen asked.

"Twenty-two thousand dollars."

"What did you do?" Elsen asked.

"I couldn't go to dad for the money, or Grace. I panicked. I told the people I owed that I needed time to pay. I was thinking I could sell drugs to other kids to get the money. I knew a dealer at school. I called him but he was cold to the idea. He didn't trust me. Then two men in a car, strangers, stopped me on the street. They knew everything about my debt. They said that if I didn't pay, our house might burn down and my family might get hurt."

"What did you do?" McDowell asked.

"I begged them to give me time. I said that we were moving, taking an RV trip to Pittsburgh.

They were suddenly interested in the trip, asked me about the RV then made me a deal."

"What sort of deal?" Elsen said.

"My debt would be erased if they could ship drugs across the country concealed in our RV. All I had to do was call a number when we got to Pittsburgh. They'd do the rest. I had no choice. They secured bundles underneath."

"What happened to them?"

"I don't know. I think they came loose when we crashed and somebody found them in the wreckage in the chaos. A lot of people pulled over, so much was going on."

A moment passed.

"What else do you know about these drug people and this deal?" Elsen asked.

"I think the drugs were part of a large shipment that came into the US through a tunnel from Mexico. They'd had a problem with some distributors. They said that an American family in an RV would draw no suspicions moving drugs from California to the east."

"We're going to need names from you and a statement," Elsen said.

"I have no idea who they are. I only know some first names and nicknames."

"That's a start."

"How did you communicate?" McDowell asked. "You talked to them yesterday?"

Blake handed her his burner phone. "They gave

me a number to memorize and told me to use burners."

McDowell passed the phone to Elsen. "Did they give you proof they had Riley?" she asked.

"No."

"Did they send photos, put her on the phone?" she asked.

"No."

"Did they make a ransom call?"

"Not yet. But they told me that they're not finished with me. I was thinking of giving a friend a tip so they would get Riley's reward fund, then I could take twenty-two to pay my debt."

The detectives looked at him.

"Don't you see?" Blake said. "We never shipped their drugs! They disappeared in the crash! I still owe them! They're pissed off and they have Riley!"

Seventy-Three

San Diego, California

Grace paced near the window in her kitchen, one hand holding her forehead while she stared at her phone. Her reddened eyes had dark circles under them. She hadn't slept. Her insides had been twisted tighter ever since John and Blake had left for police headquarters earlier.

"It's going to be okay." Sherry touched her shoulder. "Sit down, I'll make you something."

Grace stood still. Worry lines were carved deep into her face before she managed the beginnings of a smile. "Thank you for coming. I'd be alone, lost without you."

"I'm glad you called me. Don't worry. We're going to find her."

"Why're McDowell and Elsen talking to John and Blake again?" Grace raised her phone. "John hasn't got back to me, not a single word. I don't know what's going on."

"Maybe he doesn't have access to his phone.

You know, maybe they had to give them to security? Sit down and take a breath."

"I'm going out of my mind. I believed with all my heart that they'd found her in Rancho Bernardo yesterday, I mean with Caleb missing, too. But now I'm just—just—" Her eyes went around the room. "And they're still searching in Nevada. Is she here? Is she there? Do police know something they're not telling me?"

"You've got to sit down and breathe."

"I prayed last night. I prayed that she really ran off with Caleb because if she did, it means she's alive and we can get her back, but if she's not with Caleb—"

"Don't, Grace, you mustn't think like that."

"It means the creep got her, that she didn't get away, and I think of that other girl they found out there last year, and those pictures of Rykhirt, that monster—" Grace's shoulders shook as she cried.

Sherry got her to sit down then made tea and joined her, both of them looking at nothing in the silence as little by little Grace found some composure.

Rubbing her arms, Grace said, "A karmic wheel has turned. Now I'm paying the price for the things I've done. Things no one knows."

"What're talking about?"

"I'm thinking that if I confess, if I tell someone, it'll help in some way."

"Confess what? You're not making sense."

"It's about Tim, something I've been keeping locked up inside, something I want you to know."

Sherry stared at Grace. "What is it?"

"It's about what happened the night Tim died."

Seventy-Four

Nevada

That morning, some three hundred miles north-east of San Diego, Jazmin Reyna slid her forearm across her moist brow then replaced her sunglasses. Her water bottle swished as she shifted the straps of her backpack so they wouldn't chafe. Then she glanced up at the clouds streaking the sky.

It was the fifth day of Riley's disappearance. Soon after sunrise, volunteers had gathered at the Silver Sky Search and Rescue command post in the Sagebrush parking lot. There were fewer people involved and fewer news cameras now that the focus had shifted to California. But the determination to locate Riley had not waned.

"We won't quit searching until we find her," Warren Taylor had told searchers before teams headed out to their assigned areas earlier.

The fact was, they had done nearly all they could, had searched everywhere—old roads, pathways, forgotten trails and far-reaching outlying areas.

Today Jazmin's search partner was Leland Dysart, a retired lawyer who kept a few yards from her as they rechecked a zone not far from the interstate.

She welcomed a breeze of hot, dry air as they moved across the desert, threading around brush and scrub with the other volunteers in the distance. She looked at the line of poles paralleling the interstate as the highway traffic hummed. It underscored the desolation and the loneliness of the region.

Jazmin missed her daughter, Cleo. She'd wanted to be here helping, but she was with her father visiting his relatives in New York. Jazmin then thought of Riley and the news reports of the false sighting in San Diego. The agony Grace must be feeling.

Pushed by a sudden gust, a fragment of tumbleweed bounced near her and Jazmin's thoughts turned to her own anguish; how she'd lost her mother to the virus in the hospital where she and Grace worked.

I should've been there when she died. Not Grace. It's irrational, I know, but it's like she took something from me.

Then there was Jazmin's marriage and her recent separation from Miguel.

What went wrong with us? We'd been so happy.

But no matter how many ways Jazmin looked at it, she couldn't find the answers. Things between them had deteriorated around the time Tim Jarrett had died. They had all been close. Miguel and Tim had been good friends, coaching the girls' soccer team together. Miguel was devastated by his death. That's when it all started going wrong, with Miguel gradually becoming distant, withdrawn. It lingered like a sickness and when Grace married John, Miguel seemed to be unhappy with Jazmin.

She asked him what was wrong, but he didn't have an answer. She found the courage to suggest they see a marriage counselor, but Miguel refused. That's when he asked for a trial separation.

"Look." Leland pointed his walking stick. "What's that?"

Jazmin followed his direction, spotting the sun glinting on a piece of broken glass. "A bottle, or something?" she said.

Leland moved his stick with short gestures. "No, to the right, at the base of that cholla. Let's go."

As they got closer to the stand of cactus shrub, a patch of bright color flashed. Aquamarine.

Wedged against the plant was a sneaker; canvas mesh, laceless, white sole. A girl's right sneaker.

"Oh my God," Jazmin said. "It's Riley's other shoe."

Seventy-Five

"The number you have reached is not in service…"

Elsen stroked his chin while staring at his phone, which was on speaker. He'd dialed the only number that was in Blake's burner phone; the one for his drug contact.

"No surprise there," McDowell said.

"We know it's nearly impossible to get something from a burner, but we can pass this to forensic people," Elsen said.

McDowell set two coffees on the table in the empty meeting room Moore had found for them. It was down the hall from where they'd questioned John and Blake Marshall.

They'd requested John and Blake remain at San Diego police headquarters, indicating they would continue interviewing them. The detectives were aware they had no grounds to hold them. Not yet. They wanted to nail down every possible angle they could while they were in San Diego.

"All right." McDowell took a hit of coffee, sighed then began working on her tablet. "Where do we go from here?"

"We step back," Elsen said. "We look at everything; follow the strongest evidence we have. So far that's Rykhirt. We have him stalking the family in Fontana. We can place him with Riley at the Sagebrush. We have his sketch, his photos of her on his devices."

"It's strong."

"But it's still circumstantial. We couldn't get any trace, any latents from her sneaker," Elsen said. "Then we have Blake telling us the story about his gambling debt and the drugs. But we have no strong evidence so far. No ransom call, nothing giving us a clear connection to Riley but his story. All the video recordings we have show Riley with Rykhirt—no one else. We've got this burner number from Blake, which dead-ends. Some witnesses, but no names."

"We could charge him with conspiracy to traffic based on his admission and the dog," McDowell said.

"But is it strong enough to stick?"

"Maybe reasonable suspicion, maybe smuggling, just to hold him?"

"Maybe," Elsen said. "We'll talk to Blake again, press him for more information leading to Riley. We can't let his story go. We can bring in San Diego Narcotics to pursue this with the FBI and other agencies."

"And then we've got John."

"Again, no hard evidence. A lot of disturbing factors, deaths, embezzlement, insurance, all troubling dots, but it would be a stretch to connect them to a crime against Riley at this stage."

"We've got Caleb, and Riley," McDowell said. "Their texts on her phone, he's missing, one of the family cars is missing, statements from their friends."

"The runaway thing is maybe the strongest scenario with them," Elsen said.

"We've got a lot of possibilities," she said, "but nothing pointing us one way conclusively. Cards on the table: I think she ran off with Caleb."

"To me, it all points to Rykhirt," Elsen said then thought for a moment. "We have to guard against making our case fit our ideas of what we believe happened. The evidence has to tell us that."

McDowell's phone rang and she answered. It was Jackson at the command post. "Hey, Lieutenant."

"We found Riley Jarrett's other shoe."

"What, really?"

Elsen's tablet pinged with a notification, then McDowell's.

"I've just sent you photos," Jackson said.

"They found her other shoe," McDowell said to Elsen, who was already scrolling through the pictures. Crisp shots of a brilliant aquamarine sneaker in the desert brush.

"We're sure it's hers?" McDowell asked as she put her phone on speaker.

"The color, size and style all match. This is a right shoe. We already have the left. We've got the area sealed, and Crime Scene is on the way to process it."

"It's Elsen, Lieutenant. Did you find anything else at the scene?"

"Nothing so far."

"Who found it and where?"

"Two volunteers. Leland Dysart, a retired lawyer from Las Vegas, and Jazmin Reyna, a nurse and friend of Grace Jarrett's from San Diego. Hold on." Radio dispatches crackled in the background. "It was on the same side of the interstate as the first sneaker, about three hundred yards north and about forty yards from the paved shoulder." More dispatches were heard. "Gotta go. We'll keep you posted."

"Thanks, Lieutenant." McDowell ended the call.

Elsen folded his arms in front of his chest, leaned back in his chair, submerged in thought.

"This points to Rykhirt," McDowell said.

Elsen stuck out his bottom lip and shook his head slightly.

"What?" McDowell said.

"This shoe thing is strange to me."

"Maybe they were tossed from a car? Maybe he changed her appearance on the way to Vegas?"

"I can't put my finger on it, but something about this new discovery seems a little off."

Seventy-Six

Death Valley Road, California

The two-lane highway cut across the stretch of flat, empty desert for as far as the eye could see before disappearing on the horizon.

Visually stunning, Lynn Lange thought.

She would know. Lange was a news photographer who'd been laid off from the *Los Angeles Times*, yet she remained optimistic about her fading industry. Her brother-in-law was talking her up for a possible job at his paper. Smaller city, but a job's a job.

Until then she was surviving as a freelancer with magazine gigs and shooting stock. This morning she was driving to Shoshone to meet a local historian—that's what he called himself. He was going to take her to an abandoned gold mine where she'd take pictures for a Japanese magazine that paid well.

Lange had just left her motel in Baker where she'd gassed up her RAV4, bought plenty of water and food. The last sign of life she'd seen was a small, low-standing apartment building at the edge of town. Then nothing. Not another vehicle or anything. After a few miles or so, it was like she'd driven into a deserted world.

She took in the desert, the mountains, which she believed were the Silurian Hills, and got thinking about the German, French and British agencies she'd been sending her images to and how they paid pretty decent royalties.

"Look at the fantastic heat shimmer on the road ahead. What do you say we pull over and I shoot some stock?"

Her partner, Mason, a four-year-old German shepherd, barked.

"All right," Lange said, slowing down, easing her SUV to the shoulder, bringing it to a stop and dropping the windows for Mason because with the air conditioner off the interior wouldn't stay cool for long.

"Nobody here but us."

She got out and inventoried the area, loving the barren solitude, the utter silence of it, before she rummaged in her equipment for her camera, lenses and her monopod.

"I'll be quick. Promise," she said. Ready with her gear, Lange moved to the front of the vehicle while assessing the shots she wanted.

Mason barked a different bark this time, but Lange was concentrating on her work.

"Hold your horses, buddy."

Lange put everything together and took a look through the viewfinder when Mason barked again. She knew that one. He had to go.

She groaned. Better deal with it now. She hefted her monopod with her camera and lens attached, went back to the RAV and let him out, leaving the door open for him, thinking she'd give him some water before they pulled out.

"Go do your business but stay off the road. And watch out for snakes."

Snout to the ground Mason explored the fringe of the desert before moving into it, like a reluctant swimmer wading into the ocean.

Lange returned to her position with her camera and concentrated. Clenching one eye, she drew her face to the viewfinder, looking through it, loving how the highway was shimmering in the heat haze, creating illusory puddles in the road, thinking she had some great stuff here.

She ignored Mason's barks. "I'm busy," she said, her face moist now and tight to her camera as she worked lining up a shot.

But now the sound changed to his hunter's bark.

Lange was getting incredible images when she heard soft snapping, like the crunching of dried twigs, then Mason growled.

Lange turned. Mason had gone deeper into the desert by some thirty yards but was poised with his ears pricked, his tail wagging near clumps of sun-dried thistle.

Lange's first thought was a snake or coyote and

she swallowed, chiding herself for not leashing him and walking him out.

"Mason, come here!"

He remained rooted in place, barking, his attention locked on to something.

Lange moved quickly, detaching her camera, setting it in the front seat, tightening her grip on her monopod, preparing to use it as a weapon as she approached her dog, ready to grab his collar.

"Mason, come here!"

He barked as if telling her: *"No, you come here!"*

Lange steeled herself. She got within ten feet of him and froze. The little hairs on the back of her neck stood up. In a heartbeat it came into view... *a hand...arm...a corpse...*

"Jesus!"

A young woman lay on her stomach on the ground, her body bloated, hair laced over her face, bloodied foam leaking from her mouth and nose, the discharge writhing with maggots. She was wearing a T-shirt, her shoeless bloodied feet encrusted with feasting insects.

Seventy-Seven

Death Valley Road, California

Lynn Lange gulped water from her bottle. After calling 9-1-1 it took her a moment to recover from the initial shock of finding a dead body in the desert.

She was acquainted with death. Photographing shootings, fires, riots and a gamut of tragedies and disasters for the *LA Times* had enabled her to detach herself from the fact a young woman was lying a few feet from her.

Lange took a breath, brushed the back of her hand across her mouth.

Okay, maybe I can't shake this off so fast.

She didn't go back for a second look. She pushed the heartbreak to a corner of her mind. Then, driven by professional instinct, she took a few long shots, showing hair, an arm, a light-colored T-shirt blocked by the bush, framing things so that it was clear a body was in the photo.

Then she poured more water into a bowl for

Mason before taking up her own bottle again. Drinking, she heard the sirens approaching. San Bernardino County deputies, fire and paramedics arrived first, followed by a deputy coroner investigator, who introduced herself as Diane Stalling.

It didn't take long for the area to get busy as radios crackled with dispatches.

Deputy Roy McSweeney took Lange's preliminary statement then went over a few points with her.

"So it's just you and your dog, Mason, driving to Shoshone?" He copied down her driver's license, which Lange knew he would run through police databases.

"Yes."

"You stopped to take pictures and your dog went into the desert and found her?"

"Yes."

"All right, we've got an acting detective on the way from Barstow Station. She'll want to talk to you, too. We'd like you to wait here for her."

"Sure. I'll make a call, push my meeting back."

In the time Lange waited, she watched the unfolding of a process she knew well. A wide area around the body was sealed with yellow tape. The ground surrounding it was searched. Stalling suited up, brought her equipment next to the body, photographed the area and the body then examined it, pausing from time to time to wave off the flies. The mood was serene with no one else in sight.

While waiting with Mason at her car, Lange

got out her camera, went to the far side of her car and used the fender to shield her. Before anyone noticed, she quickly photographed investigators bending and crouching over the body beyond the yellow tape. Shooting a scene.

As she finished, Lange caught snatches of conversations among the investigators and overheard radio transmissions.

"…white female…teens…no obvious cause…"

Lange got back into her car, opened her laptop to review her shots, solid death scene images, when she twigged to a transmission spilling from one of the radios.

"…no identity located…missing person case… Las Vegas…call them… San Diego girl missing from Silver Sagebrush truck stop…right…put in a call to alert Metro…"

Something pinged at Lange. She remembered news reports of the missing San Diego girl. Some had raised questions about a link to another case: the murder of a California teen, her body found in Nevada, about an hour from here.

The murdered girl was from Riverside.

Lange's brother-in-law was a reporter with the *Press-Enterprise* in Riverside, where he was trying to get her a job. *This death could be related to the story—this could be the story.*

Lange grappled with her situation. She had exclusive photos of a death that could be tied to both cases. It was terrible, but it was news.

Lange powered up her windows and started her

car to switch on the air conditioner. Then, looking at the spread of her photos on her laptop, she reached for her phone and made a call.

After pressing the number, she noticed a car arrived. It bore the banner of a radio news station on its doors. Someone's been listening to a police scanner, she thought as her call rang three times.

"*Press-Enterprise*, Elliott Downey."

"Hi, Elliott, it's Lynn."

"Hey there, sister-in-law, how's it going? I'm still working on things for you. No news but my fingers are cross—"

"Elliott, listen. You know that story about the missing San Diego, girl? How it may be tied to the Riverside girl who was murdered a while back?"

"Yeah, I've been on it. Riley Jarrett from San Diego. Why?"

"I think they've found her and I've got pictures for your paper."

Seventy-Eight

San Diego, California

"You want to grab more coffee before we talk to Blake again?"

McDowell stood waiting for Elsen's answer while he studied the photos of Riley's shoes.

"What is it?" McDowell said.

Shaking his head without looking away from his screen he said: "Something still doesn't feel right about the shoes."

"Doesn't feel right, how?"

"I can't pinpoint it. I don't know."

"Maybe more coffee would help?"

Elsen thought. "Maybe, yeah." Then his phone rang. It was Lieutenant Holland from Las Vegas. "Elsen."

"Dan, we got a heads-up from San Bernardino. They've got a body outside of Baker. Looks like our missing girl."

Elsen shut his eyes and swore under his breath. He adjusted his grip on his phone then turned to

McDowell. "San Bernardino's got a body, near Baker."

"Oh no."

Elsen put the call on speaker. "Lieutenant, I got Michelle with me. What do we know?"

"They're still processing but they'll work on positive ID," Holland said.

"Okay." Elsen found his pen to take notes.

"The body's in rough shape," Holland said, "they estimate three to five days in the desert. A white female in her teens."

"Cause?"

"Undetermined so far."

"Who made the find?"

"A motorist this morning stopped to take pictures and let her dog out. The dog found it, some forty-five yards on the east side of Death Valley Road, about two to three miles out of Baker. The body was without shoes."

Elsen and McDowell stared at each other.

"The woman who made the find is an ex news photographer," Holland said, "and a radio reporter is on the scene, so this will get out fast."

"Want us to go to Baker?"

"Not yet. San Bernardino's working on ID as fast as they can. Besides, it's their jurisdiction. They'll assume the case now."

"This could be tied to Garcia," Elsen said.

"I know. I've been alerting others, including our Homicide," Holland said. "That's all I've got. I'll get back to you as soon as I have more."

"Thank you, Lieutenant," McDowell said. The call ended, and she sat heavily in the chair next to Elsen. "We'll have to alert the family soon, Dan."

"It's part of the job I hate."

"I know."

Elsen cued up photos of Riley, smiling at them as they absorbed the news. The development was a kick in the teeth. Despite all the evidence, despite the statistical odds, both of them had held on to a flickering hope that they'd find her alive. The family was not picture-perfect. They had suffered tragedies in the past. They had problems, big problems, and then something like this happens.

"Rykhirt," McDowell said. "It was Rykhirt all along."

"Fourteen years old," Elsen said. "He likely killed her within a few hours then drove to Vegas and fantasized."

Before they could even get to the question of notifying the family, McDowell's phone rang. This time it was Lieutenant Jackson from the command post. "We've got a development."

"Is it about the body near Baker?"

"No, Lieutenant Holland just called me on that."

"What is it?"

"We've got video you need to see."

Seventy-Nine

San Diego, California

"All set?" Cliff Lawton, a digital forensic specialist with the Las Vegas police, asked from the Sagebrush.

His voice echoed through the speaker of McDowell's phone at San Diego police headquarters.

After a flurry of calls Lawton and Travis Quinn, the Sagebrush's surveillance chief, had relayed to the detectives a quick summary of their work on recovering the lost security video. They had sent files and were now poised to guide them through what they had. McDowell and Elsen had readied their tablets and phones.

"Good to go," Elsen said.

"We'll start with the original," Lawton said. "Watch your screens."

Footage played of Riley moving through the Silverado convenience store, appearing to be searching for someone before leaving.

"Now we'll go to the citizen video from Margot

Winton, where we pick up Riley with the suspect, Rykhirt, in the lobby," Lawton said.

Winton and her friend appeared, standing before the Statue of Liberty mural. In the left corner of the frame they glimpsed Riley in her white *Friends* T-shirt. Then the recording captured Rykhirt taking photos of Riley before approaching her, talking to her, putting his hand on her shoulder, Riley brushing it away before they vanished from the recording.

"All right, so that was the citizen footage," Lawton said. "Now, we'll run the footage we've just recovered from the security system, picking it up from there. Stand by."

From different angles they saw Riley, appearing worried as Rykhirt talks to her, puts his hand on her shoulder. Riley brushes it away. Then the footage revealed a continuation of actions not previously seen. Rykhirt attempts to touch Riley's arm again as if comforting her, she brushes it away, takes a step back from him and raises her arm, suddenly waving to someone off camera. Rykhirt turns, follows her gaze before Riley walks off, leaving him.

"Stand by," Lawton said.

Footage tracks Riley walking alone from the lobby toward the food court before the footage dissolves into a blizzard.

As for Rykhirt, new angles change back to the main lobby, tracking him, moving alone in the opposite direction to the exit. Alone. Camera angles shift to exterior footage showing Rykhirt leaving the building as he enters the parking lot, alone. Angles shift again, picking up Rykhirt walking alone to his blue Nissan Versa. Angles shift again with Rykhirt getting into his car alone and leaving the complex. Angles shift again showing Rykhirt's Nissan entering the I-15 northbound on-ramp for Las Vegas.

"In this footage we see that Rykhirt did not abduct Riley Jarrett," Lawton said. "He's on the interstate and she's in the food court. The time and date stamp shows they separated."

Elsen and McDowell shook their heads slowly.

"Hold on," Elsen said. "So who was she waving to? Was she waving to someone she recognized?"

"We don't know," Lawton said. "We haven't tracked her inside the food court. We haven't recovered that footage yet. We're working on it."

"What you've done is excellent, critical. Cliff, Travis, thank you," McDowell said.

"We'll get back to you as soon as we have more," Lawton said.

Finished with the call, Elsen tapped his pen on the tabletop and stared at nothing.

"Do you believe this?" McDowell began replaying the new footage.

"It's not Rykhirt," Elsen said, "but not for lack of trying. He followed them from Fontana, stalked her in the Sagebrush and fantasized about her. He was hunting and had every intention of abducting her."

"But he didn't," McDowell said.

Elsen tapped his pen. "So who was she waving to, Michelle?"

"Maybe no one."

"No one?"

"Maybe it was a fake wave, a ruse Riley used to get away from him?"

Elsen stuck out his bottom lip. "Maybe. So, if it's not Rykhirt, then who?"

Eighty

Nevada

Las Vegas Officer Nate Rogan climbed into his marked Ford F-150 pickup at Metro's substation in Jean and headed for the Silver Sagebrush.

As he drove, he chewed on the update concerning Riley Jarrett's case: a body had been found near Baker.

So this is how it ends?

Looking out at the desert and the mountains, he thought, what had it been? Five days since he was alerted to her disappearance. It seemed like a lifetime. It broke his heart.

His Ford roared along the old Las Vegas Boulevard highway. It paralleled I-15 to the east with less than a quarter mile of empty desert between the two roads. Taking in the distant interstate traffic, Rogan thought of Riley, her family and how more pain was coming for them. Maybe it was better they were already home in San Diego for this, rather than out here.

The search was still in full force. But Rogan knew it would end once they received confirmation of the identity from San Bernardino. It's why he was headed to the Sagebrush now. To be there to help dismantle the operation, send everyone home with thanks.

Rogan was about a mile from the Sagebrush when he saw a flash of chrome and glass; a windshield reflecting the sun from a vehicle. But it wasn't on the road, or the shoulder. It was about one hundred yards into the desert. Odd. What was it doing out there? Couldn't be part of the search operations, he thought. They'd scoured that area several times and cleared it within the first few days. Better check it out.

Rogan slowed then left the road, heading for the vehicle, his truck jostling on the uneven terrain, brush scraping against the undercarriage and frame. As he got closer, he saw no markings to indicate if it was a state, county or corporate service vehicle. Then he thought it might be a roller who'd gambled away everything in Las Vegas then, unable to go on, drove out into the desert to end things. Sadly, it happened.

Rogan stopped behind the vehicle. He saw no one near it. It was a newer blue Ford Explorer SUV with a California license plate.

Rogan called in his position and details, requesting his dispatcher run the plate: 2GAT123.

Holding his microphone, he waited, thinking that the tag was familiar. It dawned on Rogan just as his radio crackled "vehicle sought by SDPD, CHP and FBI…missing subject Caleb Clarke…in relation to NCIC number…Riley Jarrett…"

Caleb Clarke? The boyfriend.

Rogan got out. He unclipped his holster and, with his hand on his grip, approached the SUV.

Windows were up. He went to the front passenger door. No one inside. The interior was littered with fast-food wrappers, water bottles, cans of energy drinks. A rumpled sleeping bag and blanket were in the back. No other signs of life.

Rogan turned to the desert, scanning it in every direction.

Seeing nothing, he started back to his truck when he glimpsed a figure about sixty, seventy yards in the distance, sitting on the ground, back to him.

"Caleb!" he called.

No response. No sound but the interstate traffic.

"Caleb Clarke, Las Vegas police!"

No answer.

Rogan kept his hand on the grip of his gun and headed toward the person, seeing only their back and lowered head. They were sitting cross-legged. Rogan couldn't see the person's hands.

As he got closer, Rogan said: "Las Vegas police. Raise your hands so I can see them."

The person didn't respond.

Adjusting his grip on his gun, Rogan stood behind the person. It was clear it was a young white male with his head down and mumbling.

He tried once more. "Are you Caleb Clarke, son?"

Eighty-One

The shrieking of the kettle subsided with the water grumbling to a boil. Sherry looked at Grace from the counter where she made tea. "Talking about Tim's death won't help."

"I need to say what really happened."

"But we know." Sherry softened her voice. "Tim's car slid off the road in a storm that night."

"There's more."

Sherry set their cups, milk and sugar on the table. Then she joined Grace, sitting across from her.

"It started a few months before," Grace said. "I was on the phone with Tim in Chicago when the washer broke, flooding the laundry room. Tim tells me a repair company costs too much. He says to call Miguel over. He's a contractor and friend. He can fix it. I called Miguel. He was so nice. He fixed it but wouldn't accept money, so I baked him an apple pie. Jazmin said he liked apple pies."

"That's it?"

"Miguel came back again, fixed the dishwasher and a leaky faucet in the bathroom. While he worked, I'd pass him tools and we'd talk. One time he asked if I got lonely with Tim working in Chicago." She swallowed. "It was very innocent. I said yes, sometimes I get a little lonely."

"Oh?" Sherry said with a trace of judgment.

"Nothing happened."

Sherry sipped tea. "Good."

"But there was something between us, an attraction."

"He's a good-looking man."

"One day Miguel saw me in the garden and we talked. He said Jazmin and Cleo were away. I said Riley was at a sleepover. Joking how we were both single for the night, I invited him over for wine." Grace stopped, a tear rolled down her face. "We talked, we drank…we kissed."

"Grace, you don't have to do this."

"We ended up in my bedroom." Grace stared at nothing. "It was the night Tim flew home from Chicago, surprising me…"

"Grace."

"We were undressed…but we hadn't started… you know…anything…but that's when I heard Tim downstairs. I panicked, scrubbed my face with cold water, threw on my robe. I had to get Miguel out. So I went downstairs and pretended I was sick with a cold and headache."

"He believed you?"

"He seemed puzzled, confused at first. But I'm

sure I looked the part, and he must've been tired from the flight." Grace's chin crumpled. "Because when I sent him back out in the storm to get medicine, he…he…" Grace covered her face. "He smiled. He smiled and went out to his death. I sent my husband to his death after betraying him."

Sherry's jaw opened slightly, but before she could say anything Grace's phone rang.

She looked at it, took a moment, then, brushing tears away, she answered.

"Grace, this is Michelle McDowell. Have you been contacted by the media this morning?"

Puzzled, Grace paused then said: "No, why?"

"Are you alone? Do you have someone with you right now?"

Grace glanced at Sherry. "I'm home with my friend. What's happening?"

McDowell hesitated, Grace could hear her breathing quicken. "Grace, I apologize. The reason we're not there in person is because we wanted you to hear it from us first—"

"Oh God—"

"—before the press informed you—"

"Informed me of what? What is it, please?"

"Grace, this morning…" McDowell swallowed. "Grace, this morning a young woman's body was discovered near Baker, California."

"No—" Grace began shaking.

"The San Bernardino coroner is working on identification," McDowell said. "It's not yet confirmed but you have to brace yourself— There are elements that point to it being Riley."

"NO!"

"I'm so sorry, Grace."

"Oh God, no!" Between sobs she said: "I need to see her! I'm going to Baker to see her!"

"You have to stay home. There are procedures. We expect more information."

"*I have to see her!* Please!" Her grip weakening on her phone, Grace sobbed, caught her breath. "You said it's not confirmed, so there's a chance it's not Riley."

"I'm so sorry, Grace, but that's all I can say right now, it just happened."

"You tell me when you know —*you tell me*!"

An aching groan erupted from the pit of Grace's stomach. She began pounding her fist on the kitchen table—the table where she'd braided Riley's hair, helped with homework, served birthday cakes and argued with her about Caleb.

Sensing what the call was, Sherry put one arm around Grace, catching her phone when it slipped from her hand, taking it up and speaking briefly with McDowell, sobbing as the news was relayed to her.

After the call, Sherry hugged Grace. "The detectives promised to call back as soon as they know more. They're going to talk to John and Blake so they can get home soon. Let's get you upstairs. You need to lie down."

With Sherry's help, Grace climbed the stairs,

turning to Riley's room where she threw herself facedown upon her daughter's bed. Clawing at the sheets, pulling them to her mouth, Grace sobbed.

Eighty-Two

Nevada

Holding the grip of his gun, Rogan eyed the teen. "I'd like you to keep your hands where I can see them and stand up."

Rogan knew Caleb Clarke was a juvenile sought in connection with the missing California girl; and that the body of a female fitting her description had been found about an hour's drive from where they stood. But he was uncertain of what he had here, exactly.

"Let's go. Stand up."

The teen complied.

"Extend your wrists for me."

He cooperated, staring at nothing as Rogan handcuffed him then walked him to his police truck and stood him at the hood. He patted him down for any weapons then dug into the teen's pockets, pulling out his wallet. His California driver's license showed him to be Caleb Robert Clarke of San Diego, aged seventeen.

There was also the issue of the vehicle reported missing, possibly stolen, out of San Diego, Rogan thought, not wanting to take any chances.

"You have the right to remain silent..." he began, reading Caleb his rights as he placed into an evidence bag all of Caleb's items, his wallet, keys and phone—the screen saver showed him and Riley Jarrett together, smiling at the beach.

The SUV would need processing. Rogan called dispatch with an update and request for backup and crime scene investigators.

Glancing at Caleb, Rogan wondered if he'd just killed Riley Jarrett and left her in the desert near Baker.

Finishing all he could do before other investigators arrived, Rogan looked at Caleb.

"Want some water?"

Caleb stared off at nothing without speaking.

"Where's your girlfriend, Caleb? Where's Riley Jarrett?"

A long moment passed, then with tears in his eyes he turned to Rogan.

"Don't you know?"

"Don't I know what?"

"Riley's dead."

Eighty-Three

San Diego, California

Sherry rubbed Grace's shoulders and tried to comfort her. "Nothing's been confirmed yet. We'll find her."

Grace sat up in Riley's bed, dragging her hands across her tearstained face. "I'm being punished for my mistakes."

"That's not true."

"I'm a horrible mother, a horrible wife."

"Stop, Grace, you can't lose hope, not while there's a chance."

Grace's phone rang and she tensed, staring at it. It was McDowell again.

She looked at Sherry, both of them knowing this could be confirmation—the call to tell her Riley was dead.

"Want me to answer?" Sherry offered.

Grace shook her head, gulped air and answered, her voice trembling. "Yes."

"It's Michelle."

"Is Riley dead?"

McDowell paused.

"We're still waiting on confirmation," McDowell said. "You wanted me to keep you up-to-date. Grace, there's another new development, another new factor."

"What?"

"A short time ago, Caleb Clarke was discovered near the Sagebrush. That's about an hour's drive from Baker."

"You found Caleb?" Grace said. "Was Riley with him?"

"No."

"But he must know if—if—or where she is. Can I talk to him?"

"No, I'm sorry, Grace, listen. He's being held for questioning. I know this is a lot to take in. That's the latest I can share. I promise I'll keep you updated."

After the call, Grace told Sherry what McDowell had told her.

"Caleb?" Sherry bit her bottom lip. "Okay, we have to stay positive. He must know something if he made it all the way to Nevada where the search is."

At a loss, Grace shook her head, noticing she'd missed a call on her phone from Elliott Downey, the reporter with the *Press-Enterprise* in Riverside. Thinking he might know more than what McDowell had told her, she was considering calling him back when she looked at Sherry. She was concentrating on Riley's pillow—or rather, what was under it. The corner of a tattered paperback peeked out.

"What's that?" Sherry said.

Grace reached for it, showing her. It was a copy of Shakespeare's tragic play, *Romeo and Juliet*.

"Riley loves this story." Grace fanned the pages but she stopped, noticing something unusual.

In the death scene, in every instance, the names Romeo and Juliet had been crossed out in blue ink. They'd been replaced with the names Riley and Caleb.

The book fell from Grace's hand as she released a banshee wail.

Eighty-Four

Death Valley Road, California

Diane Stalling was meticulous. As the deputy coroner investigator, she controlled the scene where the body had been discovered. She was aware of the missing person case in Nevada and the need for identification. Stalling had been thorough in her work and was nearly finished now. Positive identification had not yet been made.

The deceased was a white female, approximate age range in the midteens. Cause of death yet to be ascertained. There would be an autopsy.

Stalling had taken in the context of the surroundings, the weather, location and clothing. She had examined the body's position and lividity, searched for nearby objects that may have been involved in the death. She couldn't conclude any obvious external signs of violence or if death was natural and occurred at this location.

One unusual sign was the fact that the deceased was found without footwear. A search of the area had failed to yield any shoes. There were signs of bites on the legs and arms. That animals may have scattered shoes was a possibility, she thought, making notes and taking photos before waving to a deputy.

"I've got to turn her. I need your help."

"Sure."

Stalling passed him a set of gloves. While he tugged them on, she set down a plastic tarpaulin then pointed which way to go as she took the shoulders and he took the hips.

Hair laced and matted the face, which was bloated, discolored and crusted with maggots. The deceased was unrecognizable.

Stalling gently examined the head for wounds, finding a gash, which could have been blunt trauma from being struck or falling on a rock. Stalling would examine the corresponding area for signs of tissue, blood and hair.

The deceased was wearing a soiled white T-shirt.

Stalling examined the chest and midsection for wounds, injuries. She'd already searched the rear pockets of the shorts and found nothing. Reaching into the left front, she found nothing. Then she slid her gloved hand into the right front pocket. She felt something.

Slowly she withdrew it, looked at it, then at the deputy.

"Well, this should help identify her," Stalling said.

Eighty-Five

San Diego, California

Riley is walking away from Rykhirt and heading to the food court just as the picture turns to snow.

Rykhirt leaves the Sagebrush alone in his Nissan and drives onto the interstate north for Las Vegas.

Elsen and McDowell continued studying the security footage on their screens, while working at San Diego police headquarters.

"What if Rykhirt came back?" Elsen said.

"His window of opportunity's too tight," McDowell said. "Let him go, Dan. We can rule out Rykhirt. Our focus shifts to Caleb, his actions, the texts between him and Riley, the breakup, the emotional and psychological stresses, the statements from their friends."

"Yeah."

"The breakup was one of the last things Riley argued about with her mother. Maybe it's Caleb she's waving to in the footage and they got together and something went wrong?"

"Homicide's going to talk to him," Elsen said. "We've got to alert John and Blake about the find in Baker. We can't hold them."

"What about Blake's debt and drug-ransom story?"

"There's no direct evidence tying it to Riley. I talked to Moore and he said San Diego Narcotics and the FBI want to talk to Blake. I'm not sure when they'll do that, but Moore said they might look at conspiracy to traffic, pull some names from him. But we can't hold them."

Elsen's phone rang. It was Lieutenant Holland.

"Dan, San Bernardino's got an ID on the body. They found items in her pocket. Her prints were still good. They used a mobile scanner to confirm. I just got it officially from the deputy coroner on the scene. I'm sending it to you now."

"All right, we'll notify the family," Elsen said.

At that moment, McDowell's phone rang. Lieutenant Jackson was calling.

"I'm with Travis Quinn and Cliff Lawton in the Sagebrush operations center." Jackson's voice had an undertone of urgency. "They've just recovered more video and they're getting ready to send it your way."

"Okay, thank you, Lieutenant."

"Michelle, I've just seen it. This is a significant breakthrough."

Eighty-Six

San Diego, California

My daughter can't be dead.

Grace begged heaven, pleaded for Riley's life while struggling to convince herself that this was a dream, a nightmare and she needed to wake up.

But she wasn't dreaming. It was real and she had set it all in motion.

Grace stared at Riley's worn copy of *Romeo and Juliet* then turned to Sherry.

"What does this mean?" Grace said. "Replacing the names in the death scene. Why did Riley do this?"

Sherry shook her head. "Maybe nothing more than a dramatic teenager thing."

"It's more than that, with all that's happened," Grace said. "Is it a suicide pact with Caleb?"

"We don't know, Grace."

"Did I push things too far, making them break up, taking her away from here, knowing Riley's life was here and that she was still mourning her father? Did I do this?"

"No, don't torture yourself."

Grace's phone rang again, this time a TV news station in Las Vegas. She didn't answer.

"Reporters," she said. "I can't talk to them now."

Tears rolled down her face, and as soon as the call ended her phone rang again, another news outlet, this one from San Diego.

"More reporters. Something's happening," she said. "The press always finds out." She stared at it, letting it ring. "I can't do this now, I can't."

"Why don't we shut it off?" Sherry said.

"No, what if the police call. John's with them. Why doesn't he answer me?"

"John and Blake probably don't have their phones."

When the second call stopped, a third began. It was McDowell.

"Want me to talk to her?" Sherry asked, after seeing the caller ID.

Grace swallowed and shook her head.

Sherry took her shoulders. "Okay, be strong. I'm here."

Grace nodded, answered the call.

"It's *not* Riley," McDowell said.

Grace clenched her eyes, squeezing tears from them. "Please, are you sure?"

"There were items in her pocket. They scanned her fingerprints at the scene. It's confirmed. *It's not Riley.*"

Grace told Sherry and shook as her friend hugged her. She resumed talking with McDowell. "Please tell me. Who is she?"

"Grace, I really—"

"Please, Michelle. I want to know."

McDowell let out a long breath as if remembering her promise to tell Grace all she could whenever she could. "None of this has been released so I won't give you her name, but you must keep this confidential. San Bernardino is notifying her family. She just turned twenty. She's from Barstow but resided at Breezy Mirage Way Estates, a few miles away. She had a record for burglaries. So we had her prints. She was wearing shorts and a white T-shirt. They found sandals a couple of hundred yards away. Animals may have taken them."

"What happened to her?"

"There'll be an autopsy to determine the cause of her death. But there was a key with the apartment tag on it and a note in her pocket. She was despondent and walked into the desert."

Absorbing the tragic details of the girl, who was only a few years older than Riley, Grace's heart went out to her family and their pain. She whispered a prayer for them before coming back to her own tragedy. Riley was still missing.

"What about Caleb?" she asked McDowell. "He has to know where Riley is."

"He's not saying anything. Our detectives will be talking to him. But more new critical leads are emerging today."

"What leads?"

"We're recovering new security video from the Sagebrush. It's helping us with answers."

"How? Does it show you where she went, where she is?"

"Grace, that's all I can tell you. We're working on it now. I know it's hard, but sit tight. Now, we need to go over a few more things with John and Blake, but they should be home soon."

"Why did you have to talk to them?"

"To clarify some points."

"What points?" She could hear voices and another phone ringing on McDowell's end.

"Grace, I'm sorry I have to go."

After ending the call Grace turned to Sherry.

"Thank God it's not her," Sherry said.

"My relief comes at the price of another family's devastation."

"It's horrible, I know, and I'm sorry," Sherry said. "Did McDowell have more news? Does Caleb know anything? Should we tell them about the names in the play, just to be safe?"

"The play, you're right, I should've—" Grace shook her head as she refocused. "Caleb's not saying anything but detectives are talking to him. She said John and Blake should be home soon."

"Good."

"And McDowell sounded hopeful because they're starting to recover lost security video at the Sagebrush."

Sherry looked at Grace. "New security video

from the truck stop?" Sherry said. "That's good, right?"

"Yes, you're right." Wiping her face, Grace stood, as if buoyed, as if stronger. When her phone vibrated with a text, she looked at the screen. "It's the reporter from Riverside, the good guy. I'll see what he knows."

"You do that, and I'll go downstairs and make us some fresh tea."

Sherry left as Grace looked at the message from Elliott Downey at the *Press-Enterprise*.

Would you have time for a quick call?

Grace began a text to him before she was stopped dead by a loud, shrill scream.

Eighty-Seven

San Diego, California

Driving home from police headquarters with Blake would take no longer than fifteen minutes, but John had lost his hold on time.

Before leaving he'd texted Grace telling her they would be home soon. They'd gone about six blocks and John was still numb from Elsen's and McDowell's searing accusations, then the waiting. Then being told the news about a body and Caleb's arrest had rolled over him with tsunami force.

He was relieved the dead person near Baker was not Riley, leaving him to cling to the hope that if she was with Caleb they would find her alive. It was all he had, because his life—his tattered career—was on the verge of turning to ashes.

John didn't know how those Las Vegas detectives had found out everything but they had him nailed—making him feel that he was capable of committing any crime. It didn't matter that he'd told them the truth. That Lana's and Courtney's deaths were an accident, that he'd always feel responsible for the tragedy—*because I am and I'll never forgive myself for it.* It didn't matter that he'd made bad investments; that he'd *borrowed* money from *SoCal SoYou*, intent on repaying it before they found out.

He was not perfect.

But when Grace and Riley came into his life, it was a chance to start over and Pittsburgh would be where they would do it. Yes, he took out big insurance policies because if the worst happened, he wanted to ensure that he and Blake wouldn't have to go through the agony of grieving and worrying about money at the same time ever again. The detectives seemed to overlook that he had large policies on himself and Blake, too—to provide the same peace of mind for Grace and Riley. That wasn't illegal. John was doing everything he could to protect everyone, but he'd failed—that was what he was guilty of. That was the truth.

But Elsen and McDowell didn't care. It looked suspicious.

A horn sounded behind them. The light had turned green.

They drove a few more blocks when John's phone rang. Hoping it was Grace, he answered without looking at the number.

"Is this John Marshall, the stepfather of Riley Jarrett?"

"Yes, who's this?"

"Libby Roth with the *Associated Press*. Sir, I'm

sorry to be calling at this time, but we understand that the body of a young female has been discovered in San Bernardino County and—"

"Yes, it's not our daughter."

"Excuse me?"

"Police have confirmed that it's not Riley and I have no comment. It's not a good time."

"But Mr. Marshall, sir—"

John ended the call and kept driving.

A few blocks later he turned to Blake who'd been silent and staring straight ahead. John had no idea what the detectives had asked him.

"How did it go for you, son?"

Blake didn't turn, his face sober. "I need a lawyer, Dad."

"What're you talking about?"

"Dad, I owe some bad people a lot of money. I did a bad thing."

John pulled over and stared at Blake who, with tears in his eyes, told him about his $22,000.00 online gambling debt, the drugs in the RV.

"The police dog smelling drugs in the RV—it was all true?"

"Yes."

"And you told the police all of this?"

"Yes, they already knew some, and I told them that I think Riley was kidnapped because we never transported the drugs, the drugs are gone and I still owe the money."

John cursed. "Do police think she was kidnapped?"

"I don't know, Dad. First, they must've thought it was the creep in the video, now Caleb. I don't know. But they said that tomorrow at two, I have to report to the FBI office up in Sorrento for an interview, and a whole bunch of drug cops will be there and if I don't show up they could arrest me. Dad, they want me to give them names."

"Do you have names?"

"A couple first names, or nicknames, maybe." Tears rolled down Blake's face. "It would've been better if I drowned, not Courtney."

John looked at him. "Don't say that." He took in a hard breath and let it out slowly. "We're going to sort this out. Don't say a word to Grace, not now. Leave that with me. We need to get home. I'll make some calls, we'll sort this out."

John shook his head, raked both hands through his hair then stared at Blake for a long, anguished moment before he continued driving.

Coming up on Mission Hills, John tried reaching Grace again to let her know they were minutes away. She never responded to his earlier text so this time he called, but there was no answer. *Odd.*

He knew Grace had Sherry with her this morning while he and Blake were with police. He tried Sherry's phone. No answer.

What's going on?

He accelerated the rest of the way through Mission Hills, spotting the For Sale sign on their front yard but not seeing Sherry's white Traverse as they pulled into the driveway.

Sherry wouldn't leave Grace alone.

John pressed the remote garage door opener, the door lifted. Grace's Toyota Camry was gone.

"Looks like no one's home," Blake said when they went to the door.

"This is strange," John said as they stepped inside. "Grace! Sherry!"

The house was silent.

"Blake, check upstairs. I'll check down here."

John went to the kitchen, his office, the living room, dining room, calling and searching—

"Dad!"

Blake was on his knees at the bottom of the stairs, examining the wall and the steps. Glossy red streaks and still-wet droplets.

"This is blood."

Eighty-Eight

San Diego, California

"Here we go again," Cliff Lawton said over the speakerphone from the Sagebrush. "More recovered footage with more information."

At San Diego police headquarters, McDowell and Elsen concentrated on their screens, watching. *Riley enters the crowded food court, waving and walking directly to a woman who'd waved to her.*

The woman is wearing shorts, a T-shirt, a wide-brimmed white sun hat and oversize sunglasses obscuring her face. But it's clear Riley knows her. They embrace, speak. The woman produces her phone, offering it to Riley who declines it. The woman speaks briefly into her phone while pointing before she and Riley begin leaving the food court.

Camera angles change, tracking them as they reach an exit.

Angles change again to the exterior, tracking them walking from the exit and entering the parking lot. Angles change again, tracking them walking to a red vehicle. The woman opens the passenger door for Riley then gets in behind the wheel. The vehicle is a red SUV. Angles change as it wheels through the lot and exits the Sagebrush complex. The last images show the vehicle heading for the interstate exit for southbound traffic.

"This is it!" McDowell said. "Who is that woman?"

The image of the plate was unclear, the distance too great.

"Cliff we've got to get that plate," Elsen said. "Do you have an LPR? Can you pull up, freeze and enlarge it so we can read that plate?"

Lawton and Travis Quinn talked in the background.

"Yes, we can. Working on it now," Lawton said. "Stand by."

Eighty-Nine

Blinking back tears, her mind whirling, Grace pushed her Camry beyond the speed limit eastbound on Interstate 8. A horn sounded. She was weaving. Correcting her path, she let out a breath. She couldn't believe that while anguishing about Riley she now had to worry about Sherry.

Grace replayed the chaos from moments ago; how she'd aborted her text to the reporter in Riverside when she'd heard the scream. She rushed from the bedroom to find Sherry at the bottom of the stairs, sitting on the floor, holding her head, blood webbing from her scalp down her cheek.

"My uncle texted me. My aunt's condition has worsened," Sherry had told her. "I was looking at my phone on the top of stairs, missed a step and fell down. I'm sorry, Grace, but I should get back to Utah. I'll go home and pack for the next flight. I'm so sorry, Grace."

"No, you're not making sense." Grace examined

her head, got a towel. "I'm taking you to the hospital now. You may have a concussion."

"No, I'm fine, Grace, really." Sherry stood. "I'm sorry I startled you, and having to leave like this."

"No, Sherry. I'm driving you to the hospital. Stay here, I'll get my purse."

When Grace got to the kitchen counter, her phone rang and she answered. "This is Martin Clarke, Caleb's father in Algiers."

"Yes, hello, Martin."

"Grace, the FBI's told me that Caleb was located and arrested in Nevada."

"Yes, do you know if Riley was with him?"

"No, I know nothing. It's why I'm calling."

"Caleb didn't tell you where Riley is?"

"How could he? They won't let me talk to Caleb. Do you know anything more?"

"Not really. I'd like to talk, but this isn't a good time." She glanced around, collected her purse and car keys then caught her breath.

Through the window she saw Sherry pulling away in her SUV. Overwhelmed, Grace moved quickly through the house to the garage.

"Listen, Martin. From what I know, Caleb's okay. I'll see what I can find out and we'll talk again as soon as possible. I'm sorry, I have to go."

As she trotted to her car, Grace's phone had vibrated with a text from John. He was with Blake at police headquarters and they'd be home soon. She didn't have time to respond. She got into her car and pulled away. Sherry shouldn't be driving when she could have a concussion and be disoriented. Now here Grace was, threading freeway traffic, searching each lane in vain for Sherry's white Traverse while checking the shoulders for accidents, relieved she didn't spot any.

Taking her exit, Grace moved north on the 163.

Soon she was in Mission Valley and the beautiful section of condos and town houses where Sherry lived. Turning onto her street, she came up to Sherry's town house but there was no sign of her white car on the street. Maybe it was in the garage, or in the back.

Grace found a place to park down the block. She turned off the engine and her phone vibrated with another text from John.

Where are you? Are you OK?

She responded: I'm OK. I'm at Sherry's. Tell you more later. Sorry. Gotta go.

Then it vibrated again, this time with a text from Jazmin at the search site in Nevada. Grace ignored it, put her phone away, got out of the car, walked quickly to Sherry's door and rang the bell.

While waiting she took in the two-story town house, recalling how happy Sherry was when she got it.

Grace could hear movement on the other side of the door, assuaging her concerns for it meant Sherry was home, safe. She just had to insist she go to the hospital.

The door opened. The woman before her was not Sherry. She was an older woman Grace didn't know. "Yes?" the woman asked.

"Hi, I'm here for Sherry."

"Sherry? Sorry, you've got the wrong address. There's no Sherry here."

Grace was puzzled. "No, she lives here. This is her town house."

"No, I'm sorry, you're mistaken."

"There's no mistake. Sherry Penmark." Grace looked at the house number, 28164. "This is her address."

"No, no one by that name lives here. Have a nice day."

The door began closing until Grace's hand shot out, stopping it.

"Excuse me," the woman said.

"Hold it. I'm her friend Grace Jarrett, who are you?"

Ninety

San Diego, California

An enlarged sharp image filled their screens.

It took several long minutes for Lawton and Quinn to capture the entire plate of the vehicle that drove away from the Sagebrush with Riley Jarrett.

McDowell's eyes locked on to it as she recited the sequence into her phone. "California tag beginning Nine-Queen-Ocean-..."

San Diego PD's dispatcher was running the plate through state motor vehicle databases while McDowell and Elsen waited.

"Comes back as a 2021 red Hyundai Santa Fe, the RO is United Liberty Coast Corp. That's a national auto rental agency."

"We need an address for where it's registered," Elsen said.

The dispatcher provided the information. "Address is Admiral Boland Way, San Diego, that's at the airport."

McDowell and Elsen exchanged looks. "An airport rental," McDowell said. "The woman could've come from anywhere and taken her on a plane to anywhere."

"We've got work to do," Elsen said.

Urgent calls were made. With the help of Emery Moore and the San Diego police, the FBI and the district attorney, the investigators made their case of exigent—life-and-death—circumstances in the suspected abduction of a minor. It enabled them to get rapid sign-off for a warrant to email the legal and security divisions at United Liberty Coast Corp.'s head office in San Francisco, compelling them to immediately retrieve and provide all information concerning the person, or persons, who rented and would've had possession of the red Hyundai Santa Fe on the date Riley Jarrett vanished from the Sagebrush.

The rental corporation had been alerted, was cooperating. To save time they started work on obtaining the information they'd need to release the instant they received the warrant.

While waiting, Elsen said: "The vehicle was heading south and likely crossed into California."

"Right," McDowell said. "We'll ask California Highway Patrol if they've made any stops."

"And check plate readers on toll gates."

A short time later, Elsen received a call from Phil Matson, director of security for United Liberty Coast in San Francisco.

"We have the information you requested," Matson said. "I'll give it to you now, and we're emailing the records to you."

"Thanks, Phil, go ahead," Elsen said, his pen poised over his notepad.

Ninety-One

The woman's face tightened as she held the door. "Please step back," she told Grace.

Grace inched back. "But I need to find Sherry."

Glaring at her, the woman called out: "Andrew!"

A moment later a man came to the door. He was older than the woman, had wild white hair, a beard and looked like a wizard, Grace thought, as she got her phone and scrolled through it.

"What is it?" he said.

"This woman's got the wrong address and won't leave."

"Oh, and why's that?" he said.

"She says Sherry somebody lives here," the woman said.

"Sherry Penmark." Grace held up her phone with Sherry's photo.

The man squinted at it then nodded, nearly smiling. "Ahh. A misunderstanding," he said. "My cousin here's visiting and she's somewhat protective, I admit. But yes, Sherry lived here."

"Lived?" Grace said.

"You never mentioned this, Andrew," the woman said.

"I didn't see the need," he said to her, then to Grace, "I'm a history professor at the university. Recently, I returned from an extended sabbatical in Norway—too long, and too cold, really. While I was away I used a house-sitting service. Sherry was my house sitter. What we have is an honest mistake. I'm sorry about that. Are you her friend?"

Stunned and baffled, Grace didn't move. "I don't understand. So Sherry doesn't own this property?"

"No, I assure you, it's mine." The professor smiled. "You might try her other address."

"Other address? But I thought this was her address. I do need to reach her. There's been an accident."

"Oh my." The man held up one finger, nodded to his cousin to surrender the door, allowing Grace into the foyer as he disappeared.

Her heart beating faster, Grace surveyed the decor in a new light while struggling with questions swirling in her head.

The man returned with an envelope. It looked like junk mail, some sort of coupon offer for clothes. He studied it for a few seconds.

"I found this the other day between the fridge

and the counter. It must've fallen there during her house-sitting days. Here you go."

Grace accepted the envelope. Saw the name on it: Sherry Penmark, and a San Diego address. Trying to make sense of what occurred, Grace stared at it in her hands before thanking the professor and his cousin. Then she hurried to her car.

Grace's pulse quickened as she drove out of Mission Valley, heading for the address on Sherry's letter.

It was only minutes away.

Why would Sherry mislead her into thinking that she owned the town house? Grace remembered the few times in the past months when she'd wanted to visit, Sherry had given excuses. "It's a bad time, a water pipe burst." Or, "I'm getting a room painted." They must've been part of the deception. But why?

Confused, Grace sped south on Qualcomm Way over the freeway and multiple lanes of traffic. The road climbed up from the valley, curving into the community of North Park.

Grace navigated through blocks of neat homes deeper into the neighborhood of University Heights, passing the white stucco walls of a Catholic high school for girls.

Sherry's address led her beyond the school and into an enclave of quiet narrow streets of mostly single-level, flat homes with clay roofs, neat lawns and feather duster palms.

Getting closer, she continued down a street lined with towering palms, passed a sign that read: NOT A THROUGH STREET.

The address on the envelope was at the end. No one was in sight, as if the neighborhood was asleep. Grace parked and got out. The area was peaceful, birdsong filling the air.

Sherry's house stood on a corner lot, a white two-story frame model, built in the hope that arose after the Second World War. Its paint had blistered in places, a few shingles had escaped from the roof, the front porch appeared sunken and slats were missing from the white wooden fence that hemmed in neglected shrubs.

Parked well into the driveway and nearly concealed by overgrowth was Sherry's Traverse. All of its doors, including the rear hatch, were open.

"Sherry?"

No answer. No one was there.

Grace walked down the driveway, past the SUV to the back door of the house. She knocked.

No answer.

She knocked again, harder, and the door creaked open.

Ninety-Two

San Diego, California

Sherry Louise Penmark.

"That's the name of the person who'd rented the red Hyundai Santa Fe from us," Phil Matson told Elsen and McDowell from United Liberty Coast's office in San Francisco.

Investigators moved fast, running Penmark's name through local and national databases.

"Here's Penmark's San Diego address," Elsen said. "It matches the address on her California driver's license and the registration of a white Chevrolet Traverse."

"The Hyundai was returned to us on the date noted there, with no issues and has since been rented out. We can locate it," Matson said.

"Phil, we'll get more warrants, but we'll need to seize that vehicle and put it on a flatbed for processing," Elsen said.

"We'll work with you on that," Matson said.

The Las Vegas detectives turned to Emery

Moore, who'd joined them along with several se-
nior San Diego commanders, to determine how to
move on Sherry Penmark's address.

"We've checked Penmark's name," Captain
Kathleen Brockway said. "So far, she's got a clean
sheet, no arrests, no warrants."

Elsen nodded.

"Now that you've got this new information, we
can go a couple of ways," Brockway said. "Option
one, Penmark, being a family friend, could be har-
boring a runaway. She's misguided in her efforts
but no harm done. We could send a car over, knock
on her door for a conversation."

Elsen and McDowell didn't say anything, waiting for the captain to offer another option.

"Option two, if you believe Penmark kidnapped
Riley Jarrett and is holding her, then we set up on
her house, wait for her to come out and get rolling.
That gets her safely away from the house. We grab
her then check the house for the girl. End of story."

"Option two," Elsen said, past giving anyone
the benefit of the doubt.

"Done," Brockway said. "We'll get things moving."

Ninety-Three

San Diego, California

"Sherry?" Grace pushed the door open wider before stepping inside. She was met with a wave of stale air emanating from the darkened house.

"Sherry!" Grace raised her voice. "It's Grace, are you okay?"

Met with silence, and fearing Sherry's possible concussion may have caused her to collapse, Grace continued into the kitchen.

Pizza boxes, take-out bags and wrappers, some holding half-eaten spoiled food, littered the counter. Unwashed dishes were heaped in the sink. Flies buzzed around it all. Grace covered her mouth with her hand.

Leaving the kitchen for the living room, she stopped.

In the dim light, in the center of the room near the sofa and cluttered coffee table, were three plastic moving boxes in various stages of being emptied, *or filled*, some with clothing, others with file folders. Grace noticed a sun hat and sunglasses on the coffee table then froze. Her eyes shot to the ceiling.

A floorboard above her had creaked.

"Sherry?"

Grace went to the stairs, the worn steps squeaking as she made her way to the upper floor.

Standing in the shaded light, she looked up and down the hall. A sudden stirring came from behind a half-closed door. Grace went to it, picking up a current of foul-smelling air. The hinges grated as Grace swung the door open, her eyes widening.

Riley lay on the bed.

In that instant Grace saw her arms outstretched, her wrists bound with rope to the headboard. She was gagged, groggy. Her skin was blotched, her hair stringy. She was wearing her *Friends* T-shirt and shorts. Her feet were bare. The bed was damp, soiled. Fast-food containers were strewn about; pill bottles and water bottles stood on the night table.

"Riley!"

Grace rushed to her, Riley sputtered into her gag, shaking her head as Sherry, lying in wait behind the door, swung a baseball bat into Grace's stomach.

Grace's knees buckled.

Sherry delivered a second blow to the back of Grace's neck, knocking her unconscious.

Moving quickly, Sherry dragged Grace across the floor to a corner of the room, sat her up and used plastic zip tie handcuffs to bind her wrists and ankles. Unable to find a gag for her, Sherry went to Riley, who'd been watching in her muzzy state. She unfastened Riley's bindings before zip-tying her wrists in front of her. Then, using a firefighter's carry, she hefted Riley across her shoulders.

Sherry got her downstairs and out of the house before laying her on the rear floor of her SUV. She checked the plastic handcuffs on Riley's wrists, her gag, to ensure they were secure. Then she zip-tied her ankles.

Riley's eyes were half open, as if she was semiconscious.

"I'm sorry I had to do this," Sherry said. "Soon all this will be behind us."

She covered Riley with a blanket.

Sherry returned to the bedroom, setting a small tin can on the floor.

She bent down and tapped Grace's face until her eyes fluttered open. She struggled through her fog, looking around in disbelief.

"Sherry." Grace winced in pain from the blows. "What're you doing? Why—what—I don't—"

"How could you move across the country knowing that I was part of your family, too? You didn't think about me. You just took Riley and left me."

"*What?* What're you—I don't under—"

"I missed her so much, and when I saw that you left her behind—"

"*You followed us to the truck stop?*"

Grace's eyes ballooned when Sherry reached for the can. A red tin can. She saw the words *Paint Thinner* on it.

Pungent vapors assaulted Grace's nostrils as Sherry removed the cap.

Grace screamed. "Don't do this! You're my friend! Sherry, please!"

Riley had pretended to be drugged and docile.

For the last day—*or was it two?*—when Sherry was not watching, she'd been spitting most of the pills she'd given her behind the headboard.

She couldn't believe what Sherry was doing. Alert now, Riley squirmed out from under the blanket, determined to escape from her bindings by recalling self-defense videos she'd seen online. Wriggling her body, she sat up, examining the handcuffs on her ankles.

Riley knew plastic zip ties had a locking bar, and what she needed to do to get free was lift the bar from the tracks of the zip tie with a shim. A fingernail might work.

Steadying herself, she used her longest nail and began working at lifting the bar, applying pressure. Her nail broke.

Riley whimpered, her shoulders sagged, but she refused to give up.

She clawed off her gag for air.

Concentrating, she tried working on her ankle cuffs using another fingernail when a shaft of sunlight captured something amid Sherry's folders and papers scattered on the car's floor.

Paper clips.

With the fingers of her cuffed hands she pinched a clip, carefully removed it from a sheaf of papers, unfolded, twisted and reinforced its edge, positioned it, then began working on the lock bar on the zip tie around her ankles.

The first attempt failed.

"Come on, come on!"

Sherry's eyebrows rose ever so slightly while she held a disposable lighter before Grace, who had tears streaming down her face.

"Things happen for a reason, Grace. That's why I moved to San Diego, not to help you, but to claim what is mine."

"Please!" Grace shook her head. "I can help you! Sherry, don't do this."

"Oh, how the stars aligned." Sherry nodded with satisfaction then stood. Taking up the can she splashed a little solvent on the floor near the door.

Ninety-Four

San Diego, California

Marked San Diego patrol cars moved quickly, establishing an outer perimeter focused on the address for Sherry Penmark.

They'd sealed off and stopped all traffic in a four-block radius while unmarked units had moved to various choke points near the residence, using the layout of the neighborhood to their advantage.

Elsen and McDowell were in their rental. Other SDPD officers in unmarked vehicles were nearby, all of them concentrating on the target building.

The air was strangely quiet until the handheld radio San Diego police had given the Las Vegas detectives crackled in their car.

"We've got movement."

A woman in a large hat and sunglasses got into an SUV and began driving slowly down the street, traveling half a block before sirens yelped, emergency lights in grilles flashed, engines roared, rubber squealed on asphalt. Instantly the SUV was boxed in by two unmarked cars.

Detectives in plain clothes with badges on chains, guns drawn, surrounded it.

"Shut your vehicle off!" a detective said. "Toss the keys to the street. Get out of the car with your hands behind your head, fingers entwined."

Car keys tinkled to the ground as the frightened woman complied. Her body trembling, she was handcuffed and patted down. Within minutes police discovered the woman was not Sherry Penmark—but could not rule out that she may have been assisting her.

Other officers, with Elsen and McDowell, had gone to the residence where they found Andrew Pierce, aged seventy-two, but no sign of Riley Jarrett or Sherry Penmark.

"Dear Lord, what's going on?" Pierce, shocked by events, said to Elsen. "That woman used to house-sit here—this is not her home!"

"Where does she live?" Elsen said.

Pierce closed his eyes, struggling to remember the address on the envelope he'd given to Grace.

Ninety-Five

Backing out of the bedroom, Sherry sprinkled paint thinner on the hallway floor.

She stepped backward carefully, down the hall then the stairs, sprinkling solvent as she went. She continued throughout the main floor, the living room and the kitchen, backing near the rear door where she'd emptied the can.

Smiling, she reached into her pocket for the lighter, lit it then tossed it to the floor, igniting a fine thread of fire.

When she turned to leave, Riley swung a shovel, hitting the side of her head and knocking her out.

Riley, her wrists still bound but her ankles free, dropped the shovel, rushed around Sherry, dodging the flames, to the kitchen where she seized a knife from the cutlery drawer.

Riley sped up the burning stairs, braving the heat and smoke, navigating small walls of fire.

She flew to her mother, dropping to the floor,

using the knife's serrated blade to saw through her bindings.

As the fire grew, they both began coughing as Grace freed Riley's wrists with the knife. Their eyes stung as fire, sparks, ash and dense smoke swirled.

Small bits of the walls and ceiling fell around them, then everything turned black.

A neighbor walking her dog spotted the flames and called 9-1-1.

Within minutes sirens wailed. Emergency vehicles converged on the burning house, turning the tranquil corner of University Heights into a war zone.

Firefighters laid lines, attacking the blaze, which had engulfed the two-story structure. Crews succeeded in pulling out an unconscious adult female from the rear entrance and two more unconscious females from a room on the second level.

More sirens howled as paramedics rushed the three victims to hospital in Hillcrest.

Riley's eyes flickered. She felt the oxygen mask covering her face. In the torpid haze she had the sensation of floating on a cloud while a siren blared.

What's happening?

Through paramedic radio dispatches she'd discerned that three patients from a fire were being transported in separate ambulances.

All were alive—one was critical.

She stopped floating. Then there came the clacking rattle of the gurney's wheels extending. She was rolled through automatic doors.

Fluorescent lights streamed by on the ceiling as her gurney moved down a hospital hallway. She smelled disinfectant as her status—something about mild shock, first-degree burns and smoke inhalation—was being called out.

They wheeled her into an emergency treatment room curtained on both sides, transferred her to the treatment bed.

Masked faces hovered around Riley as she overheard voices nearby discussing how all three fire victims were now there—one on either side of her curtain.

Suddenly behind one of the curtains came tense, stress-filled orders accompanying urgent activity from the medical staff that went on for several minutes before a long, flat, resonant beep. Then switches were snapped.

A few moments later a soft voice said: "Calling time of death…"

Death?

Several more moments passed as fear flooded Riley's heart. *Who died behind the curtain?*

At some point she could hear the soft bits of conversation between two emergency people on the other side.

"…That's for the doctor…explain that her last

words when she was transported… 'Tell my daughter, Riley, I love her.'"

My daughter.

Riley lost her breath, pain catapulted her back to the night her father died. She fought for air.

Not Mom, not my mom!

Screaming, Riley pulled herself up from her bed, grasped the curtain in her fists to tear it away—*I have to save my mother—she can't leave me*—but she was seized by nurses, pulling her back.

"MOM!"

Riley fought a losing battle, sobbing, unable to breathe.

It took three nurses to subdue Riley while a fourth nurse slowly drew back the curtain on the opposite side.

Riley saw her mother. Alive.

Semiconscious, she turned her head. Grace smiled at her through her tears. Riley rushed to her side.

Epilogue

The corridor in the hospital gleamed.

Standing in a waiting area, John and Blake steeled themselves as the doctor, stethoscope collared around her, approached them.

"Riley's suffered smoke inhalation, first-degree burns to her hands, arms and feet, mild shock, dehydration, weight loss but she's going to be okay," the doctor said.

Breathing in, John nodded.

"Grace has blunt force trauma to the back of her neck. So far we see no signs of neurological injury. She has two fractured lower ribs. None of the organs appear punctured. We need to do more imaging tests. She received first-degree burns on her hands and neck and underwent smoke inhalation, as well. Otherwise, she's in good condition."

With small smiles, John and Blake exchanged glances. "Can we see them?" John asked.

The doctor removed her glasses and glanced over her shoulder. "You'll have to wait. Police are still talking to them."

"Thank you." John sat down, let out a long breath and covered his face with his hands.

Blake put his arm around his father.

Riley was sitting up in her bed, her adrenaline still surging, telling the Las Vegas detectives all she could remember.

With Elsen taking notes and McDowell recording a video on her phone, Riley recounted how Sherry had said she'd followed the family in her car across California to Nevada, noticing that she'd been left alone in the RV at the truck stop.

"I woke up, everyone was gone. I didn't see a note, I couldn't get my phone. My mom locked it up. When I went into the place to find my family, Sherry said she followed me inside.

"I looked everywhere, even back into the parking lot then back in the complex then I realized they'd left without me. I was upset, kinda scared, then this creepy guy who said I looked lost tried to get me to go with him. I thought he was a perv when he touched me. That's when I saw Sherry waving to me. It was a miracle. I was so happy, so relieved."

Tears rolled down her cheeks.

"I told Sherry what happened, that I was so friggin' angry that they left me; that I didn't have a phone and I was going to go to security or somewhere, and call my mom. Then it hit me and I asked Sherry what she was doing there. She's like, 'This is a cosmic sign, or something,' then she touches her moon and stars bracelet to the one I was wearing, the going away gift she gave me at the party, saying how it was like fate because she was driving to Utah to see her sick aunt, 'taking the scenic route' she says, and she's all like, 'Oh my God, this is such a huge cool thing that I'm here at the same time as you!'

"I said it was like a miracle for me—but I was so pissed at my family for leaving me, on top of being pissed about breaking up with Caleb and moving away. I asked her to call my mother to come back and get me, because I'm way too pissed to talk to her. So Sherry calls, tells my mom that I was too upset to talk to her and that my mom was all sorry and asked Sherry to drive me to our hotel in Las Vegas, the Golden Nugget, and we'll meet up there. Now I know that was all a lie."

Riley took a breath.

"So we got in Sherry's car—but it wasn't her car, which was weird—rented for the trip, she said—and she had a cooler in her car, she gave me a cold drink but she must've put drugs in it because I passed out and when I woke up I was in that house, tied up to the bed and she was keeping me drugged or something, telling me all this stuff that made no sense, like how I was her daughter now, that my family leaving me proved they didn't love me like she did and how she was going to take me away and we'd have new names, new lives."

Riley sobbed.

"But then she left me alone for days, saying

she had to go and she put these milkshakes with a straw near me, but I got so scared, hungry and couldn't go to the bathroom. Oh God, it was disgusting, so awful. Then she came back, cleaned me a little, fed me and the whole time I'm thinking it's just not right! I always thought she was like the coolest, nicest person, like family. But there's something wrong with her."

Riley caught her breath then told them the last of it.

"I didn't mean to kill her, but she was trying to murder my mom!"

"You didn't kill her, Riley," Elsen said. "The fire she set killed her."

The detectives were wrapping up when Riley asked about Caleb.

"He didn't get on the plane," McDowell said, "because he wanted to be with you."

"Really?"

The detectives related how Caleb took his dad's SUV to follow Riley. But he made a wrong interstate turn, got lost, abandoned the idea and started back to San Diego. That's when he learned from news reports that Riley was missing in Nevada. He drove there to help search. Knowing Riley's mom wouldn't want him there, he searched alone at the fringes, keeping out of sight before he learned she might be back in San Diego.

"Then came a radio news report of a body found near Baker, California. He thought it was you,"

Elsen said. "We found him alone, distraught in the desert."

Riley covered her face with her hands.

"He's fine," McDowell said. "He's not facing charges. He's with Family Services in Las Vegas. His mother is on her way there, and his father is flying back from Africa, to help him."

McDowell and Elsen then talked to Grace.

She recounted everything. They told her how they thought Sherry had joined the search after Grace told some of her friends about faulty security footage, and that Sherry placed Riley's shoes in the desert to thwart the search and investigation.

When they were done, Riley, John and Blake had a tear-filled reunion around Grace's hospital bed.

The story became international news, drawing headlines for weeks.

In that time, the FBI, Las Vegas and San Diego police continued investigating.

Following an autopsy on the body of Sherry Louise Penmark and using fingerprints, DNA and some of her documents recovered from the fire, investigators learned her true identify: Etta Dolores Orenscu.

McDowell and Elsen received calls from investigators across the country fearing there were other cases involving "Sherry" as they continued probing her background.

One day, McDowell and Elsen arranged to meet Grace at her home in San Diego. Stunned by the revelation that her friend was an impostor, Grace had questions. The detectives had answers but warned Grace to brace for what they'd learned.

"Not everything was lost in the fire." McDowell slid her tablet to Grace. "We recovered videos and a video diary from her laptop."

Heartbreak and humiliation twisted Grace in knots as she watched a video of Sherry and Tim, naked in bed together. They were having sex in the bed at his Chicago apartment. The apartment Grace had visited with Riley—the bed where she and Tim had made love.

Wiping away tears, she swiped to another file and Sherry's face filled the screen.

"Another entry because you, Dear Diary, will know the truth," Sherry began. "Tim was lonely in Chicago and looking online for company. That's how we met. He told me Grace was suffocating him and he was going to leave her. That's why he took the job. He said he loved me. He promised me a life together, but Saint Tim LIED!"

McDowell and Elsen said nothing as Grace listened.

"I couldn't let him get away with what he'd done," Sherry said. "I called him that night, begging, pleading. You know what that saintly family man said? He told me to go to hell. He never wanted to see me again." Sherry laughed. "But he *was going to see me again* because what he didn't know was that I was parked down the street from his perfect home in San Diego. I'd seen his plane tickets and knew when he'd be back in San Diego. When he got here I was waiting for him, prepared to end my life and take him with me."

Grace covered her face in disbelief.

"So the night Tim got home I watched the house from my car, waiting in the rain for the right time." Sherry paused. "I knew it could've been the next day, or the next week. But lo and behold, Tim comes out almost as soon as he went in, and drives off alone.

"I followed him to the drugstore, waiting, realizing this was the time. Few cars were on the road when he started home. I raced ahead, pulled a U-turn, mashed my foot on the pedal and drove at him head-on, shutting my eyes, ready for the impact that never came. Saint Tim swerved, crashed and, well, you know the rest."

Tears streamed down Grace's face.

"Grace got the best of Tim and I got the worst of him." Sherry shook her head. "But, things happen for a reason. That's why I moved to San Diego, to claim what is rightfully mine, little by little! The life I was promised! The life I was owed, a good life with the daughter I was meant to share with Tim. Ever since Tim died I listened to Grace mourn and praise him while I seethed, because I knew the truth."

Grace was shaking her head, sobbing, devastated.

"We know this is painful," McDowell said.

"Orenscu targeted your family with an obsessive fatal attraction because Tim rejected her," Elsen said.

"And it wasn't her first time," McDowell said.

Her DNA matched a sample collected in a cold case investigated by homicide detectives in Boston and Maine. That's where Orenscu had lived before moving to Chicago after assuming a new identity, using records of Sherry Louise Penmark, who drowned in Rochester, New York, at age two, but would now be similar in age to her.

In the Boston case, Orenscu had stalked and wormed her way into the life of a Boston man. In the months that followed, the man's wife and young son died in a suspicious cabin fire in Maine.

The man confessed to having an affair with Orenscu that she'd refused to end because she wanted to start a family with him. Police sought to question her, but she vanished.

The sickening truth of Tim and Sherry's deception had gutted Grace—yes, she accepted that she was not perfect, had almost cheated on him. Still, she couldn't believe that Tim had done what he did, betrayed her and Riley. It was mortifying. Deepening the wound was the awful truth that Sherry—or Orenscu—had tricked her into believing they were such good friends. Sherry had seemed warm, honest and true, helping Grace and Riley endure so much pain over the years, while secretly intending to destroy her.

Can you ever really know a person?

The detectives tried to help her find consolation in the fact that she had Riley back, and that her case had helped solve the tragedy of another teen who would never be coming home. For in continuing their work on Rykhirt, Las Vegas forensic experts, combing through his 2015 Nissan Versa, found a fingernail fragment and traces of hair and blood. Analysis determined that it matched the DNA of Eva Marie Garcia, aged seventeen, of Riverside, California.

The online reward fund for information to find Riley had surpassed $83,000. Grace closed it and requested contributors redirect their donations to the Garcia family. Nearly all did and the family set up a memorial scholarship in their daughter's name.

John got Blake an attorney who advised the teen to cooperate with police.

In exchange for immunity from charges, Blake continued helping federal agents. Studying photos and surveillance footage of known cartel members, Blake worked with investigators, identifying suspects, which ultimately led to a series of arrests, including those to whom Blake owed gambling money.

In a related development, several weeks after Riley was rescued, Arlo Compton parked his Ford pickup in a visitor spot at Las Vegas police headquarters. Unshaven and wiping his moist brow, Compton went to the reception desk.

"I gotta talk to one of your drug people right now," he said.

After a brief back-and-forth—"don't got an appointment but you better get somebody, please"—Detective Rico Flores from Narcotics came down and took Compton aside in the main lobby near the memorial plaque for officers slain in the line of duty.

"Now look, my family's got nothing to do with that missing girl case, Riley Jarrett, now that it's all done with. I want that understood."

"All right," Flores said.

"Way back when their RV crashed on the interstate near Jean, my no-good, shiftless son-in-law and his no-good shiftless cousin took something from the wreckage."

"What's that?"

"It's in the back of my truck and I want to return it in exchange for a promise they don't get charged with nothin'. What they did was wrong and I'm here to make it right."

"Let's have a look," Flores said.

They walked to Compton's truck and he drew back a canvas tarp in the bed, revealing four bundles the size of small pillows, wrapped in plastic and tape.

"It's drugs," Compton said. "They stole it when they stopped to help people clear the wreckage. They were fixin' to sell to Lord knows who when all the attention died down. Hid it in my shed.

When I found it, I got the truth out of them, don't ask me how, but I got it."

Staring at the bundles, Flores shook his head, knowing the substance would need to be analyzed and Compton's story verified.

He looked at Compton. "All right. After I get someone to tag and process this, you and I will go inside and talk further."

John and Blake moved to Pennsylvania without Grace and Riley.

Having never learned about his troubled parting with *SoCal SoYou*, the Pittsburgh company welcomed John into its operation and he secretly started repaying his debt.

But Riley's ordeal had fractured Grace and John's relationship because it had unearthed secrets about John, Blake and Grace, too. It resulted in a breakdown of trust leading Grace and John to agree to a trial separation, to battle their ghosts and determine if they had a future as a family.

Grace and Riley remained in their San Diego home, taking it off the market. They underwent intense therapy and worked to come to terms with the trauma of what happened with Sherry, Tim's affair and all the tragedies of their lives.

But what they realized was that when it came down to the final moments, they'd saved each other. It drew them closer.

After detectives had processed and returned the

moon and stars bracelet Sherry had given Riley, Riley and Grace took a trip to La Jolla. They went to the beach, and Riley tossed the bracelet into the Pacific.

Grace allowed Riley to spend some time with Caleb, but it amounted to another break, a long goodbye, before he moved to Paris where his dad got a new job.

Eventually, through an attorney, Grace and Riley agreed to tell their story through a book to be written by a celebrated true-crime author who lived in Orange County, California. It would go on to become a *New York Times* bestseller and a Netflix miniseries, entitled *Search For Her*.

It took time and overcoming their trust issues, but Riley resumed dating boys her own age, and Grace returned to nursing. Caring for her patients and her daughter helped her to heal.

* * * * *

Acknowledgments & A Personal Note

In writing *Search For Her*, I aimed to make the story as realistic as possible. Very early in 2020, I traveled to California and took the same route on Interstate 15 that the family took from San Diego to Nevada. Researching the book, I met, or was in touch with, a number of experts who kindly made time to suffer my questions.

My thanks to Sergeant Matthew Botkin of the San Diego Police Department; Dan Letchworth of *San Diego Magazine*; Officer Larry Hadfield, Las Vegas Metropolitan Police Department; Tina Talim, Chief Deputy District Attorney, High Intensity Drug Trafficking Area, Clark County District Attorney's Office; Sandy Breault, Public Affairs Officer, FBI Las Vegas Division; Trooper Travis Smaka, Nevada Highway Patrol; Guinevere Hobdy with the Nevada Department of Transportation; and Donald Moore and Erin Pavlina, with Red Rock Search & Rescue.

If the story rings true, thanks go to them for their generosity. For any errors, blame me for taking creative liberties with police procedure, jurisdiction, the law, technology, geography and the virus. In fiction you stretch reality. I did my best to keep it real.

In bringing this story to you, I also benefited from the hard work and support of a lot of other people.

My thanks to my wife, Barbara, and to Wendy Dudley for their invaluable help improving the tale.

Very special thanks to Laura and Michael.

My thanks to the super-brilliant Amy Moore-Benson and the team at Meridian Artists, to the outstanding Lorella Belli, at LBLA in London, to the ever-talented Emily Ohanjanians and the incredible, wonderful editorial, marketing, sales and PR teams at Harlequin, MIRA Books and Harper-Collins.

This brings me to what I believe is the most critical part of the entire enterprise: you, the reader. This aspect has become something of a credo for me, one that bears repeating with each book.

Thank you for your time, for without you, the story never comes alive and a book remains an untold tale. Thank you for setting your life on pause and taking the journey. I deeply appreciate my audience around the world and those who've been with me since the beginning who keep in touch. Thank you all for your kind words. I hope you enjoyed the ride and will check out my earlier books while watching for my next one.

Feel free to send me a note. I enjoy hearing from you.

Rick Mofina
www.Facebook.com/rickmofina
www.Twitter.com/rickmofina
www.RickMofina.com